Praise for LYING

"I devoured Kristin Wright's southern gothic romantic suspense *Lying Beneath The Oaks* in a single fabulous sitting. I loved the setting, the mystery, but I particularly loved her heroine, Molly, who is strong, delightfully human, and fun! Give this book a try. Once you pick it up, you won't be able to put it down—and you'll enjoy every sultry and exciting minute."
—Linda Castillo, *New York Times* bestselling author of the
    Kate Burkholder Mystery Series

"Wright's southern gothic will keep you turning pages as you unravel all of Molly's secrets—and those of the family she accidentally married into. I couldn't put it down."
—Sally Kilpatrick, author of *Oh My Stars* and 2018 Georgia
    Author of the Year in Romance for *Bless Her Heart*

"I fell in love immediately!"
—Elly Blake, *New York Times* bestselling author of *Frostblood*

"A well-crafted southern gothic romantic suspense with atmosphere and voice to spare."
—Mary Ann Marlowe, author of Golden Quill-winning
    A Crazy Kind of Love

"An enthralling read that weaves a vivid Southern setting with sizzling chemistry and page-flipping suspense. Simply wonderful."
—Kelly Siskind, author of *My Perfect Mistake*

LYING
beneath
THE OAKS

KRISTIN WRIGHT

BellaRosaBooks

BellaRosaBooks

LYING BENEATH THE OAKS
ISBN 978-1-62268-143-3

First Printed: January 2019

Library of Congress Control Number: 2018956751

Also available as e-book: ISBN 978-1-62268-144-0

Cover design by Jennifer Church and McBratney Marketing

Book design by Bella Rosa Books

Printed in the United States of America on acid-free paper.

BellaRosaBooks and logo are trademarks of Bella Rosa Books.

10   9   8   7   6   5   4   3   2   1

To Frank, who started me dreaming

To my boys, who are the reason I dream

To Mary Ann, who kept me dreaming

To Sarah, who made the dream come true

LYING
beneath
THE OAKS

BEFORE

Blood pumps between my fingers and trickles over my knuckles; it's slower now. I press the towel hard to stop the flow, but it's sodden and useless. I imagine I can push the blood back into her body. The ambulance is taking too long. There's no sound. Her skin is bleached of color. Her stilled eyelashes fan out over her cheeks. I'm bewildered by blood like this: I've seen minor cuts. A scraped knee. A crimson dot or a slash, blotted easily. This is a salty red ocean. I pray the wound is sealing up under my hands. Cooling blood soaks my legs where I kneel. Everything shines wet and red. It's like being inside my own heart.

I can't feel the throb of her pulse anymore; only my own, roaring in my ears. I don't dare move my hands to check my watch. It's been too long. My fingers begin to stick together.

In the distance the sirens wail. At last.

CHAPTER ONE

Marrying a stranger was hardly the worst thing I'd ever done.

What happens in Vegas stays in Vegas, they say, though I hadn't a clue how on earth that would apply to a legal marriage and a wedding ring that's too cheap to pawn and too nice to throw away.

I woke up with a stiff neck in the thin white light of morning in a parking lot. Muscles screamed as I un-wedged my head from the crevasse between the passenger side window and the headrest of a Ford sedan that smelled like two thousand miles of cigarette smoke and Febreze. Some worrisome brown substance stained the front of my jeans and cheap pink scoop-neck top. Only one flip-flop remained on my feet.

On my left hand, a too-big gold ring with a tiny stone of some kind slid toward my knuckle.

My head throbbed and my vision twirled and twisted. *This must be a hangover.* I hadn't had one since I was a teenager, because I'd always been careful not to get drunk for fear of what could happen. I tried to swallow but came up short of saliva, and groaning with every millimeter, turned my head to glance at the driver's side. The intake of breath hurt my head.

A man sprawled there asleep, his khaki pants and Vineyard Vines T-shirt rumpled and stained to match mine. He had messy chestnut hair with gold streaks. A straight nose over well-formed lips. A fit body. No noticeable tattoos or ridiculous jewelry. Something about him screamed To the Manor Born—maybe the khakis. They belonged on a boat deck or a golf course or something. He snored, his breath fanning fumes of alcohol that churned my stomach. He wore a gold ring on his left hand as well.

Oh, my God. What had I done? What had *we* done?

What had I said?

For a horrible throbbing heartbeat, I couldn't come up with his name.

Cooper. It clunked into place. His name was Cooper, though I had no idea what his last name was.

I poked him. He grunted and shifted in his seat. Yep, I remembered right. His voice was low and rumbly and did things to me. Had we . . . ?

"Hey," I said, poking him harder. His upper arm was solid.

"Whassgoinon?" he muttered, backhanding his mouth and nose like a child. Apparently I wasn't the only one with a hangover, because his eyes squinted tight in pain. They opened, revealing green-brown irises in a sea of red.

"I think you'll see what's going on when you wake up." I pushed on his shoulder again, holding up my hand to show off the ring.

He sat up, blinking against the daylight and what had to be a whopper of a headache, and took in the situation. "Oh, holy God." He looked at me, eyes full of remorse and—to my surprise —kindness. He stretched out his own hand where the matching gold ring told the tale. "Did we get married?"

"I think we did." I pointed to the small white fake chapel in front of us, deserted at this hour.

"Do you remember it?" he asked in his musical drawl of an accent, carefully trying not to give offense.

"No." A few hazy memories assaulted me, but not enough to put together a picture. Another couple kissing passionately in the hotel lobby. A flash of skin. A sense of terrible fear and longing and then a ride in the night with the windows all open, my hair blowing. None of it made sense. Fear—of myself and the lost time—stood the hair on the back of my neck on end. "You?"

"No." He glanced, wincing, into the backseat, handing me my missing flip-flop and pulling a sheaf of paper forward. I leaned in to look as he flipped through. A fancy-looking marriage certificate with bad calligraphy, suitable for framing. A brochure for the chapel, with an inflated price list for wedding attire, a photographer, and hair and makeup. An instruction sheet for the licensing place. Another sheet explaining that our real marriage certificate would be mailed to us.

"Edward Cooper Middleton. The Fifth. Your last name is Middleton," I said, to have something to say to cover the memory jolt of my first communion at age six. I wore a white dress that resembled a bride's. I'd dreamed of my future wedding, then, but that dream had been dead for over fifteen years.

"It is," he said. "No relation to the princess, though. I get that a lot. I go by Cooper. Edward—Ted—is my dad. You're Molly Todd."

"Molly Middleton, now, I guess," I said, choking back a gasp of disbelief. This man was my husband. *Husband.* And I didn't know him at all. If I had to be honest, though, he should probably be more worried that he didn't know me.

Much more worried.

I'd met him—what?—three or four days before. I'd been fired from my job six hours earlier and had curled up in the hotel bathroom crying, wondering what in the hell I'd do next. Whatever it was would almost certainly involve ramen for dinner and defaulting on some bill or another. I should have spent the time calculating how I could continue to pay for my month-to-month lease, how to save money on groceries, and where I could find another job quick.

Instead I cried, and a kind woman named Nikki turned from the sink where she was washing her hands to listen. When she heard the part about the ramen, she invited me to join her and her husband and their friends at the buffet for dinner. I wiped my tears away with a cheap brown paper towel, asked her not to mention what I'd told her, and followed her.

At the table were two other women, three husbands, and one single man named Cooper who'd all come to Vegas from South Carolina for a Clemson University reunion of sorts. In an instant, I understood why Nikki had thought I might fit in—she made up some story on the spot and pointed me straight to the chair next to Cooper. They were having a good meal and a good time and the longing for both overwhelmed me. If Cooper hadn't looked up at that moment of weakness and caught my eye and smiled, I might have been able to walk away.

But he did—and when he waved me over, I went. I turned off my desperation long enough to let myself enjoy it. It had been a long time since I'd spent an hour with someone attractive who thought I was attractive, too.

Cooper paid for my dinner, and I let him.

My conscience had fought me over that: it jabbed and whispered that, deep down, the things I'd done in my life barred me from simple pleasures like this.

The friends—all Clemson grads in their early thirties, except one woman who took a lot of ribbing for having gone to the rival University of South Carolina—welcomed me into their group and did everything but physically shove me at the single Cooper, who'd been divorced some years before. They were easy to talk to and laughed and teased each other and bought lots and lots of drinks. I joined their pack and we all stayed pretty well drunk as skunks, going from casino to buffet to bar to hotel to casino, for three days. I slept on the sofa in someone's hotel suite.

They were kind. None of them knew who I was. What I was.

I didn't remember what happened last night. My memories grew hazier as the weekend went on. I hadn't drunk alcohol in so long that my tolerance had dropped to nothing. In high school, I'd been known for saying too much when I drank. I prayed I'd grown out of that. I couldn't afford to say too much anymore. There were things I had to keep secret.

"You have red hair," Cooper said now, trying to stretch his lanky frame in the seat of the small car. "Last night, I remember your hair. Something about your hair, anyway." He trailed off.

"It's too dark to be red," I said, self-conscious now.

"Okay. Auburn, then. It's pretty."

"Thank you," I said, prim as a nun. Prim had no place here: the stranger I'd married probably knew the curtains matched the carpet. Um. In a manner of speaking.

"Oh, holy God," he said again. "We've really screwed up now, haven't we?" He leaned back against the glass of the driver's side window, throwing sunlight onto his sculpted cheekbone. At least I'd picked a good-looking stranger.

I liked that he didn't blame me, though most likely he should. I guaranteed I had more to gain through this marriage than he did. Even if I didn't remember how we decided to first get a license and then arrive at this extra-sleazy chapel, I doubted I'd objected to it. The memory of the longing returned.

"It's probably my fault. I do impulsive things sometimes." Not true. I hardly ever did impulsive things, and that's what worried me the most. "I'm sorry. What do you want to do now?" I asked.

"First things first. Let's hit a gas station and get some water and some hardcore breakfast to sop up all this alcohol. My head is killing me. Yours can't be much better."

Cooper reached out a hand and squeezed mine.

Later that night, we sat side by side at the airport gate, surrounded by Cooper's luggage and my tiny duffel bag. I didn't own much, and it hadn't pained me to terminate my lease this afternoon and save myself the upcoming rent. While we packed and cleaned up in his hotel room, he texted his friends some explanation I never saw and bought us both plane tickets to Charleston.

I'd chosen more wisely than I'd realized. Cooper didn't ask any questions—or not the right ones, anyway—and said he couldn't let me stay alone in Vegas until we got all this straightened out. He assumed I was on vacation, like he was, and that I wouldn't need to be anywhere until the Monday after Thanksgiving, now a week away. Nikki had kept her word and never told the others about how I'd lost my job, or what it was. He didn't know I didn't need to be anywhere at all.

It seemed crazy that I'd pick up and go with this stranger-husband across the country, but somehow, I trusted him. I trusted him at a basic bone-deep level, and I'd never trusted anyone before. Instincts had been one of the few things in life I could count on. I tried not to question the strong ones.

We were on our way to his home in some small town in South Carolina I'd never heard of, where we'd see if annulments were a real thing. I'd never even been to South Carolina.

Six hours of flight, a layover in Charlotte, and an hour of driving from Charleston ought to give me a chance to figure out first who I'd married, and then to figure out what to do from there. I felt bad that Cooper had paid for my plane ticket, but he said he'd take care of it. I certainly couldn't afford it—it cost more than a month's rent on the apartment I no longer had. I glanced at his phone as he read articles on the internet: the latest model iPhone. Leather luggage. Nice watch. He hadn't had to borrow money for the plane ticket.

"Listen," I said, as he spoke at the same time. I let him go first. I'd prefer if he did most of the talking.

"Molly," he said. "I know this is deeply awkward and bizarre. I wanted you to know—I'm not a psycho criminal. I'm a regular guy with a good job and a normal family and a place to live. I'm sure you're worried for your safety and I want to make sure you know you'll be safe with me, until we get this mess all straight. If it makes you feel better, you could call my sister before we get on the plane."

I had to force myself to keep up my tough-girl face. Tears welled and I blinked them back. Nobody had ever said anything to me as thoughtful as that. So far, I'd been safer with Cooper than I'd ever been before. "Thanks. I trust you. If you'd wanted to kill me, I guess you'd have done it by now."

"And I also want you to know," he continued, his hands open and loose on his lap. "I'm not an alcoholic. I haven't gotten drunk like that since college. I don't normally behave like that. I swear I'm a responsible adult. When I'm with those guys, it's like we're all twenty-two, not thirty-four. You'd never know it to look at them, but Craig is a banker in Columbia. High up on the pay scale, too. Jon's a high school teacher and football coach in Beaufort, and Jeremy works for a drug company. The corporate kind. We were all close in college and then they met the ladies and well . . ."

he said, trailing off. "We are actually grownups."

I chuckled, trying to calm my emotions and stop my brain from worrying about the next step and the step after that. They'd been great. If they'd noticed my inexperience with any kind of party, they hadn't commented, not even when I made the mistake of letting my amazement show the first time I tasted a mixed drink. After that I remembered to cover my lack of sophistication. I didn't think they'd been aware I had no knowledge of ordinary fun that was normal for regular people.

Cooper echoed my laugh. "Yeah, I can see how you might think Jeremy was running a pot farm the way he carried on here. Without the ladies, we'd have been even dumber. Reliving the days when we all still had hair and no gut."

While I waited for some kind of response to occur to me, I took the opportunity to study him. If his hair had thinned in the last decade, then there'd been way too much of it before. It was thick and came in many colors from dark brown to light caramel, and I had a dim memory of maybe having rubbed my hands through it.

My eyes drifted downward. "Umm. How skinny were you? Because now, you're . . . that's not much of a gut."

The flush lit up his beautiful skin once again. "Uh, I run. I play basketball when I can find guys to play with. And in college I was too skinny."

An overwhelming urge to run my hands up his flat torso to his shoulders shocked me out of nowhere. I sat on my hands.

"What about you?" Cooper asked. "What do you do to stay in such amazing shape?"

I glanced down. The boobs. He must be talking about the boobs. 36D, noticeable on a relatively thin frame. They'd never done a single good thing for me since the day they'd made their unwelcome appearance at age twelve. "Oh, I eat regular meals and no snacks. I walk whenever I get a chance, too. I got lucky, I guess. With my metabolism."

"Whatever it is, it's working."

Heat shot through me. He met my eyes. The contact held and

simmered. For a wild second I thought he might kiss me. He swallowed and looked away.

Better that way. It would be better if I didn't get any further emotionally entangled with someone who'd use all the legal efficiency money could buy to remove me from his life within the next few days. This couldn't last. Even if I'd married him on purpose in a fit of alcoholic idiocy, I knew that much. These days were a gift. A little time to try to figure out a life plan. At age thirty-three, better late than never.

"Cooper, I—" I bit my lip. He didn't need to know my history. There'd be no point in telling him and taking us from awkward to awful. "What's the name of the town you live in again?"

"McClellanville. It's about forty-five minutes north of Charleston. In the Lowcountry, on the marsh."

"How long do you think it will take to get this straightened out?"

He put away his phone to give me his full attention. The worst of the hangover had disappeared. His skin tone had returned to a healthy tan and his eyes had cleared of the red. "Well, now, this is Thanksgiving week. I doubt we can get in to see a lawyer tomorrow, and then it's almost the holiday. I'd say we've got to stay married at least a week. Or more, depending on what they say when we do talk to them."

"Oh. Should I stay in a hotel?" I asked, terrified he'd say yes. I didn't have much money for a hotel. "You don't have a girlfriend or something, do you?"

"Nope. No girlfriend right now. I do live at my family's house with my dad and sister and her little girl, though. She and her husband split up about six months ago and she's back home. We've got room, in any case. House is old, but it's plenty big. More than enough bedrooms. You can stay with us."

I pictured our entrance. We'd walk in. Cooper would say, "Hello, Father. This is Molly. I married her during a three-day drunk. I don't know the first thing about her."

Oh, God.

"What will you tell your family?"

He sat back, long legs stretched out in front of him, and laughed. "If it were just me, I'd tell the truth. Caroline'll think it's funny. Dad'll try to take control of the situation no matter what."

"What do you mean, 'take control'?"

He rubbed the tip of his nose. "Oh, Dad is one of those guys who has to be in charge of every situation. You know. If he thought we got married drunk, he'd want to ask a million questions to find out whether you took leave of your senses as a child or only recently, and whether I need to check in somewhere to dry out."

"Oh." A million questions sounded bad.

"It's nothing. Dad's just like that. You can't let him bother you. I'll leave it up to you, though. What do you want to tell them?"

"I have no idea. I shouldn't care what they think, but I'd hate to have your father think I'm an alcoholic gold digger. Or a nutcase."

"He'll probably think you're terrible anyway, but not for that. Do my ears deceive me or is that a Northern accent?"

Heat rose up my chest into my cheeks. "I'm from Michigan. Does that count?"

"Yup. That's what I thought. Somewhere Midwest. North of the Mason-Dixon line. Dad's got a few old-fashioned Southern prejudices."

"Great. So he'll hate me the instant I say hello. Before we even explain."

"Tell you what. If you're up for it, we can pretend that we weren't drunk. We can pretend we had some kind of love-at-first-sight situation and got married stone cold sober. Let him think what he wants. Then we work on the annulment all quiet-like and I tell him what happened after. You'll be gone and you'll never have to see him again. How's that?" He ran his hands through his hair. It fell back into place in perfect waves.

I stared at him, unable to make sense of someone so easy-going. "Cooper, why?" I cleared my throat, the words escaping me. "Why would you do this for a total stranger? The plane ticket? Taking me home to meet your family?"

His brows met in confusion, then his gaze dropped sheepishly. "Well, as you say, you're a stranger, but you're also my wife, for the moment at least, and you seem kind of . . . lost, maybe. Like not enough people have taken good care of you in your life. It won't hurt me a bit to do that a few days until we get all this mess straight, and like I said, the annulment will be easier if we can go to the lawyer together and just get it done."

I was so overwhelmed with the generosity of this plan—his kindness—it delayed the realization that it would seriously complicate the sleeping arrangements at his family's house. Which took my mind to another unanswered question. "Um. Last night. Do you know if we . . ."

"Huh?"

"Did we have sex, do you know?" I forced out the words, unable to meet his eyes. I didn't think we had before last night. The first couple of nights, we'd crashed along with his friends in whatever hotel room we fell down in. Nikki had shared her suitcase. "I mean, I wouldn't be upset . . . you know, if . . ." Son of a bitch. I made it more and more awkward every word I spoke.

"Uh. I don't remember," he said, rubbing his temples. "I honestly don't. When I packed up my hotel room, I didn't see . . . anything that would make me think we did," he said, delicately. "Though that doesn't mean we didn't. Because I would have wanted to." Now it was his turn not to meet my eyes.

"Right."

"So," he said, uncomfortable now. "Do you have family you need to call?"

I'd need to tread carefully here. "Um. My dad was never in the picture. My mom died when I was a teenager, and my grandma died six years ago. I never had any brothers and sisters."

"I'm sorry," he said. I glanced up. He meant it.

"It's all a long time ago."

"What do you do for a living?" he asked, showing off his skill at the basic manners I lacked.

I did not lack skill at lying, however, and this lie I'd practiced. I'd told it to several people I met in Las Vegas during my time there. No one would understand my real job. "I'm an interior decorator."

"Oh, that must be interesting. Annoying as hell, too. People who can afford help with interiors are usually pretty demanding."

"Are you one of those people?"

He colored and spread his hands flat on his thighs. "I guess I am. Or my dad is, anyway. That's the second blunt question you've asked in five minutes."

"Yeah. I do that, I guess. Does it bother you?" Bluntness was good cover: people never think blunt talkers are hiding anything.

Sometimes they are.

"No, not exactly. I'll get used to it." He leaned his elbows on his knees. "I'm a Realtor."

"Oh." I couldn't think of the first thing to ask about that.

He studied his fingernails as I desperately scrabbled for anything to say.

"Welcome to American Airlines Flight 355 to Charlotte. We'll begin boarding with our first class shortly."

I'd lost my train of thought. "Thank you. For what you said. For taking me home." *For so much else I can't say.*

"Ha!" he said, his low-pitched laughter rumbling. "Don't thank me until you meet my family."

"No, it's amazing what you're doing. Everything. Nobody . . ." I owed him more. I owed him some of the truth. "I-I'd been having kind of a tough time when I met you. I lost my job recently. I came to Vegas to try to forget things. To be somewhere new. I don't think I've ever been that drunk before. I've certainly never married someone before."

He absorbed that, taking it in stride. "Well, good. No need to apply for extra vacation time after all. You don't have a boyfriend who's going to turn up at my door, shotgun in hand, do you?"

"No. No boyfriend."

"You know I was married before. Got a divorce after Lynette left and stayed gone for a year. I never heard from her again. My lawyer had to put a notice in the paper. She never responded."

"What happened?"

"I don't honestly know. We'd been married two years. I thought we were happy enough. Dad used to give her a hard time about being a Yankee—she was from Virginia, so it was his joke —and occasionally we argued about me spending too much time at work or hunting, but that's it. She was a first grade teacher. Not the kind you'd think would be impulsive, but one day she was gone. Took a bag and left. A plane ticket to Charlotte showed up on our joint charge card. Then nothing else. She must have cut up the card."

"Did you look in Charlotte?"

"Charlotte is a major airline hub for flights all over everywhere. She could have flown on anywhere. My dad hired a private investigator and he never found anything."

"No contact with her parents?"

"Nope. She only had a dad. He was in a nursing home with Alzheimer's by the time he was fifty. That part was odd. When I checked there, they said they'd call if she ever visited him again. They never called."

"That is odd. Are you okay?" I asked, searching his face, finding that I cared whether he was hurt by this, and worried that I cared.

"Yeah, now I am. I was torn up about it at first, no question. But it was five years ago now. I hope she's happy somewhere. And look. I've moved on. I'm remarried." He laughed.

Something inside me lifted knowing he was the sort of person who could already find the humor in it, less than twenty-four hours later. If I had to be married to a stranger, at least he was a kind stranger.

"Now boarding, American Airlines Flight 355 with service to Charlotte. All rows."

"Are you ready?" Cooper asked, shouldering the carry-ons and extending a free hand to me.

I took it.

CHAPTER TWO

McClellanville, South Carolina, was off the beaten path. Like, far off. After flying all night, Cooper and I drove out of the busy Charleston airport onto Highway 17 North. We blinked in the morning light as we passed chain restaurants and a mall and thinning subdivisions. It didn't take long before only an occasional grungy-looking roadside eatery broke the ceaseless line of tall pine trees.

"Don't let those fool you," said Cooper, into the silence. I didn't know how he kept the truck going in a straight line. I could barely keep my eyes open. "That restaurant on the left there looks like a dive, but it made the pages of *Southern Living* last year."

"Oh. What do they serve?"

"You know. Meat and three. Fried green tomatoes. Red rice."

"Meat and three?" It sounded like food, but I'd never heard of any of it.

"Meat main dish, three vegetables. Southern staple. You know."

"Oh. Right. I've never been to the South."

"Never?"

"No. I haven't done much traveling. Las Vegas was my first trip anywhere."

"Seriously?" he said, not taking his eyes off the road. "No matter. Well, try to keep an open mind."

"I can do that." Open mind was no problem. Opening my mouth would be harder.

For a full twenty miles, the pine barricade rose straight and intact on both sides of the highway, offering only partial glimpses of houses. We turned right where a blinking yellow light slowed traffic for a couple of gas stations and wound through shady residential streets. In an instant, I'd been transported into a movie. Every ten feet or so, another huge, wide-branched tree crouched over the road, dripping some grayish-brown Southern-looking stuff from every branch.

"What are those trees?" I asked, my breath almost stopped by their beauty—and by the simultaneous hint of threat that somehow underlay their gnarled branches.

"Live oaks. They're native around here, but the town plants them and keeps them up. Beautiful, aren't they?"

"I don't even know what to say. Beautiful isn't a big enough word for those trees." We passed house after house, all old, all large, all well-cared for, but it was the trees that made me feel unworthy. They made me feel guilty, somehow.

"See that plant, growing on the branches? On the tops?" Cooper took a hand off the wheel of his pickup truck and pointed. "That's resurrection fern. When the weather's dry, it wilts and dies off, all brown and dead-looking. Rain comes, though, and it wakes up again, just as green and alive as it was meant to be. It can live a hundred years without water and still come back. I always liked that."

I liked it too. Actually, I loved the idea of something so indestructible. I wanted to climb one of the enormous trees and go to sleep in a crook of its branches with the green carpet of ferns as a mattress. Maybe the ferns could tell me the secret of invulnerability.

"This is where I live."

We turned down a sandy driveway, lined on both sides by live oaks so immense they had to have been there when George Washington was alive. "Wow, Cooper. How old are those trees?"

Cooper chuckled. "Supposedly they're two hundred fifty years old. This is what they call an allée, which I guess is a fancy French word for alley." Pride in his surroundings, in his home, radiated from him.

"They're spectacular."

We'd entered a cathedral of green, with the allée of live oaks for the pillars and aggressive green shrubbery and impenetrable tangled woods as the walls. A white frame house with a shadowed porch and green shutters dominated the far end where the pulpit would be. Beyond the house, water and glinting sun etched the stained-glass window. It looked nothing like Michigan.

"Don't the trees lose their leaves? It's November."

"Nope. They're evergreen. That's the house."

"Wow." The house sprawled so wide I had to turn my head to take it all in. "Holy crap, Cooper." Leather luggage, ha. He could buy every item I'd ever owned with his pocket change.

"Thornwood Oaks. That's the name of it. No idea who named it that, though it fits. There are plenty of plants out in these woods that'll cut you up. This house has been here since about 1850. The last one burned to the ground."

"Does your family know you're coming?"

"Yeah. At the baggage claim I sent Caroline a text. Let her know I had a surprise coming with me." He gave me a leer and an eyebrow wiggle, so cartoonish it made me laugh.

"Oh, my God." He hadn't given them any time to prepare. A drop of cold sweat ran down my spine.

"She'll love you." He stopped the truck in the circular driveway and we got out, Cooper again carrying all the luggage, what there was of it.

A yellow dog, streaked with mud, wiggled out from under the front porch and galloped up to Cooper, tongue lolling. He got down on one knee to greet him. Or her.

"Mary Jane! Hey, girl. I missed you." Cooper dropped the bags to rub the dog behind her ears. Dog and man got reacquainted, both wearing identical expressions of delight.

"Mary Jane?" I asked.

Cooper rubbed his own nose, evoking a kid with his hand in the cookie jar. "Yeah, I got her from Jeremy when she was a puppy and he moved into a condo that didn't take dogs. He had a little hobby, back before Nikki. Which . . . well, uh, you might be able to guess what it was."

Mary Jane sat back on her haunches and studied me. Cooper

watched her.

"She's a great dog, but she's slow to warm up to new people. Give her time."

On the last word, Mary Jane moved forward, slipping her yellow head under my hand. The message was clear. I petted her gingerly.

"Well, I'll be damned. Look at that. I guess she warmed up quick today."

Mary Jane removed all doubt about that by shivering under my hand with what appeared to be pleasure. Her mud streaks nuzzled dangerously close to my jeans-clad leg.

"Can't believe it. She can be a little stuck up. She won't have anything to do with Dad. Even Caroline gets the cold shoulder every now and then," said Cooper, giving me an admiring glance as he collected the luggage. He ruffled the dog's ears. "Come on, girl."

As we approached, the wide black-painted front door swung open. A man I assumed must be Cooper's father stood there. He stepped out onto the porch, closing the door behind him.

"Hello!" he called.

"Hey, Dad," said Cooper, climbing the steps to greet him. "This is Molly. We met in Las Vegas."

I caught the lack of the word marriage. Cooper's dad was as tall as Cooper, in his early seventies but fit and hearty with a full head of close-cropped gray hair. His face was weathered to a ruddy tan, making his eyes blaze bluer above his immaculately-pressed plaid button-down shirt. He radiated command and power, and some other quality I couldn't pin down. Charisma, maybe.

"Molly. Good to meet you. I'm Ted Middleton. Call me Ted. Come in," he said, gesturing at the closed front door. "Mosquitoes, you know. Around here we can't leave a door open."

I glanced at Cooper, who silently seconded his father's gesture with the smile that had been missing from the older man's face. Though he tried to hide it, I caught trepidation behind the smile. He was nervous.

Inside the house, the air dried up. I hadn't realized how soupy and humid it had been outside until I stepped out of it. Beyond the front door, a tremendous U-shaped staircase rose two stories, surrounding an ancient chandelier with sharp-pointed crystal that looked too heavy for the dull brass fixture in the ceiling to support. Anyone standing under that thing if it fell would be sliced to ribbons.

For the moment, though, I was too tired for the chandelier to arrest my macabre imagination. I longed for a bed. Any bed. The flight and its connection, not to mention my nerves at flying for the first time and the surreal situation I'd gotten myself into, had kept me awake and staring all night.

Not yet, though. We followed Ted into an expansive living room, full of heavily-carved Victorian-type furniture I guessed was the real thing. I suspected it had bruised many an unwary shin in its day. Some kind of textured fabric in beach colors had been used above a paneled chair rail instead of paint or regular wallpaper, the better to display a collection of glass cases containing various oddities I desperately wanted to examine. The case closest to me held a dragonfly, caught in eternal mid-flight by the jeweled pin that had stabbed it through the heart. The room was like a museum—the deep pile of the rug silenced all movement. Great. I wouldn't want to do the get-the-paternal-blessing-interview anywhere that wasn't fabulous. Nerves threatened to sink me, until I remembered it didn't matter what Ted thought of me. This wasn't a real meet-the-parents thing.

The opposite wall of the room had huge floor-to-ceiling windows with no coverings, and no wonder. The view was spectacular—green and yellow marsh grasses that met blue water sparkling in the morning sun. A long wooden dock bisected the grasses almost to the horizon. A single boat bobbed at the end. It looked like a landscape painting. The golden wash made the outside scene seem almost as if it didn't exist in the same world as the heavy-furnished house—like a view through a telescope. The urge hit from nowhere: I wanted to get outside. Out of this house.

Now.

I shoved down the irrational impulse to flee and sat on the

severe-looking tweed sofa next to Cooper opposite his father in an imposing wing chair. I swung my calf free of a carved wooden rosette at the sofa's edge. Cooper scooted over, closer. Right. We were going to pretend this was real.

"Where's Caroline?" asked Cooper.

"Don't know. Upstairs, I expect," said Ted.

"I want her to meet Molly."

"I'd like to do that myself," said Ted, pointedly.

"Your home is lovely," I said, in my best imitation of someone from HGTV, trying hard to stop running my fingernails along the ridged tweed of the sofa over and over.

Ted stared at me, a half-smile making him look mischievous. He turned to Cooper. "A Yankee?" Then to me, "Where is your home, darling?"

That was a loaded question. Here we go. "Michigan, originally."

"What part?"

Cooper hadn't asked me that. I hadn't prepared. I blurted out the truth. "Ypsilanti. And Detroit, when I was young."

"I feel like I've missed a couple of steps, son. When did y'all meet, exactly?"

We glanced guiltily at each other. Cooper took my hand. Courage shot up my arm from where our hands touched.

Cooper cleared his throat. "We met in Las Vegas. No better way to tell you this than straight out. We had something special right away and we got married yesterday in one of the chapels."

"Do what?" said Ted, his face going slack. I gathered "do what" was Southern for "what in the ever-loving fuck."

"We're married. Molly is my wife."

I'd been punched in the gut before, more than once. Ted looked like that feels—helpless and without air. He took time to collect himself, gripping the turned ends of the chair arms. "Well, of all the damn fool things you've ever done, and you've done some damn fool things, this beats them all."

A whole flood of disappointment and worry and anger and frustration queued up behind that relatively mild statement, and I braced for the deluge, clinging to Cooper's hand like a life preserver.

"Cooper! What is the surpr—" came a breathless voice from the hall. A woman about my age, with beautiful gold-flecked chestnut hair to match Cooper's, skidded into the room. "Oh! Hi." She halted uncertainly, taking in us on the couch and her father's reddening but still shocked face.

Cooper stood, tugging me up with him by the hand, a wicked glint to his eyes. He was enjoying this. "Molly, this is my sister Caroline. Caroline, this is my wife, Molly Middleton." He grinned at her.

"Are you joking?" she demanded, her eyes narrowed.

In answer, Cooper held up our hands, rings showing.

Her eyes lit up. I got a quick assessing look, and then she attacked me. My defenses, long used to wary watchfulness, went up and I stiffened, arms up to block an assault.

Instead, she enveloped me in a hug. A huge hug, the kind that meant something, the kind that said welcome, the kind I'd experienced infrequently enough to count on one hand. She stepped back, grinning. My matching grin surprised me.

"Well, hi! Welcome to the family!" She glanced at her father, still stone-faced in his wing chair, his crossed-leg pose rigid. "Oh, look. You've turned Daddy into stone."

"Yes," said Ted, a single syllable. Cooper squeezed my hand even tighter. Ted cleared his throat. "I think we'd like to hear all about how it happened, son. Get to know your bride."

Was I the only one who heard the sarcasm on that last word?

"Sure," said Cooper, relief on his face. "Molly's from Michigan. She was vacationing at the same hotel we went to. She's an interior designer."

Yep. There it was. The sum total of what he knew about me, and most of it wasn't even true. Cooper had done nothing but offer me kindness, and I'd done nothing but lie, by omission at least. He was pretending to care about me for the two people in the world most important to him.

"And you just fell for each other? Like that?" Caroline clapped her hands together in delight. I estimated her to be a few years younger than me. Maybe late twenties. She had the kind of looks that turned heads—endless legs, bountiful shiny hair, tasteful clothes that came from expensive stores. "That's so romantic. Not like you, Coop. What came over you?" she teased.

"Yes. Not like him at all," said Ted implacably, giving me the once-over. "And I can imagine what came over him. Caroline, why don't you go fix us some tea?" Translation: get out. Ted's voice left no room for ambiguity.

Caroline read something on his face and departed without another word.

"Now, Ms. . . . what is it?"

Automatically, I said, "Todd."

"Middleton," said Cooper. He was doing this all the way. Gratitude washed over me. I should let go of his hand but I wanted the warmth a little longer.

"Right. Molly. What exactly do you do?" asked Ted.

"I'm an interior designer. I'm between jobs right now, though." I made sure I met his eyes as I told the lie. Ted seemed like the kind who didn't miss much. He'd be the kind who watched for body language tells. I'd been watching his, and other than the brief shock brought on by the news, he'd been careful to give nothing away.

"Of course. Charleston is full of interior designers. I'm sure you know of Bitsy Waterman. Close friend. That profession is a small world, isn't it?" He grinned, but unlike the sunshiny smiles of his children, his grin hid tiny things that sting.

A test. Before I could decide whether such a person as Bitsy Waterman existed, he went on. No sweet doddering old man here. "Who are your people? Do you have family up north?"

"No. All my family is gone." Knowing he'd consider this too blunt, I went on in a vein he'd understand. "It must be wonderful to have your family so close-knit."

"Yes. I like to have my children close. Caroline has recently extricated herself from an unfortunate situation. I do hate seeing my children in unfortunate situations."

"Dad. Give me a break. There are no unfortunate situations here," said Cooper, good-naturedly.

Despite my best efforts to hold it in, I yawned. Cooper smiled.

This time Ted's shoulders relaxed into a posture of warmth and comfort, only a shade off from convincing. He glanced at Cooper, whose grip on my hand relaxed. "You're right. Darlin'," Ted drawled, "I'm a bit overprotective. Looks like you've come to the right place if you've got no family to spend Thanksgiving with. And it looks like you don't need tea, right now. You need to sleep. Coop, take her on up to your room. Get her settled. We'll talk again when you've caught up on your rest."

With alacrity, Cooper stood and extended a hand. He probably was as anxious for the interview to be over as I was. "Thanks, Dad. It was a red-eye flight. We're pretty tired."

I skirted the potential crash zone below the chandelier and followed Cooper up the creaking stairs. The upper hallway looked like a hardened wedding cake—moldings thicker than my waist adorned the tops of the walls and every window frame. Two long hallways branched off from the main chandelier hall, each with doorways farther than I could see. Three doors down the left hallway, Cooper set our luggage down in a large room with a queen-sized bed in the middle. The enormous four-poster faced a pair of tall windows with open drapes and a view of the marsh and the water.

"Wow. Is this your room? It's beautiful. Look at the view!" I said.

"Yep," said Cooper, waiting on my reaction.

The room had ordinary blue paint on the wall, and a couple of modern framed posters advertising shrimp festivals and an art show in Charleston. Here, no cushioned hush silenced everything. The light streamed in, dispelling the gloom from downstairs, leaving behind only my nervousness at how to handle the bed situation.

"Yep. Look. I know this is weird. In retrospect, maybe we shouldn't have done it, but now we've told them we're married for real. They won't believe it if we don't sleep here together. Dad is

. . ." He trailed off. "Don't worry, though. I'll sleep on the floor." He stowed the luggage next to the dresser and unzipped a bag, his back to me.

"Wait," I said, touching his arm to stop him. "I'll sleep on the floor." The thick patterned rug was nicer than most of the beds I'd slept in. "This is your house and your bed and you've been so nice to bring me here and everything. You could have walked away in Las Vegas. Most guys would have."

"Ha. Doesn't speak too well to the guys you've known." He pulled out a phone charger and plugged it in. "The way I see it, it took two people to get married. I couldn't just leave you there. I feel responsible. Maybe it sounds stupid, but I married you. For now, at least, you're my wife. It'll be easier to see the lawyer together and get it all straightened out here rather than send papers to sign back and forth all the way between Nevada and South Carolina. Or Michigan, I suppose. You'd have been going back there."

"No," I said, feeling that concerning need for honesty again. Too much of that would ruin everything. "I wasn't. I went to Las Vegas looking for work. I needed a change of scene. I had a job there but it didn't work out. Money's tight." I couldn't meet his eyes, sure I'd see calculations of the cost of the meals he'd bought and the hotel room where we'd done . . . whatever we'd done.

After a beat, he said, "Aw, girl, I didn't know that."

I glanced up. Doubt was written on his face, and I hated it.

A desperate urge to make him understand made the words spurt out of my mouth. "But I really am not a gold-digger. You have to believe that." Despite my hatred of tears, the lack of sleep had destroyed my ability to squelch them. They burned the corners of my eyes. "I never meant to . . . to trap you into marriage. Only an idiot would think you'd let yourself stay in that trap. I let you get dinner, but I never wanted . . . or thought—"

"Shhh." Cooper sat down on the edge of the bed. "I know. I wish I'd known at the time that you needed help. I would have given it." He patted the bedspread beside him. "Come on. You need sleep."

Exhausted, I melted more than sat next to him. Who was this man? I believed him. He would have helped me in whatever way I needed. He rubbed my neck and shoulders briefly, shooting warmth and relief and something else into all the parts of me. I closed my eyes.

Without warning, Cooper pushed my shoulders down into a prone position. Adrenaline shot to my arms and legs and I struggled. Bad things could happen in prone positions. Too vulnerable. Panic rose and I pushed his hands away, before I met his eyes and saw only surprise and the total lack of malignant intention there. He only meant for me to sleep.

His lips twitched, misunderstanding me. I let him and forced my breathing to calm.

"Don't worry," he said. "I wouldn't even think it. Sleep." He stood to make room to pull my legs up onto the bed, and removed my shoes. A blanket folded at the bottom of the bed I hadn't noticed drifted over me. He took one pillow from the headboard and lay down blanket-less on the rug beside the bed.

"Um. If you want, you can sleep up here. We could put a pillow between us," I offered, hating the idea of him sleeping on the floor in his own room.

"No, ma'am," he said, a smile in his voice. "Too much temptation."

"Oh."

The odd noises that go with a strange house kept me awake for a few minutes. The low rumble of his voice penetrated the last shreds of my consciousness.

"You should know I wouldn't say no another time."

CHAPTER THREE

Cooper and I slept much of the day and woke groggy and disoriented around dinner time. Neither Cooper's father nor his sister was home, so we rode in Cooper's truck to the Subway housed in one of the gas stations at the blinking yellow light on Highway 17 and took the food back to his house to stare glassy-eyed at the TV until crashing again. I stuck close to his side, afraid of getting lost in the dim hallways of the silent house, never to be heard from again. This time I insisted he take half the blankets and all but one of the pillows.

In the morning, I woke first and got out of bed on the side opposite where Cooper and Mary Jane lay curled on the mat on the floor. I padded to the window, marveling at the way the rising sun colored everything—marsh, water, sky—golden. The Middleton house had no neighbors I could see: a small garden shed, a boat garage, and a larger work shed kitty-corner from back right corner of the house spread out to the right of a formal garden with manicured hedges lining a diamond-shaped path that stretched almost to the water. Mary Jane stood with a jingle of her collar tags and pushed her warm head against my leg, spreading calm with the simple touch. The water didn't extend far in front of us. There must be some peninsula or island or something beyond it, but it was all marshland and trees as well. You could walk naked in front of this window and nobody would see unless they came by boat, binoculars in hand.

Speaking of naked, I had on my own scoop neck shirt without a bra and a pair of Cooper's athletic shorts. I needed the bra, but how to put it back on with Cooper in the room? Blanket. I'd sit on the floor on the other side of the bed from Cooper and put it on under the blanket.

This plan worked beautifully in my mind, but not so smoothly in real life. The blanket smothered and tangled with my clothes, and that's how I didn't notice when Cooper, awake and soundless on bare feet, peeked under the blanket at a point in the proceedings where I'd gotten the bra back on but not the shirt.

"What in the name of God are you doing under there?"

The blanket slipped to the floor. Helpless, I sat there holding the shirt to my chest. Cooper's curious eyes widened. He whirled away. I tossed the blanket aside and whipped the shirt on. No point in modesty now.

"Cooper, I'm sure you've seen it before. You know, in the hotel. I'm sorry."

"I haven't seen it sober before." He let out a low sound of approval.

At the appreciation in his morning-scratchy words, a hot streak of yearning shot through me. It had been so long since I'd had sex . . . that I could remember. A memory that refused to show itself whole danced before me: Cooper shirtless, broad honed planes of tanned chest, wide shoulders, no fat on him. The memory slipped away and dissolved.

Across the room, he crouched by the window, keeping his gaze fixed on the horizon and rubbing Mary Jane's back, worn T-shirt obscuring my view. He cleared his throat. "Ah. Thought we could get dressed and get on into Charleston today. I've got a buddy from high school who's a lawyer. Might be willing to see us on short notice."

"Okay."

"Are you decent?" He turned around at the window, sunlight spilling across his cheekbones, lighting the gold streaks in his hair. "Good. I'll go start some coffee. You take the shower first."

Ninety minutes, a pot of coffee, and a whole lot of extra-careful politeness later, we were back out on Highway 17 heading south to Charleston. Cooper handed me his phone and told me to find the phone number for Gibbes DuPre, the man who'd be able to turn this faux marriage into no marriage.

"We went to Porter together. He's a lot brighter than me, though. Went on to Duke and then Harvard Law."

"Here it is." I handed back the phone and he pushed the green button.

"Yes, good morning. I wondered if Gibbes was around? Cooper Middleton. Thanks."

He waited.

"Gibbes. I need a lawyer. ASAP . . . Yeah. For me . . . Yeah, man. I've descended into a life of crime. Offed Dad and Caro. You've got to save me from the chair . . ." He grinned at me, laughing into the phone. "No, of course not. What do you take me for? No . . . Can you do today? . . . Oh. Sure. We can do that . . . See you then. Thanks." He ended the call and tossed the phone into the truck console.

I focused on forcing my nervous hands to still. "Well?"

"He can see us at one this afternoon. He's got court this morning."

"It's only eight-thirty. Should we turn around?" We'd been driving no more than fifteen minutes. Charleston was another thirty minutes further south.

"Naw. Let's go on. You've never been to Charleston, right?"

"No. Is it nice?"

Pride and love shone in his face. "Charleston? Might be a little biased, but I like Charleston pretty well. Do you like history?"

I did. Or I had, when I studied it in school. I nodded.

"It's well-preserved. Lots of old houses from the 1700s and 1800s. Some you can tour. We could do one of those, if you want. They also have carriage tours. The Battery walk by the water. Museums. The Exchange. It's all walkable. You up for a tour?"

Only a truly horrible person could say no to all that downplayed enthusiasm, and I might be horrible, but not that horrible.

"Sure. That sounds fun."

It sounded like a date. A date that would climax with a visit to an annulment attorney.

Nobody had ever said I led a boring life.

Three hours later, I'd fallen in love. Hopeless, desperate, forever love—the kind I knew I'd never recover from.

For Charleston. We crossed the most spectacular bridge I'd ever seen and inched down Meeting Street past beautiful old houses with their sides turned to the street. We wandered the streets reading plaques and peeking at gardens through wrought-iron gates. We toured one house, marveling at its spectacular spiral staircase spanning the foyer supported by nothing but air for two hundred years. From the seawall along the Battery, Fort Sumter was a black speck out in the enormous harbor.

By the time we reached the Exchange, an imposing old building Cooper said was used as a custom house back when the city was the major port in the colonies, I had developed the eerie feeling I'd been in Charleston before.

Cooper bought us tickets and a tour guide led us through the expansive and ornate upper floor rooms of the Exchange. The building had been built before the Revolution and had been used by the colonists to plot and plan South Carolina's revolutionary tactics and to ratify the Constitution.

"Is that the whole tour?" I asked Cooper, as we descended the stairs back toward the gift shop.

"Nope. This is my favorite part. The prison in the basement."

We descended into a dank, windowless, low-ceilinged brick room, stuffed with miserable-looking mannequins dressed like colonials and pirates. I swallowed wrong and doubled over to cough. Cooper's hand flew immediately to my back.

"This was a prison, too?" I managed, as I got my breath back.

"Yeah. Supposedly it's haunted by dead pirates. I used to beg my parents to bring me here when I was at the height of my elementary school career as a paranormal investigator." His sheepish smile put a dent—a small dent—in my tension. He registered my shortened breathing. "Hey, are you okay?"

"I'm fine. It's just that, um, it's a little claustrophobic in here."

I wanted to run, and my heart acted as if I'd already started. "Would you mind terribly if we went on up before she finishes?" I said, pointing to the tour guide.

Cooper's obvious worry made me feel worse about my white lie. "Of course." He waved apologetically at the tour guide, mouthing the word "sick" so she wouldn't feel bad about her tour-giving ability. The casual thoughtfulness of it took me aback. I'd never known anyone who would have cared about the feelings of an unknown tour guide. In a moment we were back in the sunshine. Cooper, to his everlasting credit, said nothing more about my "claustrophobic" episode.

I couldn't tell him the real reason I'd freaked.

Cooper knew everything about Charleston, and he told me stories of violent deaths by duel, of slave markets and abolitionist sisters, of earthquakes and bombardments and elopements and yellow fever epidemics. I'd never really thought about all the generations of people who'd lived and suffered and loved and cried and died before us, but in Charleston it was somehow easier to imagine them staring at us from the time-worn shaded doorways or in the wind whistling through the mossy churchyards. A shiver twitched my shoulders.

At almost the moment when my feet burned so badly from walking I'd have to beg for mercy, Cooper stopped in front of an old house converted into a restaurant.

"Hungry for lunch? My treat," he said.

"What is this place?"

"It's called Poogan's Porch. The restaurant is named for a dog. See, there's his grave right there. Only place to eat in the city that's haunted by a dog that I know of."

More tension drifted away at his boyish delight in ghosts. "Is everything in Charleston haunted?"

Cooper laughed. "So they say. There's hardly an inch of ground where there aren't bodies buried. They find them every time they build a new parking garage. The ghost tours at night make plenty of money."

"Yeah, but dog ghosts?"

"Yup. Here, anyway. They say if you're lucky, you can feel Poogan brush against your legs under the table, looking for scraps."

"Seriously? That's not what I'm accustomed to feeling brush up against my legs under a table," I tossed over my shoulder, figuring a little flirtation couldn't hurt. As practice.

Inside, the restaurant hadn't yet filled up for the lunch crowd. A hipster server with a buzz cut and a long beard saw us to a table by the window immediately and was back in minutes to take our order.

I followed Cooper's recommendation to get the shrimp and grits—classic Lowcountry cuisine, he said, and better at Poogan's Porch than anywhere else in town. Generally, I'd eat anything, though the menu was full of words I didn't know: "tasso" and "pimiento" and "sorghum" among them.

"Do you spend a lot of time in Charleston?" I asked.

"A fair bit. Most of my clients are here. My office is in Mt. Pleasant, though I work out of the house most of the time. My mom was from Charleston. When I was a kid we came down all the time to see my grandparents. They lived in one of the old houses South of Broad. We passed it."

"Are they still alive?" If they were, they'd be pretty ancient. Cooper was thirty-four.

"No. My grandfather died when I was eight. My grandmother died a couple of years later." He ran a finger around the rim of his water glass. "Caroline is five years younger than I am. She hardly remembers them. Or our mother."

"She was young when your mother died?"

"Yeah. She was six. I was eleven."

"What happened? Was it cancer?" I wanted to know, but as soon as the words were out I wanted to kick myself. It was none of my business.

He swallowed and gave me a long searching look. "Mama committed suicide." He shuddered visibly.

"Oh, God. That's terrible. Oh, Cooper." I had a sudden desire to take his hand or come around the table and hug him, and it wasn't all altruism. Part of me needed to move my mind away from this topic for my own mental health.

Cooper played with the edge of the tablecloth. "It was around this time of year. She didn't leave a note. I didn't understand it at the time. I was a kid. I'd said a cuss word in front of her the week before, and somehow I got the idea that her death was my punishment. Obviously, I know now she must have been depressed. Dad said later he'd found her crying a lot, and she never said why. She never let us see it, though." He gave me a tentative smile.

"You remember her differently?" I asked, wanting to let him talk about the good things. Anything to encourage that smile.

"Yeah. She was so great. She read to Caroline every night. She came to all my baseball games and practices. She even played video games with us. She'd just decorated the house for Christmas. She was always there to listen to all my problems and she always knew when I needed a hug. Nobody understood it."

"And your dad? Was he okay?" It was difficult to picture Ted and his commanding presence handling two grieving kids.

"Dad was a wreck. Torn up in a big way. He stayed in his room or his office with the door closed for two weeks except for the funeral. Plus he had no idea how to cook or take care of a house." Cooper's smile was rueful. "It was a mess there for a while. Eventually, he had to hire a lady, Etta was her name, to work full time." With his eyes downcast and the memories he was reliving, he looked every year of thirty-four. None of those years had made any of this easier for him to bear.

"I'm so sorry I asked you. Made you tell me." I clenched my fingers under the table. I wanted to reach for his hands.

"Don't be. It was a long time ago. Dad can't bear to talk about her. He can't even say the word 'suicide' at all. But I think it's better to talk about it. When I was in college I volunteered at a hotline. Keeping quiet about stuff like that makes people less willing to get treatment when they need it."

"That's true," I said, though I'd come from a family where the preference had been to tell nothing at all to anyone about anything. Though I shared with Cooper a natural inclination to straightforwardness, I'd spent a lifetime keeping my mouth shut.

"I found her," said Cooper, slowly, not meeting my eyes. The water glass in his hand vibrated. His Adam's apple moved convulsively.

"You . . . you did?" A passing server stepped on a creaky floorboard, making me flinch.

"Yeah. I came home from school and saw. I dropped my backpack and called her name. I had a good grade on a test to show her." He ran an index finger in a track over the tablecloth. "Then I saw her leg, behind the sofa. It was anti-freeze."

Unbidden, a fragmented memory flashed of our tiny living room, blood on the sofa, Ma on the floor, the stark contrast between the pale skin of her arm and the blood everywhere.

I swallowed, forced the memory away as I'd done a million times before.

Cooper looked up. "I didn't even need to touch her. I remember the feeling in the room, like she was gone, like she wasn't there anymore. An empty room, even while I stared at her pink polo shirt. It's funny, you know. The house still feels like that to me. Like there's . . . something missing. I hate going in that room to this day. Have you ever seen anyone dead before?"

"Yeah. I have," I said, adding nothing more.

He looked at me, registering that nothing more on that topic was coming. "How old were you when your mother died?"

"Seventeen." Move off the topic. Cooper might be able to talk about all this, but I wasn't. "I'm so sorry all that happened to you so young. To lose your grandparents and then your mom all so close together."

"Well, I haven't had a bad life. I had Mama for eleven years and I've still got Dad and Caroline. Haven't had to do without. It's been good. Dad did pretty well after Mama. He kind of threw himself into fixing up the old house for a few years afterwards. You might get him to give you a tour later, you know, because you're an interior designer. The house was in a magazine once."

The magazine had to be called *Southern Mansions That Look Like Slightly Creepy Museums*. At the next table, a bald man eating alone dropped a piece of silverware. I turned my head in time to see him lean back. He'd been listening to our conversation. I shoved down my unease. He must just be nosy.

"Right," I said, dropping the volume a bit. "That might help me get him to hate me a little less, anyway." Relieved he'd taken us so firmly off the topic of dead mothers, I struggled for something interior design-ish to say. "I love the emphasis on the view. The lack of drapes on all the waterside windows was a good choice."

"Yeah, though it's not always great. Once I'd come up after an evening run to get a shower and had pulled off all my sweaty stuff near the windows in my room. There were two guys and a woman I didn't know in a fishing boat right outside, probably lost their way in all the creeks and channels. With the lights on, I'm sure they got a real good view," he said, rubbing the back of his neck, eyes sparkling.

"I doubt she minded," I said, opting for reckless flirtation again. It paid off immediately, as I watched the pupils of his green eyes dilate. A pulse of heat shot south.

The moment stretched and lingered, the eye contact fixing me in place, water glass raised halfway to my mouth. He swallowed. I put down the glass. The contact held, until I began to feel invisible delicious fingers on my skin.

Invisible things on my skin. "Whoa," I said, breaking the contact. "I think maybe I felt the ghost of the dog on my ankle. You?"

"I felt something, all right."

It wasn't the ghostly dog.

CHAPTER FOUR

After lunch, we walked four blocks in a silence punctuated only by two comments about the weather, one wobble on a cobblestone, and three thank-yous for lunch. The whole situation was so surreal I couldn't think of anything to say. Cooper led me to the law office of Gibbes DuPre, on the third floor of a nondescript building on Meeting Street.

I could have sworn I saw the same bald man who'd dropped the fork at the restaurant crossing the street as we entered the building, but he disappeared before I could get a good look. Certain Cooper would think I was paranoid if I mentioned it, I stayed silent.

In the dark wood and leather waiting room, we sat in two separate armchairs, trying to act like eating lunch together and seeing an annulment attorney in the same day were compatible activities. The silence began to make me sweat. I grabbed the first magazine I touched to kill the awkwardness.

Cooper's knee bounced. I glanced at his foot and my cheeks heated. When I looked up, he was watching me with steady green-brown eyes.

The small man who opened the door behind the receptionist's desk wore a conservative gray suit, white shirt, red tie, and tortoiseshell glasses. He also had unruly sun-kissed hair and a tan. He spent time outdoors.

"Coop! Long time no see, man. And who's this with you?"

I stepped forward. "I'm Molly Todd."

Cooper let it pass this time. Weirdly, a twinge of regret flickered though me at the sound of my own name.

"I'm Gibbes DuPre. Nice to meet you, Miz Todd," he drawled,

dragging out the vowels into something like music. "Come on back."

We followed him to his office and sat. Gibbes leaned back in his chair with a creak and steepled his hands under his chin. "Now, what can I do for you, Coop? You sure you didn't rob a bank or something?"

Cooper relaxed in his seat, an easy grin making his face light up. "Nope. Sorry. Nothing so exciting. It seems that Molly and I may have had a little too much to drink in Vegas last weekend. We found ourselves squinting at the sun with hangovers . . . and a marriage certificate."

I had to give Gibbes his props—he had a good poker face. I'm sure it came in handy in court. He held his interested and helpful expression without change. He turned to me. "Now Miz Todd. You sure he didn't slip something in your drink? Because let me tell you, this old dog ain't good enough for you." Back to Cooper, he said, "I know you must have done something criminal, Coop. No way this little lady would take you on otherwise." Then he let the serious face slip and started a cackle of a laugh, so rat-a-tat and froggishly rusty-sounding I couldn't help but laugh myself.

"Thanks, DuPre," said Cooper, though he laughed along with us. "Appreciate it."

"Known him for years. He's a damn fool," said Gibbes, making clear that for him, a damn fool was a damn good thing. "Coop's famous for getting up to some nutty stuff back in the day. Did you tell her about your Battery run?"

Cooper clamped his lips together in mid-laugh. "Uh, no. You don't really need—"

"Oh, I do." Gibbes grinned devilishly, and Cooper leaned back, resigned. "Senior year of high school, Coop here had a thing going with a bunch of guys where we'd dare each other to do crazy things. His were always the most over-the-top, but eventually a buddy of ours came up with a humdinger. You see, Cooper held the school record for the two-mile in track."

"It was the thirty-two-hundred meters," said Cooper, suppressing a grin.

Gibbes stared at him as if he were an irritating fly. "Uh. Whatever. So our buddy dared Coop to wait for the day of the Charleston Garden Tour, you know, when all the tourists come from wherever to see all the flowers and things, and run nekkid as a jaybird down the Battery from the Exchange to White Point. It's only half a mile or so—no distance at all for him." The cackle went off again. I giggled automatically. Some people have a laugh that is funny all on its own. Gibbes DuPre was one.

"Did he do it?"

"Well, now. I guess that's as good a test of your marriage as any. What do you think?"

It didn't take a spouse to judge, given Cooper's red face and fidgeting hands. Surprising joy burst free. "I think he probably did?"

"You'd be right! He sure did, and we drove along beside him behind a carriage full of tourists, watching his shining white ass dodge families with strollers and old couples on anniversary trips and blue-hairs from the garden clubs. Best day of my life. Ahem. I mean after my wedding day. And of course the births of my two children."

"Cooper. You didn't." We'd walked the Battery earlier in the morning. Even on a random Tuesday in November, dodging the tourist throng had required agility. Cooper had a wild streak. I shouldn't have been so unexpectedly delighted; he had gotten married drunk in Vegas, after all.

"I did," Cooper said, his face red but proud. "My honor was at stake. Fortunately, back then I could outrun the cops. Jumped into some clothes I'd hidden in a tree at White Point and went on my merry way. Also fortunate that back then nobody had cell phone cameras, or I'd be famous from coast to coast."

We grinned at each other, long enough for the thing between us from the restaurant to start burning again.

Gibbes cleared his throat, an eyebrow raised. I'd forgotten him. "So what is it exactly you need me to do?"

"We needed to ask about an annulment. How do we go about doing that?" asked Cooper, dropping his gaze and getting back to business.

"You sure you want one?" asked Gibbes, jesting on the surface but with an undercurrent of something edged in iron. He was reading our interaction like a billboard. Gibbes had mastered the good old boy impression, but in that moment I knew he was a hell of a lawyer, the kind that was as rare as a unicorn.

And I should know.

"How do you get an annulment?" I asked. "What are the steps?"

With an oblique look, he went to his computer and did some clicking. "I've got to look it up, you see, because annulments are rare these days. Used to be the thing if you were opposed to divorce. Now, nobody seems to care if you've been divorced three times. Uh, sorry, Coop. I forgot about Lynette."

"It's all right," said Cooper.

"Here it is. You have to have the right grounds for an annulment. One of you has to have been a resident of South Carolina for over a year to file here, so you've got that. The grounds are: fraud, duress, bigamy, incest, mental incompetence, underage, and no consummation by living together. Well, I'm hoping we don't have a bigamy or incest situation, and I think you're both old enough and clearly you're mentally competent. So. Any of those others fit?"

"What does duress mean?" I asked. I thought I knew the meaning, but I also knew enough to know that lawyers made words mean different things than they actually meant.

"Duress means did he hold a gun to your head. Did you threaten to kill his family? That kind of thing. It's for people forced into marriage somehow. Alcohol doesn't count."

Cooper and I exchanged glances. "No."

"What about fraud?" I asked.

"Fraud means one of you lied about something, or didn't tell the truth about something pretty big."

That fit. Before I could say anything, or figure out how to say something without giving anything away, Gibbes continued. "But for an annulment proceeding, that thing has to be something to do with the marriage. You know, like one of you knows you're infertile and didn't tell the other. You're not required to tell each other everything pre-marriage; only the stuff that can affect the state of the marriage."

"Oh," I said, untoward relief mixing with the worry that Cooper would be stuck with me. "Then that probably doesn't work."

"Y'all living together?"

"She's staying with me, and Dad and Caro, but we only got married three days ago. Or two. I don't remember which side of midnight it was."

"Let me be frank. In the old days, they used to call this consummation. I don't guess I need to spell that out for people of your intelligence. If you haven't had sex since you woke up married and you keep it that way, you can use that ground."

We looked at each other again. I tore my eyes away and gave Gibbes my best "thank you very much" smile. "That one might work. We're strangers, or we were."

Gibbes took off his glasses and shined them on the front of his pristine white shirt. "Well, then. I can draw up a complaint for annulment and get y'all squared away in no time. Today's Tuesday, and my wife and I are taking the kids to her mama's in Greenville tomorrow for Thanksgiving, Lord help me. So if y'all want to come on back on Monday, we can get it filed. On your way out today, stop by and see Ada. She can get all the info, Social Security numbers, birthplaces, all that, to get it started. It's not difficult. Then there's a hearing sometime later. If I can sweet talk a clerk, I could get you in within a couple of weeks. After that, poof! No more marriage."

"Thanks, Gibbes," said Cooper, standing and extending a hand for me. I loved that he did that every time.

Gibbes missed nothing, watching the gesture. "You're welcome," he said. "See you Monday. Y'all have a nice Thanksgiving. Pray for me in Greenville."

He moved around the desk and opened the office door for us, as Cooper put his hand on my lower back to let me go first.

"Oh," said Gibbes, as if it had just occurred to him. "Keep

your hands off each other in the meantime."

That night, we ate at T.W. Grahams in McClellanville, with Cooper's father and Caroline, and Caroline's four-year-old daughter Mia, who'd been visiting her father in Charleston but had returned home for Thanksgiving. Mia didn't resemble her mother at all, with her black hair and eyes, though they were equally beautiful. I assumed Mia's father must be Asian.

T.W. Grahams, like the restaurant Cooper had pointed out on the road from the airport, had gone with an intentionally "been here forever" exterior and an interior with basic tables and chairs combined with walls full of fishing boat curiosities. Cooper assured me that T.W. Grahams was regularly written up in *Southern Living* and that people drove from Charleston to eat the fresh-caught shrimp and flounder from the town's fleet of fishing boats. A friendly woman in a black T-shirt showed us to a round table in the center of the noisy restaurant.

Ted went to some effort to avoid sitting next to Mia. He didn't seem to have the knack of talking to children and didn't bother to hide his annoyance when she asked for different colored crayons or talked out of turn, oblivious to the grown-up conversation. Caroline's hands stayed in constant motion, handing Mia things or righting what she knocked over. My heart squeezed as Caroline dropped a lingering kiss on Mia's dark head.

Ted watched Caroline's head disappear below the table disapprovingly. She caught his expression as she popped up. Whatever she'd retrieved had landed closer to Ted than to Caroline. Ted had made no move to help pick it up.

"Dad," she said, checking to make sure Mia's attention was on a placemat art project. "I promise you won't catch anything too life-threatening."

Her tone was mild, but she made little effort to hide her sorrow. Ted didn't like Mia and Caroline knew it. I didn't know if it had to do with a general incompatibility with small children, anger at Mia's father, or worse, race issues, but no matter what the reason, I'd have a hard time liking a man who couldn't love his granddaughter.

It took forever and lots of earnest negotiation for Mia to decide what to order, though she eventually went with what Caroline said was her usual—fried flounder and French fries. I caught Ted rolling his eyes when Mia demanded that Caroline admire the way Mia had colored her paper pirate placemat.

"She's adorable," I said to Caroline. "She lives mostly with you, I take it?"

"Yes," said Caroline, from under the table as she picked up a dropped crayon. Re-emerging, she covered her mouth and whispered, "Though some people would like to change that. It's a constant battle."

She was talking about her ex, not her father. I glanced at Ted, who had angled his body away from Mia as if he didn't know her. Given the way he was acting, Ted would probably help Mia's father get custody. I forced myself to stop grinding my teeth.

"How long have you been apart?"

"Not long. Six months. Married six years and together for seven." She rolled her eyes.

I really wanted to ask her what happened, and it looked like she'd like to tell me, but it would be bad to have that conversation in front of Mia. I hadn't spent much time around children. There were, it seemed, a wealth of things one couldn't discuss when they were present.

Caroline gave me a wavery smile. "Though . . . I guess I still hope. Well. Anyway."

Ah. So she hadn't wanted the separation.

A gray-haired man in the signature black T-shirt came to our table, greeting all the Middletons by name. The owner of the restaurant, I imagined. Ted stood up to clap hands and shoulders. They chatted, not keeping their voices down, about how busy they were—"Worse problems to have!"—and how the shrimping season had gone well. Two other men came over to join them, all wearing the local uniform of pressed khakis and polo shirt or button-down with belt.

"What does your dad do?" I asked Cooper, who'd taken his turn admiring Mia's picture and hadn't stood to do the glad-handing thing with his dad's friends.

"Oh, a little of this and a little of that. He's part-owner of a couple of shrimping boats. He owns a lot of property—two or three businesses out on Highway 17. He's got a share in a gas station. I think maybe also a self-storage business or two in Georgetown. I'm sure I don't remember it all."

"Wow. That is a lot."

"Yep. Back when I was little, he was a structural engineer for a company in Charleston, but he retired from that when I was in middle school. Now he enjoys sticking his fingers in as many pies as he can find. Town might die without him. Just look at him."

A jovial and boozy crowd had surrounded Ted. Frequent guf-faws punctuated by back-slapping and elbows to the biceps made clear Ted's importance to these men.

"He seems popular," I said, watching.

"Mostly," said Cooper, following my gaze to where a younger man stood a bit apart from the herd, arms crossed. "He's got a few enemies. Dad's not always good at compromise. Fortunately, most of these guys are okay with that."

"Also," added Caroline, "we eat here probably three times a week. Everybody in town comes in, and Daddy does half his deals holding a drink."

Cooper scooted his chair closer to mine, ready to tell me some story that had his eyes lit up.

"Cooper," called Ted. "Come tell Floyd about that property you've got listed out on the Isle of Palms. His daughter wants to move out to the beach."

"Duty calls," said Cooper, putting his napkin back on the table. "Dad's responsible for most of my referrals. Sorry." He stood and was welcomed into the pack with more back-slapping.

A woman headed our way from the bar area. Unlike the other preppy women in bright twinsets and printed capri pants seated elsewhere, this woman wore jeans with ballpoint graffiti all over them and a black ribbed turtleneck, like the kind that had been popular when I was in high school. This outfit might not have been jarring on a young woman, but she was old. At least sixty, and possibly much older than that. She had a generous streak of pure white in the front of long iron gray hair worn layered like a much younger woman. No way to tell her exact age.

She plopped down in Cooper's chair and blew Caroline and Mia kisses. "Caroline, will you do the honors?"

"Yes, of course. Miss Aurelia is our honorary mother," Caroline said to me. "Miss Aurelia McClellan, this is Molly Middleton. Cooper's new wife." Caroline glanced at Cooper, but he'd been sucked into the aging testosterone huddle.

"What?" Miss Aurelia's eyes widened. "Did you say Cooper's new wife?"

"Yes, ma'am." The "ma'am" didn't come naturally to me unless I was confronted with a person whose authority could not be questioned. I'd only just met Miss Aurelia, but she fit in that camp without doubt. In fact, she might own that camp. "We've been married three days."

"Something told me I needed to get up and come on over here. Looks like I was right," said Miss Aurelia, rubbing her hands together. "And three days? No honeymoon?"

"Well, we got married in Las Vegas, so I guess we kind of already had the honeymoon."

"Did you now?" She narrowed her eyes, taking her gaze off me only long enough to click a pen she pulled from a back pocket to make an illegible note on an empty spot near the left hem of her jeans. What in the hell? "Don't mind me," she said. "My memory is shit and I can't remember anyone's name."

The profanity shocked me. I'd heard—and used—far more than my share of cuss words in my life, but it wasn't as common here. Cooper hardly ever used it and so far I hadn't heard Caroline say anything stronger than "crap."

Caroline glanced at Mia who'd either not heard the curse word or ignored it. Once reassured that Mia's innocence remained mostly intact, Caroline gave Miss Aurelia the classic "oh, please" look. Huh. Whatever she'd scribbled just now, it must not be my name. Not that it mattered. The odd thing here wasn't what she wrote on her jeans. It was that she wrote on them at all.

I'm sure it wasn't what Caroline would have done, but I did it anyway. "It's Molly. M-O-L-L-Y."

Miss Aurelia grinned, knowing I'd called her on her lie. "Well, M-O-L-L-Y, let me buy you a celebratory drink. I'd buy one for Cooper too, but it appears he's busy keeping his Very Important Papa happy. Caroline, Mia, you'll excuse us for a minute?"

"Sure. I've got to take Mia to the bathroom anyway." Caroline said, as Mia pulled on Caroline's hand. "See you in a few."

Miss Aurelia and I found an empty corner away from the table. She flagged down a passing waitress and told her to put two glasses of pinot grigio on her tab. "I've known the Middleton family since I was two years old. Ted pulled my ponytail for the first time before I went to kindergarten. His wife Barbara was one of my closest friends from high school. I was a bridesmaid in their wedding and I babysat those kids whenever Barbara needed a minute to herself."

"Oh." Though all that was intimidating—Miss Aurelia was clearly a close "family" member—her brown eyes were kind. She meant me no harm—as long as I meant none to her and hers.

"I also knew Cooper's first wife about as well as anyone in this town."

Intense curiosity washed over me as I accepted my glass of wine. Why would she bring up Cooper's first wife? What was the deal with this Lynette who'd married Cooper and stayed two years before disappearing forever without a trace? Something about the way Miss Aurelia avoided saying her name set off alarm bells. There was a story here. I glanced across the room at Cooper, hands down the best-looking man in the room and so far, the definition of kind and easy to live with. What had happened between Cooper and Lynette?

Miss Aurelia went on, taking note of my awareness of Cooper. "And given that, I want to tell you that if you need anything, anything at all, you ask me. May come a time when you have questions and can't ask a Middleton. If that happens, you run right on over. Give me your hand."

I stuck it out obediently, mind whirling. Her tone was urgent. She didn't expect me to come over and borrow a cup of sugar. Her words were code for something I didn't know to look for yet. She took my hand, turned it over, and whipped out her ballpoint. When I pulled back my hand, numbers were written on it.

She laughed at the question I must have worn all over my face. "That's my house number on Pinckney Street and my phone number. I'm serious, now, girl. You get in touch if things get odd."

"Thank you."

This time her laugh was more of a bark. "I wish you could see your face. You're thinking the only odd thing around here is me, and you're right, for now. Come on. Your food will be here soon."

Miss Aurelia ushered me back to the table, to which Caroline and Mia had returned. She kissed Mia on the top of her head. Before I sat, Miss Aurelia held her hands out. Not knowing what else to do, I took them. "Cooper is the best of men. You could have done a lot worse. I think Caroline would say the same. Cooper took care of Caroline during a bad time. If I know him, he'll do the same for you."

She squeezed my hands tight and reeled me in so she could speak into my ear, only to me. "And from the look in your eyes, you need it." To cover it, she gave me a smacking kiss on the cheek. With a queenly wave at Caroline and Mia, she saluted me with her wineglass and disappeared into the throng of people holding drinks while waiting for tables.

What on earth had just happened?

I took a good long look at Cooper, still explaining some real estate opportunity to the man named Floyd. He caught my eyes and did a frustrated grimace, but Floyd hadn't finished with him.

Caroline surfaced from under the table again, this time holding a dropped napkin. She gave me a knowing smile. "Don't mind Miss Aurelia. She's the closest thing to a real-live small-town eccentric we have. She's harmless, but she knows everything. She'll have your rank and serial number in addition to your name before the turkey is carved on Thanksgiving."

A shudder passed through me. I hoped not. "What is the writing on her jeans?"

Caroline giggled. "She's always done that. It's her notebook, she says. She must own fifty pairs of jeans, all scribbled over like those. Her handwriting is so terrible nobody can read it without doing a deep dive into her personal space, but the theory is she writes down little pieces of info she wants to remember. It's not names, I don't think. She's got a memory like a steel trap for names."

"I kind of got that." Under the table, I glanced at the neat numbers on the palm of my hand.

"I shouldn't have said all that. It sounded flippant and glib," said Caroline, a dent creasing her brow. "I love Miss Aurelia. She never married or had kids, so when my mama died—Coop told you about that, he said—Miss Aurelia sort of took charge. She spent hours with us outside, showing us how to identify plants and trees and birds. She fed us she-crab soup and red velvet cake and gallons of sweet tea. She kept up with our homework until Etta got situated. I owe her a lot. She's done more for me than anyone besides my family. She's there for pretty much everyone in town."

The food arrived, and Caroline broke off to cut up Mia's flounder. She glanced up when she was done, as Cooper slid into his seat.

"Just never assume you can keep anything secret from her," Caroline said.

"Who? Miss Aurelia?" asked Cooper. "Nope. She's got enough info written on two pairs of jeans to destroy the lives of half the town." He waggled his eyebrows. "Now. Let's eat."

CHAPTER FIVE

Ted spent the whole meal shaking hands, giving sugary compliments to wives, and otherwise asserting his dominance for everyone in the restaurant to see. Cooper and I didn't have much chance to talk, because once the food arrived, Mia abandoned her crayons and her iPod game and peppered everyone with questions. After we'd eaten all we could of fresh shrimp and some sinful gooey chocolate-y thing called Pawley's Island pie, we took a drowsy Mia home. Inside, Caroline took Mia up to bed. Ted retired to his walnut-paneled study, weaving a little from the many drinks his fellow townsmen had bought.

"Want to watch some TV or something?" Cooper asked.

It was too early for bed at only nine p.m., so I shrugged and followed Cooper to the family room down a hallway hung with a collection of photographs a hundred years old or more, all featuring ancestors with blank, staring eyes. He sprawled on the light-colored sectional—this room was done in cream and navy with a nautical flair—and clicked the remote. I sat a careful distance away, noting, and then looking away from, the shape of his muscular knees in his khakis.

"Anything you want to watch? I didn't ask the other night what you liked," he said, as he flipped channels.

"I'm good with most things."

"Usually when I turn on the TV it's to watch football, but Clemson doesn't play until Saturday. What team do you root for? Or do you?" He paused on the sports channels, apparently dissatisfied with the offerings there.

I almost laughed at his last afterthought of a question. Clearly, he had difficulty imagining a person who didn't root for a football team.

"I grew up in Michigan. Never heard of Clemson. Is that a high school?" I kicked his bent leg with my toe, to indicate I was teasing. In Las Vegas, in a group of drunk Clemson alums, I'd heard enough about Clemson that I could now sing the fight song.

"Whaaat? Clemson is the finest institution of higher education in the land. It's only the best football team in the nation." His horror was thirty percent comic effect, intended to mask the seventy percent of real horror.

"Everyone where I come from roots for either Michigan or Michigan State."

"Did you go to one of those schools?"

"No. I didn't go to college." It may have been my imagination, but in shifting his weight, he inched a millimeter or two closer.

"You didn't? I've got to admit, you seem like someone who's been to college."

I couldn't speak. I'd been an excellent student in high school. I'd done well in all the limited advanced course offerings we had in the Detroit Public School System. My eleventh-grade English teacher, a young woman who was part of Teach for America, had encouraged me to think about college. My family hadn't believed that college was necessary or even desirable—my mother had thought it was ridiculous that I didn't drop out of high school when I reached the legal age—but inside, in the quiet moments, I'd dared to dream about applying.

I never applied. Some dreams—a lot of dreams—don't come true. In the end, I did drop out of school, though I had no trouble getting my GED later. Cooper's unthinking compliment warmed me enough to cause the corners of my eyes to sting. In that one sentence, he'd restored to me a tiny piece of the identity I'd enjoyed for those few short school years as a "brain."

"Thanks. That's a nice thing to say," I said, concentrating on not letting my voice waver.

"Where'd you go to high school?"

"In Detroit. It wasn't unusual not to go to college." I considered the relative risk of continuing, then said anyway, "We didn't have the money." And my mom died during my senior year. I didn't add that. I'd already told him I'd been seventeen. Mentioning it now might be seen as a bid for sympathy. More importantly, it might let him begin to connect the dots.

I waited for the usual exhalation of pity: people imagined Detroit high schools festooned with razor wire, populated by drug-sniffing dogs, with burned-out faculty yelling assignments over the sound of violent gang fights in every classroom. That hadn't been my experience at all. On the contrary—many of my teachers had chosen to be there over the better-paying suburbs. In our east-side neighborhood, we lived close to the border of a particularly wealthy suburb, close enough that our houses, though small, were mostly well-kept.

Mostly. My mother hadn't been a fan of washing dirty dishes, let alone repairing the fallen gutter or doing more than covering the missing shingles with a blue tarp.

Cooper surprised me. He either had never heard of Detroit, had learned to conceal his emotions like an A-list movie star, or didn't pity me for being a product of an inner-city school system. In my confusion, none of these options seemed possible.

Actually, he looked guilty. He ran a finger down the seam of one of the couch cushions, eyes down. "I . . . I don't know what that's like. I was lucky. My family had the money for college—without loans, even. My mom's parents—the ones from Charleston—were wealthy."

"When we were in Charleston, you said they had a big fancy house there."

"They did. Built in 1814. I remember the attic, especially. It had all these trunks of ancient clothes. I used to try on the World War One uniform in there. There were old tuxedoes, and even a top hat. The house was on a tour at one point. I remember being there once when it came by. I loved the feeling of being part of history. Feeling like I belonged to it."

"It didn't pass down in your family?" Somehow, I didn't resent him for his wealth like I'd resented so many others. He didn't act entitled to it. He seemed honestly upset that our resource levels were different.

"Oh, it did. When my grandparents died, they left it to Mama. She was an only child. After she died, Dad inherited it and sold it. A white elephant, he said, with termites and a cracking foundation. Some Yankees—excuse me, people from Vermont—with a fortune in quarrying or something bought it and fixed it up. Now it's on the garden tour." His lips tightened. "It was in our family for eight generations."

"I'm sorry," I said, trying to imagine any eight-generation family history. I didn't know the names of anyone further back than my grandmother. Cooper quit tracing the seam, letting his hand fall open on the cushion as if defeated. The loss of that house bothered him, though not for its value.

I inched a little closer, intending to pat his shoulder. Instead, he took my hand, and my breath along with it. Startled, I met eyes that held a hint of the loss, but maybe something else besides. "Um," I said, trying to cover my awkwardness. "Shouldn't it have gone to you and your sister when your mom died?"

"No. Mama left everything to Dad. We were kids anyway—not like we could have taken care of the house. I'm not even sure it's legal for a minor to own a house. Guess Gibbes would know the answer to that," he said, a hint of babbling in his voice. "Though it doesn't matter now."

He gripped my hand tighter and urged me closer, his forest-colored eyes wide, the pupil growing larger. "Do you remember anything about Las Vegas?"

"I remember the buffets," I said, self-conscious laughter coloring my tone. "There was a lot of food. And . . ."

"And drink. But we shared a hotel room, didn't we? At least once? I could have sworn . . ."

"What?" Oh, my God. What had we done in a hotel room?

"Nothing."

"Oh, no. No. You have to tell me. I'm imagining the worst possible things." Just the mere mention of those worst possible things had caused my pulse to speed up in a pretty delicious way.

"Well, then, I want you to tell me what you're imagining," he said, mischief making him look younger than thirty-four.

"No. You first. Please." The words came out breathy with anticipation. I didn't mind.

He yanked me a little closer. I went, feeling the heat of his body now. My bent leg twined with his. My shoe dropped on the floor.

He leaned toward me, his wine-scented breath stirring the hair at my temple. He was going to kiss me. My lips parted in response as I reached to fill my hands with his hair as I'd wanted to. As I might have done. In the hotel room.

"You made the bed," Cooper said, lips not kissing but instead softening into a laugh.

"What?" I asked, too dazed by his nearness to register what he'd said.

"You made the bed. In the hotel room. I've never seen anyone do that before. You did a great job, too, but I couldn't figure out why you'd bother. It's a hotel. They have people for that."

My spine went slack as if melted and I slumped backward onto the sofa. Talk about a buzzkill. Could I put this next part off? "Well, I like things to be neat."

Cooper ran his knuckles up my arm. "Come on. There's neat, and then there's professional. You made that giant bed up with hospital corners and everything. Like you could bounce a quarter off the middle. Where'd you learn to do that?"

"Um," I said, stalling.

"Were you in the Army? Don't they make you do that there?"

"No." There was no way out. I'd have to give him a piece of the truth. "I wasn't in the Army. I'm not really an interior designer. As a matter of fact, I am a professional bed-maker. I worked at the Palace Hotel. In housekeeping. I'd been there about two weeks when I saw you."

Now was the part where he'd stand up, brush off his pants, and dash to his computer to send a reminder email to Gibbes DuPre to get on that annulment complaint right away.

"A maid," I continued, determined to get it over with. "I was a hotel maid." Or had been, until I quit the Palace after a man in one of the expensive rooms decided I was the dessert he'd ordered from room service instead of the bringer of towels I was supposed to be. His lips had been shiny with moisture. I remembered that much.

Which brought me to the buffet where I'd seen Cooper.

Cooper didn't stand up. He didn't scoot his knee so it wouldn't be touching the help. The servant class. He didn't blink or flare his nostrils. He only asked, "How on God's green earth did someone as smart as you end up in Las Vegas cleaning hotel rooms?"

"That's what I did in Michigan, before I left. But there aren't as many hotels, and I'd never traveled, so I checked with—" Someone. Someone I didn't need to mention right now. "A guy I knew and he made arrangements for me to go out to Vegas. Vegas is Hotel-Cleaning Nirvana. But it was somewhere different. A new start."

"I can see that," said Cooper, scratching his chin in an appraising kind of way. He shook his head sadly. "Though I don't think you were ever going to be the champion of the bed-making racket. I noticed there was one corner where the sheet gapped away from the mattress edge a little bit."

I stared at him. A tiny hitch to his lips hid a smile there. He was kidding. He didn't care that I'd been a hotel maid. "It did not. I'll have you know, one of my bosses once used my bed-making as a lesson for new maids."

"Naw. You? Sloppy. Sloppy as hell," he teased.

I thwacked him on the shoulder. "Am not. I could kick your ass any day of the week at bed-making."

He grabbed my hand, gently moving it to his shoulder. "I've got to admit it," he said, turning the full force of his spectacular eyes on me. "This champion bed-maker stuff is kind of turning me on. You know, all that perfection destined to be undone, over and over." He moved closer, enough for me to feel his skin warming mine even before he touched me.

Something inside clicked, like metallic clock parts fitting into perfect grooves. Memories danced, elusive, on the edge of my consciousness, at the corner of Cooper's lips. I gave up trying to fight them, or him. His long eyelashes swept closed as I stopped resisting the pull and swayed toward him.

Our lips met, uncertain at first, then harder, with consuming force. He pushed his fingers into my hair on either side of my head, his thumbs tracing the whorls of my ears as lightly as if they were spun glass. The long muscles of his back bunched and gathered under my hands as he pulled me closer. The kiss grew deeper, harder. The memories that had frustrated me for days pieced themselves back together. We'd done this much before, and we'd done it well. Our noses knew which way to go. Our mouths fit together. His tasted familiar: clean and healthy. His body—so honed and perfect everywhere I touched—understood what to do for mine. And mine—against all odds—had learned what it should have known all those years.

He pulled back, questions in his eyes. "We've done this before."

"I think so."

"But I don't remember if we . . ."

"Neither do I." My memories stopped with a bare chest, in the late-day sun from a hotel window. "I don't think we . . ."

He put one hand on my lower back to pull me closer, using the other to arrange my legs over his lap, where evidence grew undeniable that he might prefer his beds unmade. The second kiss shot adrenaline over every inch of my skin, making my clothes feel too tight and hot. He slid his hands up under my sweater, pushing it north. I worked on the buttons of his Oxford-cloth shirt. A humming urgency made my fingers nimble.

"Oh, get a room," came an affable voice from the doorway. Caroline. "Or, I guess, go to it."

We broke apart. The disconnect felt sudden, sharper, more difficult than I would have thought, like we'd come unstuck. Cooper backhanded his nose and mouth. I ran a nervous hand over my hair.

Caroline plopped down on the far end of the sectional and blew her bangs out of her eyes. "Glad to see you were having a better time than I was. Mia claimed she couldn't sleep without hearing *I Love You Forever* four times. Is it me, or is that the creepiest children's book ever written?"

Cooper let out a chuckle, apparently familiar with the book and in agreement with Caroline's assessment of it. "We were going to watch some TV," he said, giving me a sideways glance. "But I'm kind of sleepy now. Molly?"

A thousand fluttering wings of panic clogged my lungs at the thought of taking this to the next level. I stood, smoothing my pants over my legs and sliding my feet back into my shoes. "Um. Would you mind if I go for a little walk? I need some exercise. Lot of time in the car today. I'll be back in a few."

"Wait. I'll go with you," called Cooper. I'd already made it to the door to the front hall.

"No need. I want some fresh air."

"Molly. Wait. You need . . ."

I cut off his words with the thump of the heavy front door. Outside, a slight chill reminded me that it was in fact Thanksgiving week. All the green here kept letting me forget. My feet sank into the unfrozen lawn as I hiked toward the allée of live oaks. Dim light from the moon helped me find the brown crunch of the driveway, but also illuminated the ghostly tendrils of moss hanging from the trees. I had no idea where I was going, but I needed to go somewhere.

I'd let him kiss me. No, I'd kissed him. Without the excuse of alcohol. Without any of my barriers of protection. Without the ability to disappear into the night like a ghost.

I'd let it go too far.

The pull I felt toward Cooper scared me, but it could never work. No matter what Gibbes said, if anyone was not good enough in this pairing, it was me. Cooper deserved better. Far better than me. Cooper needed to end up with one of the Southern women I'd seen in the restaurant: twinset, pretty-but-practical heels, and simple pearl earrings. The kind with shiny hair. The kind who knew how to tailgate and call people "Sugar." The kind who had a whole host of loving relatives around every corner. The kind who'd fit perfectly into a picture on Cooper's real estate company brochure.

He would never end up with someone like me.

Ha! End up with me? That was a joke and a half. If he knew about my past, he'd kick me out of his house—and his town—as reflexively as he would swat a mosquito.

I was the kind of person a gentleman like Cooper would cross the street to avoid. The kind Caroline, much less Mia, had never met before in her life.

I was a person who'd spent all of her adult life in a maximum security prison.

For murder.

A bird sang in the distant branches of the live oak next to me. I went up to the trunk of the vast tree and leaned against it, trying not to panic, trying not to scream or beat my hands against the rough bark. I'd let it go too long. I should have told him before we got on the plane. Hell, I should have told him before the first meal he bought in Vegas. He'd brought me into his home. Where his family—including a child—lived. True, I'd done my time and completed my parole, but that didn't mean I wasn't a felon. I was a violent felon, and I'd stay one until the day I died. Afterward, too, if my grandmother had been right about purgatory.

I should have told him, but I'd wanted to pretend for a little while that I wasn't alone. That I wouldn't always be alone. That I was just like everyone else.

Against my spine, the enormous tree trunk was more wall than plant. Two hundred fifty years old, Cooper had said. How many prison terms did that add up to? How many families had lived their lives from cradle to grave within sight of its branches? How many people had been born and buried in that time?

I climbed easily to a low-hanging branch as thick as most tree trunks. The greenish-brown leaves of the fern Cooper had pointed out coated the top, but I figured this late in the year there probably wouldn't be too many bugs hiding in it. I pulled my knees up to my chest, mind searching for a way out.

I had almost no money. I had no job. I had no transportation. Everything would close for the four-day holiday weekend starting tomorrow. I had no choice at all except to stay here through Thanksgiving and wait for the annulment to be filed. On Monday, I'd ask Cooper for a small loan and get a job in Charleston, where there were plenty of hotels to clean. Without the help of my parole officer, job availability would be close to zero, but maybe I could call him and beg for another referral.

Meanwhile, I'd keep my comments about my personal life to a minimum and my guilt level dialed up to a thousand.

CHAPTER SIX

Cooper appeared in the kitchen where I helped Caroline wrap sweet potatoes in foil, and made a beeline for the coffee pot. The grace with which he moved registered low in my spine, the pull undeniable as he regarded me. Like a big cat, his footsteps were silent. He stretched a hand up to rub the back of his neck, showing me the bicep and pulling the T-shirt up to display a little hipbone. I swallowed. Undeniable, yes. Possible, no.

He didn't say a word until he'd gulped half an unadulterated cup, then he took in the scene. "She put you to work, huh? Well, fair's fair. I've peeled enough potatoes in that spot."

"We're not peeling," I said. "Apparently we bake them first to loosen the skin."

Caroline lobbed one at his head. He caught it with a snap of reflexes, a millimeter before it hit his forehead. "Seriously, I'd help, but Dad says I'm going hunting with him. He's already in the woods and has been since before dawn. He texted me to get my 'lazy ass' out there."

"In the woods?" I asked. "I thought hunters hunted in trucks. I've seen them, beside the roads."

"Some do," said Cooper, tossing the potato from hand to hand. "I don't. I like being in the woods. A lot of hunters do."

"Oh. What do you do with the meat?"

"Freeze it and eat it all winter, or give it to Hunters for the Hungry. I've never been a fan of shooting more than can be eaten."

"What's Dad after today?" asked Caroline.

"Oh, just deer. No hogs today."

"You hunt for pigs?" I asked, shocked.

Both Middletons laughed. "No, not pigs," said Caroline. "Wild hogs. Haven't you ever heard of wild hogs?"

I shook my head.

"They're a nuisance," said Cooper, now spinning the sweet potato in his palm like a top. "They're aggressive and dangerous to animals and people, and hard to hunt. We've got a lot of them around here in the Francis Marion National Forest and down on the river deltas. Hunting doesn't do much good, anyway. Their litters are so huge that unless you took out every male in the state, the population would keep increasing. I'm not a big hunter, but Dad is. At the holidays he likes for me to go with him. I'd invite you along, Molly, but Dad's funny about women being along on a hunt."

"Because I know that to be true, you're excused," said Caroline, hands out to catch the return of the sweet potato. "But get back early enough to help with the pies. You're better at crust than I am."

"You bake?" I goggled at him. Granted, I didn't have a lot of domestic experience with men, but I somehow hadn't pictured Cooper rolling out pie crust.

"Yep. Miss Aurelia taught us. She coming tomorrow?" Cooper tossed the potato back to Caroline, who nodded.

Miss Aurelia unsettled me. I'd have to concentrate on keeping my mouth full of whatever this was we were cooking to avoid spilling all my secrets.

"Good. Well, ladies, wish me luck." Coffee in hand, Cooper padded out of the kitchen, trailing a hand along my shoulders as he passed. It left an invisible scorch mark.

"Better him than me. Though I've never been invited," said Caroline, handing me the remainder of the washed potatoes. "Dad's a sweetie, but he's kind of sexist. Like it's 1954, maybe. He got pissed at Miss Aurelia for teaching Cooper to bake."

"Oh," I said, noncommittally, while filing away the raging misogyny for reference later. I liked Caroline—and Cooper—enough not to comment.

"My ex, Danny, is a nurse at MUSC, in Charleston. You should have heard Daddy going on about that when we started dating. Nursing is for girls, he said. Always wanting to know why Danny thought he couldn't hack it in medical school."

"I'm sure."

"I wish I could say Daddy stopped giving him a hard time after we got married, but you know."

I could imagine. I concentrated on preventing my eyes from rolling. "How'd you and Danny meet?"

Confirming my suspicion that she wanted to talk about her husband, Caroline's face softened. "Not long after college, I got assigned to work on a landscape design project for the hospital. Danny ate his lunch outside every day, and it wasn't long before I realized he was doing it on purpose to see me. We used to live in Charleston near the hospital until we . . . Until he left. He doesn't have family here—his family is in Chicago—so we agreed I'd take Mia and move back here and let him have the apartment." Her voice wobbled and her eyes grew bright.

If I were another girl, with a different history, I'd have hugged her, but hugs weren't really in my repertoire. I wished they were. I'd always wanted to have the kind of friendship women in movies did. "Hey. It's only been six months, you said? Maybe he'll change his mind. You never know. Stranger things have happened."

"I know. I don't usually get this emotional, but last year at Thanksgiving I thought everything was fine. We were so happy. I hate that Christmas is coming, and Danny won't be here, and Mia will have to travel back and forth. I hate it." She sniffled. "And . . . and I miss him."

"What happened?" It did seem odd. She clearly loved him. Had there been another woman?

"I don't know. I asked him, and all he would say is 'I can't do this anymore.'" Caroline's hands dropped uselessly to her sides. I stood to turn off the water and watched helplessly as she sat.

"Is there someone else?" I asked, worried my bluntness would kill whatever connection we'd made.

"No, that's the thing that is so odd. I've had a couple of friends whose husbands left like that, not saying why, claiming there was nobody and then lo and behold, a month later there's a serious girlfriend. Or boyfriend, in one case. But with Danny, it's not that. Mia would tell me if there were anyone around during her time with him."

It was written all over her, but I asked anyway. "Would you take him back now, if you could?"

She let out a mirthless chuckle and fiddled with a dish towel. "God. I should have some more self-respect, or something, but yeah, if he showed up here, I'd take him back in a heartbeat. I fantasize about going to the hospital and sitting on that bench, with his favorite chicken sandwich, and begging."

I wished I knew how to hug her. "I hope he sees the light."

"Me, too." Caroline turned to the pile of foil-wrapped potatoes, all business again. "Okay, let's toss these things in the oven. After an hour, we'll pull them out and when they cool, the skins slide right off."

"Then what do you do with them?"

"We mix them up with a whole bunch of sugar and butter and cinnamon, and bake it with an absolutely decadent brown-sugar bourbon pecan crumble on top. Tomorrow, we'll warm it up."

I did like sugar, even if I hadn't completely discarded my suspicion of sweet potatoes. "Do you do all this every year?"

"Yeah. Well, Etta did it when we were younger and even used to come over and help me do it after she didn't work here anymore. I've been handling it for the last four or five years. Hey," she said, a new thought occurring to her. "You're an interior designer. Today's the day Leandra Scott, Dad's decorator, comes to do the Christmas decorations. Maybe you'd like to help her."

My first impulse was to let my jaw hang open and marvel that this family was so rich they paid someone to decorate their house for Christmas. But if I did that, I'd both offend Caroline as well as make clear I wasn't an interior designer.

"Oh, no, if she's already scheduled to come today, she'll have her plans and her, um, materials all ready. I wouldn't want to mess her up."

"Don't be silly. You wouldn't mess her up. She'll be here after lunch. She'll love to talk shop with a fellow house aficionado."

Oh, dear God.

After I helped Caroline make ginger cranberry sauce from actual cranberries, convert healthy sweet potatoes via butter and sugar into a decadent dessert masquerading as a side dish, prep leftover cornbread into what I called stuffing and she insisted was dressing, and bake two dozen red velvet cupcakes without a cake mix, she released me from the cinnamon-scented kitchen.

I grabbed an apple and a book from the loaded family room shelves and headed for the door, in the hopes that I could skip lunch and avoid being in the house with the decorator. She'd know in a heartbeat I didn't have a clue, and while Cooper already knew I couldn't tell jacquard from a jaguar, he also knew about—and was complicit in—the lie of our marriage. I didn't want Caroline or Ted to spend Thanksgiving dinner viewing me as the liar I was.

I wanted a real Thanksgiving dinner for once. Just this once. I ignored the stab of conscience when it helpfully reminded me that a desire for normal had gotten me here in the first place.

The lies about the marriage and the career were nothing, however, compared to the other problem. My criminal history was a secret so huge that hiding it felt worse than lying. I'd never tried to hide it before. I hadn't expected to feel so dishonest, even though I knew I shouldn't have to explain it to every single person I met in my life.

"Molly!" said Cooper, coming around a corner and catching me before I figured out how to work the heavy brass door lock. "Where are you going?" He leaned against the wall, casual in a T-shirt and jeans. "Are you okay? Did Caroline get in your face too much this morning?"

Unexpectedly, tears burned at the corners of my eyes at this last. Caroline hadn't gotten in my face. She'd included me. Talked to me. Been friendly to me. With nothing to gain and no ulterior motives.

I hadn't spent hours with another woman gossiping and laughing, with no agenda, in years. Almost half a lifetime ago, I'd gone to a high school football game with a friend. Shameka and I had ignored all the plays and giggled over the reactions of a certain boy. Then I went home to a strange car in my driveway and the night when everything broke apart. After that, nothing was the same. No matter what happened after the annulment came through and I left here, I'd remember a morning spent cooking with someone who knew how. Someone who took me at face value and accepted me into her family traditions.

Someone who didn't look at me and think about violence.

"No," I told Cooper. "I had a great time. I just thought I'd . . . um, get out of the house a bit."

"Are you hiding from the decorator?" he asked, putting his hand on my chin to turn my face toward his.

"Maybe?" I said, scooting away a little to put some distance between us.

"If you want to stay here, we've got some rooms we don't decorate where you can wait her out." Cooper lifted a hand and brushed my lips with a finger.

"Sure. That sounds great," I babbled, shaken more than I'd expected from that slight touch. "I could use some alone time." I'd much rather closet myself in an unused bedroom with him, but that was a bad idea. I could lie and cheat my way through life, but I definitely couldn't withstand the uninterrupted blast of Cooper's attention. I couldn't let him kiss me again without telling him, but I hated imagining his face when I told him he'd been harboring a felon in his house. The pain might kill me.

A faint ripple of hurt showed on his face. "Alone, huh? Well, okay." Cooper stepped closer and ran his hands lightly down my forearms to clasp my hands. At this range, the rumble of his voice vibrated in my spine—and elsewhere. "Are you sure?"

I wanted to, so much that I had to concentrate on not letting my teeth chatter with the longing. I'd been attracted right away in the casino—he ticked every box on my list of attraction. The hair. The height. The eyes. And the kindness. No wonder he'd gotten me to a marriage chapel or, more likely, tempted me to drag him there.

As I swayed in indecision and Cooper tugged me infinitesimally closer, my stomach gave a growl that sounded more like a dinosaur's roar than any sound that should ever be emitted by a smallish person. My laugh rang with more gratitude than embarrassment. I showed him the apple I held. "Yeah. I'll take this and stay quiet up there." I said.

Cooper knew when he was beaten and retreated like the gentleman he was. "All right. Come on." He led the way up the stairs and down the hallway opposite from his room. I lost count of the closed doors we passed before he ushered me into a small bedroom with a view of the driveway and a huge bookcase crammed full of volumes. "Tell you what. While Leandra is here, I'll make excuses for you." He laughed self-consciously. "Say you have a headache or something."

"Thanks. Really. For being understanding about that and not blaming me for lying about my job. I'm sorry I lied."

"Don't be. I get it. Though being a hotel housekeeper is honest work. Work that people need and appreciate but never think about. You have absolutely nothing to be ashamed of."

Right. Nothing at all to be ashamed of.

He closed the door on his way out.

I bit into the apple while examining the framed items hung on the walls—an interesting collection that included rice sales receipts from 1761 and 1765 with the Middleton name on them, an old map of something labeled Cape Romain that showed creeks and water channels in a nightmarish maze, and an 1800s photograph of a toddler lolling with its eyes closed in a white-linen bedecked chair. I hoped the baby was sleeping, but I suspected it was dead. They took pictures of dead people in those days, didn't they? I shuddered and turned to the bookcase.

Downstairs, the front door closed with a thunk and Caroline's muffled but enthusiastic greeting was echoed by another feminine voice. I glanced out the window. An understated SUV of the sort with surround sound and leather seats now sat in the driveway.

The Decorator had arrived.

The bookcase could occupy my attention for the duration. This must be where the books no one wanted on display went. I giggled as I noted a few 80s-era bodice-ripping romances. Other books, histories of South Carolina and the Civil War mostly, were in bad condition and had torn spines. Someone had hidden the entire collection of *Twilight* books here as well as a good variety of the "For Dummies" series: *Computers for Dummies, Crosswords for Dummies,* and even *Fishing for Dummies.*

On the top shelf, the books were mostly old *Reader's Digest* volumes of the kind my grandmother had collected one at a time. At the far-right end, five fabric-covered spines drew my attention because of the lack of titles. I pulled the middle one out at random.

It was a journal, and not an old one. The handwriting, in ball-point pen of different colors, looped and squiggled in the manner of a young girl, Caroline's, I assumed. I flipped to the front cover to see if there was a name. Only a date, approximately twelve years before. I read a few entries at random. A girl had written sporadic descriptions of sorority parties, final exams, wearing orange to football games against the University of South Carolina. Clemson. I scanned it—yes, there they were: toward the end Cooper's name appeared more and more often and not as a brother. This wasn't Caroline's; it must be his first wife's college diary. I eagerly grabbed the last book in line. The date in the fly leaf was six years before. Doing the math quickly, I figured this must have been written after Lynette and Cooper married but before she left.

I paused. I should not read another person's diary once I knew it was a diary. It was wrong.

Or was it? Cooper said Lynette packed a bag and left, five years before. If this journal meant anything to her, surely she would have taken it with her. She'd never contacted Cooper to get it back. Someone in the family, probably Caroline, had stuck it here to get dusty and forgotten. Maybe it held the answer to where she went and why. I flipped to the last page she'd written before I could stop myself, then sat back with a disappointed huff. It was nothing but musings about the way a nurse at her father's nursing home had spoken to her and whether she should report her to the head of nursing. Nothing about Cooper or divorce or departure at all.

Regaining the shreds of my own ethics, meager as they might be, I re-shelved the book and reached for *Twilight*. I'd read it in prison, but it was better than being tempted by things that were none of my business.

"Molly!" called Caroline, closer than from downstairs. "Where are you? Come on and meet Leandra!"

Damn. If I didn't answer and she found out later I'd been in the house and ignored her, I'd destroy whatever tenuous connection we'd forged. I'd rather be caught than destroy that. I put the book down and followed her voice.

Leandra had already been busy. The handmade magnolia-leaf-and-pinecone garland now artfully draped on the stairway banister heralded a Christmas perfection that didn't exist anywhere outside of a Bing Crosby movie. In the hall, Caroline—with Ted standing by—carried on an animated conversation with a pretty blonde woman about her age whose hair shimmered with the glassiness produced only by expensive hair products. She wore tight jeans and a cashmere sweater. An interesting choice for the dirty work of hanging natural Christmas decorations, but to each their own.

Cooper, no doubt having heard Caroline hollering my name, materialized from the back of the house.

"Hey, y'all! Where've you been? Cooper, you remember Leandra, I'm sure."

Huh. He clearly did, and unless I missed my guess, there was some attempt in the past to get them together. Cooper's face twitched into a perfunctory smile, guilt written all over it. Leandra lifted her perfect chin a little higher and pointedly smoothed the front of her shiny hair with a left hand adorned with a giant diamond.

"If he doesn't remember you, little darling, Coop here's not much of a gentleman, and I raised him better than that. Didn't you all have a little thing, couple years ago?" asked Ted, delighted to wade into the tension. He watched my face. He was testing me.

Caroline gave Ted a death-ray glare that did about as much damage as a snowball on a brick wall. "And this is Molly, Cooper's new wife. They just got married last week. Can you believe it?"

Leandra's eyes widened despite herself. I caught the flick of her lashes as she checked my hand. Though it was hard, I resisted the temptation to copy her hair-smoothing gesture.

"Molly's got a vicious headache. She's been resting upstairs. I probably need to go find her another Advil," said Cooper.

I shot him a grateful glance. Caroline, on the other hand, was having none of it.

"Oh, shoot. I'm sorry, honey. Probably all that work this morning. But wait. Leandra, Molly is an interior designer from Michigan."

Leandra had an expressive face, and I could practically hear her thinking Cooper was a cliché with a thing for women in the interior design business.

I needed to get back upstairs and behind that door. Now. My stomach clenched. How had I gotten myself into this crazy stew of lies? I had a secret from each and every person in this room. Worse, I was desperate to keep it that way. I'd do anything to avoid watching Cooper's and Caroline's faces fall. How had I managed to let myself care?

"I'm so sorry, but my head is killing me. Let me get an Advil and I'll be right back," I said, praying they'd let me go.

"That's amazing, Molly. What a coincidence! What have you worked on?" gushed Leandra, with that fakey tone that I'd heard used in movies to maneuver the main character into position for a pig-blood shower. One good thing about prison: nobody bothers with that tone prior to the humiliation. The whole thing is straightforward.

"Um, mostly houses. Small-scale projects," I babbled. "You wouldn't know any of them."

"Oh. Too bad. Are you a traditionalist? Modernist?"

"Probably traditionalist," I said, picking one at random.

"Great!" She must have double the normal number of perfect

white teeth. "You can see I am, obviously. Ted wouldn't have any of those New Age Christmas decorations here, would you, Ted?" she asked, simpering.

"You talking about that hippie stuff with the bare twigs and the burlap nonsense? Nope, I like my Christmas to look like Barbara used to do it."

Barbara. Their mother. Cooper went still and Caroline let out a tiny sigh. "I'd love it if you'd help me decorate the tree later," said Leandra to me, something malicious in the glint of her eyes. "Ted insists I put all the decorations in the exact same place that Mrs. Middleton used to, even the individual ornaments on the tree. I work from a picture of the tree taken when she . . ." She thought better of where she was going and stopped.

"Oh . . . Oh, sure. If my headache is better. You know. Later."

Caroline came forward and squeezed my forearm. "Leandra, are you good a minute?" To me, she said, "Come on with me to my room. I've got the Advil in there. Cooper doesn't know where it is." She began steering me toward the magnificent and pine-scented stairway. Leandra must have cut down a full-size magnolia tree to get a garland that lush. "Cooper, can you check on the turkey brining? I should be doing that. I'll get Molly some Advil."

I nodded to Cooper. He knew I didn't have a headache, though he'd have one if he took me upstairs and I put him off again. Even better.

Caroline's room was a calming oasis painted a beautiful gray-green with white moldings, dark wood furniture and a white textured bedspread—and no alarming wall hangings. The oppressive gloom of the rest of the house didn't extend into either Cooper's or Caroline's rooms. Once inside, Caroline made no move toward a bathroom or a dresser drawer. She sat down with a bounce on her un-mussed bed and grinned. "Do you really have a headache?"

Flummoxed, I flailed verbally before she took pity on me. "Um. Well, ah . . . I don't . . ."

"Okay. I'll get you an Advil if you need one, but first I want to know what you really do for a living. Is it exciting?" Her eyes shone. "Are you a stripper? A showgirl? Or is it some boring thing like CIA agent? Come on. Tell me."

"How . . . how did you know?" Tentatively, I came a little closer and leaned a hip against her nightstand.

"That you aren't an interior designer? Pssssh. Easy. You said you were 'probably' a traditionalist. That's like saying you're a little pregnant. People who are into interiors are decidedly in one camp or another. You know nothing about interiors. Obviously. Does Cooper know?"

"Um. Yeah. He does. I'm a hotel housekeeper. You know. A maid. I didn't tell you because— Well, I didn't tell you."

"Aw, honey. Only a jerk would care about that." She stood, gave me a quick hug, and dislodged me to root around in her nightstand drawer, extricating a bottle of Advil. "Though Leandra will have figured it out, too."

"Will she tell your dad?"

"I doubt it. She'd have nothing to gain with him. I'm sure she'll try to tell Cooper, though, just to be petty, but if he already knows it won't matter. She and I went to school together. She's got a great eye for decorating and there aren't many who'd be willing to follow Daddy's directions to do Christmas exactly like Mama used to, but Leandra can be mean. She didn't take it well when Cooper didn't call her after going out with her on one date I set up a couple of years ago."

"What happened?"

"Nothing major, I don't think. He prefers girls who can talk about something other than themselves. Leandra, sadly, doesn't fit in that group."

Well, I did, in such a big way it made a caricature of Caroline's description. Given the things I'd have to say if I did talk about myself, he might well prefer the silence.

CHAPTER SEVEN

I surfaced from sleep with a gasp, as if I'd been too long underwater, out of a fast-paced dream of the sort that populates the three-hour nap. Late afternoon light filtered into Cooper's bedroom under and along the sides of the pulled shades. How long had I slept? I'd hidden from everyone by pretending to sleep to cure my "headache," but then I'd fallen asleep for real. Cooper's bed was a dream: the mattress a cradle, the sheets high thread-count, the blankets downy and soft. I untangled myself from its cocoon to read the alarm clock. Four-thirty.

Below, the house was silent. When I'd pretended sleep earlier, Leandra's hammering and the thumps and scrapes as she dragged boxes of decorations through the house had been interspersed with the family's voices and Mia singing Christmas carols. I swung my legs over the side of the huge bed and went to the bathroom to fix my hair, wild in the front and matted at the neck. The navy eyeliner I wore to highlight the blue of my eyes had spread out underneath to make me look like a cast member of a zombie TV show.

Once I'd gotten myself more presentable, I crept downstairs and peeked out the sidelights beside the front door, now crowned even on the inside with a huge magnolia-leaf wreath. Leandra's car had gone, as was Cooper's truck. I wandered into the kitchen, but Caroline had finished her work and disappeared. Pies sat cooling on racks and the refrigerator had been stuffed full of baking dishes with plastic wrap neatly tucked around the corners. Headed for the TV room, I met Ted in the hall.

"Good morning, Sleepyhead," he said. Wow. I hadn't heard that one in real life before. He ditched the fatherly tone. "You look like you could use a stiff drink. Come on. We'll have a little happy hour before supper." He didn't check to see if I followed him as he headed for his study.

What the heck.

"Where is everyone?" I asked as I sat on the leather sofa that faced an oversized dark wood desk meant to scare people. As expected, the study was a monument to outdoorsmanship: a huge elk head, gigantic antlers intact, glared angrily from the wood paneled wall behind the desk. On an opposite wall, a flock of fading butterflies had been pinned to curling brown paper and glassed over. "It's so quiet."

Ted snorted, turning from a mini-bar next to the credenza with two cut-crystal glasses of an amber-colored liquid I suspected would make me cough at the first sip and then stinking drunk by the second. "It always gets quiet when Caro takes Mia off to piano lessons. That kid can talk forever. I don't know where she gets the lung power. Oh, and Coop got a call about a property somebody home for Thanksgiving wanted to see. They'll all be back in an hour or two. Coop said he'd bring supper so Caro could get out of the kitchen for a while."

I wondered if Ted had at any point volunteered to prepare any food. I imagined not. He looked like the type who didn't know you needed to open a soup can before heating it up. I took a sip of the drink he handed me and managed to cover the cough with a tiny laugh. "Caroline is quite a cook."

"Not used to whiskey, are you, darling? That's all right. You're a Yankee. I'm sure you're not too delicate for it."

Yep, there was an insult buried in there. To Ted, being a non-delicate Yankee lumberjack or whatever he thought women did up North was about the worst thing he could think of. "It's delicious," I lied, taking another sip to bolster my claim. The smell alone would make me tipsy.

A coffee table with a glass display case containing an astonishing quantity of shells and coral and an actual skeleton of a small alligator sat between us. Ted set his drink down on it and guffawed. "I wish you could see how your pretty little mouth is screwed up. Still, it's good whiskey and I appreciate the compliment, sincere or otherwise."

"I've never had it before," I said, with a note of apology. I had no doubt that his whiskey was top of the line.

"Never? Are you more of a wine-drinker, then? You can't be a teetotaler," he said, gesturing at the glass I held on one knee.

"No. I got drunk once or twice as a teenager, but since then . . ."

I'd been forcibly kept dry by the State of Michigan correctional system? Nope.

"Since then, I've pretty much stuck to water."

"Except, I'd imagine, for a weekend in Vegas?"

Damn. How had he found out? "Yes. Except for that." I turned the glass around in my hands, running a fingertip along the rim. "About that, Mr. Middleton. I never meant to . . ."

"Call me Ted. You'll make me feel old."

"Ted. I want to apologize." I had a lot to apologize for, but I'd have to settle for what I could say. "I'm sure it was quite a shock when Cooper brought me home, and I want to thank you for your hospitality. I don't usually drink like that. In Vegas, things got a little out of hand." I looked down at my lap, preparing the lie. "Well. I don't regret how it came out, with Cooper and me . . ."

Oh, my God. It wasn't a lie. I didn't regret it.

Ted cleared his throat. I'd ventured into uncomfortable territory, and not only for him. "Well. Yes. An unconventional start, but I'll say this. Cooper is a chip off the old block. Just like me, he's been, since he was a kid. Always following me off into the woods, out on the water. And of course, he shares my excellent taste in beautiful women." He raised his glass to me. "Traditional, Coop and me. Both of us."

What did that mean? Should I run and get an apron and a pearl necklace? Cooper hadn't struck me as being much like Ted so far. I wasn't accustomed to receiving compliments from men of Ted's generation, but somehow that one made me uncomfortable.

Ted cleared his throat again and went to the mini-bar fridge, returning with a can of ginger ale. He offered it to me: a test. I thought for a second, reflexively looking for the right answer, and cracked it open and poured it into my whiskey glass. He smiled in grudging admiration. I'd passed.

"Bring it with you. Come on out to my workshop. I've got some things to do for Caroline's dinner tomorrow before she gets home. Keep me company?"

I didn't want to go. Something felt off about spending time with Cooper's father when he wasn't around. Though of course that was ridiculous. Ted had to be seventy years old and a widower. He was probably lonely. I stood and, drink in hand, followed Ted through the silent house outside through the slanting sun to the large outbuilding I'd seen from Cooper's window.

"My workshop," said Ted, gesturing at it as he dug for his keys. "You young people would probably call it a man-cave. I built it back when the kids were little and I needed someplace to go that didn't smell like baby powder. Probably won't surprise you to know that I got the electricity out here right away. Man's gotta have a TV. Got the water a few years ago so I could have a sink. I could live out here if I wanted to."

Inside, the building was a simple rectangle. A long wooden table ran the length. A large refrigerator and utility sink sat next to movable cabinets. A TV was centered on one wall, and Ted hit the remote. ESPN blared through speakers unobtrusively mounted in corners. Two recliners sat in front of it. The entire area reeked of booze. I associated both the recliners and the booze with my mother's house and my stomach roiled.

I registered all this with only part of my attention. It was a bit hard to tear my horrified eyes away from one corner, where there was a large hook in the ceiling, over an empty cement space about four feet by four feet. Most of that square footage was covered in newspaper, and all of the newspaper was soaked in . . .

"Is that blood?"

It took everything I had to keep my face still and normal as memories threatened and screamed and fought me to run, to cry, to curl up in the fetal position. I turned away, as slowly as if I were stepping over a land mine, to hide that weakness from him.

"Yup. Got lucky this morning. Shot a big old buck. Ten-pointer." He pointed to a black bucket beside the refrigerator, out of which a set of impressive antlers sprouted. I went over to peek and blanched. The entire head of the deer, still with the flesh on it, looked up at me through some foul-smelling liquid.

"Oh. Um." My stomach turned over. The faint metallic smell of the drying blood made me sick. People in Michigan had hunted, though not many in Detroit—the distance to the country was long. No one in my house had ever voluntarily gone outside for any reason or owned a gun. I'd never seen a dismembered deer before. I tried to push down my horror and act as if I ran into decapitated woodland creatures every day. "Where is the rest of it?"

Ted laughed, noting and enjoying my discomfort. "I cleaned and butchered it earlier this afternoon, while you were taking your beauty rest. Got rid of the carcass already. Meat's in the fridge. That's what I've got to do—cut up the tenderloin so Caroline can fry it up to eat along with the turkey tomorrow. I prefer to refrigerate it first. It tastes better that way. Makes it easier to slice, too."

"Oh, right. Yeah."

"Guessing you don't know hunters, either," said Ted, chuckling at my retreat away from the bucket as he rummaged around in the fridge.

"No."

He thumped a blood-stained package of paper and plastic wrap onto the table and found a cutting board and a long, vicious-looking, serrated knife. Without thinking, I took a step back, putting the table between us.

Ted missed nothing. "Aw, now, Miss Molly, I'm cutting up deer meat, not Yankees, today." His grin, atop a slaughterhouse tableau like that one, did nothing to lighten the mood.

It occurred to me that this was another test. For the courage, I tossed down three quick swallows of my whiskey and ginger ale. He planned to put the city girl through her paces. Watching me swallow the alcohol made his grin even larger.

Before opening the package of meat, he washed his hands with soap and water at the utility sink and got ready a plastic zip bag to store the pieces. Working efficiently, he sliced the meat into thin pieces about the size of a rice cake.

"There's nothing like getting a deer," he said, his voice hushed into reverence. "You wait, sometimes for hours, freezing in the cold and the dark, and you're afraid to move, even to blink, for fear you'll miss that movement out in the woods. You see that twitch of a tail, and you know it's yours. Nothing more beautiful than a whitetail deer in the wild."

I looked at the pile of meat on the table. Nothing beautiful about that.

Ted was still reliving his hunt, and from his expression, I realized it might be even more than that. Bloodlust. "You raise your gun, and you hope the deer won't sense your movement and bolt. In the sight, you can practically see the veins pulsing, and then you squeeze the trigger and pray. There is little in life that makes you feel more powerful."

Or sick. Unable to look at him, at the rapt face or the knife in his hands, I assessed the meat. It didn't look different from other meat I'd cooked before. I'd handled plenty of raw meat in my life. I'd never been a squeamish meat-eater, but then, killing an animal to eat and killing it for the joy of killing seemed like two different things to me.

"You ever eaten deer meat before? We coat it in breading and fry it. It's delicious."

"No, I don't think so." All I knew about it was that it was supposed to be "gamey," not that I knew what "gamey" tasted like.

"Caroline does a good job with it, but you should have tasted Lynette's deer meat."

"Lynette?"

"Cooper's first wife. Oh, man, could she cook. Everything that came out of her kitchen tasted like manna from heaven. She'd take one of these slices and fry it up some way or another where there wasn't any grease left behind. Caroline has to blot hers with paper towels."

I tried not to show how excited I was to hear about Cooper's mythical first wife. "Did she live here, with Cooper?"

"Y'all haven't talked about Lynette?"

"Not much."

"Naw, they didn't live here. I offered, but they rented a house right down from T.W. Graham's, little two-bedroom thing. Cooper fixed up the kitchen for her, all granite and white and what-have-you, and she used it. She was a genius in there."

"Where did he meet her?"

"Clemson. She was a year or two behind him. A cheerleader and sorority girl he met at some mixer or another, and an elementary education major. I told him at the time, Coop, you can't do better than a woman who wants to work with little kids. She'll be a good mother and she'll be home with the kids when they're home. The traditional kind."

Right. No doubt this Lynette wore pearls with her apron. Pearl necklaces didn't go well with orange jumpsuits, though, and I still wore the orange jumpsuit mentally and probably always would.

Before I got too depressed, I narrowed my eyes. This was Ted talking, not Cooper. Interesting that he'd admired his son's wife that much. His turn to take a test. "What did she look like?"

He paused, looking off into the distance. "Beautiful as a branch of wisteria. Long thick dark blond hair, deep brown eyes. She was a right little girl, kept that cheerleader figure. I believe she'd done some beauty pageants back in the day. Cute as anything."

I'd watched a lot of faces in my life. It's the best way to figure out what people are capable of. When they're about to attack. When they might feel something they don't want other people to know about. Faces are worse at lying than voices. Ted's face right now—rosy, softened, eyes shining—didn't look like a father-in-law talking about an ex-daughter-in-law. Or even a daughter. Or anyone about whom he had a remotely fatherly feeling—or should have. His efficient meat-slicing had stopped; the knife loose in his hand as he reminisced.

No way could I come right out and ask him if he'd been in love with his daughter-in-law. But I didn't need to. The evidence was right in front of my face. A couple more questions and I'd be certain.

"Did you enjoy doing things together—you and Lynette? And Cooper?" I asked, concentrating on his reaction.

He started, as if realizing he'd drifted off into some rose-colored memories of a woman the same age as his daughter, who'd left Cooper years before. He squinted one eye at me and resumed slicing, one corner of his mouth lifted sardonically. He knew exactly what I was asking—and why. "We did, as a matter of fact. She hated hunting, but she used to come out here to help butcher the kills. Summertime, weekends sometimes, when she was off from school and Cooper was at work, she'd come by here. She liked baseball. We used to watch the Braves games on the TV." He peered at me, blue eyes slitted. "You Yankees are so inquisitive. I'd say yes. The answer to your question is yes."

Nothing in what he said was remotely inappropriate, yet something was off. His tone, maybe, or the tiniest twitch of a lip. There was a note of innuendo there. Sirens and flashing lights filled my head. Had Ted and Cooper's first wife had a thing?

I watched his hands, deep in the juicy flesh of the deer that had run in the woods last night; tried to imagine them, wrinkled and weathered, moving on a tiny, much younger female figure. I hit a wall of nausea.

He said she spent all her time with him in this awful little room. If she felt the way I already did about him, she couldn't have done that. Had they been sleeping together? That made no sense to me. Why would anyone sleep with Ted if she had Cooper in her bed? That situation would have blown wide open and fast. But Lynette did run away, and no one had any other theories as to why. Maybe she had run to keep Cooper from finding out. Cooper had never hinted at anything like what I was thinking when he talked about Lynette. I didn't think such a thought had ever crossed his mind.

I hated that I looked for grit and sordidness everywhere. No. I had to be wrong. Prison had rewired my brain to look for the underside of everything. That was all.

"Why did she leave?" I asked, hoping he'd tell me an innocent reason I could believe.

"No idea." Ted put the last piece of meat in the plastic bag, sealed it, then turned to wash his hands once again. "May have been some problems in the marriage. Cooper had changed his office hours. Started working from home more, so he could spend time with her. According to him that upset her instead of made her happy. I saw a lot less of her after that."

"And then she just . . . left?"

He cleaned the cutting board and knife, drawing the dishrag along the blade. "One day Cooper came home from an all-day open house down in Mt. Pleasant, kind of late, and nobody had seen Lynette since he left her asleep in the bed that morning. She was gone. Bag packed, plane ticket, just gone."

I stood there, gripping the table edge, fighting for the courage to ask what I needed to know while my heart pounded.

"Did you and Lynette . . . have a . . . a . . . ?" I couldn't get the words out. I'd always thought of myself as blunt, but apparently there were limits to the things I could force myself to say.

After a moment of stillness, Ted threw back his head and guffawed. "You asking if she and I fooled around? What an imagination you have, girl." He held the eye contact, though, in a way that seemed odd. He'd finished my still-unspoken thought. He hadn't said no. Somehow there hadn't been enough shock in his reaction. *Oh, my God. They had.*

"What happens if I tell him?"

He put on a grotesque innocent mask that resembled Cooper's easygoing smile. "Tell him what, your lurid sex fantasies? I don't think so."

"He might be able to connect some dots or something," I sputtered, knowing I was beaten. Ted had been careful. He hadn't said a damn thing that would justify what might indeed be nothing but wild imagination. If I said anything to Cooper, he'd think I'd lost my mind.

Maybe I had lost my mind.

"You must be joking. Cooper and I are thick as thieves. There aren't any dots to connect, and if there were, connecting them isn't Coop's forte." His half-smile was knowing and contemptuous.

I began to feel dizzy. He'd given me nothing to go on, but I didn't have a shred of doubt anymore. Ted and Lynette had been sleeping together. I could practically smell the self-satisfied testosterone rising off him.

He'd sent up alarm bells from the minute I met him. My prison-honed clairvoyance had told me he wasn't to be trusted. It hadn't failed me yet. Ugh. All those people in the restaurant, slapping his back, wanting favors, needing recognition from him. All the time he was the guy who did his son's wife.

"I'd better go take another Advil. My headache seems to be coming back," I said, letting my scorn and derision show. I searched for my forgotten glass so I could return it to the kitchen. Who was Ted to me, anyway?

As I reached the door to the workshop, a hand shot out and grabbed my wrist as I turned the doorknob.

"Hold on, now," said Ted. He insinuated his body, once no doubt as good as Cooper's but now gone to seed, between me and the exit. "Calm down."

"I'm calm."

He laughed. "Like hell you are."

"What do you want?"

He stood watching me, scanning for movement, like the hunter he was, waiting for me to realize he had me cornered. When I stilled, he did the scariest thing yet in an afternoon full of insinuations and knives and blood and dismembered animals.

He stepped close, a breath away, like a lover. Soft as velvet, so lightly I couldn't even tell if his hand was hot or cold, he laid his open palm against my cheek.

Oh, holy Mary Mother of God.

I stepped away. "I'm going to pretend you didn't do that."

He laughed. "You do that, if it helps you."

CHAPTER EIGHT

I'd learned early to force unpleasant thoughts out of my head. Ted had terrified me, but I knew well how to compartmentalize the terror so I could show a normal face to the world.

The rest of the evening, I went for a walk through town with Cooper, Caroline, and Mia out to the docks where the tall-masted shrimp boats waited for spring and the town residents had access to the public boat launch. Cooper and Caroline pointed out an giant live oak, estimated to be over a thousand years old, that dominated a grassy green. We took turns pushing Mia as she swung on a tire attached by rope to a mighty branch, me marveling the whole time that the tree predated not only me, but McClellanville, this state, the United States, the printed word, and the bulk of recorded history. When we got home, we played a simplified version of Pictionary while ESPN hyped Clemson's weekend prospects in the background.

In the bedroom with Cooper, I yawned ostentatiously. I owed him the truth about my history, but before I gave it up I needed to figure out what I should do about the other truth—the one about his father. Even if I was wrong about Lynette—and I wasn't, I knew it, I would run straight for those diaries to confirm it the first chance I got—Ted had put his hand on my face. He'd crossed a major line. Nothing coherent would come out of my mouth while I still felt that touch. Cooper accepted my purported exhaustion without complaint and contented himself—and me—with a slow caress of my hair and a neck massage before spreading out his pallet on the floor.

I breathed a huge sigh of Procrastinator's Relief, though I didn't get away scot-free. As I drifted off, his low rumble reached

my ears in that netherworld where consciousness had outlasted
the power of speech or movement before sleep.

"In the morning, we're going to talk."

I slept the sleep of the guilty: damp twisted sheets, dreams full
of dread, and rose before Cooper with an aching neck and tense
jaw. I peeked down the hall toward the room with the diaries, but
Ted's early morning coughing from that general direction made
me change my mind. I rocketed downstairs without waking anyone, racing on sock-muffled feet down the heart-pine stairs to the
kitchen and the sanctuary of Caroline, up early to organize the
Thanksgiving meal. Cooper wouldn't dare to try to have a meaningful conversation while Caroline whizzed from oven to fridge to
sink and back.

"You're up early," said Caroline, washing a huge roasting pan
at the enormous farmhouse sink.

"Yep. What can I do to help?"

"Well, dinner's at three, so the turkey doesn't go in until ten-
ish, but if you want to chop onion, that would be amazing. Daddy
won't eat celery in the dressing, but he will eat onion."

I made a noncommittal face. Maybe I could ask Caroline about
Ted and Lynette and swear her to secrecy. Maybe she could help
me figure out whether Cooper knew anything about it. I watched
her, cheery yellow rubber gloves with a purple Life is Good T-
shirt warding off the bad.

How could I tell someone in a Life is Good T-shirt her father
had—what? hit on? scared the shit out of?—one daughter-in-law
and might have done far worse with another?

Caroline was still focused on the onion-only stuffing. As if
worried I might judge the fact that Ted had control issues reaching all the way down to celery, she continued. "He's so picky. I
shouldn't cater to him like that, but Mama used to. And it's
Thanksgiving."

Right. The heavy weight of the secrets I'd thought to lighten
with sharing settled onto my shoulders. It was Thanksgiving. A
holiday devoted to family togetherness—the kind I'd never experienced before—and a huge meal around one table. With Ted. And

both of his children.

Even if I could figure out a way to say something to Caroline, I couldn't do it now and ruin this meal she'd worked so hard on.

I might not ever be able to describe the scene in the workshop to Cooper. He'd known me a week. He'd never believe me over his only living parent. Still, that living parent had told me some disturbing things. Ted had sucked me into this family's backstory, whether he'd intended to or not.

I had gotten involved in these people's lives. The realization hit with a heady mix of terror and guilty elation.

Glad to have somewhere to look and something to do with my hands, I sliced off the ends of the onion. During a stint in the prison kitchen, I'd learned—not without a certain irony—to wield a kitchen knife effectively, and as a result, could chop an onion in record time. When finished, I joined Caroline at the sink to wash and peel potatoes, ordinary white ones this time.

Cooper clattered down the stairs, dressed in frayed khaki pants and a long-sleeved T-shirt that bore the name of a local outdoors shop. "Caroline. I'm taking Molly. No more potato peeling. She's a guest and we're on our honeymoon. It's warm today. We're going out to hunt shells."

"No, Cooper, I can help. It's not fair to Caroline to . . ."

Caroline laughed and nudged me away from the sink with her elbow. "Oh, please. I can cook this meal in my sleep. I don't cook much but I've got this one down. Hope you like it. We're eating the same thing for Christmas. Off you go," she said, looking at my yoga pants and T-shirt. "Though you'll need to change if you're going out to the beach."

Cooper looked me up and down, and I could have sworn his eyes lingered on my ass. "Yeah, the beach is an empty barrier island with no dock. We have to anchor the boat and wade in. You'll get wet feet at a minimum. Caro, you have some shorts she can put on under her pants? And something warm?"

"Sure. Third drawer from the bottom, in my closet. All the boat clothes are in there. My water shoes are in the bottom cubby. Get a windbreaker too. Even on a warm day, it can be chilly this time of year on the boat."

Within forty-five minutes, I was outfitted like a born sailor in water shoes, polypro underwear, and windbreaker, and Cooper had backed a large white motorboat into the water from a trailer attached to his truck at the public boat ramp we'd seen the night before. The house dock, he said, was for Ted's exclusive use. We weren't the only ones out, even in November. Other trucks and boat trailers filled the lot, parked in neat rows. I held the boat in place as it bobbed in the water until Cooper had dispensed with the truck. He hopped in with a grin.

"Safety first, okay? Here's the pole you can use if for some reason I fall overboard." He kicked at a long wooden pole on the floor of the boat.

"Are you likely to fall overboard?" I said, suddenly concerned.

"Nope. See this? This is the kill switch. The engine can't run if this thing isn't plugged into the console." He held up a small key-like device and inserted it into a slot next to the ignition key. A long fabric strip with a clip on one end extended from it. Cooper clipped the end onto his shirttail. "With it attached to me, if I were to fall overboard, the key comes loose and the engine dies. You'd have time to fish me out, right?"

"Don't fall overboard."

"I'll try not to," he said, laughing.

My God, Cooper looked good in a boat. The breeze off the water ruffled his hair and the sun turned his skin to gold. He'd spent his life on or near boats: that much was obvious from the ease with which he started the motor and navigated around the end of the boat launch without even paying attention. I'd never been out on open water before and might have been afraid, but his obvious skill made me feel as safe as if I were in a bathtub. His capable brown hands on the wheel took my thoughts down a road that would do me no good. I squeezed my knees together on my perch.

"You're from Michigan, so I assume you've been out in a boat before? Lakes, right? You don't get seasick, do you?"

I yanked my attention off the way his forearms curved and the width of the T-shirt across his shoulders. He seemed unaffected by the chill. Under my hands, I bet those shoulders would feel warm to . . . "Um. No idea. I've never been in a boat before. We lived near a suburb where the boats outnumber the cars, but my part of Detroit was pretty far from the lake."

He laughed. "Right. I thought maybe a ferry at least. Well, we'll see how you do. I'll speed it up gradually, but you let me know if you feel bad or we're going too fast."

"Okay."

If I threw up from seasickness, it would be worth it. Being on this boat made me feel more alive than I'd felt in years. The day, though definitely not hot, was crystalline blue. The water sparkled a reflected blue with black depths in channels like roads, the marsh grasses to the sides as thick and green as if it were June and not November. Long-beaked birds swooped and dove over the water like a squadron of World War Two aircraft.

"What are those?"

"Those?" Cooper turned. "Oh, those are pelicans. They're everywhere. They're fishing."

"Cooper, it's beautiful out here."

His face split into a relieved grin. "You think? This is my favorite place. Dad likes the woods."

The mention of Ted was a sign. "Um. About your dad. Yesterday, he . . ."

"What?"

"He took me out to his shed, or man-cave, or whatever it is, and cut up a deer in front of me, and then . . ."

Cooper interrupted me by laughing. "Oldest trick in the book. Dad always loves it when a city slicker or a Yankee, or better yet, both, visits. He loves to shock people with the country boy thing. He didn't make you gut the deer, did he?"

I shook my head, at a loss for speech. "No. Just showed me the head, antlers and all, in a bucket."

"Sounds like him. Once, when we were in college, I brought Jeremy home one weekend—he's from Atlanta—and Dad got out a deer heart and acted like that was going to be the main course for dinner. Jeremy said he almost puked right on the spot. Dad cackled for days about that one."

"No, this was . . ." What was it? Had Ted merely been trying to intimidate me? To shock a city Yankee? Was that possible? I hadn't looked at it that way. "It was nothing. You were saying? Something about the woods?"

Cooper glanced at me, open and smiling. Whatever Ted had been doing, Cooper wasn't a part of it. The Ted-unease disappeared. "Yeah. Dad likes the woods, but I've always liked the water better."

"I like the water better, too." Something about that murky knotted mass of green unsettled me.

"Are you doing okay? Warm enough? Not sick?"

"No. Not sick." Happy. For this moment, I was happy. Drunk with the simple pleasure of existing in this place. The motion of the boat as it bounced over the waves, the smell of the soil at the base of the grasses and the saltwater, electrified me like nothing ever had. I swallowed.

"Look!" Cooper slowed the motor and pointed off to the right, his raised arm swinging as he kept it fixed on a point near the marsh grass. "A dolphin. Unusual this time of year, but it's been warm. Keep your eyes on that spot and wait for it to surface. Watch."

With a longing I didn't expect, I stared out over the water unblinking, even when the roll of the water sent a sunbeam straight into my eyes. It didn't take long before my concentration was rewarded. The heads of not one but two dolphins rose and fell, one after the other, like merry-go-round animals I'd seen at a church parking lot fair near my house once. It felt like magic. A perfect thing that shouldn't be real.

"I could stay here all day. If I lived here I would. I can't believe how beautiful it is," I breathed, afraid to break the spell with a too-loud voice. Cooper's cheeks went rosy and he reached a hand to me. I took it, letting the warmth of his skin spread over me. I'd worry about the messages I was sending later.

Far too soon, a low-slung spit of land approached. Water, calm here, lapped against the empty ribbon of a barrier island, too thin and sandy for habitation. Cooper turned off the engine, unhooked himself from the engine kill switch, and tossed an anchor into the water, pulling on the rope to check the hold. For a moment the only sound was the insistent beat of the water as it slapped the bobbing boat.

"What is this place called?" I asked. "Does it have a name?"

"We've always called it the beach. Its official name is Lighthouse Island." He pointed. "See the lighthouse down there?"

In the distance, an old-fashioned brick lighthouse painted in black and white vertical stripes loomed alone, miles from anywhere.

Cooper rummaged under the seat, dropping his phone and keys into a clear plastic box. "When we were kids we used to be afraid of the Cape Romain light."

"Why? It's pretty."

"Well, there's a pretty dark story about this one. The lighthouse is more isolated than most: on an island, miles offshore. It was a tough life for the keepers' families, who lived totally cut off from other people. Dad used to tell us the story of how back in the 1870s or so, a keeper named Johnson killed his wife in the house next to that light. She'd gone to the bank to collect her jewels, supposedly, so she'd be able to leave him. Before she could, he slit her throat from ear to ear with a huge knife. Somehow it got ruled a suicide. The keeper told the police, once they rowed all the way out to investigate, that she slashed her own throat. My guess is they looked the other way, because it was hard to find a keeper for a light on an island eight miles from shore."

"Is that a true story?"

"Yup, that's what I've always heard. The story says her ghost haunts the island, looking for her lost jewels. Caro and I used to make Dad avoid going by the lighthouse when we'd come out here to the beach. The light hasn't worked in my lifetime. They abandoned it decades ago, and then storms washed away the dock. The keeper's house is rubble now, and the stairs inside the light are falling in. It's amazing how fast things like that disappear." He stood, feet wide apart. "You ready?"

I scanned the water. The closest point of the sandy strip was at least fifty feet from the boat.

Without any further ado, Cooper hopped overboard, landing with a splash.

"Cooper! What are you doing?" My heart thrummed wildly, causing the first sick feeling I'd had all morning. How deep was it here?

He straightened, eyes sparkling. The water came only to his waist. "Did I scare you? It's only two or three feet here. Not too cold." He peered at me, noting my unusual level of panic. "Wait a minute. You can't swim, can you?"

"N-no. I never learned."

"You should have told me. I would have made you wear a lifejacket. You will, on the way back. Anyway, it's not deep here. You'll get your legs wet, but if you want to take off the long pants, you'll dry faster in the shorts."

Suddenly fearful, I gazed out at the waves. They made the boat rock like a cradle. If they could do that to something this large, would they knock me down? What if I couldn't right myself? "I . . . I'm not sure."

"Hey. Hey," said Cooper, coming around to the back corner of the boat where a ladder dropped into the water. "Molly. Don't worry. I can carry you that far. Can't promise to keep your butt high enough to stay dry, but I'll do my best. Grab a couple of the plastic grocery bags from under the console there, for the shells. Come on."

Bags in hand, I stripped off the long pants and left them on the seat. Before I could decide whether to go or not, Cooper swept me off the ladder, one arm under my knees and the other around my shoulders. "Put your arms around my neck. The bottom is murky and I don't want to drop you if I step on a sharp shell or something." He took careful steps forward toward the beach, holding me as easily out of the water as if he'd picked up a small child.

His strength and bulk made me feel safe. A lot of guys in this position would drop a girl, just to watch her sputter or get wet. Cooper would never drop me.

And then everything changed faster than a glint of sun on the wave.

He'd draped me across his torso, and in this position, I could feel his entire upper half—hands around the sun-warmed skin of his neck, a breast tingling where it pushed against his chest, hip bumping against the tensile strength of his lower abs. Warmth spread through the windbreaker and burned down my thighs.

I could swear his thumb rubbed against the underside of my bare thigh more than necessary for carrying. I had to resist the urge to shift so his hand would slip higher.

Steps from dry land, I glanced up at his face. His pupils had contracted in the sunlight so that the black-rimmed green of his irises took what breath I had left. He stopped moving as his eyes met mine, his lips parting, leaving no doubt that he'd been affected by the proximity too.

"Cooper, I . . ." *I want you.* "I-I . . ." *I want to run my hands all over your chest and shoulders and hair and cheeks.* "I can take it from here."

He blinked once, then bent and placed my feet in the sand. "Okay." He stood back, letting me see what I'd missed before, his face quiet and waiting.

Oh, holy Mother of God. His frayed khakis were wet to the waist. They hung off his honed hipbones and molded to the long muscles of his thighs, leaving nothing to the imagination —nothing at all. No underwear obscured the view, and the view was impressive as hell. He held my gaze, knowing I was looking, and dared me to react.

I wanted to. How to react wasn't a problem at all. Oh, I wanted to climb him like a flagpole and press against him with my whole body. I could almost taste the longing. My fingers tingled with the need to touch him again. Blood shot down to my long-neglected lady parts and left no doubt how my body thought we ought to approach this. No one was around. No boats. No houses. No people. I could strip off all my clothes and his and have him here, on a pillow of khaki-colored sand. Judging from the view, I'd bet he'd join in with enthusiasm.

There were repercussions for acting on impulse, though. I'd learned long ago to shut that down. I owed him the truth.

Some of the truth, as much as I could tell him, anyway.

And that wasn't much.

CHAPTER NINE

After a short silence, Cooper splashed ashore and bent, avoiding my eyes, to roll up the hems of his pant legs.

He was disappointed. I wanted to give him something.

"It's amazing out here. I feel like we're the only people in the world."

He put his hands in his wet pockets to give things some breathing room. "Molly, you know you're killing me, don't you?"

"I know," I said, approaching him tentatively, like a wild animal, to give him a grocery bag. "And I'm sorry. I need time."

"Okay," he said, giving me a speculative glance. "We'll take it slow. Slower, anyway. Come on. The shells aren't hard to find. All we have to do is cross over to the ocean side—you practically trip over them."

He was right. We hadn't gone twenty yards before I happened upon a huge spiral shell, unbroken, chipped only a little, eight inches or more long. The kind I'd only ever seen in stores or in pictures. I picked it up.

"Let me see it," said Cooper, reaching for it. "No, you don't want this one. Look, it's missing the edge here. Trust me. The shelling here is amazing, especially at this time of year when nobody comes out here for days."

Within twenty minutes, I'd acquired a bag full of intact spiral shells of the kind Cooper said were whelks—anywhere from five to ten inches long, in blue, cream, perfect white, black, tortoiseshell, pink, and brown. Cooper found a shiny-smooth armadillo-shaped cowrie, a fragile unbroken angel wing, a broken loggerhead turtle eggshell, and four pearlescent moon shells, similar to overlarge snail shells but far more intricate. The joy of collecting them, something I'd never gotten to do as a child, lightened my feet. I took far more shells than I had any use for. More than I could carry away when I left South Carolina.

One blue whelk was smaller than the others. I pocketed it. Surely I could keep one.

When the bags were full, we sat in the sun to watch the stronger waves roll in on the ocean side of the island. The sun rose higher in the sky. Sandpipers ran busy and intent into the waves and back. Eighteen inches of sand stretched between us and every one yawned with yearning.

Cooper rolled a moon shell around in his hands. "Is it that you feel like you don't know me well enough?" he asked, staring out at the water, his voice barely loud enough to be heard over the crash of the surf.

"No, not exactly. It's more that I don't feel like you know me well enough."

"I know enough."

"No," I said, with feeling. "You don't."

"Well, tell me, then. Who was your last boyfriend?"

Tears pricked and burned in the bridge of my nose. Another thing I could tell him only part of. "Um. His name was Anthony. He . . . he worked at the hotel in Detroit with me, though he was a prep cook in the kitchen." He'd been a fellow parolee, working through the same program. He'd done only five years, however, for driving the car his buddy jumped into after an impromptu armed robbery, so he'd had a little more life experience on the outside than I had.

"What was he like?" asked Cooper, pulling his arm back to throw the shell into the ocean. It went so far I lost it in the sun. With the movement, I caught a whiff of sun-warmed skin, salt air, and Irish Spring.

"He was younger than I am—like five years younger."

"So you're a cougar, huh?" Cooper's over-serious face made the teasing clear.

"Right." I snorted. "Not quite yet. Though it's weird how much difference there was between twenty-seven and thirty-two.

He loved fixing up cars. Always wanted to take me to body shops to hang out. I think he wanted to be one of those guys who—what do you call it? It used to be 'pimping a ride,' but I'm sure that's outdated now."

Cooper chuckled. "Yeah, those cars are groovy, no doubt."

I elbowed him into silence. I hated it when I didn't know the current terms for things. Everyone in prison, the long-timers anyway, got caught in sort of a pop-culture amber. We watched TV, of course, learned from new prisoners or visitors, and kept on top of most of it, but it wasn't the same as living it.

"Anyway, we lasted about four months, and then he . . ." Got off parole and changed jobs. "He quit the hotel job and dumped me for a nineteen-year-old two weeks later. Who's the cougar now?"

"Me, I guess. You're a whole year younger than me."

I laughed. A year's difference did not a cougar make.

He cleared his throat repentantly. "So, how long ago was that?"

"Spring. I didn't date anybody this summer, and then I went to Las Vegas."

"Which brings you to me." He inched closer, eighteen inches between us dropping to more like twelve. Possibly eleven.

You should tell him right now. I pushed down the voice of reason by coming up with all kinds of ludicrous reasons why not. He might get so mad he'd leave me here on a deserted island. He might drop me over the side of the boat. He might bring me back but make a spectacle of kicking me out of the house during the Thanksgiving dinner.

Give me a break. I just didn't want to watch his face as I became a criminal in front of him. I'd spent a few days not being reviled. Was it so wrong I wanted to keep it going a while longer?

"Tell me who you've dated, then."

"Well, you met Leandra. I went on exactly one date with her, but I got tired of hearing about how much money each of her clients had. She seemed to know it in great detail. Creeped me out."

"And?"

"For two years I went out with Kara Leigh Lawless."

"Was that really her name?"

He laughed. "Yeah. She was a nice girl. She was in chef school, though, and she moved to Texas for a job when she finished. We broke up. She got married last year. Most of the rest of them since my wife left have been short. Couple dates here and there."

"Lynette, right?" I couldn't resist asking him, probing to see what he knew about her relationship with his father. He ought to know, but I couldn't bring myself to tell him. Maybe I'd get lucky and Cooper already suspected.

At the mention of her name, Cooper's lashes swept down and he dug his fingers into the sand up to the first knuckle. "Lynette. Yeah. We'd been married only two years. I thought we were happy —well, at least as happy as my parents were."

"And you weren't?"

"We went to school together, got matched up at some stupid Greek system thing, and to be honest, I married her because we'd been seeing each other a while and she was nice and pretty and I couldn't think of a single damn reason not to. But in the end, she never got comfortable with anyone her age in town, or Dad, or anything. Back then Caro was finishing up school. I used to think it might have been better if Caro had been home more. They got along, when they saw each other. We lived in a little house and Lynette taught at the elementary school on Highway 17, and that was about it. She didn't go anywhere much. I wasn't home a lot and she never wanted to come along when I had to do client dinners and things in Charleston."

"I'm sorry." He had no idea. Ted had been right: he had not connected any dots.

"It didn't work out. While I wish she'd said something, suggested counseling, something, at least a goodbye, I guess it would have ended up like that anyway. Divorced. I would've at least liked to give it a try, though, first." He allowed the sand to run through his fingers, looking up at me, abashed. "I hate that it didn't work. I always thought I'd have kids by now. I'd like to have kids."

"I'd like kids, too."

He considered me, then looked away, at the horizon. "She was from Virginia. Early on, she tried to get me to move with her back to her hometown in the mountains. I made some excuses about my job, you know, family. But I couldn't move that far from the water. I feel bad about that. Maybe if I'd been able to, things would have been different. It sounds stupid, I know, but the saltwater feels . . . vital, or something. Like oxygen. I'd never want to live anywhere but here."

"It doesn't sound stupid." In fact, the sounds of the tide coming in as we sat sounded like music, like white noise people needed for sleep. I could see how it wouldn't take long for it to seep into my soul.

"After that, I don't think she was happy. She pretended to be, some, but I guess she missed her home too much and knew I'd never go with her."

"Did you look there?"

"Yeah. I went there, pretty place called Abingdon, to find her when we were looking to serve the divorce. Nobody had seen her. Her dad in the nursing home died about six months after she left. None of the nurses remembered seeing her in a while. No address. No Facebook page. Nothing."

"Something must have been wrong with her, to want to disappear like that."

"It's funny, you know. She said that, a few times, when we'd argue or she was tired or upset. 'Sometimes I just want to disappear.' Southwest Virginia is a big place with lots of mountains and terrible internet. I guess she meant it."

"I guess so." It wasn't hard to imagine why she hadn't wanted to be found. She hadn't wanted to explain to Cooper what happened between her and his father. I couldn't blame her. I didn't know if I could find the words to explain it either.

I wanted to ask him so much, but the subject was obviously still sore. The mystery. The unexplained loss. No matter how much I wanted to know, I couldn't bring myself to interrogate him. Glass houses, and all that.

Cooper hitched the leg nearest to me up so he could turn to

me. "Molly. It's been five years since she left." He looked away to throw a pebble into the ocean and licked dry lips before continuing. "I know our circumstances are odd, and maybe we didn't start off the usual way, but don't you think there must have been something . . . some reason we went to that chapel? We have a connection, I think. Don't we?" He reached out and touched my bent knee—the contact of his hand on my bare skin shot fiery arrows into my resolve.

I blew out a careful breath, trying to remain still. I should pull my leg away and keep the boundaries up. Everything inside me wanted to push my knee further into his hand. I'd had so little touching in my life.

"You're cold. You should have said." Cooper scooted closer, his body large and warming me in more ways than one.

"I'm not cold."

"You didn't answer my question." He moved the hand to my chin, tipping it up so he could search my face.

"What question?"

"Am I wrong that we have a connection?"

"No," I whispered, my lungs too focused on continuing to breathe to give any volume to my voice. "You're not wrong."

Slowly, he threaded his hand through my hair, careful not to pull or tangle it, lowering his head to mine. The charge, the magnetized pull of his lips, rippled over my whole skin. I wanted to give in. It wouldn't hurt. We'd already kissed. His sun-flecked hair, the light on his cheekbones, the total solitude, even the sound of the waves echoing the blood rushing in my head, called me as if by hypnotism.

I closed my eyes, knowing my lips would find his. His kiss surprised me—soft and tentative and asking nothing of me. This communion lingered in that place where sweet gives way to passion, almost introductory, while a foregone conclusion at the same time. His fingers in my wind-blown hair moved slowly, reverently, caressing and protecting. The waves crashed onto shore beyond us, mimicking our heightened breathing. He wrapped a large hand around my waist, to pull me closer. I opened my eyes to find his open as well, mossy green and wide with wonder.

You owe him more than this.

"Cooper. Wait." I put a restraining hand on his shoulder. "Yes. Yes. We have a connection." I met his heated gaze head-on. He deserved this truth, at least. "I want you so much I can barely keep my hands off you. But there are things about me you don't know. Things I've done in my life. Important things; things that would change what you think of me. If you knew those things, you'd be ready to sign that annulment paper so fast the cops will pull you over speeding down to Charleston. We can't do this. I want to, so much, but I can't do it to you."

He didn't give up easily—or make it easier for me. His sensitive fingertips trailed over my hair, down my spine, over my shoulders, convincing with every inch, though merely sitting next to him meant I was already drowning in a sea of persuasion. "Then tell me. Tell me now, and let me decide."

Dizziness made the horizon tilt before me at the prospect of the relief of unburdening myself, but it changed quickly into grim knowledge of what the relief would cost me. Disgust. Horror. Revulsion. Loathing. He'd jump up. He'd wipe his hands off where he'd touched me. What fragile connection we had would break. He wouldn't be able to look at me. He would . . . despise me.

Again, I tried to convince myself I was virtuous—waiting to tell him would save his Thanksgiving holiday—even as I knew I was the vilest of cowards for putting it off. The bravery inside me cowered, begging me to put off its appearance so that I could look into his beautiful eyes, even without touching, a little longer. One day more. Or two. Then we'd be getting that annulment and I would never have to tell him.

Never before had I been in the habit of putting off the unpleasant. Life had been full of the unpleasant and I'd always faced it straight-on. I didn't recognize this desperation to have just a little more time, but I needed it. I could not tell him.

"I can't," I said, dropping my gaze to the sand. "I can't bear to have you think badly of me. I think it's best if we try . . . if we stay away from each other and get through this weekend and get the annulment. I'm not for you. Trust me."

"Why do you get to decide that? You're not letting me be a part of it. You've made up your mind I'll judge you without giving me a chance." Cooper stood, jumping up exactly as I'd imagined, tension radiating where before there had been warmth and safety.

"You will judge me. You'd have to."

"You don't know that." He kicked a piece of broken shell away down the beach.

"Yes," I said, miserably. "I do."

He said nothing, hurt bleaching his skin, the kind that isn't easy to wipe away.

"I can't. I just . . . can't." I bent my head onto my knees, unable to look at the pain I'd already caused.

"You mean you won't," he said, resignedly. With effort, he replaced his frustrated expression with a more pleasant one and extended a hand to me. "Let's go. We'll be late for dinner."

CHAPTER TEN

"Pass the potatoes!" yelled Mia, adorable in a smocked red velvet dress already liberally smeared with gravy goo.

"Not if you persist in that unladylike tone," Ted said, crossing his arms.

Mia stared at him with her index finger in her mouth, the vocabulary, if not the tone, lost on her.

We sat around the enormous mahogany table in the formal dining room. Caroline had gone all out—nice silver, fine china, linen tablecloth, wicker cornucopia centerpiece with apples and squash and mini-pumpkins spilling out of it, cloth napkins embroidered with fall leaves. Mia sat, as far from Ted as the table permitted, in front of a plastic plate, placemat, and a cup with Pilgrims dancing merrily around the edges.

The festive table helped distract me from the oil painting of a Civil War bayonet charge, full of riderless horses and smoke from cannons and chaos and carnage, that hung over the mantel facing me.

The ancient table legs did their work: they supported the weight of enough food for twenty people. I'd been seated between Cooper, who'd put up an impenetrable wall of wounded politeness only I could see, and Miss Aurelia, who'd worn a cashmere black turtleneck and chunky necklace with her written-on jeans to acknowledge the festiveness of the occasion. I smiled across the table conspiratorially at Mia and passed the potatoes to Caroline, on her left.

"You need to teach that child some table manners, Caroline," said Ted, nostrils flaring at being thwarted. I shot him a passive-aggressive glare. He volleyed right back. "Miss Molly, have some venison. It's delicious." Without waiting for permission, he passed the plate to Miss Aurelia to hand to me.

She gave the plate a perfunctory wave in my direction before putting it down again, out of Ted's reach. "Molly doesn't want your deer meat, Ted. This is Thanksgiving. Turkey day. I've never understood your obsession with messing with tradition. Would you like more turkey, Molly? Cooper can give you what you need."

I mumbled a demurral at her, wondering what she knew. Did all that have a double meaning? She turned to give me a sunny smile, then resumed eating her green beans as if nothing had happened.

Caroline replaced the bowl after serving Mia. "Cooper? Aren't you going to pass Molly the turkey?"

Cooper, who'd devoted himself wordlessly to clearing his plate in minutes, gave me an oblique look charged with electricity. His hand hovered over the turkey platter with utmost politeness. "Molly? Can I pass you anything?"

I shook my head, trying to calm my thundering pulse and focus on the unbelievable deliciousness of the bourbon topping on the casserole I'd helped make. Granted, I'd never eaten a fancy Thanksgiving meal before, but in no way had I been expecting as many undercurrents at the table as were happening here. Did all rich people do this at the holidays? Use innocent side dishes as metaphors? My dinners with my mother had been frozen meals, but we watched TV in silence and didn't impart special meaning to the gravy mix.

"Aurelia, we haven't heard much from you lately. Where've you been, darling?" asked Ted, turning the full blast of his charm on her.

"Oh, you've got some newlyweds in the house. It's usually best to leave them alone." Aurelia enunciated the last part and took a delighted bite of her yeast roll. I gathered she and Ted had sparred before.

"Oh, now, you know I haven't interfered with them," he said, spearing the venison on his plate.

"I know nothing of the kind," she said, while Caroline glanced back and forth like a spectator at a tennis match who didn't know the rules.

"Uncle Cooper and Aunt Molly went on the boat today, Miss Aurelia," offered Mia, waving her fork full of food dangerously close to her mother's hair.

"It was a bit chilly today. Did you get wet, Molly?" asked Caroline. Her eyes widened slightly as a second meaning of her words hit her, too late.

I choked. *Oh, my God.* I stared at my plate, unable to meet anyone's eyes.

Ted stabbed at his food like it was trying to escape, his lips in a thin line.

Miss Aurelia didn't miss a beat, grinning at Caroline. "Well, if she went to the beach with Cooper that would hardly be a surprise."

The heat of my face threatened to scorch the food remaining on my plate. "Umm. Well, we . . ."

Cooper set his fork down with a clatter, his face red, his mortified eyes wide. "The surf was a little rough."

"I can't swim," I said. "I was afraid."

"I wish you'd told me."

He definitely wasn't talking about swimming. *Oh, God.*

"The beach was beautiful, though," I said, desperate to turn things around. Despite my best efforts, I'd ruined Thanksgiving for Cooper anyway. "I'm glad I went. I . . . I loved it."

Cooper's brows met in suspicion. "Did you? That's something, at least."

"Cooper . . ." Oh, why were there all these people here? People probably didn't stand up and walk away from Norman Rockwell Thanksgiving dinners to have a private word. Even I could guess that much. I'd seen movies.

He gave me one last searching glance, then turned to his sister. "Caro, I'm driving in to work tomorrow morning. Do you need me to deliver the package for you?" He inclined his head at Mia, busy decorating her uneaten dinner with lima beans.

Meaning dawned along with relief on Caroline's face. "Yes. Thank you. That would be great. He's expecting . . . it . . . tomorrow morning about ten. I'll pack the stuff tonight."

I gathered Mia's father got custody back for the rest of the Thanksgiving weekend since Caroline had her for the actual holiday.

"You're taking Molly, too, right? It's Black Friday tomorrow. She'd love to shop in Charleston while you work, I'm sure. Wouldn't you?" asked Caroline.

"Um. Sure. If it's not too much trouble," I said to an impassive Cooper.

"All right," he said, standing to gather plates. I jumped up to help. "No, no. Sit down." He left no doubt he didn't want my company.

"There's dessert," said Caroline, watching her brother disappear through the door with a worried expression. She spared me a quick speculative glance and followed. I made another move to go after them. Miss Aurelia pushed down on my thigh under the table, keeping me in my seat.

"Speaking of the beach," she said breezily while keeping an iron hand on my leg, "last time I rode out there, I cut my foot all to hell on a sharp shell buried under the sand. Limped for a week. Should have worn my water shoes, but I forgot 'em. Anyway, I knew right away my foot was bleeding, because it hurt like a damn devil and the shell stuck out of it like a dagger. You know what? That was one of the most beautiful shells I ever saw. Perfect white channeled whelk. Huge. Unbroken. Still got it on my mantel."

"That's a beautiful story, but what on earth does it have to do with anything? You're two years younger than I am—and too young for a senior moment." Ted folded his napkin impatiently.

"Don't be obtuse, Ted. Point is, that sometimes the beauty's worth the pain."

Dessert, in contrast to the meal, was eaten in silence unbroken by anything except approving comments about the food and Mia's assertion that one of her teeth was loose. Afterward, Miss Aurelia claimed to need my help getting up from the table. Once she'd reached her feet, she didn't let go of my arm, gripping it with a pincer like a crab.

"I believe I need a turn around the yard," she said, in a terrible fake accent that managed to be a cross between British Madonna and Scarlett O'Hara. I wasn't the only one who caught the parody. Caroline's mouth dropped open. Cooper mumbled something unintelligible into his plate. With the grace of a panther, he vaulted out of his chair and out of the room.

"Molly? You willing to help an old lady walk off some pie?" Aurelia asked, gripping my arm.

As if I had a choice. Or wanted one, for that matter.

"Yes, ma'am. Some fresh air would be good. But, Caroline, are you sure you don't need me to help clean up?"

"You go on. Coop will help. Mia too, right, sweetie?"

Mia nodded solemnly.

Ted, apparently, did not need to enter the kitchen for any reason.

"See? Off we go," said Miss Aurelia.

Outside, Miss Aurelia dropped the old-lady-walking act. She let go of my arm and set off down the allée with the arm-swinging posture of a regular speed-walker. I jogged to keep up.

"Miss Aurelia, slow down. What happened to needing help?"

"Oh, now, you didn't buy that, did you?"

"Did anyone?"

"No, I'm sure not, but it got you out here, didn't it?" She cackled, a rusty croak that made me smile.

"Yes, ma'am, I suppose it did."

"I want to talk with you about that shit show in there, and I want to do it without a room full of Middletons listening. You've walked into a damn mess."

"I-I'm sure I . . ."

She barked a laugh, not slowing down one iota. My flip flops weren't up to this level of fitness walking. "You're sure of absolutely nothing. How'd you meet Cooper? You said you got married in Vegas—had you known each other six whole hours beforehand?"

I stumbled over a slight dip in the ground in surprise. I should have known she'd figured it out, but I was still curious. "How did you know?"

"My dear. It's obvious. He's besotted with you—I've never seen him behave that way at a meal, and I've eaten a damn year's worth of food at that table. But it's not a married kind of besotted. It's a third-date kind of besotted. Y'all have just met. It could work, but it's touch and go, I'd say, at least at this point."

"We met in Vegas, when he went with his friends. We'd never seen each other before. We all got sloppy drunk and Cooper and I woke up in a rental car with a marriage certificate." I wasn't sure whether to trust her with the information that we had no plans to try to make it work. That we'd already been to a lawyer to start the annulment process. That as far as we knew—or remembered— we'd never slept together.

She thought he was "besotted" with me. I'd never dared imagine that word in connection with me. Anthony had been a warm body in my bed for a few months—taking the virginity he'd never known about—but he'd certainly never been besotted with me. Or even all that interested. Miss Aurelia was seeing what she wanted to see, nothing more than that.

"Ah. Interesting. A quickie Vegas marriage is a damn odd thing for Cooper to do. I don't know you well, my dear, so I have no idea if that is out of character for you, but to my knowledge, Cooper, despite his good ol' frat boy appearance, has never done a truly irresponsible thing in his life. At eleven or twelve, he was taking care of his sister like a parent. He had perfect attendance and perfect grades and won every sportsmanship award on every team in high school. Oh, he's no saint—he'll take a dare, and he drinks enough to be a gentleman, and he used to drive too fast when he was younger—but I'd never have pictured him at a Las Vegas wedding chapel. Not in a million years." She slowed down enough to give me a head-to-toe speculative look. "Must have been a hell of an inducement."

The heat set my cheeks afire. "I don't think so. Not the kind of inducement you're thinking of. W-we never . . ."

"Are you serious? The air between the two of you would scorch my socks, if I wore any. Getting wet at the beach, indeed.

Clearly you're not gay. Why the hell not? Are you already married?"

"I . . . no. I'm not married. But I'm not the right one for him. He deserves better. I can't bring myself to tell him the things that would convince him, though."

"Well, what are those things?"

I opened my mouth to tell her, but then she put her hand on my arm. Her touch was kind and comforting—like a mother. A real mother. A mother from a book or a family sitcom, not like my own actual mother's touch. She didn't need to know either. I'd rather be thought well of after I was gone if I could manage it. I wanted to leave behind a few people in the world who wouldn't associate me with wrongness and evil.

"Um, some things I've done. Places I've been. He doesn't need to know. He'll be better off when I'm gone."

"You think so, do you? And how will you be after you're gone? Huh. Your plan is to nobly leave him as he was, but go away a mess yourself? Looks to me like only a person who cared quite a bit would want to protect him like that. You ought to tell him. Give him a chance to decide if he needs protection from whatever it is. He's a pretty tough kid. He's had to be. He lost his mama early, and his father is . . . Well. Ted is Ted."

There was a note of something there. Disgust, maybe, or hidden knowledge of some kind.

Hope rose. Maybe if I asked her about Lynette, she'd help me figure out what to tell Cooper and Caroline.

"About that . . ." How to begin? Blunt? Smooth? Pray she'd read my mind?

"About Ted? Can't believe you could have been in the house three hours without figuring him out. What'd he do?"

Okay. I'd go with blunt.

"Miss Aurelia, was there something going on between Ted and Cooper's first wife?"

With no warning, Miss Aurelia stopped walking so abruptly I shot five paces past her and had to boomerang back. "What are you saying, girl? Did he do something? Did he say something?"

"Yesterday afternoon, Cooper had gone to work. Ted asked me to come to his workshop. He cut up the venison and talked about Lynette. It isn't that he *said* anything out of the ordinary. Nothing I can put my finger on. It was just . . . odd. There were hints. Things he said . . . without saying, if that makes sense. It made me wonder."

Miss Aurelia sighed, looking older than her years where minutes before she'd seemed younger. "I've always wondered, too. Lynette was alone a lot. She was the kind to put up a lot of barriers. Introverted. She didn't warm up easily to others. She'd been a sorority girl and she could pretend, but it was hard for her here. I used to go over to their house when Cooper was gone so much, bring her a cake, a tin of rosehip tea, something to let her know that we cared."

"She wrote a diary. Did you know that? I found them upstairs, hidden away. I only read enough of one to figure out it was hers. It talked about Clemson."

"Oh, Lordy. Yes, I did know she had a diary, but I didn't know they were still in the house. I'm damn sure I wouldn't have been able to resist reading them. I'm impressed."

Heat rose in my cheeks. "Well, I actually ran out of time. I probably would have read them. Since she left them behind and all."

She ran a hand distractedly over her wild mane of hair. This topic troubled her. "After about a year of marriage, I'd find her sleeping more often than not. Depressed. She admitted to being depressed when I asked her. Meanwhile, Ted said a few things about her or around her that raised my hackles. I've known Ted all my life. We both grew up in this town. Went to school together. His wife, Barbara, and I played basketball together in school, down in Charleston." She grinned at me. "Yeah, even old ladies can be former athletes, you know."

"I never doubted it," I said. "You nearly ran me into the ground getting out here."

"I did, didn't I?" she said, pleased. "I still got it. Anyway, Ted's been a dog all his life. He was as good-looking as a Greek god when he was young, and he had all the confidence that goes with that. He never saw a girl with any looks at all without getting in her pants, or trying to. Barbara had a time of it during their marriage, but she was the kind of woman who'd been taught to look the other way. Her daddy was the same, so she took it as normal. Of course, Barb died when Cooper and Caroline were young enough that they never knew he was a cheater. He didn't marry again."

"Probably for the best."

"You could say that. Barb, on the other hand, was faithful as the day is long, and absolutely devoted to those kids. It must have been tough, though. The last one of Ted's women before Barb, uh, died was a close friend of hers. I assume it got to be too much, one day, for her to handle."

Rage flared. Ted apparently thought all women on earth existed to serve him—in bed or elsewhere. I balled my fists and kicked a convenient tree root, regretting it when I remembered I had on flip flops.

"Lynette, though," continued Miss Aurelia. "I don't think she was interested, or if she was at first, she wasn't later. I'm not sure he'd have left her alone, even if she'd been the kind to tell him baldly to stick his dick back in his pants, which she definitely wasn't. I've always thought Ted drove her off. That she ran, rather than have to tell Cooper that his own father was a horny goat."

"I was trying to decide whether to say something to him. After Ted went on about Lynette's looks, he put his hand on my cheek. Made it clear that he wanted—"

Miss Aurelia let out a long hissing breath, but she didn't look shocked. "Oh, dammit, my dear. I'm sorry. Like I said, he doesn't hesitate when he sees someone attractive. I'm not sure he gets that he's supposed to make sure she's interested first, or cares, if he does. He's a dog. And you're more than attractive."

"Um. Thanks?"

She gave me a rueful smile and went on. "I'll be honest, I've never known whether to say anything about my suspicions to Cooper either, because it wouldn't change the fact that Lynette is gone and they're divorced now. It would only make him think badly of his father, and he's only got one parent left. Ted is an oversexed bastard, that's for sure, but he hasn't been a bad father to those two. I never said anything because of that."

"That's as far as I got, too," I said, relieved she looked at things the same way I did. I was enjoying the workout that walking with Miss Aurelia allowed.

She reached up and smacked a slim branch of a nearby live oak, dislodging a few leaves. "But you . . . this is different. You'll have to make it plain to Ted you don't want him and wouldn't have him even if he were wrapped in gold and dipped in a chocolate fondue."

"How do I make it that plain?"

"Knee him hard in the balls. That's what I did, back in high school. If you can't shut Ted down, and make him stay down, you'll have no choice but to tell Cooper."

"I know."

Or I could follow Lynette's example and get the hell out of here.

After Miss Aurelia drove off in her tiny Toyota, I went back to the kitchen, where Caroline and Cooper had almost finished cleaning up. Mia sat like a mesmerized zombie in front of a cartoon on TV in the family room.

Cooper's back straightened into a ramrod at my entry. Caroline took one look at him, drew her brows together, and said, "Cooper. Can you take the turkey carcass out to the woods and dump it? Then stay out. I need some girl time with Molly."

He gave me one searing glance that communicated all the frustration and hurt and desire he'd kept zipped up during the meal, pressed his lips together and went, the turkey carcass in a plastic garbage bag.

"Let me help," I said, my voice coming out uneven and breathy.

Caroline handed me a pot to dry. "Oh, honey. It looks like

you're the one who needs help. What's going on? I couldn't get Cooper to talk."

"It's nothing. A spat. We'll figure it out." If I couldn't tell Cooper, I definitely couldn't tell Caroline. "Did you have a nice Thanksgiving?"

She waved off my question. "Mama used to do all this," she said, gesturing at the mostly clean pots and pans drying in the rack and wrapped leftovers waiting to be put away. "Every year at the holidays, I miss her. I was only six when she died, of course, but I always wonder what it would have been like if she were here."

"It was a beautiful meal. I can't believe how much work you did. In my family . . ."

A cell phone in a pink case plugged into the kitchen charger rang, saving me from whatever ill-advised admission I'd been about to make about my own past. Caroline washed her hands and dried them quickly to get to the phone before it stopped ringing. I stood near enough to see the name on the phone was Danny Kim. Her ex. The one Cooper had offered to take Mia to during dinner.

Caroline held up one finger to me making clear she wanted me to stay.

"Hello? . . . Yes, I . . . Well, I thought . . . No, I didn't . . . Yes, at ten. I know. Cooper is bringing her. We . . . I was thinking . . . Only to say Happy Thanks— . . . Fine."

Caroline's voice was breaking and she fought for control.

"Danny, I just wanted to say Happy Thanksgiving . . . of course I do . . . I'm not the one who . . . Fine. Ten o'clock." Her face had gone white, and the tears would roll soon.

There was a long pause, while I watched the remaining joy of the holiday drain out of her. "Goodbye." She hit END and plugged the phone back in, carefully, with slow and weary movements.

"Your ex?"

"Yeah. Making sure I planned to have Mia to his house on time for her second Thanksgiving dinner in two days."

"I'm sorry."

"God, I hate this. I never wanted . . ." The first tear made its appearance.

Most prisoners learned in the first twenty-four hours not to cry. Touches could be easily misconstrued. Experience or no experience, though, it was time for me to take a tentative step into the world of personal contact. I laid a tentative hand on her shoulder. She wiped at the tear with hot-water-reddened hands, the gesture tiny and inexpressibly sad.

The hand wasn't enough. Slowly, I held out my arms to another woman for the first time I could ever remember. Caroline came willingly into them and cried onto my collarbone. An odd kind of glow spread through me, making the corners of my own eyes well with tears.

She gathered herself and stood back. "I'm the one who's sorry. It's really hard. He's so cold to me and I don't know why. I called him, earlier, because I wanted to say Happy Thanksgiving, and he acted like I had some kind of nefarious motive for everything, and I don't know why. I want us to be together. I've always wanted us to be together. I hate that Mia is caught in the middle."

"Divorce sucks." Many of my fellow prisoners' biggest regrets wasn't their crime, but the fact that their imprisonment meant that they'd had no choice but to leave behind a child or four to be raised by a hated ex or a hated mother or a hated in-law. Though I'd never had a father, I felt the absence of one, like a lost tooth. I used to fantasize that he'd have taken care of me. And in prison, I'd heard plenty of anguish like Caroline's before.

"I never knew how much it sucks," said Caroline, shoving food into the refrigerator. "People always say it's hard for kids, and it is, but gosh. It feels like I've been dumped all over again every single day. For six months. It's supposed to get easier. But on days like today, days that are about family, it only gets harder." She sniffled. "I'm so glad you're here. Daddy and Coop are guys. They feel bad, but for them it takes the form of wanting to . . . to punch Danny, or something. I don't want that. All I want is . . . him."

"I know. I'm so, so, sorry. If there's anything at all I can—"

Ted entered the kitchen, carrying a glass of whiskey. "Caro, I'm sure you've got this under control. I need a word with Miss Molly. In my study."

CHAPTER ELEVEN

A finger of discomfort ran icy down my back. If Ted got me behind the closed door of his study, would he try something? Oh, holy shit, I'd actually have to knee him in the balls. It would be hard to return to "please pass the turkey" after I'd kneed him in the balls. At the same time, I had to admire his strategy. He'd asked Caroline's permission, making it totally aboveboard.

"Sure. I'm done," Caroline said. "Thanks for your help. And, just thanks."

"No problem," I said, giving her a smile before following Ted down the hall, knee at the ready.

In the study, I sucked in a deep breath: tobacco, leather, and oddly, the mud of the marshland. I sank into a wing chair where Ted couldn't join me.

Romance didn't seem to be at the top of Ted's list today, however. He sat behind his desk and opened a laptop.

"What is your full name?" he asked, dropping any pretense at the kindly old father figure.

Oh. I glanced between him and the laptop. Ted had been Googling.

Shit.

"Molly Kathleen Todd." That was a lie. My legal first name was Mary. My grandmother had nicknamed me Molly at birth and everyone had called me that all my life. Mary was the name that would show up on the Internet with the convictions and the sentence and the news articles, though in my drunken stupor, I'd told the marriage certificate guy "Molly." Ted hadn't found "Mary" yet, obviously, since he hadn't thrown me out of the house. "Excuse me. I haven't gone to the Social Security office yet, but I suppose it's Molly Kathleen Middleton, now." There you go, Ted. Right in your eye.

He snorted. "Your occupation? Could be I misheard you the first time."

"I'm an interior decorator."

"Interesting. I thought you said interior designer at one point. There's a difference, you know. One requires a certification. Do you know which one?"

I sure as hell hoped it was the designer one. I had mixed it up, not knowing the distinction. Almost certainly, I'd said both at different times. "Designer requires certification," I said, with as much knee-him-in-the-balls confidence as I could muster.

"Correct. You are not listed anywhere in any registry of certified designers. Now you say you're a decorator? Who did you work for? I'd like a reference, please."

Who the hell did he think he was? I stared him down, practically feeling the acid shoot out of my eyes, and forced my voice to remain calm. "Do you always summon your Thanksgiving dinner guests into your study and interrogate them? Wouldn't it be easier to have a form we could fill out before the turkey is carved?"

His lips thinned until they disappeared. "I don't need that backtalk, young lady. You've worked some magic on Cooper, but I'm not so easy to take in. If he's too bamboozled to protect himself, I'll do it for him. A client reference, please."

Please. As if this had to do with protecting Cooper. Yet at the same time, Ted as an enemy lit a fire within me. I'd never tried fighting back before. Now, when I had nothing to lose I wouldn't lose anyway, might be the best of all times to practice. "I'd hardly think you'd want to change decorators at this point, Ted. Leandra does a fine job. Couldn't do better myself."

"Who is your employer? You must have one."

"Actually, I don't. I worked for myself. No boss. I find it grating, having other people order me around." I spit out the last three words so he couldn't mistake my meaning.

He ground his teeth. Hard. "When I Google you, all I get is some long-distance runner who is approximately fifteen, and a woman in Australia who runs an insurance agency. How is it possible to leave no trace on the Internet in this day and time?"

"Apparently, I've done nothing worthy of mention."

"You have no Facebook page. No Twitter. No website thing where you post constant vanity pictures of yourself."

"I guess I'm not vain. And I don't like social media. It's a waste of time. I'm flattered, though, Ted. I'd think you'd have better things to do than to sniff around after your son's wife."

Ugly red unfurled up his neck, but he didn't change expression. I'd made an enemy, but the exhilaration made it hard to care. The vanity in this room belonged all to him. "Cute. The Yankee's got a bite." He stood, slapping the laptop shut. "Listen to me, Miss Todd," he said, all silky control. "You're under my roof. Not Cooper's. Not Caroline's. You'd do well not to forget that."

"I'm married to your son."

"Who is a guest here as well. Cooper's clearly not in his right mind at the moment. Been a while since that boy got laid, and he's being led around with a ring through his pecker. Anyone can see that."

Heat crept up my chest, though I didn't move a muscle. Adrenaline sizzled through me, snapping all my synapses, but I remained composed on the outside.

The wing chair I sat in angled a foot or two opposite Ted's desk. He came around the huge piece of furniture and perched, with great care, on the front edge. Keeping eye contact, he scooted forward, until his knees were an inch from mine. I shifted, and his knees followed.

"The same day you arrived, I called a friend of mine down in Charleston," he said, watching me fight not to give in and jump up, a half-smile reminding me grotesquely of Cooper's, "I told him, I said, I got someone needs checking out up my way."

Ah. The man who'd dropped the silverware during our lunch at Poogan's Porch.

"He's been digging. He's good. Cooper said you were a year younger than he is. That gives me a birth year, a state of birth, and a city to start in. Your middle name is unusual. Too unusual to be made up. I expect we'll start with that."

"I'm guessing you want me to ask you what I can do to get you to tell him to stand down."

"Nobody ever said you weren't smart," he chuckled, running his moccasin-covered toe down my calf, the smooth leather making my skin crawl. "Yes, ma'am, I think you know the way. I don't think you're dumb enough to need it spelled out." His gaze dropped to my chest, more on display than usual in a blue V-neck sweater I'd borrowed from Caroline for the holiday dinner, and lingered there, making a point. He kicked off his shoe.

Enough. I sprang to my feet and backed around the chair, the movement instinctive and practiced from a childhood full of putting pieces of furniture between me and danger.

"You embarrass yourself," I said, my voice shaking now. "I'm not interested. Not in you. Not ever."

His laugh was a low rumble that reminded me of a twisted version of Cooper's. "Oh, when I'm ready to get what I want, I can get it. Don't you worry. It's a lot easier than you think. For instance, I could tell Cooper his mother was a slut. That she slept with everything that moved—and a few things that didn't. I'd hate to have to do that."

My mouth went dry. Cooper worshipped his mother's memory. "Ridiculous. She didn't do anything of the kind. Everyone in town would know that. Cooper wouldn't believe you."

He chuckled, the sound untroubled and skin-crawling. "Maybe, maybe not. So I don't tell him that. I tell his real estate partners that he's developed a drinking problem. Or drugs. Whatever." Without a ripple, his face turned old and tragic, the long-suffering father of an addict. My breath deserted me. *My God.* He was good. "See? When it comes down to it, you wouldn't want to force me to say something that would ruin his life, would you? I know you wouldn't. You already care too much about him."

He was a monster. He wasn't even threatening—only explaining what he could do if he wanted to. He'd sully anything, at any time, to get what he wanted. I had to get out of here.

"Google away. I dare you. I don't have any secrets."

He stood, but made no move toward me. His grin was contemptuous, but no less full of desire.

"Aw, now. You don't need to be scared of me." He backed off, hands up.

I made it to the door. From behind me, he laughed quietly. "I'll take that dare any day of the week, darling. Because I've never seen anyone hiding as many secrets as you."

I turned and fled for the safety of the allée.

I walked for an hour, emptying my mind of everything but the beauty of my surroundings. Figuring Ted wouldn't be anywhere near the back staircase, I crept in that way. The bed called to me—even at this early hour, I could read and hide from everyone. Cooper would no doubt stay away until late, given that he wasn't speaking to me. In any event, if I heard footsteps outside the door, I could pretend I'd fallen asleep with the book on my chest and the bedside lamp still on.

This plan would have worked like a charm, except that when I entered the room, Cooper lay on the bed, reading, in my place. He sat up. His lips relaxed naturally into a smile of greeting until he remembered he was angry. He swung his legs over the side of the bed, slapping his book shut.

"I'm sorry. I'll leave," he said as impersonally as I used to when a hotel guest arrived when I was in mid-clean. "You stay."

"No, wait," I said. I'd taken his room, his bed, his food, his money, his holiday, his house. I was so tired of taking without giving, and the lack of anything to give frustrated me all over again. "You stay. It's your bed, after all. I can't keep taking everything from you. I'll go to a guest room."

Someplace where Ted wasn't.

I made a move to his side, to reach a pillow to take with me. He stopped me with a gentle hand on my forearm.

"Molly. I don't want to fight. I'm sorry."

"I don't, either."

"I was thinking about what you said this morning," he said, his voice low.

Part of me longed for the not-too-distant day when I'd never see him again—the pull of him overpowered me when he was near me like this. There would be relief in not feeling that wrench of connection whenever I got within five feet of him.

Most of me dreaded it, though.

"Which part?" I asked, not moving away even though I knew I should.

"The part about you wanting me. Was it true?"

I swear the vibration of his vocal cords echoed in my body. I had to swallow before I could speak. "Yes."

"Then tell me again why we can't." He gestured at the bed. "I mean, we've probably already . . ."

"Because you don't know who I am. You don't know enough about me."

"And I said I knew enough."

"You don't." I pulled away, out of his electromagnetic field, and retreated across the room to the window.

"What does it matter? I don't need to know your secrets. Don't tell me. But that doesn't mean we have to stay in this room and act like monks. We're adults. We aren't seeing other people. We've seen each other naked before. Why not?"

I closed my eyes. "Because, Cooper. It's gone too far. I can't."

"What do you mean, 'it's gone too far?'"

With a sickening lurch, my brain figured it out. Hopelessness opened up in a yawning chasm before me. Maybe in Vegas I'd had meaningless sex with Cooper, but I couldn't have meaningless sex with Cooper anymore. I cared about him too much. Over a short span of days, he had become important to me. I'd never get back the little piece of my soul I'd lose if I let him touch me when the meaning was only on one side. It ached already, trying to explain why not without admitting how much I cared.

"I mean we are getting an annulment. We are going our separate ways. We should not get entangled. It'll be easier not to."

He approached slowly, hands at his sides, letting me decide. "It might be better not to, but it won't be easier. Getting entangled, at least for tonight, sounds like a hell of a good idea to me."

Oh, it did. He and his orbit had sucked me in. I'd give anything to be able to throw out my feelings and go eagerly to him. I squeezed my hands together to keep them from touching him now that he was within reach.

"You are so beautiful. I can't think about anything else, all day, but touching you. I feel you under my hands when you're not even in the room. I might burn up if you don't let me touch you." His fingers burned a path along my jaw. His eyes blazed with desire. "Please."

And with that one word, all my defenses fell into rubble at my feet. Suddenly, the choice between virtuously avoiding meaningless sex and having carte blanche to touch him wasn't a choice at all. All the options disappeared. There was only him, the sound of his breath, the heat of his body, the smell of his skin, in front of me, around me. Everywhere.

In answer, I spread my palms out over the planes of his chest, solid under his plaid button-down he'd worn to dinner. As my hands drifted slowly outward, he shivered and wrapped his arms around me, pulling me close. I'd never felt a response like this, demanding, leaving no room for thought. My skin hummed with yearning.

"I've been dreaming about you at night," he said, into my hair, the low timbre of his voice rusty and hoarse. "I don't know if it's memories or imagination. But I want you so much I can't even tell them apart."

He lowered his head, the kiss starting at the corner of my mouth, working its way over until our lips met, soft at first, but then harder. Unwilling to wait, his thumb pushed gently on my chin, opening my mouth. He tasted my lips, his tongue slipping skillfully in to dance with mine. He knew what he was doing. He knew everything good about kissing. I dug my hands into his shining hair to pull him closer, smelling his skin, sharing his warmth.

To my surprise, he disentangled my hands and brought them down to the buttons on his shirt. "I need to feel you. Your skin. Against mine." His hands moved to the hem of my sweater, pausing there, asking permission.

I nodded, breathlessly managing two buttons before the sweater swept up over my head and I had to stop to free myself of it.

"Oh, Molly. Look at you. You are perfect," he said, pulling back. "Those breasts belong in a museum."

I giggled. "You've got to be kidding."

"No. I'm very serious." He palmed them reverently over my bra, lifting them, taking their weight, rubbing his thumb over the nipples. His touch was sure but worshipful, and a wave of pure lust shot down my spine to my nether regions, lighting them up in ways Anthony never, ever, did.

"My turn." I tried to ignore Cooper's roving hands to concentrate on unbuttoning and casting aside his shirt. He wore an undershirt underneath, which I stripped him of as well. At last, my hands could explore: up and up they went, over ridges of muscle and smooth skin to his rounded shoulders. Memory materialized. "I remember this. You, without a shirt, in that hotel room . . . You're not the only one who wondered where the line between dream and fantasy was. Oh, my God, Cooper."

His was the chest that ought to be carved in marble for the ages. Defined pecs, a hint of a six-pack, grooves above his hipbones. He paused in his wanderings—and oh, what wanderings— to let me explore, before crushing me to him for another kiss, like he couldn't get enough, couldn't stand to be apart.

Before, I'd never felt like this. Never so out of control, never this intense longing, craving, to be naked and horizontal. My thoughts became so disjointed and lost to sensation I didn't even notice he'd undone my bra and brought a breast to his mouth— and then I was helpless to do anything but pant as his mouth did acrobatic things at the peak.

"Oh, God. Like that. Do that forever," I said, robbed of breath and close to knee-buckling weakness. I'd never known my nipples were so sensitive; he'd taken me halfway there merely by suckling.

He reached for my hand and pressed it to himself. His khakis strained with the strength of his erection, and it dawned on me where we were going. Eight feet or so, to be exact, directly to that top-of-the-line mattress. And sex that would curl my toes and my hair, too. I knew it even before I'd experienced it.

It would be the kind of sex I'd never forget. I'd never forget the guy who gave it to me, either. It might already be too late to walk away unscathed. I wavered as his tongue did magical things to my other breast. If I was already . . . scathed, then what would it hurt?

It would hurt my ability to walk away at all—scathed or otherwise. We would be fully and properly married.

Consummated. Married for real. Screwed, quite literally.

It took a while for me to find the strength to pull away from his kiss, much less his talented hands on my breasts. He looked up, his lust-glazed eyes trying to focus. The broken contact stung, made me feel vulnerable and lost. "We shouldn't do this."

"What?" He kissed me again, biting on my earlobe, trailing down my neck, causing a full-body shiver. "No. Come on." He put his hand on a place that made me melt into him.

"I want to. My body is screaming yes, Cooper, but we should stop. You don't want to be married to me. You don't . . ."

You don't love me.

Fear woke and yawned inside me, clearing my head. Oh, God. I wanted him to love me. And he didn't. He was attracted to me, but he couldn't love me. Not yet. Not rationally. We hadn't known each other two weeks. "If we don't stop, we can't get an annulment. We'll have consummated the marriage." My hands belied my words, moving over his chest and following the narrow line of chest hair south.

"Nobody has to know if we do." He licked my neck. I gasped, procrastinating. The skin-to-skin contact made me swallow convulsively.

"Gibbes will be able to tell."

He twined his hands through my hair, ran a thumb over my cheekbone, pulled my mouth to his. I didn't want to stop. I swayed back toward him. "He won't."

"No!" I pushed him away, bending to find my sweater and holding it to my chest. "No. We can't do this. We've gone as far as we can go. We have to get the annulment. We need the grounds to be real. They'll make us swear to it in court. On a Bible."

"Okay," he said, a hurt expression crossing his face. "If you want to be rid of me so badly, we could just get a divorce."

"No. A divorce is a big deal. You'll be twice divorced at thirty-four. It will take forever and cost a bundle. I'll live somewhere else and it'll all have to be done by mail. We don't want that."

"You're serious."

"Yes." I turned away, but regret and longing kept me talking way past the point of sense. "If . . . if you still want me after the annulment goes through, give me a call."

He barked out a laugh that left no doubt nothing at all was funny. "You've made it pretty clear that you don't want me." He ran a hand through his hair and backhanded his nose, looking for his undershirt.

Tears pricked the corners of my eyes. Sex was a big deal to me. I'd only slept with one person before, and I'd never learned to think of sex as simple or easy. Cooper clearly viewed this whole interlude as entirely physical, something we could do before acknowledging or even expecting to have feelings for each other, and that knowledge choked me. I'd thought I could get past it, but I couldn't.

And then I knew why. I loved him.

Pain exploded like a bomb in my chest. I wanted to drop down and hug my knees to my chest and squeeze until I disappeared. How had I let that happen?

"Fine," I said, pulling my sweater over my head. "You want the truth? I do want you, but wanting each other for sex is a lot different from wanting each other for life. This may not be a big deal to you, but it is to me. I don't sleep around. I don't have sex for 'fun.' That may be the way they did it in the Clemson frats, but you'll need to find a bimbo ex-sorority girl for that."

A silence fell.

The air in the room stopped moving.

What a thing to say. His face. Lynette had been in a sorority. I didn't remember it until the words were out of my mouth. I had n't meant to . . . I'd hurt him, and badly. Nausea roiled my stomach. His skin drained of color as if he'd been gut-punched.

I'd done that to him.

"Oh, Cooper, I didn't mean it," I babbled, my mouth going dry. "I forgot that Lynette . . . I'm so sorry. Please . . ."

He blinked and pressed his lips together, snatching a pillow and the top blanket off the bed. "Enough," he said tonelessly. "I'll find somewhere else to sleep."

CHAPTER TWELVE

Sleep came late and unwilling after that, so I woke far later than usual to sunshine streaming in the window where Cooper and I had . . . what? Given in? Fought? I had no words, and nowhere near enough experience, to know what the hell kind of summary would cover what we'd done the night before.

The house stirred as I lay in bed, hiding like a coward. Mia clattered down the stairs; her piping voice singing what I could swear was a Beyoncé song. Caroline's more distant one issued directives about teeth brushing and finding a lost book.

The rug beside the bed where Cooper had been in the habit of setting his pallet was bare. A streak of pain or illness or longing or all three sliced through me. I sat up, pushing hair out of my eyes, prepared to face another day as an imposter.

The door opened. Cooper stood there, pillow and neatly-folded blanket in hand.

"You're awake," he said, barriers up, his face impassive.

"Yes."

"For what it's worth, I can handle taking things slow. That's not a problem. I didn't expect the things you said to hurt as much as they did." He turned his back to me to put the bedding away. "That's on me, I guess. We're strangers, after all. I won't forget again."

"Cooper, I said it before I remembered that Lynette was in a sorority. It was insensitive. I have no excuses."

"I'm sorry I suggested lying under oath. In the light of day, I see how bad an idea that would be," he said stiffly. Then his lips softened almost imperceptibly. "Last night, I wasn't really considering good and bad ideas."

We stared at each other, awkward after our formal apologies.

Cooper cleared his throat. "If you want to ride along to Charleston, you'd better get ready. Danny can be a dick if Mia is late coming back to him." He went to the door, hand on the knob.

I nodded, unsure whether it would be better to ride to Charleston with a possibly wounded and silent Cooper or stay here to be Google-hunted by Ted.

Uh, yeah, dumbass. That choice was easy. Without another word, I slid out of bed, grabbed my things, and headed for the shower.

Thirty minutes later, I sat in the passenger seat in the leather-upholstered luxury of Caroline's SUV. Cooper's truck didn't have a backseat where Mia could sit safe from the airbag, so he had to borrow it. I passed twenty charmed minutes listening to Mia's story about a princess and a magic horseshoe and how the princess and her faithful horse save the poor baker's son from the evil king with a spell that shot out from the ends of the magic horseshoe.

"Did you make all that up, Mia?" I asked, amazed. Were all kids that bright?

"Yes. I like horses. And princesses."

"That was really good. Better than any Disney movie. You should write it down."

"Silly. No!" she said, as if only an idiot would expect her to write anything. "I'm four! I can only write my name!"

"Oh." Her emphatic tone and adorable disgust with my cluelessness made me laugh. I had no experience with kids at all. "Well, I could write it for you, if you'd like."

"Yes! You can write my book! Uncle Coop, do you have any paper?"

"No, I don't, not here in the car. Tell you what. Molly and I will get some later and we'll have it all written up for you when you get back Sunday night. Okay?"

"Okay. Can I have my iPod now?"

When Cooper nodded assent, I unplugged it from the dashboard charger and handed it to her. In a moment, she'd blotted out the world as tinkly music emitted from its miniature speakers.

Though he was about as approachable as a growling dog, I figured it was up to me to put us back on a level of basic civility. Something about being away from the house, maybe just the radio DJ announcing the weather, lessened my unease. "Do you have to work all day?"

A muscle in his cheek twitched, and his oh-so-casual grip on the wheel tightened. "Not all day, but at least until mid-afternoon. You can take the car if you promise to pick me up when I'm done."

I got my driver's license at sixteen like most teenagers, though it had never done me much good. My mother owned an ancient Ford Escort with a hole in the floor big enough to watch the pavement go by and a pair of wipers that acted independently and looked like they were attempting drunken sex with each other. I drove it on the rare occasions she'd let me, or when she was too drunk to notice I'd taken it. After that, however, I'd gone to prison, and after my release, I still hadn't amassed enough cash to buy a car. I kept my license current but I hadn't driven more than two or three times in sixteen years. This SUV was a new model, with a push-button start and a fancy Bluetooth music system. No way. I'd die if I damaged Caroline's car.

"No, thank you. I'll walk around Charleston until you're ready to go. I-I don't drive."

That got his attention. Surprise softened his jaw a touch. "What? How is that possible? Aren't you from Detroit? Isn't that the whole purpose of Detroit? Cars and driving?"

It would be so easy to tell him there aren't roads in prison, even in the Motor City, right now, but I glanced into the backseat, where Mia manipulated the iPod figures marching across the tiny screen.

"I learned when I was a teenager, but access to a car has been kind of spotty. I used to take the bus to get to work."

A certain flat sense of resignation settled over me. Even without prison, even without the crime for which I'd gone there, the gulf between Cooper and me would have been daunting anyway.

He'd had everything he wanted all his life. I'd never had anything. They had a bus system in Charleston—I'd noticed one when we were there before—but I'd be willing to bet that Cooper had never been on a city bus in his life.

To my surprise, he stopped clenching his teeth. His hand relaxed on the wheel. "Right. I forgot. Well, if you want to get some practice, I won't tell Caroline if you don't." His lips settled into their more natural good-natured expression. "You lived with your mom, right? She never took you out driving?"

"No. She . . . she wasn't particularly maternal."

Cooper checked the empty stretch of highway in front of us, then took his eyes off the road to give me a sympathetic glance. He patted my forearm. "I'm sorry."

It would kill me to walk away from him. Even in his anger and confusion over what happened last night, his default was still caring and concern for others. The more I tried to separate myself from him, the more he reeled me in, without thought, without planning, without trying. Once he had, he'd be able to play with me and toss me back. I'd be left gasping for air. It was time to reset.

"Have you heard from Gibbes's office? About the annulment?"

His jaw tightened again. "No. He said it would be Monday." He glanced at me. "Let me check on him. Can you find his number in my phone?"

He hit the green button when I located it and waited. From the way he spoke, it must have been voicemail. "Yeah, Gibbes, this is Cooper Middleton. I know you're off upstate with your family, but I was wondering if maybe your secretary could speed things up and get the annulment paperwork moving before the weekend instead of after." I watched his cheek move as he ground his teeth. "Molly is ready for this to be over. Give me a call when you get this, or Monday morning, whichever is earlier." He repeated his phone number and hit END.

"What's a nullment?" asked Mia.

Oh, damn.

"Nothing, Pix. A grown-up piece of paper, that's all," said Cooper.

"Pix?" I asked.

He colored, faint rosiness spreading across the tan of his cheeks. "When Mia was born, she looked like something out of a fantasy. Tiny. Huge eyes. I said she looked like a pixie and it stuck."

"What is Aunt Molly ready to be over with?"

"Aunt Molly thinks we need the grown-up paper right away. She's had enough."

"Oh." Mia went back to her game.

"Cooper, I . . ." *I'd had enough?* He wanted the annulment too. Didn't he? I had no idea what to say. "It's not that."

He pinched the bridge of his nose. "Stop. Just stop trying to explain. You don't want . . ." He checked the backseat through the rearview mirror. "It's obvious what you don't want, and you don't want the person who offered it. In any form. We'll get the damn paper and we'll move the—" He checked himself again. "We'll move on. That's what you want."

All the things I wanted to say were dammed up behind all the things I couldn't bring myself to utter. I'd have to suck it up, now, though. There was no point in trying to make up with someone I was about to leave.

The outer sprawl of Charleston had crept up on us. Only the sight of the soaring white Ravenel Bridge, with its supports like huge tall ship sails in the distance, brought me back to noticing my surroundings again.

Mia's game and its music like fairy dust was the only sound as we crossed the bridge and wended our way to downtown Charleston. Slightly away from the fancier areas where tourists walked and the buildings were renovated within an inch of their lives, we drove through a more lived-in neighborhood and stopped in front of a huge Charleston-style house with a slightly sagging porch and chipped gray paint.

"This is Danny's place. He has the second floor."

I stayed put in the passenger seat while Cooper went back to the lift-gate so he could retrieve Mia's overnight bag and the pillow that had to go back and forth to each parent. Suitcase in hand, he opened the back door to release Mia from her booster seat. A man banged out of the front door of the house, looking perturbed.

"Cooper," he yelled, dark hair flopping over his forehead, every line of his trim body full of nervous energy. "You're late."

"Nice to see you, too, Danny," said Cooper, as Mia sprang out of the car, gave the man a quick hug of the legs, Cooper a quick wave, and ran inside. "You know how hard it is to get Mia and all of her things out the door on a tight schedule." The two men squared off, wary.

I lowered my window, out of some desire to say something helpful and friendly.

"Who's this? New girlfriend?" asked Danny.

"This is Molly. My new wife."

My mouth fell open in shock. He'd still call me his wife. Even after everything.

"Wife? You got married again?" Clearly this news dumbfounded Danny, whose confrontational body language melted into shock.

"Nice to meet you," I said from the passenger seat. "Mia is adorable. She told us a story she'd created on the way here. She's talented." I smiled at him, wishing I had the power to fix this marriage for Mia—and for Caroline.

The sincere compliment had an instant beneficial effect on Danny. His hands relaxed at his sides and his posture eased. "Thank you. That was nice of you to say. How long have you been married?"

"Didn't Caro tell you on Tuesday? We got married last weekend. In Vegas." Cooper glanced at me, as if trying to decide whether to pretend we were in love. He apparently elected to go with total neutrality.

"Uh, no. We . . . we talked about other things."

"You mean you fought," said Cooper. I watched the body language. These two men had once been friends. They were upfront with each other and, under the circumstances of a custody exchange, reasonably comfortable.

"Yeah, we fought." Danny glanced back at the house as if Mia might reappear. "That's what we do." He blinked and bit the inside of his cheek. I knew it. He hadn't moved on either. "Congrats, man. And to you, Molly."

"Anyway," said Cooper, clapping a hand to Danny's bicep. "We'll see you. I've got to get to work." He walked around the car and got in, starting the motor. Danny didn't move.

"Wait," I said to Cooper, putting a hand on his to stop him from taking the car out of Park. "Hold on, okay?"

"What are you . . . ?"

"Just hold on." I hopped out of the car after Danny, who'd turned toward the house. "Danny. Do you have a second?"

He stopped, waiting, no doubt with bated breath to hear what this total stranger brand-new ex-sister-in-law might have to say to him.

Damned if I knew. I only knew I couldn't let it go. Caroline's tears swam in front of my eyes.

"I know I don't know you, and I only met Caroline this week. It's absolutely none of your business, but she missed you yesterday. Like, a lot."

"You're right. It's none of your business." His face closed over, but there was something there, something that made me keep talking despite his words.

"I thought you ought to know. That's all." I shut up then, more out of loyalty to Caroline than anything forbidding about him.

"You're blunt," he said, with a certain degree of admiration in his tone. "I'll do you the favor of bluntness. I assume you've met Ted?" he asked, his face changing from distrust to outright dislike.

"Yes." I left it at that.

"If Cooper is still living there and you love him at all, you need to get the hell away from Ted."

"What do you mean?" Did he know about Ted and Lynette?

"Ted didn't like his pretty little Caroline being married to a

Korean. A Korean who was also a nurse. He made things . . . difficult. You're white, though. Maybe he'll like you. Most likely he won't. He's not a fan of outsiders coming into his perfect little family. If he doesn't like you, trust me, he'll get you out of there one way or another. I guarantee you've got some weakness he can exploit. Mine is Mia."

His forthrightness shocked me. "So it wasn't anything about Caroline."

"It was, in that she couldn't see the truth about Ted. Refuses to see the truth about Ted. She's an adult, though. I had to do something for my daughter. Surely you've noticed how he treats her like furniture, poor little half-Middleton that she is. Seriously. It's not too late for you two." He jerked a thumb at Cooper, sitting mystified in the front seat of Caroline's car. "Get him to move. He's not a hopeless case. Get him out of there. You'll have to if you want anything to last with him."

"Caroline's not a hopeless case. Give her a chance."

"Hummmph." A flash of pain reddened his cheeks, before he schooled his face back into impassive.

"Did you know Lynette?" In for a penny, in for a pound.

"Yes. A little. She was married to Coop when I married Caro. She was a nice person. Smart."

"Smart?"

Cooper leaned out the window. "Molly. I need to get to work."

"Yeah," Danny said, stepping back to indicate this conversation was over. "Smart. She left, didn't she?"

CHAPTER THIRTEEN

I was dreaming but I couldn't stop it. I knew this dream, but all I could do in my netherworld of sleep was wait for the dread to play out. I was nine and small for my age. A permission slip for a long-awaited field trip to the Henry Ford Museum had been ignored, and the teacher called my mother at home to ask why. My mother took it the way she took everything—as criticism. She screamed into the phone that we didn't have money for no Henry Ford Museum, that she didn't give a shit if I learned about the Wright Brothers or the assembly line, that I could spend that day getting shit done at home, that the teacher was a slut and a bitch and ten other names that made me cringe and dread going back to school the next day.

She hung up the phone and advanced on me, her breath stinking of onions and alcohol and floating ahead of her like a miasma of danger. "Little cunt-ass bitch, you sicced her on me, didn't you? You know we ain't got no money for that."

I backed around the recliner, a mistake. It put me against the wall with nowhere to run. I glanced at the door, calculating the distance like always.

She hated me. Her ruined voice was a hiss of loathing as she stalked me. "Now that fucker is gonna go to the principal and tell them about me. That was your plan all along, weren't it? You think your life would be better in fucking foster care? Foster mothers are worse'n me. I hear they beat you every day with a belt. Keep you in line. I shoulda been doing that. I can start now, though."

With no warning, her drink-palsied hand shot out. My scalp burned as she grabbed a handful of my hair. She yanked me over the arm of the recliner. I dropped in a heap of limbs to the floor. She kicked me several feet across the worn linoleum. One kick got my ribs and air deserted me.

I struggled to breathe: a ball on the floor, legs high to protect my stomach, face between my knees. She kicked me and slapped me, over and over. With fingers knotted in my hair, she hauled my head free. Pain exploded as she smashed her open palm into my cheekbone. I couldn't get a breath; my lungs sucked at nothing. I was dying.

Somehow, she held a knife. Without air, I couldn't scream. Slowly, inexorably, it moved toward my exposed throat. All I could do was—

I woke, as I always did from this dream, a real scream tearing from my uninjured throat. Moonlight spilled from the uncovered window across the bed in neat pane-shaped squares. My limbs clenched so tight they wouldn't release right away. I gasped for air, begging my lungs to work again. The darkness shimmered and rippled with threats of attack.

"She's dead. She's dead. She's deaddeaddead." I gabbled the mantra that sometimes dissipated the terror the dream left behind. She had never slit my throat and she could not do it from the coffin.

"Sssh." A weight shifted the mattress, and a warm hand reached to smooth my hair. I reacted like a wild animal, snaking away under the hands to the safety of the headboard. I crouched there; alert now, eyes wide, adrenaline roaring, as Cooper, wide-eyed, pulled a long leg in flannel pants up onto the bed.

Cooper. We'd returned from Charleston, making polite small talk like people do in a doctor's waiting room. We avoided each other at the house, going into the kitchen to scrounge dinner from Thanksgiving leftovers separately. We'd gone to bed in silence, Cooper back on the pallet and me in the bed.

But now he was on the mattress. With me. The bulk of his body promised eventual comfort, but while the shards of terror from the dream still cut me, his body, any body, meant threat and flight.

Holding very still, he spread his hands out on the rumpled sheets, palms open and unthreatening. He had no intent to hurt me. He changed and deflected the dark.

"Molly." The word held everything: fear, concern, caution, awareness. "I'd never hurt you. You know that, don't you? Come here." He held out a patient hand, making no sudden movements, letting me be the one to move toward him. I stayed squeezed into a ball, but less tightly wound, forcing my brain to replace the violent dream with the gentle reality. I relaxed enough to sit, knees bent protectively before me. He brushed the front of my calf and dropped his hands to his own knees. The house was silent. I'd woken no one else.

"Molly. You were dreaming. Tell me what happened."

"It was nothing. Just a dream. I'm fine now." As if he'd believe that: sweat dotted my upper lip and my voice still carried the high-pitched remnants of my shriek. I felt for the covers, folding the sheet into an accordion to anchor me to this bed.

"You screamed. I've never heard anyone scream in a dream before. It's not fine."

"I'll be fine. Really. I'm sorry I woke you. Go back to sleep. It's still the middle of the night." This time my voice sounded more normal. Almost persuasive enough. I curled my hands into fists to hide their trembling.

In the silvery pale light from the moon, he blinked. "No. That was more than a dream. Something happened to you."

"It was a long time ago. Bad memory."

"Hell of a memory. Look at you. You're shaking. What did you dream about?" He inched closer, hand out as if he wanted to gentle a horse. I squeezed my knees tighter to my chest, arms locked around them.

"N-nothing."

"You said, 'she's dead.' Who, Molly? Your mother?"

I pulled my face sharply from my knees, alert again. "Why do you say that?"

He sat back. "I . . . I guessed. I dream about mine sometimes."

With those five words, I was lost. Misery overwhelmed me.

Tears flowed down my face as I grieved for a grown Cooper's dreams about his mother. For a boy on the cusp of his teen years who'd come home from school to stumble on her lifeless body. For the loss of a mother who'd hidden depression and hung magnolia wreaths and cooked sweet potato casserole and played basketball with Miss Aurelia. For a mother who'd loved her kids enough to stay with Ted, even as he humiliated her at every turn.

And I grieved for myself. Sobs wracked my shoulders. I'd never had any of that. No Christmas decorations. No food-as-love. No love at all, not from her, that I could remember.

Yet his mother and mine were equally dead.

Cooper scooted up the bed until he'd pulled me into his arms, gently, little by little. I relaxed my knees to one side as I leaned into him. Minutes or hours passed and my sobs slowed. He rested my head on his T-shirt-clad shoulder and rubbed circles on my back. He let me cry, saying nothing, until the sobs became whimpers and then subsided altogether.

I could let him rub my back, but I couldn't handle the pity. I'd never been able to handle the pity.

"No. The dream was nothing," I said, trying to think of what normal people might dream about in their nightmares. "A woman was after me. That's all. A faceless woman." I'd never told Anthony, never told my friends at school, never my cellmate or any of the other prisoners about my mother and what she'd done to me. What she'd done over and over. Silence was the code I'd lived by all my life. If I let the words, the concept, leave my lips, the words would rip me open. I'd be flayed. Bare. I'd be disloyal, though even I knew how ridiculous it was to worry about disloyalty to a dead woman who'd spent a lifetime proving how little she deserved it.

We breathed together, as his hand continued its lazy movement on my back. He applied the slightest pressure with the hand that rested on my shoulder, giving me strength.

"Your life before now hasn't been easy, has it?" Cooper asked, barely audible. "It wasn't just a dream, was it?"

I shook my head into his chest. His hands tightened, pressing me closer.

I took a long, shuddering breath. His heat, all around me, flooded my senses with comfort and safety. It felt almost like love. If I concentrated hard enough, maybe I could convince myself that it was love. Real love that might last.

He took my shoulders in both hands and pulled me away enough to see my face. "I want to apologize. I was horrible to you today, because I got offended. Felt rejected. I made it all about me. I know you're not ready to tell me about your nightmare, and that's okay. It was a dick move, today, to treat you the way I did. Obviously there are things bothering you. You had things going on last night I didn't take into account."

"You're right. I have stuff that happened, but it isn't new. I'm not dealing with anything I haven't been all my life. That's not why I . . ."

"Oh, I know. The annulment. You want the annulment, and I get that you don't want to lie under oath. Actually, after you said that, I felt even worse. You're a better person than I am. I would have lied. Because . . ."

"Because why?"

His voice was all rough gravel. "Because I wanted you so much I would have lied about my own name."

For nine heartbeats, I let those words wash over me. "The annulment isn't the reason I said no. Not all of it," I said, knowing the words were reckless.

"What, then?"

"At first, last night, I thought wanting was enough. I thought I could let you touch me when you don't care about me and I could ignore it. That it wouldn't matter. But I'm not that kind of person. I'd like to be, but I'm not. I can't do it. I need to be with someone who cares. I can't do it just for fun. At least, not if I . . ." *Not if I love you.*

Anthony and I had not loved each other. We'd cared about each other almost exactly the same amount, which is to say, not a lot. It worked for a while.

This imbalance was growing by the hour.

Cooper's fingers slipped gently into my tumbled hair, cradling my head. The other hand came to my face, where he used a thumb to wipe away some leftover moisture next to my nose. His touch was infinitely reverent. His voice was barely audible in the silent night.

"How can you think I don't care about you?"

I took in a breath with a sharp hiss.

"Of course I do. Look at us, Molly. Look where we are. I'm holding you in my bed. You've trusted me to take care of you. It's killing me that I can't wipe away those memories as easily as a tear off your face. I care more about you than I have any woman since . . . since Lynette." He ran a hand down my upper arm, tenderness in every fingertip.

He did care. It was apparent in every touch, every hand he'd extended to me, every bag he'd carried, every time he'd told someone I was his wife.

Caring isn't love. But it might be enough.

I reached for him, ready to find out. He stilled, brushing my hair with a light palm.

"No, Molly. You don't owe me that. Not as some kind of payment for basic comfort." He smiled and kissed my temple like a brother. "I told you once I wouldn't say no another time, but I guess I am. You need calm now. And sleep."

I'd never known anyone like him. I'd never even heard of anyone like him. I bowed my head until it rested on his collarbone. He held me like that, making circles on my back with a gentle hand.

At long last I pulled away enough so he could hear me. "Stay with me."

Cooper nodded and swallowed. We rearranged ourselves under the covers. He pulled me close, so I could rest my ear on his chest.

I fell asleep listening to the slow thud of his heartbeat.

Some hours later, I woke. The moon had shifted and now cast a dim glow across the bed. I'd thrown off the covers and found a new source of warmth. My leg nestled between Cooper's. I'd curled on my stomach tight against him as he lay on his back. My right hand lay loose on his hipbone. The awareness of the contact caused a fine shiver to begin in my arms.

The moonlight gleamed bright enough to see Cooper's thick lashes on his cheeks. He breathed deep and peaceful. His beauty struck me dumb. The line of his perfectly-carved lips and nose in profile made me take in a sharp breath.

Under my hands, he twitched at the sound. His breathing changed. His lashes swept up and he turned his head to look at me, eyes wide in the darkness.

He'd said he wanted me. Enough to lie about his own name.

I'd done a lot of bad things in my life, but I'd do them all again for one night with him. Suddenly, my body's need blotted out rational thought. Raising myself onto an elbow, I put my hand on his cheek, asking permission. His lips parted.

Even so, a shock of surprise jolted him as my lips touched his. He'd let me make the initial move, but he adjusted easily, fitting his mouth over mine and upping the intensity all at the same time.

He broke the contact only once, a gentle breath in my ear, to ask, "Are you sure?"

In answer, I moved my mouth down to his neck and kissed the depression between his collarbones. "I'm sure."

"My turn, then." He tipped my head up and kissed me, softly as if I were breakable, on each of my closed eyelids, on the tip of my nose, on the crest of each cheek, then detoured for a long and lavish kiss of my lips before stopping to look at me in the dim light. His kiss robbed me of breath. He threw off the remaining covers, long limbs like a landscape painting all my own. "You are so beautiful, Molly Middleton."

This time, I didn't let his use of the name send me down the dead-end path of wondering where we were, what we meant, where we'd end up. Instead, I sat up to yank off the shirt I'd worn to sleep in. I wore no bra underneath. For a beat, Cooper stared, unmoving, his eyes glittering. Then his shirt hit the wall behind him, and he pulled me close with a groan of satisfaction. "I could stay like this forever. You are perfect." My hands and fingernails explored his back and shoulders, sketching my terrain, and he shivered. His skin was like satin, his muscles firm and defined everywhere I could reach. I bent my knee between his, pressing my thigh against his heat.

His hands were urgent, pulling me closer with every touch. Again, as he had before, he took my breast in his mouth, this time unhurried, devoting attention to the slopes and the tip with his lips and hands, then giving the same care to the other. He suckled each nipple in turn, back and forth, keeping the pleasure from building too fast. Each time he returned he stayed for a longer and longer time until I began to feel the burning and clenching of an oncoming orgasm before he'd even touched my sex.

I needed more. I interrupted his feasting by tugging on his pants, wanting him bare. I wanted to see. To taste. I hadn't been able to give him anything in return for his kindness, but I could give him this.

His chuckle was quiet in the dark as he gently stopped me. "You're impatient." He kissed his way down a slope to my belly. "I think ladies should come first."

In an agony of longing, grasping for any relief, I reached for the elastic waistband of my own running shorts instead.

He caught my hand, stopping me again. "Let me. I want to." Slowly, too slowly, he held my gaze as he pulled down the shorts and the underwear beneath while I lifted my hips to free the fabric in a haze of desire. Once he'd tossed the last of my clothing aside, he cupped my ass with big hands and lifted me to his lips. His tongue worked magic, and the wetness, his and mine, drenched me. Mindless sounds of ecstasy escaped me, embarrassing me, but he had no mercy. He did have skill, though, and within seconds or hours under his mouth I was grasping his hair and stifling a scream at my release.

"Again," he said, pulling a condom from his nightstand as I melted, boneless, into the mattress. He was beautiful in motion— lean and strong as he pulled off his pajama pants.

As they dropped, I knew. We hadn't had sex before, because if I'd seen then what was on display now, there was no way I could

have forgotten it. My breath caught. Watching him roll the condom down his length almost undid me. I couldn't wait any longer
to have him inside. I pulled him down to me and with a smooth
gasp-inducing slide, he filled me. He waited a beat or two while I
stretched for him.

Yes. I would have remembered this. My body would have remembered this. He was all around me, in me, everywhere.

"Holy God, you feel so good. I knew it would be like this." He
braced one muscled arm beside my head, smoothed an errant
strand of hair from my face, and leaned down to nip at my breast.
The beauty of his face combined with the eroticism of my own
nipple in his mouth dazzled me in the glow of the moon. I
touched a finger to his lips, wanting to make sure he was real. He
sucked hard on the finger and the nipple at the same time, shooting a pulse of energy straight to the place where we were joined.

Then he started to move, and I lost myself as he stroked me,
the pleasure building even more powerful than before. Each
thrust brought forth a moan, mine and his and mine, until it didn't
matter anymore whose sounds belonged to who. A sheen of sweat
made us slippery. Faster and stronger, he pounded into me as
everything around me disappeared. With a last burst of energy, I
reached for a piece of joy and held on with everything I had.

Afterward, I came to rest curled again into his side, head on his
chest. His heartbeat thudded steady under my ear. He dropped a
kiss onto my hair, unable to move any more than that.

"We've done it now," I said, sense returning to me as my
breathing slowed.

"Yes, we certainly have," he said, sounding inordinately
pleased, his low-pitched chuckle making his chest vibrate.

"But, Cooper, we've killed the annulment ground." Anxiety
quickened, dissipating the afterglow.

"Yup. And I'd do it again." He rolled to his side, bringing our
faces close together. He leaned in for a lingering kiss, then fell
back onto the mattress. "I will do it again, as soon as I recover my
strength."

"But what about . . ."

"Shhh. It's four-thirty in the morning. Let's sleep. Here. Both of us. Together."

"I don't know . . ."

He rolled to his side again, then over me, kissing me into silence. "Shhh. We'll talk about it in the morning. Come here." He pulled me close, my back to his front, and dropped another kiss onto my hair. Inside a minute, he fell into the sleep of the sated, his breathing easy and slow in my ear and his arms tight around me.

Sleep didn't hover quite so close for me. It took every ounce of restraint I had not to slither like a fish out from under his arms, into my clothes, and out into the night forever. The room dimmed as clouds made slow progress across the moon.

We were married for real now.

I'd done it. I'd slept with him: in plain disregard of the need for annulment when I knew perfectly well he'd want one—hell, demand one at the top of his lungs—when he found out about the murder. He'd said he didn't care about the annulment ground, but he didn't have enough information to make an informed choice. And it was my fault that he didn't have the information. He'd asked for it. I'd withheld it.

I'd had the power to prevent this from happening, but as I lay there, pinching the sheets in agitation, maybe I hadn't. The physical pull of Cooper was strong. Even now, glancing down at the heavy arm across my midsection, the memory of what his hands and tongue could do liquefied my insides and caused me to back up tighter against him.

No matter. I'd needed this and wanted it, and now I'd gotten it. No matter how he reacted when I told him, no matter how devastating his horrified face would be, this night had happened and could never be undone.

In the light of day, I would tell him and all this would end, as I'd known all along it would. The prospect was slightly less scary, because I'd decided to ask Miss Aurelia if I could stay with her until I had enough money to get on a bus back to Michigan. Something about her go-to-hell streak of white hair and the written-on jeans that contrasted so much with the other women's attire in this town made me think Miss Aurelia might be able to take an ex-con in stride.

I'd have to ask Gibbes the next time we talked. Fraud was an annulment ground, though he'd said it had to be something that directly affected the marriage. I was a convicted felon and I'd hidden it. Convicted felons didn't exactly have their pick of high-paying jobs. Surely Cooper would agree to testify that he hadn't known before the marriage that I was virtually unemployable and would be unable to contribute to the marital income. Surely that would count as fraud.

The knowledge that I might still be able to free Cooper helped me relax toward sleep. Though I was the last person entitled to it, until dawn I'd enjoy being held as if I mattered. As if I were beautiful and clean.

It almost felt like love. I could pretend I was loved.

Only for a few more hours.

I closed my eyes as the first raindrops hit the tin roof, nestling closer to the sleeping Cooper, who reflexively tucked me even nearer.

The memory of this night belonged to me. Though I didn't deserve it and would be punished for it when I told him, when I was banished I'd take a perfect memory with me. I would have that much, at least, forever.

And nobody could ever take it away.

CHAPTER FOURTEEN

Sunlight warmed my closed eyelids by the time Cooper woke. I resolutely pretended to be asleep, a prison skill coming in handy as I tried to appear unaffected and comatose, even through a lingering kiss on my unmoving lips. That, on the other hand, had never happened in prison. Thank the Lord.

"Okay, Sleeping Beauty. I'm going to hide in my office and get some work done. Got an offer out on Isle of Palms. I'll see you later," he murmured, a smile in his voice. Possibly I hadn't fooled him. Sheets rustled as he slid off the bed. "You can't hide from me forever."

I kept my eyes shut as he opened and closed drawers in search of clothes. He murmured to Mary Jane and her claws clicked across the threshold. Cooper shut the door quietly behind himself.

I waited a beat before jumping out of bed. I threw on jeans and my remaining clean shirt without much care for attire. Miss Aurelia wouldn't care, and I'd be making a beeline for her house. I needed her help. Then I would tell him. Then I'd have to tell him.

Caroline's door was still closed. Mia was in Charleston with her father. Cooper should be in the back of the house in the office. I glanced down the hallway to the unused bedroom where I'd found Lynette's diaries. On sock feet, I tiptoed down the hall. No sound. Nothing. As I put my hand on the doorknob, a cell phone rang downstairs, making me jump. I had no business in this part of the house, but I slipped into the room anyway and pressed myself against the closed door. The photo of the possibly-dead baby made me recoil. I turned away to let my heart rate calm.

Then it sped up again. The top right corner of the bookshelf was empty. The *Reader's Digest* volumes were still there to the left.

Twilight and its progeny lurked immediately below, but the spot where the five fabric-covered volumes of Lynette's diary had been was empty.

Someone had taken them—but where, and why? I'd mentioned them to Miss Aurelia; maybe she'd decided to satisfy her admitted curiosity. But when would she have gotten them? I hadn't told her which bedroom. I'd only said "upstairs."

Something odd was going on in this house.

I slipped out of the room and listened for noise in the hallway before making for the massive staircase, moving like a thief across the foyer. Ugh. The thought of thievery made my stomach clench. They'd be horrified even if I were only a thief. Nausea rose as I reminded myself that what I'd done was so much worse. I got the front door unlocked, but it creaked as I eased it open.

My lifetime allotment of luck had never been enormous. The pattern continued. Ted appeared in the front hall.

"Miss Molly, as I live and breathe. Where are you off to so quietly on such a fine—and early—morning?" Ted's delight was evident, and delight, on Ted, already scared the crap out of me.

"I was going for a walk, as a matter of fact. Did you want something?

"Oh, a walk'll be so refreshing."

"I thought so. I'll be going, then."

His hand shot out and stopped mine from turning the door handle. "Ypsilanti."

"Sorry?" He was getting closer. The women's prison where I spent fifteen years was in Ypsilanti, Michigan. He'd kept up his research.

"It's a funny name, Ypsilanti. Nobody in the world would ever guess how to spell it if they didn't know. You say you grew up there?"

I had no recollection of what, specifically, I'd said. I'd have to brazen it out and stick as close to the truth as possible. I owed Cooper the truth, but I desperately wanted to tell him myself. Being outed by Ted first would be the worst possible scenario. "It's named after a Greek person, I think. Lots of places in Michigan have hard to pronounce names."

"Funny. You didn't answer my question. Did you grow up there?" He laughed. "Look at you. Like a rabbit in a snare. I'll help you out. I didn't find any records of any graduate named Molly Todd at any high school in Washtenaw County. Still from Ypsilanti?" he asked, the odd word rolling with satisfaction off his tongue.

"I went to high school in Detroit. I lived in Ypsilanti until a year ago. I never went to school there. I have to admit, Ted, this kind of prying is hardly the Southern hospitality I've been promised. Now, if you don't mind, I'd like to go for a walk."

"Two big employers in Ypsilanti. Eastern Michigan University and a state prison. Do they need a lot of interior decorators in Ypsilanti?" His breath, smelling of coffee and bacon and other, less savory, things, choked me.

"They need some." If I didn't get away, I'd faint. Or scream.

"Any more info you'd like to volunteer?"

"No, Ted," I said, moving into his space. "Most fathers do not ask for the social security number of their son's new wife. Let's get together and have coffee later," I said, as politely as I could manage, not that it would help much now. Ted was a hunter and he'd caught the scent. "We'll gossip. Right now, however, I'm going for a walk. See you."

I slid past him, afraid until I made it off the porch that he'd reach out and grab my arm, but he let me go. I'd given him enough, now. He'd look for graduates named Todd in Detroit, though maybe I'd bought some time by not telling him I hadn't graduated. He'd make the connection between Mary and Molly—not an uncommon nickname for Mary—and then he'd have the story.

I had hours, at the most.

The day was chilly, but pretty. It had rained hard in the night, drumming on the tin roof, and the ferns on the branches of the live oaks unfurled new green. They were so resilient they were almost immortal. Drying and renewing, over and over. I plucked a bit of one off into my hand from a low-hanging branch. I could use that kind of strength for this next conversation.

Miss Aurelia lived in a light green Victorian house on the main street through town, a little less than a mile away from the end of the Middleton allée. She might listen to me and have pity on me, but soon I'd be back to the yawning and empty feeling of being totally alone in the world.

Michigan's correctional system doesn't dump you on the street after prison. The parole system had helped with the transition. My parole agent, Jeff, had found me a job through their programs and a place to live. At first, it was a house with several other recently-released inmates and a housemother to watch over us. Later, I'd been allowed to live in approved housing with a roommate, another parolee, at least until she'd re-offended and gone back to prison. I'd been lucky enough—or unlucky, however you looked at it—to be cleared to be off parole after the minimum one year. I'd never had a positive drug test, never been drunk, never been late for work. I'd never even taken a sick day. I'd saved nearly every penny I'd earned. I'd never associated with my roommate or anyone else who participated in any kind of criminal enterprise, mainly because I'd kept to myself and not associated with anyone at all except Anthony.

Anthony dumped me for a younger woman, that was true, but when he broke up with me, he told me it was because I never gave him the impression I wanted to spend time with him. The break-up hurt, but less than it might have, because he was right. I didn't want to spend time with him. I didn't know how to talk to him. I had nothing in common with him.

Three months later, Jeff said I was coming off parole. It felt like being thrown out into the winter naked as I lost the only support I'd had. Jeff had cared. It hadn't mattered to me that he was paid to care. After parole, I was allowed to leave Michigan. Jeff helped me find the job at the Palace and made sure I had transportation to Las Vegas. Then he closed my file. Less than an hour after our final interview, I got on that bus and I was totally alone.

I had a panic attack somewhere near Joliet, Illinois that left me sweating and gasping for breath. I couldn't shake the terror of the realization that not a single person anywhere in the world cared whether I lived or died. I'd never dared make a connection with anyone. I was a ghost, existing in a world where I was absolutely invisible.

Yet the bus kept moving.

Walking the shady blocks of Pinckney Street to Miss Aurelia's house, the panic woke and rumbled, pushing scaly hands on the inside of my ribcage.

Within hours, I'd be back to drifting alone. With a herculean effort, I forced my mind away from the familiar terror and concentrated on concrete things. The uneven sidewalk. The broken limb from a live oak lying across a yard. The boxwood Christmas wreath on the door of a house. A loose board on Miss Aurelia's porch.

With a relief not unlike grabbing a life preserver, I lifted the knocker on Miss Aurelia's door. Muffled thumping and a curse echoed behind it. "I'm coming!"

The door swung open. Miss Aurelia, in her uniform of black turtleneck and script-covered jeans, stood there, wincing. "Well, Molly. Hello. Don't mind me. Banged my damn toe on the hall table. Come on in."

I faltered, trying to put this off, then entered and sat in the most peculiar living room I'd ever seen. Leandra the Decorator had never set foot in here. A huge stuffed owl, dusty wings spread wide and threatening, hung over the mantel. It wore a pair of purple earmuffs. In a place of honor on a side table sat three vast Lego constructions: one Millennium Falcon, one Army-green all-terrain vehicle, and Hogwarts Castle. None of the furniture matched, though all of it was comfortable and overstuffed. One piece was a taxicab yellow vinyl chair shaped like a fishhook that could have been constructed no more recently than 1975. On the battered coffee table sat a metal sculpture with pieces that whirred and rotated like something a clockmaker would build.

"Legos?" I managed, trying to think of something to say.

"Oh, I didn't build those," said Miss Aurelia, perching on the edge of the fishhook chair. "Elijah did. He's twelve. Lives three doors down. He loves to show me his Lego things, and when his mama said he was too old for Legos and they were getting dusty, I offered to let him keep them here. He visits them every so often. I don't mind dusty. As you can see."

I gave her a smile I knew didn't really qualify as a smile.

"What's going on, honey?"

The kindness in her voice undid me. I burst into loud, noisy sobs for the second time in hours, unable to speak or move or do anything except cover my face with my hands and let the tears flow through my fingers. I sensed more than saw Miss Aurelia leave the room, then return and sit next to me. She pulled a hand away from my face and pressed a cold glass into it.

"Drink. It'll help."

Eyes streaming, I took a sip. Tea. The Southern cure-all. Cold and so sweet my teeth hurt, flavored with mint and something else. Though I'd never liked iced tea, the contents of this glass suddenly became the only liquid in the world that could quench my thirst. I gulped it, fighting the sobs and the hiccups the sobs left behind.

When I'd drained the glass and the hiccups slowed, I raised a bleary and burning gaze to her.

She sat still, like people do with a wild animal that might bolt and run. "Now. Can you tell me what's wrong? Is it Ted?"

I opened my mouth, to say the words I came to say, to tell her I was a felon, less of a person, part of one of the few remaining groups it was still okay to despise and shrink from, and shocked myself by saying something even more hopeless.

"I'm in love with Cooper."

"I kinda thought," said Miss Aurelia, taking my glass and setting it down directly on the wood of the coffee table, coasters be damned. "And why on earth is that wrong?"

"Because . . ."

"Because?"

"Because I . . . I'm a felon. I spent fifteen years in prison. For murder."

She sat there, eyes narrowed as if she were figuring out a puzzle. "Who'd you kill?"

"M-my mother."

She considered that. A tiny curl of hope began to rise. She hadn't ordered me out of her house. "How old are you, girl?"

"Thirty-three."

"So you were a teenager?"

I nodded.

"What? She didn't like your boyfriend? Tried to take away your cell phone? Told you to put on something decent?"

I looked down. My clothing was decent at best, dowdy at worst. "No. She came after me. With a knife. I don't remember what happened after that until the ambulance came. I . . . I blocked it out, or something. I remember sitting in a pool of her blood, trying to stop the bleeding. I found out later I stabbed her."

"Who said that?"

"Everyone. The police. The prosecutor. My fingerprints were on the knife. And there was a witness, a friend of hers. He testified he saw it."

Miss Aurelia snorted. "Did he see her chase you with a knife? Did he testify about that?"

I froze. Shock soured my stomach. It had never occurred to me that no one had asked the man that on the stand.

As if we weren't talking about the defining event of my entire life, Miss Aurelia idly pushed on the metal sculpture, making its parts whirl and click again. "Growing up, I used to hear my daddy say that some people needed killin', and I expect he was right. Some people in the world get what's coming to them. Did your mother need killin'?"

Aghast, I goggled at her, at a loss for speech.

"Way I see it, a grown woman coming after her own teenage daughter with a knife, who she's supposed to protect and love, might could have needed killin'. She beat you up lots of times, didn't she?"

"She . . . she was . . . It wasn't the first time. With the knife."

Miss Aurelia patted my hand, as if I'd admitted to a secret dislike of Brussels sprouts instead of matricide.

"I expect you've seen the news, even in prison. Got a lot of home-grown terrorists coming into places they don't belong and shooting innocent people. Makes the nightly news every few weeks. You think anybody misses those scums when they die in the police shootout? You think anyone would care if somebody shot them down in cold blood, days later?"

Again, I stared at her in amazement.

"I, for one, wouldn't care. If your mama was the kind to do what you say—and I bet she did a whole lot more than what you've said, then I don't believe I'll waste a lot of energy mourning her, either."

A memory stirred. In prison, in my third or fourth year, a woman had been admitted into the general prison population despite some recommendation that she shouldn't be. Later, I'd wonder if that was actually an oversight. The woman stared at the world with malevolent silvery eyes, cold and flat with nothing behind them, almost as if she had no soul maybe. Word got around that she had killed her children. Teenagers, all three of them. Supposedly she'd gone with the insanity defense and it failed, and no wonder, looking at those wintry eyes. She'd stabbed each of them in the middle of the night, in their beds, dozens of times. When it was over, she'd brewed coffee, dumped the grounds, put her mug in the dishwasher, and gone to work like nothing had happened.

Many of the other prisoners had left beloved children behind. Most were in for drugs, armed robbery, or accessory offenses, but not all. It didn't take long. One afternoon the guards found the woman with the frozen silver eyes dead in the shower, bled out from a stomach wound from a rough shank. No search was mounted. No inmates talked. The guards didn't ask. We went on with our lives and they cremated her unclaimed body.

No one mourned her. No one felt guilty about not mourning her.

"Miss Aurelia, I . . . I . . ." I swallowed, struggling for the words. "Thank you. For not—"

"Not screaming? Not throwing you out the door? Not calling the police? Not taking a shower? Aw, my dear, I expect you've seen all that and more. You won't get that here. You're the same person you were at Thanksgiving dinner, only a little more battered than I thought."

"But it was murder. I killed her. Well, second degree murder. And Cooper—and Caroline, and Ted—don't know. Your reaction isn't . . . Well, it isn't the usual one."

"Couple things. First off, you must have had a damn fool lawyer. I won't ask what idiotic thing he did or didn't do, but I'll say this. Child who's chased by a knife-wielding adult and fights it off should get a parade, not a prison term. Had he ever even heard of self-defense?"

"I told him that I used to dream about her being dead. To get away from her. So she wouldn't hurt me anymore. I couldn't testify, he said, if I didn't remember it. The witness said I stabbed her. I couldn't say different, he said. And the dreams were proof I'd had motive."

"Hmmph. There's tree stumps out in the swamp smarter than that moron. Of course an abused child dreams about getting away from the abuse. Any decent lawyer would've looked at that as a challenge, not a roadblock."

She shook her head. Relief mingled with a vague feeling of nausea. My lawyer had done a much worse job than I'd known. I would have liked to have had Miss Aurelia for a lawyer.

"Second of all, you must tell Cooper. I think you'll be surprised. Once he knows, you can decide together whether to tell Caroline. I'd recommend against telling Ted, but . . ." She couldn't restrain a grimace.

"He's on the trail. He's doing a lot of Internet research."

"That sounds like Ted," she said, snorting. "Well, that only means you need to tell Cooper before Ted gets there."

"Ted will throw me out."

"I expect so. Well, that's no matter. You come on over here. You don't mind Teensy, do you?"

"Teensy?"

She gestured at the owl. "Teensy. Named her after my sister. She was always kind of a know-it-all. Fact that she hates owls is the icing on the cake."

"Do you mean stay with you?"

"Of course I do. My home is open to you as long as it takes until you find a better place to be. Matter of fact, probably wouldn't hurt you to go on and move your stuff over here. I've got four extra bedrooms. You can take your pick."

"What about the town? They'll find out. Won't they make it hard for you if you take me in?"

"Eh. This town is as much mine as it is anybody else's. My great-great-however-many-greats grandfather settled this town. And I'm eccentric. I highly recommend eccentricity, by the way. It allows quite a bit more freedom than conventionality, that's for damn sure." She gestured at her jeans. "The whole town thinks I either have some secret code on these jeans, or that I write down notes to remember things. Hell. I remember everything anyway. The jeans are proof."

"Proof?"

"Proof I'm eccentric enough to do whatever the hell I want. A prop, sort of. People expect their eccentrics to look eccentric. Kind of fun, too. I'd say I get away with murder around here, but I won't," she said, winking at me, "because that would be insensitive. But I do."

"What do you think Cooper will do?"

She leaned back, smoothing out the ancient upholstery along the back of the sofa. "One of the things I like best about you, girl, is that you're straightforward. Blunt as hell, actually. Straightforwardness is an underestimated quality in a woman. It saves so much time, I've always thought."

I took in her frank face, with its crow's feet and smile lines, and her wild black and white hair, feeling something like love. The kind I hadn't felt in my life for anyone except my grandmother, years and years ago. She must have seen it in my face, because she took my hand and squeezed.

"So, I expect you can handle straightforward coming from someone else. Cooper is going to have to make a choice here. I think he feels much the same way about you as you do about him. I've known him for a lot of years, and he's a good boy. One of his best qualities and the worst at the same time is that he sees only the good in the people he loves. That's going to help you, after he gets over the initial shock. Then it's going to hurt you, when Ted gets all wrath-wreaking angel on you. Cooper will have to choose. Choose between two people he loves. I guess it remains to be seen which way the wind will blow."

Despair deadened my limbs. "Cooper doesn't love me. He finds me attractive. It's not the same thing."

"That's where I *think* you're wrong. But thinking ain't knowing. We'll know, soon enough."

She patted my hand, indicating all the wisdom was done for now. "Come on now. If you're going to stay with me, you need to learn to make proper sweet tea. You're a Yankee. Yankees have no appreciation for the finer things in life. Sweet tea is one of those things. Life is short. Let's get going."

CHAPTER FIFTEEN

Miss Aurelia drove me back to the Middleton house two hours later. My veins buzzed. I persuaded myself it was the sugar in the tea we'd made (a cup and a half in a gallon!), but that wouldn't account for the way an uncontrollable shiver vibrated my ribcage. I kept putting on and taking off the cardigan I wore when my body temperature swung wildly between sweaty and frozen. I had to tell Cooper, right now, and get it over with, or I might stroke out.

The tires squealed as she pulled to an irresponsibly quick stop. Ted was out in the yard, facing a bush, doing something that might have been public urination. "Go get Cooper, honey. Do it quick before you lose your nerve. Then come on back to my house. I'll distract Ted."

"Huh?" The unbuckled seatbelt went slack in my hands. I pointed toward Ted. "Is he peeing?"

"Of course he is, honey. All Southern men pee outside like dogs, the ones who live in the country, at least. Marking their territory, I suppose. Watch and learn." She jumped out of the car. As I watched, she underwent an extensive change in her body language. She leaned helplessly against her car door, seeming to lose bulk and all her energy merely by the change of posture. "Oh, Ted!" she called, unbelievably bringing a fluttering hand to her chest. "Ted!"

Apparently finished, he obediently approached, wearing an outdoorsman's fleece vest for the day's chill over his button-down, brows drawn together. He spared me a quick glance conveying all manner of suspicion, then turned his attention politely to Miss Aurelia. "What can I do for you, Aurelia?"

"My car is making a clunk-clunk noise I simply can't tolerate. I'm terribly afraid it might quit on me, out on a deserted stretch of Highway 17, when I'm all alone and helpless. Could you come and see if you can figure out what it is? I'm sure you'll know right away if you drive around in it for a while. Please?" Though she wasn't short, she managed somehow to look up at him, eyes wide.

I choked back laughter. Miss Aurelia probably knew how to take apart and put back together an engine as easily as the Legos in her living room, but Ted bought it, lock, stock, and barrel. Cooper must have heard our voices because he came out the front door and leaned against a column. "Do you need me to look, Miss Aurelia?"

"Oh, no, honey. You stay here with Molly. Ted will help me, won't you, darling?"

"Sure will. Come on in."

We all went into the foyer. Cooper said nothing. He kept his hands clasped behind him.

"Let me get my wallet," said Ted, "'case we need to take it up the road to Jimmy." Ted disappeared into his study where the click of a key turned in the lock of his desk. He absolutely was the kind to keep his home desk locked. Figured.

Miss Aurelia winked. "Being blunt saves time. But it's not the only way."

"What . . . ?" asked Cooper, clearly mystified. I glanced at him. He didn't meet my eyes. Something was off, and unrelated to Miss Aurelia's antics.

"Shhh, honey," said Miss Aurelia, waving him away with an airy hand. "This is girl talk. Ah, Ted. I'm so glad you could help." She took his arm and steered him straight out the front door.

A silence fell. Cooper remained where he was, his face impassive, his arms crossed in front of him. Something was very wrong. A cold chill went through me. Maybe this wasn't the time to tell him.

No. Miss Aurelia would expect more. She'd done all that play-acting for Ted to make it possible for me to do this now. I needed to do this now.

"Cooper, can we talk?"

"I think that's a great idea. Let's talk," he said, not moving.

"It's a pretty day," I said, my voice wobbling despite my best efforts. "Want to go out to the end of the dock?" No one else could hear us at the far end. Also, according to my grim calculations, the water lapped under the dock no more than two feet deep. If he pushed me off when I was done, I probably wouldn't drown.

Cooper shrugged his assent.

Out in the marsh, the sun sparkled off the water in a million points of light. At least I wouldn't lose the water right away if I went to stay with Miss Amelia. No Middleton could keep me off the public dock near the boat launch. No sign banishing felons had yet been posted there. "Is there a name for that smell? The marshy smell?" I asked.

"That's pluff mud. It gives off that smell at low tide."

"It's nice."

"Is that what you want to talk about?"

"No. No, that's not it." Aghast, I heard the catch in my voice at the end.

Cooper sat on the end of the dock, legs dangling, waiting. I sat next to him, preserving protective space between us. He didn't touch me.

Here it was. The whole truth should come out of my mouth in three, two, one. "I . . . I . . ." I couldn't make it come out. It had been so much easier with Miss Aurelia.

"Maybe I can help," he said, lips pressed together.

I stared at him, taken aback. "Wh-what . . . ?"

His expressionless mask slipped. Underneath lay pain and betrayal and loss. Nausea roiled low in my stomach. "You know, Molly, there's almost nothing you can't find out if you spend enough time on the Internet." His hands clenched.

Oh, my God.

He knew.

Ted and I had raced, and Ted had won. "Did your dad . . . ?"

"Dad? What is it with you and Dad? This has nothing to do

with him."

He'd found it without Ted? "Is it that I'm a felon?"

He raked an angry hand through his hair and stood, pacing in a tight circle. "A felon? Is that what you call it? Oh, holy God." He tried to speak, failed, and then tried again. "I Googled you. I wanted to find out about your mom. I knew she was in your dream last night. I wanted to find out what she'd done to create that kind of terror. You weren't ready to tell me, so I figured I'd see if anyone named Todd had a criminal record for abuse, or assault. You know they keep records online of every crime listed by defendant?"

He glanced at me, fury in his eyes. I didn't respond.

"Surprise!" he said, gesturing like a mad magician. "I didn't find her. I found you. Mary Kathleen Todd, your age, your city. I went to school with a girl named Mary who went by Molly. Michigan Mary Todd was busy, all right. I'd just landed on it when I heard Miss Aurelia pull up in the driveway. Second degree murder. Incarceration. Holy shit."

"I-I was going to tell you, right now. That's why I . . ."

"Oh, bullshit. You've had days to tell me. You could have told me in Vegas. I don't even know that it would have stopped us from hanging out with you, but it damn sure as hell would have stopped me from marrying you."

I would have been nothing but a party girl to them. Not a human being.

"I can't even . . . You even lied about your name. Mary. It's been Mary all along."

"I've always gone by Molly." It felt stupid, paltry, so far from enough.

He let out a disgusted breath.

I pressed my thighs, trying to still the shaking that had moved to my hands. I'd predicted revulsion and horror and now I had it. Loss and jagged pain ripped through me and tightened my chest. Cooper, who'd held me so tenderly and rubbed my back last night, would want to wash his hands now. He'd be just like my old landlord. And the hotel head of housekeeping. One of the other housekeepers had refused to work on the same floor as me and they'd accommodated her. She told them she had children to think of and they patted her back and gave her a better shift.

I had absolutely nothing to lose now. For the next few minutes, at least, I could take the guard off my words. I could say anything. I forged ahead with perfect honesty. "I was seventeen. I went to prison for second degree murder. I served fifteen years in the state pen in Ypsilanti, and one on parole in Detroit."

The water sparkled with a mocking glint, when it should have dulled to gray and flat.

It took him long moments to speak again. While I waited, I wondered idly if skin was supposed to lose feeling like mine had. Shouldn't I be used to this by now?

He pulled his legs to his chest, away from me, closing himself off. "Are you trying to act like second degree murder makes some kind of difference?"

Actually, the degree mattered a lot. It meant many fewer years in prison. It meant even without my memories of the event, memories I'd give anything to get back now to offer him as atonement, no one thought I'd planned it with diabolical precision and a total lack of concern for the taking of a life. It meant it had been spur-of-the-moment, sloppy, unexpected, traumatic. I didn't remember everything, but I knew it had been traumatic.

It should matter, but it clearly didn't now. Cooper raked his hands through his hair again, pulling at it agitatedly. He knew all he needed to know; all he wanted to know. I'd taken a life. Broken the commandment. Become untouchable. There was no point. I'd known all along I'd be walking out of here with nothing but my pride, under the repulsed and loathing eyes of everyone in the house. Anything I said now would sound like an excuse. Cooper had found it first. I should have told him. He might have understood, like Miss Aurelia, if only I'd told him first.

"Never mind," he said. "It doesn't make a difference if it was second degree or first. You . . . you killed someone. Oh, holy God. Who did you kill?"

"My . . . m-mother."

At that, he lost the power of speech and looked sick. I'd sort of thought after I told him about the crime and the prison, I would tell him that my mother had been abusive for years—but not now. Cooper had lost the mother he loved. He'd apparently wondered if my mother was abusive because that's how he'd found the conviction, but if I mentioned it now it would sound like I thought it was fine to kill your mom if she hadn't won Mother of the Year.

"I don't know what happened," I said, hating myself for groveling even that much. "I lost the time. The memory."

He said nothing. He sat frozen, only a single blink letting me know he was still alive.

"Still, I did do it, and I went to trial, and then to prison for fifteen years." I didn't know why I felt the need to repeat it—maybe only as penance to counteract the groveling. I couldn't protect myself from being reviled, but I could at a damn minimum not beg for kindness.

"W-with a gun, or . . . ?" Cooper stared out at the water.

"With a knife. She got it from the kitchen and chased me with it. She had me by the hair." That much I remembered.

Another blink was the only sign that he registered the fact that it had occurred immediately following a threat to my life.

"Oh. Oh."

He fought hard to hide his horror but he was way, way out of his depth. He was well past appreciating the nuance of the reasons. I'd seen this expression on others so many times before and it killed another small piece of my soul every time. I couldn't even look at him, but I could give him a break. Bring this to a close.

"Look. I'm going to take my stuff and go. Miss Aurelia said I could stay with her. I understand, truly, I do. This is hardly the first time I've had to tell someone I was in prison."

"Except you didn't tell me."

I could tell him again I'd planned to tell him, but he hadn't believed me the first time. What good would it do? "You're right. I didn't. But we were going to get an annulment. You had no reason to know anything about me and I wanted . . . dammit. I wanted just a moment of something normal in my life. I stole that mo-

ment from you. You have so many moments of normal; I didn't
think you'd miss one. So I'm going. Before I do, though, we need
to talk about the annulment."

He was silent.

I filled the silence, words in a dead-sounding monotone but
still desperate to escape. "We . . . we can't go with the one Gibbes
suggested, obviously, but there's fraud. This isn't the same as lying
about being able to have children, but it should be close enough.
Being a felon means most jobs are closed to me. Employers all do
background checks now. I did okay when my parole officer
vouched for me, but now I'm on my own. I can only get jobs
where they don't check, or don't care, and there aren't many of
those. Manual labor, or farm work sometimes. I heard Mc-
Donald's hires felons. Sometimes."

"Is that true?" he asked, clearly on auto-pilot. A fault line had
opened under his feet and the ground was still shaking. There was
no telling what emotion he'd land on when it stopped. "You were
a hotel maid. That's a good job. Why can't you do that again?"

"I got the jobs in Detroit through the work transition program
on parole. The one in Vegas was as a personal favor to my parole
officer. He knew the guy. I quit the day I met you, because . . .
Well, never mind why, even knowing I wouldn't be able to get
another one."

"Why did you quit, Molly?" Maybe I imagined it, but a fine
thread of impersonal iron laced his tone now: blame where there'd
never been blame before.

Honestly. What would it hurt? The only silver lining to this
level of humiliation was not having to worry about what I said.
He'd already shouted and gone cold and grim. But the surprise
bomb had exploded and rained down its ash and I was alive. He
hadn't hit me. Or run. The worst had to be over.

I pulled my legs tight to my chest. "I quit because I walked into
a suite, one of the high-dollar ones, to bring extra towels and the
guy in there pushed me against the wall and ripped open my uniform top. Thought he was entitled to me as a hotel perk, like he
was entitled to high thread count sheets and free salon shampoo."

"Why didn't you report it?"

"Right. Who'd have believed me? I was a hotel maid and a former criminal. He runs one of the country's most famous companies. Even I recognized him. He's on TV all the time. I turned in my uniform. They took the cost of the repairs to the front of it out of my last paycheck. I met you less than six hours later."

"Molly. I'm sorry about that."

I lifted my head, thinking I heard an echo of the caring, but his face was a frozen mask. The dull ache returned and I went back to picking a seam of my jeans. "Anyway, I got off track. For fraud, I think you could testify that I didn't tell you I was a felon and therefore I lied—fraudulently—about my ability to contribute money to the marriage. I'm sure that would—"

Off in the woods to our right, a gunshot echoed, then two more behind it, making me jump. "Was that someone hunting?"

"Probably." He had to be ready to be done with this and rid of me. I watched as, at my eye level, he opened and closed his fists by his sides. Like there was something dirty on them.

Something about his closed-off face, his impatient posture, the damned gunshots in the woods, the hopelessness that flooded my senses all at once, made me lose whatever grip I still had on the flapping of my tongue. I jumped to my feet.

With the swiftness of a cobra strike, anger shot through my synapses. It was so unfamiliar and hot and unpardonable I didn't know how to grasp it. Felons aren't entitled to anger. We're supposed to be thankful we were released, that worse wasn't done to us. We're supposed to be grateful others will condescend to speak to us, employ us, serve us food, occupy the same room. We grovel for what others will allow us to have. Anger has to be hidden at all costs when people are waiting for you to confirm you are capable of violence.

The worst of it was that I was as angry at myself as I was at Cooper. Blood roared in my ears. So much rage, because . . . because he'd seen only my outside after all and cared nothing about the rest.

Because I'd let myself believe he cared.

"I guess we're done here."

"Well, I don't know what to say to that." Hurt had written itself across his face.

"I feel like you have a lot to say, actually."

"You're expecting a lot if you think I can process this and be fine in ten minutes." He clenched his hands into fists at his sides again.

I bit my lip, forcing back tears. "I'm still the same person I was last night."

He blinked. "Last night you knew things I didn't know. Things I'd asked you about. Things you didn't tell me until I brought it up."

I couldn't leave it alone. The frustration at not being understood boiled out like steam. "You have no idea the kinds of things everyone around you is hiding all the time."

"Stop it. You went to prison. For murder, for fuck's sake. It's not the same as finding out that you evaded taxes or something. You killed someone. You killed your mother. Holy God, this can't be real. You didn't tell me I was sleeping with someone who's killed."

That hurt like a gut punch. I gasped for air, and when I had it, my voice came out in gravel and ash. "There isn't a day that goes by that I don't think about what happened in that kitchen. Not an hour I don't wish I knew what happened, or why. Not a single night I don't wake up sweating at least once, or screaming."

He blanched. It hadn't been twelve hours since he'd seen me do it.

"It's easy to be you, Cooper. Worst you've ever done was run up a street naked. You have no idea what it's like. Killing a person, whatever the circumstances, means becoming the scum of the earth for the rest of my life. That doesn't even count the guilt and the certainty that when my life is over I'm going to burn in Catholic hell. You don't care. You're exactly like everyone else. For a little while last night, I thought you might be different. I thought maybe you'd be able to continue to see me as a person if I told you, but no. I didn't want to tell you because I was afraid you'd react exactly like this: like you'd been dropped into a sewer and denied a shower. Everything else about me, all that stuff you liked, eclipsed, erased, like that." I snapped my fingers. "Even if I knew how it happened, it wouldn't make any difference to you, would it? If I could tell you it was an absolute accident, you wouldn't care. She's still dead. She couldn't have killed herself. It had to have been me. That was good enough for the court system. For everyone else in the world. It would be good enough for you, too. You wouldn't care."

He did care. The tightness of his jaw relaxed a bit. And there it was in his eyes, behind the horror: remorse and pity. "Don't turn this around on me. You were the secret-keeper."

"I didn't tell you at the beach because I was afraid you might leave me there."

His face whitened around the nose and mouth, defensiveness and fear and disgust mixing into a familiar mask of judgment.

"Can you say for sure you wouldn't have? You can't, can you? No way to deny it—I've gone from beautiful to repulsive in the blink of an eye. I see it in your face. But it doesn't matter. I can live through this," I said. "I'm going to Miss Aurelia's. I'll get my stuff and be gone in thirty minutes."

"Wait. You don't need to do that. You can stay in the guest room until we get the annulment." No. No pity. Being horrifying was far better than being pitiful.

"Not in a million years. Tell your family whatever you want. I'll stay at Miss Aurelia's until we can find out from the lawyer if fraud works or if we have to get a divorce. I'm not going to lie and say we never slept together. Maybe you could lie about that, but I've spent a lot of time in court and I've never lied once. I'm not going to start now."

Cooper ground his teeth, body taut as a wire. "Fraud it is. I know where to find you."

My insides—throat, lungs, heart—dried up in the scorching heat of the pain from my chest. "Okay. Goodbye, Cooper."

CHAPTER SIXTEEN

That night, Miss Aurelia fed me overcooked pot roast and green beans, and then a steady diet of reality TV that allowed for scornful asides every now and then but no real conversation. I wanted to kiss her in gratitude. If she'd showed even the tiniest hint of sympathy, I'd have melted away like wet cotton candy into a weeping puddle on the floor. She seemed to understand that and confined herself to remarks about insufficient vocal talents and the relative ratio of intelligence between one catty bachelorette and a hedgehog.

She showed me to an old-fashioned gable room with a twin-size iron bed and an old quilt an ancestor had probably sewed by hand. A battered dresser and a ladder-back chair were the only other furniture. I loved it immediately. It reminded me both of the sparseness of my cell and the room I used to imagine Anne Shirley lived in at Green Gables.

I'd always been a light sleeper. I'd had to be, both at home because of my mother, and in prison, where things happen in the night sometimes, but that night I slept like a dead person with no dreams. The sun had already angled above the roof by the time Miss Aurelia shook me awake.

"Get up, honey. Assuming you went on to sleep when I left last night, you've been asleep for near twelve hours. You need to get cleaned up: Caroline is coming and she wants you to go with her to church up in Georgetown. It's a fancy one, so if you've got a skirt, I'd wear it. If you don't, I'll give you one to borrow."

"Whaaa?" I mumbled, into the pillow. "Caroline? Coming here? Does she know?"

"Couldn't rightly tell. She sounded like her normal chipper self.

No gloom and doom."

"Oh, I can't. It's been years since I went to church. I'll embarrass myself."

"I hate to point this out, but you're still lying there, horizontal and wearing the ugliest damn T-shirt I ever did see. You'll definitely embarrass yourself if you don't get that perfect little ass out of bed and into the shower." She gave my ankle a yank. "Come on now. I've got cereal downstairs. Oh, and this house is falling down around my ears. The shower's got mixed up handles. You need to turn on the cold tap for the hot water."

She banged out of the door.

I sat up, pushed my tangled hair out of my eyes, and tried to adjust to my new temporary reality.

Dressed in Miss Aurelia's surprisingly chic black sheath dress and a pair of her heels, miraculously only one size too small, I sat on the couch as if auditioning for a part as a statue. Somehow, it seemed obvious that I couldn't be nervous if I could stay totally still.

Five minutes later than planned, the doorbell rang. Miss Aurelia, in jeans and with no plans to do anything as proper as going to church, opened it.

"Oh, my gosh, I'm so sorry I'm running late." Caroline burst into the room, adorable in a blue print wrap dress. "I usually blame that on Mia, but she's still at Danny's and I totally have no excuse. We'll have to hurry. Ooh. You look beautiful. Georgetown is about thirty minutes away. Come on!"

Well. No way she'd act like that if she knew, but what had she been told about why I was here instead of there? With a perplexed exchange of glances with Miss Aurelia, I followed Caroline out the door.

In her SUV, I barely got the buckle clicked before she peeled away from the curb. "I'm the worst driver in the world," she said. "I've got a terrible lead foot. So many tickets. I try not to be so bad when Mia is in the car, but I can't seem to help it. She's starting to notice now, too. 'Mommy! It's only thirty-five here!'"

I laughed and noted her expression. Cheerful, unguarded, the same as it had been since I first met her. "Sooo. What did Cooper tell you?"

"About why you left him?" She laughed, making my jaw drop. "He said you had a big dramatic fight and you were going to stay with Miss Aurelia. I followed him all around the house and drove him nuts, but he wouldn't say any more than that. Daddy tried to get it out of him, but he zipped his lips good. So I figured I'd corner you."

My emotions tried to run in three different directions at once. He hadn't said. He hadn't told them I was a felon—no, a murderer. Why? Why wouldn't he tell the two most important people in his life something like that? It would be a shorthand explanation that would make immediate sense to them and pave the way for the annulment, and instead he'd gone with simple domestic spat, even under—given Caroline's sunny persistence—what had to count as torture.

Hope, that underhanded backstabber of an emotion, the one that gave birth to almost all the pain I've ever felt, lit again like one of those horrible trick birthday candles.

But now I'd be on the other end of Caroline's Spanish Inquisition. Fear and dread shouted for my attention instead.

"Caroline. You know I can't tell you any more than what Cooper said."

She waved away marital privilege with an airy hand. "Oh, sure you can. It must have been a humdinger, for you to leave him. You're coming back, right, when he apologizes?"

I had to laugh at her woman-of-the-world expression. "How do you know it isn't me who needs to apologize?"

"I grew up with him, dork. It has to be him. Let me guess. You said you wanted to wait to have children. That would do it. He'd be a jerk about that, no doubt. He wants kids like some people want to win the lottery."

"No. That's not it," I said, momentarily distracted by a rush of raw longing for the children with dark-lashed green eyes like

Cooper's. For the man who wanted them so desperately. "Caroline . . ."

She took her eyes off Highway 17 to assess me. "Okay. Something he never told you about himself. He dropped out of medical school, you know. Couldn't stop throwing up when he had to look at the dead bodies."

"Um. No." He'd never mentioned that to me. Though, considering the way he found his mother, it was hardly surprising. It broke my heart a little more, like when you step on a shard after dropping the glass. "Listen, let's not do this. It was upsetting and it's still upsetting and . . . and it hurts, okay? It wasn't a little spat. I wasn't being dramatic."

Her face bleached of color and she reached over and touched my hand. "I'm sorry, honey. It was insensitive of me. Gosh. I'm not usually so horrible. I just couldn't imagine that there could be anything seriously wrong between you and Cooper. Not when you look at each other like you do."

"Like we do?" I said, fighting the rush of feeling that warmed my skin.

"Oh, please. It's gross because he's my brother, but you and he totally look like you're two shakes away from ripping off each other's clothes half the time. The other half, it's what we used to call googly eyes. You know. Like this." She took her eyes off the road again, widened them until the whites around her blue irises showed all around, and then fluttered her eyelashes until we both giggled.

"Okay. Obviously I need to work on my subtlety," I said. "But Cooper never looks like that."

"Don't be silly. Of course he does. I've been teasing him about it mercilessly all week."

The blood in my veins took a detour and missed a few stops. My head felt too light. Why hadn't I claimed a headache and stayed behind? She would have believed I was upset from the fight. "I don't think . . ."

"It's such a relief, you don't even know. Oh, I know you fought and you're upset right now, but you'll make up. You have to. You're the first woman who's made him look like that since Lynette. He and Lynette had issues, that was for sure, but when she left him without a word, no note, nothing but a plane ticket on the Visa, it hurt him so much. He didn't date for forever. He's had so much trouble trusting anyone again. It makes my heart sing to see him with you. Ooh. I love this song. Do you mind if I turn it up?"

No. I didn't mind. I sang with her, my mind yowling along in a discordant wail of agony. He'd cared about me. Enough to let his sister see that he did. *Oh, damn, damn, damn.* I knew I'd leave here limping and broken, but I'd thought I could leave here and not hurt him. I'd thought I could leave him untouched. But I would hurt him. I already had hurt him.

Prince George Winyah Episcopal Church, built in 1750, was a huge steepled structure in a cozy residential neighborhood. An ancient walled churchyard spread out around it, filled with graves with impressive stone memorials carved with macabre images of skulls and scythes. I'd have loved to explore, but we were late. Caroline locked the car and we rushed inside. The church's beauty —all elaborate molding and carved wood—took my breath away, and would have even without the decorations for this first Sunday of the pre-Christmas Advent season. Many people greeted me as Caroline guided me to her family's traditional pew—a wooden waist-high box with a swinging door separated from other family areas. We sat and adjusted our skirts.

The service was mostly familiar. As a child, I'd gone a few times with my grandmother to her Catholic church. A procession of priest and acolytes kicked things off. There was a lot of kneeling and standing and repeating of passages from the novel-length program, and then it was time to go up to the front for communion.

I hadn't taken communion since the day I was charged with murder. I'd always done it before, with my grandmother, who'd handled what existed of my religious training, when she had time.

Religion is available, even encouraged, in prison, but I'd avoided it.

I still felt too dirty. Unclean. Unworthy to be in a church—this one included—with all these people on a maintenance-free escalator to heaven, busy living their blameless lives. I couldn't take communion alongside them. Like spitting in the eye of the God I'd hoped might watch over me, once.

Ugh. I never could decide whether I was more afraid of offending God and causing him to do worse to me, or mad at him for not protecting me. Both, maybe. Either way, communion was too much to ask.

I thought for a moment I could go up there and pretend. I even uncrossed my legs in preparation for standing. Then I sagged. "No. You go. I can't."

Caroline stood, waiting for the aisle traffic to clear. "Are you Catholic? In the Episcopal Church, everyone is welcome. Come on."

"Yes, I'm Catholic, sort of, but I can't. Go on."

"Okay." With one backward glance, she stepped outside the pew into the flow of bodies up the aisle.

The rest of the service passed quickly and in short order we were out in the sunshine. Caroline greeted friends. A young and preppy priest, who'd been in the procession and done a reading but not given the sermon, approached.

"Are you a visitor, miss?"

"Yes. I'm Molly. I enjoyed the service." I left off the last name, in part because of the confusion. Part of me wanted a few minutes of anonymity.

He inclined his head, indicating I should step away from the crowd with him. I did, balancing Miss Aurelia's shoes on an exposed tree root.

"I noticed you didn't take communion. I hope it wasn't because you didn't feel welcome."

"No. Everyone was nice."

"I'm John MacIlroy," he said, simply, no distancing title. He reached into the voluminous pocket of his robe and came up with a business card, making me smile when he pulled it out like a magician. He pressed it into my hand. "I hope you'll call me, or any of the others on there, if you need to talk. God welcomes everyone. Never feel like you don't belong in our church."

My throat thickened and I had to clear it. "Thank you."

"Call if you want to talk."

Caroline rushed up. "Oh, you've met John. He and his wife are the best. Where is Marnie, anyway? John, this is my new sister-in-law. Cooper's new wife, Molly Middleton."

My heart sank and I realized that I'd actually been contemplating calling him to talk about my issues with God. Now I couldn't, though, because his loyalty would be to the Middletons.

"Oh!" His eyes widened, and not in pleasure, before he could hide it. "You didn't say that, Molly. Well, you've chosen wisely. Cooper is as good a guy as they come. It was nice to meet you." Another parishioner approached, wanting a word with him.

Caroline nudged me. "You ready? I'll start the car."

"Wait." Before I could follow her, John grabbed my arm and whispered urgently into my ear, "If you're a Middleton, remember what I said. Hold on to that card. Use it if you need it."

What? Invoking the Middleton name got some alarming reactions. Miss Aurelia had written on my hand. This unknown clergyman had momentarily restrained me. What was going on here? Blank with shock, I backed away, stumbling slightly over the tree root. I followed Caroline to the car.

"Ugh," she said. "I love going to church, but afterwards everyone always wants to know what's going on with Danny. 'When is that boy going to come to his senses?' 'Do you think there's someone else?' I know they mean well, but ugh, anyway." She started the car and before pulling away, she checked me over. "Are you okay?"

Shaking it off, I nodded. "Fine. Thanks. It was a beautiful service." Why had John been so urgent about the card and the need for pastoral counseling even more after he found out I was Cooper's wife? He didn't know we were done. He knew nothing about me, except that I was married into the Middleton family.

As Caroline handled the vehicle in the rush of traffic leaving church, flinging faux curse words like the chirping of a bird, the pieces began to fit. The church knew all about Danny leaving Caroline, probably down to the date, time, and color of suitcase he'd packed.

Maybe they also knew about Ted and Lynette. I'd forgotten what founts of knowledge congregations can be. Something about Caroline's sure hands on the wheel decided me. She was a fully-grown adult. She would find out shortly that I was a felon. Life was going to throw some tough things at her. It was time.

"Caroline, Miss Aurelia hinted that there may have been something off about Lynette. That she and your dad had an odd relationship."

A sharp intake of breath. "Wait a minute. I'd better not try to drive while we talk about this." She signaled responsibly, then zoomed into a grocery store parking lot and yanked the transmission into Park with a clunk. She turned to me with narrowed eyes. "What did she say, exactly?"

"She said . . . she thought maybe something was going on."

Pain flitted across her features and her blue eyes dimmed. "I don't know. Coop and Lynette lived in that little house. I lived at home, but I was so focused on Danny—I'd just met him, it was that part when he's all you can think of—I didn't pay much attention to Lynette. I did see—"

She broke off.

"What?"

"Once, I went looking for Daddy. I don't remember why. I couldn't find him in the house, which wasn't unusual, so I went out back. Lynette shot out the shop door, crying. Her face was red and she wouldn't tell me what was wrong. Brushed past me without stopping. In the shop, Daddy . . ."

I waited. She closed her eyes. "He was straightening his clothes."

Agony for her made me close my eyes. What a thing for a daughter to see.

"Oh. Did you tell Cooper?"

"No. I was never sure that . . . I did waver about it a lot, but then a month later she was gone. How did this come up with Miss Aurelia?" A woman with two small children passed the car on the way into the store. Caroline waved.

"Um. I mentioned to her that your dad said some things about Lynette that kind of raised a red flag or two."

"Oh, gosh. Oh, no." Caroline put her hand on her stomach as if struggling with nausea.

"If they did have a thing, do you think it was . . . ?" I stopped. "Do you think she wanted to?" We both delicately refrained from saying the words, as if not saying them would make it easier for Caroline to bear that her father may have gotten naked with his daughter-in-law.

"Well, at the time I thought maybe she did. The time I saw her, she was out there with him, after all. But the crying, and then when she left, I thought maybe not. I never said a word to Daddy. It's hardly the kind of thing you can ask about. 'Hey, Dad, were you doing my sister-in-law?'"

My eyes widened and my mouth dropped open at the matter-of-fact way she said it, shooting straight past all the polite dancing around we'd been doing. "Caroline! Holy crap!"

"What? Will not talking about it make it not true? Both my grandfathers had a little trouble with the 'faithful' part of the vows. Granddaddy, Daddy's father, was famous throughout the land for his total inability to keep his thing in his pants. It's probably not a shock that Daddy was the same. He'd been single a long time, then. And now, I guess. Anyway, I wonder if that's why Lynette ran off."

"Do you think it would help Cooper to know the truth? Or would it make it worse—she'd still be gone and he'd have to know that your dad . . ."

"Banged his wife?" Caroline gave me a cynical look, all wrong on her sunshiny face. "Yeah, I held off all this time, saying anything. I'd only ever seen that one thing that bothered me. But now . . . I think it might be good for him to know why. If that had anything to do with it. It might help him get some closure. I don't

know what y'all fought over—and I know, I know! I won't push
—but I'd bet my bottom dollar it had something to do with his
trust thing after Lynette. Let's do some digging. See what we can
find. I don't want to say anything to Coop based only on a guess.
We'll need more than that. Are you with me?"

"Are you sure? Cooper and Ted seem close."

"Coop and Daddy are close on the surface. Coop's a good boy.
A good son. He knows his role. But underneath, he and Dad have
had some major issues. Dad got super mad about him dropping
out of medical school. Holds some of the real estate business hos-
tage, sometimes, for no obvious reason other than to rile up
Cooper. Cooper's still upset that Daddy sold off Mama's family's
house in Charleston. All the old heirlooms in it, too, in a giant
auction. Coop really had a thing for that house. I don't remember
much about my grandparents on that side, but he does. It's something he's never forgiven Dad for."

"And you? Are you okay with doing this? He's your dad, too."

"I already know it, don't I?" asked Caroline. "Danny used to
say . . ."

"What did Danny say?"

"He used to say that Daddy wasn't what I thought he was.
Well, I knew he wasn't perfect, but he's . . . well. He's the only
parent I have left. He's done everything for me. He bought me my
first car, paid for my college, got my landscape design business
started, gave me and Mia a place to live after Danny left. I suspected that something was up with Lynette, but she's gone and
he's here."

"Aren't you worried that you might find something you don't
want to know?" I hated the thought of Caroline knowing Ted's
real proclivities and losing respect for her only remaining parent.

"I think I owe it to Danny."

"Danny?"

"Danny kept trying to get me to talk about Daddy. About his
attitudes. About things Danny said he did or said. I always
brushed it off. I said Daddy was born in another time. That
Danny needed to accept Daddy for who he was. I wonder if he

was trying to tell me something more important. And I refused to listen."

Based on my short interaction with Danny, she'd almost certainly hit the nail. Cooper had reacted the same way as Caroline described when I'd even hinted that Ted had some dark depths. Not the time to discuss that, though. "What happens if we tell Cooper about this?"

Caroline threw the transmission into Drive, signaling responsibly to pull out of the lot. "Then Cooper knows what we know. Though we don't know anything for sure, right now. But it's worth it to check it out a little more. I think Cooper blames himself for Lynette leaving. I'm afraid he can't move on if he never knows why. I think we have to do it. He and Daddy will have to have it out. Daddy and I will have to have it out, too. Secrets aren't healthy."

No. Secrets weren't healthy.

Okay. As Caroline merged back out onto Highway 17, I put my hand in my pocket and ran my fingertips along the edges of the card of Pastor John MacIlroy.

CHAPTER SEVENTEEN

After a quick lunch in Georgetown, Caroline dropped me off at Miss Aurelia's.

"I hate that you won't come home with me," she said, slowing down for the small-town streets of McClellanville.

"I can't," I said. "I can only come home with Cooper, and he hasn't asked me."

"Semantics. Temporary semantics." She pulled to a stop. "Okay, seriously. I'll go see if I can find the stuff Lynette left behind. After she left, I boxed it up. I don't think Cooper's looked through it in years. I don't know if there'll be anything of interest, but it won't hurt to see what's in it."

"She kept a diary."

"Diary?" screeched Caroline. "What diary?"

"You didn't know? I saw it. A bunch of volumes. It used to be on the bookshelves in the room with the picture of the dead baby. You know the one."

Caroline wrinkled her nose. "Yeah, that's Great Great Great Aunt Dolores. They used to take pictures of people after they died. Ew, right?"

"Focus!"

"Right! What do you mean, 'used to be'?"

"The diaries aren't there now. I went to look for them and they were gone."

Caroline's face went through an array of expressions as she tried to make sense of it. "I'll look for them."

I described the little books to her and got out, leaning into the open window. "I'll call the church guy."

"John." She picked a Cheerio off the console and tossed it in the backseat. "You really think he might know something?"

"He said . . ." Doubt crept in. "He said something odd, there at the end."

"Okay," she said. "I'd love to know what, but I'll try for once in my life not to be so nosy. Let me know if you find anything. I'll talk to that mule-headed brother of mine."

"Don't, Caroline. Please. It's between us."

"Darn it. I knew you'd say that."

I waved to her. She drove off, too fast.

Inside, I accepted a glass of sweet tea and told Miss Aurelia about the odd remark the priest had made.

She slumped into her seat, looking older as she ruminated.

"Lynette loved that church. She went every Sunday. Dragged Cooper with her when he could go—you know Realtors are pretty busy most Sundays—and also went to all the little things they have up there: ladies' meetings, Sunday school, Bible study. John MacIlroy's a good one. Grew up in Georgetown, nice family. Went to Sunday school sometime in there with Caroline and Cooper—can't remember which one he's closer to in age. He might know something." She looked me up and down. "After you call him, get changed and I'm taking you for a picnic lunch. Phone's in the kitchen."

The phone, an ancient wall-mounted model in Harvest Gold, matched Miss Aurelia's messy laminate countertops and actually had a rotary dial. It gave me the oddest feeling that I was dialing the past direct.

"Hello?"

"Reverend MacIlroy? This is Molly . . . Middleton. We met at church this morning?"

"Oh, yes, Molly, of course! Please call me John."

"John, then."

"I'm glad you called. What can I do for you, Molly? It felt this morning like you were a little lost at church."

Oh, shit. I'd forgotten. He'd want to counsel me. Straight-up interrogation of him wouldn't work.

"Um. When you found out who I was, you said . . ."

"I should have said you might need this phone number even more." His chuckle over the line was warm and well-used. "Apparently you figured that out on your own. Here you are."

Desperate to make the connections before I had to say something that would prove I had no idea what he was talking about, my brain whirred and popped. He'd made his jarring remark after Caroline had said I'd married into the family, and he clearly liked Caroline. He'd said Cooper was a good guy and I'd chosen wisely. That left . . .

"It's Ted. Cooper's father. I needed to talk to someone. This is all confidential, isn't it?" I remembered from the trial that what I'd told my useless lawyer was supposed to be confidential, and enough from going to confession with my grandma to know that the priest wasn't allowed to repeat what I'd told him. Given the kind of things I'd had to tell both of them, this assurance had stuck in my head. "You won't repeat what I say?"

"No. It's confidential. Everything."

"Ted has expressed interest in me. He touched my face. I think . . . he might want . . ." Words failed me. I couldn't say "fuck" to a priest. Even I had enough raising to know that, but what Ted wanted from me bore no resemblance at all to "making love." Or, frankly, to anything I could say to a priest. "This is uncomfortable."

"Ah." The syllable held knowledge and worry. He wasn't surprised. He'd heard this before. Adrenaline flowed, heating my skin. I'd guessed correctly. I wound my fingers in the old-fashioned curly phone cord to stop them from shaking.

"Please don't feel uncomfortable," Reverend MacIlroy continued. "Do you return Ted's interest?"

"No." Bile rose in my throat. "Not at all."

"Have you tried telling him that you're not interested?"

"Yes. I've been clear. He . . ." I might as well go for it. "He seemed to imply he had a relationship with Cooper's first wife and he expected something similar from me."

A silence burned over the phone lines. He took his time, choosing words. "I never saw evidence of that, but then again Ted is only an occasional church-goer." He emphasized the word *saw*. Not much, but enough. I hadn't imagined it.

"Did you know Lynette?"

Another pause. "Yes. She hardly ever missed a service. While she lived here, anyway."

"Did she tell you about Ted?"

He must consider every word out of his mouth. "You're aware that for the same reasons this conversation is confidential, anything Lynette said to me is also confidential."

Dismay weighed my shoulders down. He knew everything and he couldn't—or wouldn't—tell me anything. I had to try, though. "So she did talk to you."

"I didn't say that." I caught the distress in his tone; he was afraid he'd said too much. I'd give anything to see his face and read his body language right now. "Merely that if she had, it would be confidential."

Okay. Let's cut the crap. "I am asking you as a counselor: am I going to be able to tell Ted no and be done with it?"

This time the silence lasted so long I thought he might have hung up. "My advice to you, Mrs. Middleton, is to say no. Say it a lot and say it loud. Call me whenever you need to." Two seconds elapsed. Then two more, before the words flowed in a rush, the cadence of a man who wasn't able to stop himself. "And under no circumstances should you ever be alone with him. Do you understand me?"

I swallowed as the implications hit me. "I understand you. Thank you for talking with me. I enjoyed the service this morning."

We said our goodbyes, and he hung up.

As Cooper would say, holy God. Lynette's tears had not been shed over nothing.

The heavy weight of the old-fashioned receiver made a loud clunk as I hung it up.

"Well?" asked Miss Aurelia from the living room.

Still trying to make sense of what John had said, I wandered around the corner. "He couldn't say much, but he told me to make sure I was never alone with Ted. Don't you think that's a little . . . over the top?"

"What I think will wait until we eat. Go get changed."

"Where are we going?" I asked, as Miss Aurelia's little car hurtled north on Highway 17 and then turned left, down a two-lane road leading away from the coast.

"You may have noticed I don't do church in Georgetown with all the proper Southern ladies and gentlemen. I do church my way. I wanted to show it to you." After a short stretch on the road, she turned left again onto a straight dirt road into unrelieved pine forest.

"This little track might not look like much, but 'George Washington was here,'" she said, grinning. "This is the old King's Highway, and it was the coastal highway for most of the 1700s. Can't you picture the carriages coming along here? Patriot guerrillas shooting at Redcoats?"

I could. There wasn't a single modern thing in sight.

"The first European settlers in this area built their church on this highway—St. James Santee is the name of it. When the road moved, the church got left behind, untouched. Coming here is like religion and a time machine all rolled into one. I manage to come by about once a month. Here we are."

The impenetrable woods gave way enough for a small brick church with Jefferson-style columns, tall round-topped windows, and a tiny walled churchyard with grave markers.

I carried the no-frills cooler and set it on the church porch as Miss Aurelia slid a heavy bolt on the door and led the way. Inside, the utter stillness of the empty sanctuary took my breath. This was a church similar in age to the one I'd attended with Caroline—it had the wooden box pews and a raised pulpit—but time had left no fingerprints on this building. No paint or varnish on the dark wood. No microphone. No bulletin boards or fancy crosses or paintings. Only the wooden pew boxes and the majestic symmetrical ceiling-high windows, and the sunlight that slanted in as it had for almost three hundred years.

"Miss Aurelia. I don't know what to say."

"It's beautiful, isn't it, the things that last through time? One trip through this door is better for my eternal soul than an hour with some busybodies and a stuffy pastor."

"You can feel the history here." I felt different here. Better. More worthy.

Miss Aurelia had made a valiant effort but couldn't maintain the reverence any longer. "Yup. Thought you'd like it. Everyone does. Now. Let's set up outside and eat. It's a warm day and this time of year the mosquitoes might leave you enough blood to survive. Don't come here in July without an entire can of Off. Just a tip."

We spread out a blanket in the churchyard and munched on sandwiches and sweet tea. One of the antique graves caught my eye. "That one's old." The carving had worn away to become almost illegible. "Do you know whose that is?"

"Daniel and Margaret Huger. They're among the earliest settlers here. Huguenots, traveled here from France. I believe they both died before 1720. Had a dozen children too, and outlived all but two of them."

"A hard life, back then," I said, trying to imagine it.

"Yes, I expect so." Miss Aurelia gave me a sidelong glance and gestured at the gravestone. "I don't have a clue if it's true, but I like to think the Hugers loved each other and supported each other through everything. Love can carry you. I believe in love. You have to. If one kind doesn't work, there's always a chance for a replacement kind."

Something in her tone made me search her face. "Did you have a love that didn't work?"

She let out her sharp bark of a laugh. "I'm as subtle as a brick to the face, aren't I? Yes, I had the star-crossed love as a young woman. It didn't work. It never was going to and I knew it all along. I never forgot it and I never quite moved on, but I ended up with plenty of love and who knows? I'm not dead yet. For now, Cooper and Caroline are my loves, and Mia. And Elijah, who visits his Legos. And half a dozen others. Anyone in that town who needs something—a friend, a co-conspirator, a mother—I'm ready. That's my role. It's been enough."

"I'm sorry."

"Don't be. Sometimes love doesn't come in the package it should, or the one you expected, but it's out there if you let it find you. The universe is pretty fair, most of the time. I'd bet good money there's something worth having coming up for you soon."

I squeezed her hand, astonished at my own familiarity. "I'd love to have you for an honorary mother."

"Done." She laughed and began stowing the remains of the picnic in the car while I gathered myself.

An unaccustomed warmth lingered and my chest loosened a bit more. It wouldn't last, but I hadn't felt blameless even for a few minutes since I was seventeen. Had I done right? Or at least not wrong? Gingerly, I poked at the memory and to my shock, more of it showed to me than ever before. Only a fragment, but for the first time, I remembered the feel of the wooden knife handle in my shaking palm, down by my thigh.

I hadn't raised it to her. At least not in the sliver of memory that had come back.

It wasn't a lot, but it was more than I had before.

Miss Aurelia returned from the car. "When you were on the phone at the house I sorted through things that maybe didn't make sense at the time, or that I thought didn't mean anything." She grimaced, her face awash in concern and guilt.

"One time when I went over to have tea with Lynette, she wasn't asleep. It was during the time when she slept a lot, a month or two before she left. I remember it because it was September and hot as Satan's furnace outside and she'd built a fire in the fireplace. She was feeding paper to it. She said it was her high school journal, and Cooper had read part of it. You said you'd seen her journals in the house?"

"Yes, the second day I was there I hid from the decorator in a spare bedroom. There were five. I flipped through one and it was all college stuff. The last entry in the last one was dated sometime around the time she left and didn't say anything except that she was upset with the care her dad was getting at his Virginia nursing home. Nothing about Ted."

"I'd like to take a look at those."

"I would, too, but when I went back to look, they were gone. I thought you might have picked them up."

"Nope. I didn't."

"You . . . you didn't?" *Then who?*

"No. That's more peculiar than a five-legged dog. Well. It'll be a job to hunt those down, but I think we must."

The prospect daunted me—searching for five little books in that vast house full of oddities. Books Ted must have moved. I hadn't a clue how I'd manage it, especially while living with Miss Aurelia.

"Anyway, I thought it was strange and out of character for Cooper to have read Lynette's journal without her permission, so I asked her. Gave her the third degree, I expect."

"You?" I asked, smiling at her.

"Me. I liked Lynette, and I felt bad for her, but I love Cooper like my own. It was a hell of an accusation. I couldn't make sense of her answer. She said something that gave me the idea that Cooper hadn't searched out the journal, but that he'd been given pages from it. That he'd read it without knowing what it was somehow."

"Ted? Would Ted have done that?"

"If Ted thought he could use that information to get something he wanted, he sure as hell would." Miss Aurelia sipped her ever-present tea. "Poor girl. Apparently Cooper found out that way that she'd once participated in some little girl-on-girl demonstration at a boozy high school party. Of course she'd never told him that. I don't know that he had a problem with it, but something was making her destroy that journal."

"I bet Ted found the diary and was using some other little story in there to manipulate her. I'd bet everything I don't own that she had no interest in him and he forced her to do what he wanted." He'd certainly done that with me to keep me from telling

Cooper about Lynette—he was a master manipulator. He'd figured out that I didn't want Cooper hurt, and he knew what would hurt Cooper the most.

"He might could have been. Damn," Miss Aurelia said. "No wonder she ran. I wonder what else was in that journal for her to feed it to the fire."

"Something big, I guess. We need those diaries."

CHAPTER EIGHTEEN

I took a nap after the picnic and woke to late afternoon sun and Miss Aurelia calling me to the phone.

"How is it you don't have a cell phone, girl?"

I passed her in the hall, pushing my hair back into place. "It got smashed in Las Vegas right before I met Cooper. Replacing it hasn't been a priority. Who would I call anyway?"

"Hmmph. Gonna have to do something about both of those things. Here. Caroline's on the phone."

I took the receiver from her, and she laid a warm hand on my head. Almost before I could register the comfort, it was gone.

"Molly?" Caroline's voice was agitated.

"Hey. What's up?"

"Can you come over here? I found something, I think. In the box of Lynette's stuff. It's freaking me out."

"No, I can't. Cooper might—"

"Cooper's not here. He's gone to Charleston to get Mia for me. School tomorrow. He said he might take her out to eat at Jack's Cosmic Dogs. That's her favorite. He always gives her a million dollars in quarters to play video games. He'll be gone until after dinner. Daddy's gone, too. Out to dinner with some business people in Mt. Pleasant. Something about buying a lot for a Piggly Wiggly. Come over and eat leftovers with me."

"Okay, if Cooper isn't there. I'll come over." The walk was a pleasant one and I'd grown to enjoy it.

Fifteen minutes later, I raised a hand to knock on the door, but Caroline opened it before I even made contact with the knocker.

She yanked me unceremoniously over the threshold. Mary Jane looked up from her doze on the floor and stared at me curiously, but not curiously enough to get up to greet me. Caroline steered me upstairs by my arm to a bedroom I'd never seen, clearly used for storage and guests. And extra trophies—two antlered deer heads on plaques watched silently from one wall, on either side of a swordfish caught in a jump from which it would never land.

"This is all Lynette's stuff." A large blue Rubbermaid box with the lid off had been dragged out of the walk-in closet. Some of the contents—a winter coat, a plastic basket full of crumbling make-up, some outdated phone charger cords, a glasses repair kit and cleaning wipe, instruction manuals for things I didn't catch a glimpse of—lay on the floor next to it. Caroline had obviously spent some time going through it. Two huge piles of loose copy paper, mail, printed emails, and flyers teetered, the kind of stuff you'd get out of a desk or junk drawer.

"What did you find? This all looks like pretty normal stuff."

"It is. I remember most of it from when we packed it up at their house. We kept it because we thought maybe there was a chance she'd come back for it, but anyway. Here's what's freaking me out. Sit."

We sat on the floor by the box and Caroline spread out a piece of paper. "Look. The day she left, Lynette bought a plane ticket from Charleston to Charlotte. Showed up on their joint Visa. Right? She drove to the airport and then we never saw her again. But look at this. It's a travel reservation through one of the online sites. She printed out the schedule and the receipt. It was in here in a huge pile of paper."

"So?"

"Look at it."

I picked up the paper. A flight had been reserved from Charleston to Roanoke, Virginia, with one stop at Washington, Dulles. I handed it back. "I don't think I understand."

"Look at the dates. She bought a plane ticket to Charlotte and disappeared on October 21. We never saw her again. This flight to Roanoke was scheduled for October 23. When she bought the ticket to Charlotte, she already had a plane ticket that hadn't been used. She must have bought it way back in September. She printed the email on September 15. See at the bottom?"

"That's near the date in her diary. Oh, God."

"So did she say something about a plane ticket?"

"No. Sometime in September she wrote that a nurse wasn't taking care of her dad right in Virginia."

"Well, that would explain why she bought this first plane ticket to Roanoke. It's the closest airport to her hometown and the nursing home."

Caroline waited, while my sluggish brain tried to make sense of it.

"I'm not seeing what you're seeing."

"Why would someone with an unused plane ticket to Roanoke who suddenly decided to go to Charlotte not just change the ticket she already had? It's what, a hundred dollar fee to change a ticket? Cooper could have afforded two plane tickets, but Lynette didn't grow up with money. She was frugal. She'd have hated spending money that wasn't necessary. Why would she have done it?"

"Could she have forgotten about the Roanoke ticket?"

"A five hundred dollar plane ticket to her hometown for a flight two days away? No way. Lynette remembered everything. Why buy a second ticket? Why go to Charlotte at all? Why not wait two days and go home?"

A silence hummed, as my thoughts tried to keep up with an unease that tightened my throat.

"I don't know." A terrible thought, the kind that liquefies your insides and threatens to bring up the contents of your stomach, occurred to me. "Do you know for sure she made it to the plane to Charlotte? How did she get to the airport? Did she actually get on the plane?"

"Oh, my gosh." Caroline wrung her hands. "She took the car to the airport and left it there. I remember a while later we went to look for it in the structure and bring it home. But I don't know if she got on the plane. I don't think we checked it. Cooper was angry at the time, and I assumed she must have since she went to the airport. It never occurred to me to ask. Would they still have the info after all this time?"

"We can check, though if she got to the airport, where else could she have gone?"

Caroline sat back on her heels. "Well, this is a heck of a mess. What should we do?"

Slowly, I pulled my knees up to my chest, thoughts whirling. "I guess we check on the airline."

"Caro?" called Cooper, from the foyer. The front door slammed.

"Mommy!" yelled Mia, in a joyful howl. "Uncle Coop wrote my princess story!"

Caroline looked at me. "Oh, no. I'm so sorry. Do you want to wait here and try to sneak out? I can distract them in the kitchen."

"Mommy!" yelled Mia, more insistent now. "Where are you?"

"I'm coming down, sweetie!" Caroline stood, but held still, waiting for my reaction.

"I'll come down. I'm a grown-up. I can be one if he can." Grim determination to be unaffected by his presence mixed with the undeniable swooping thrill of hope.

She laughed. "You might be asking too much. Come on."

Running feet pounded up the stairs, and Mia burst into the room and straight for Caroline's thighs. "Mommy! I missed you!"

Caroline bent down, hooked her hands under Mia's armpits and lifted her for a tight squeeze. I didn't catch all the words she spoke into Mia's ear, but most of it was choked-up expressions of love that squeezed my heart. Mia clung like a baby koala as if they'd been separated much longer than three days.

I tried to think if anyone, ever, had missed me like that. I'd have given almost anything for one more hug from my grandmother at that moment.

Caroline moved to set Mia down, but Mia climbed back up, arms tightly knotted around Caroline's neck, face buried in her hair. "Okay, baby. Let's go tell Uncle Coop thanks for getting you, all right?" Thus weighed down, she headed for the stairs. "Coming, Aunt Molly?"

I snorted in response to her over-sweet tone. "Absolutely."

Though I was nervous enough to pee my pants, I got a ridiculous amount of pleasure out of anticipating Cooper's face when he realized I was in the house. He couldn't be angry. He hadn't kicked me out. He'd gone out of his way to say I could stay.

"It's getting cold out there," Cooper said, carrying Mia's stuff in from the car. He glanced up the staircase, saw me following his sister, and his face turned red. He closed his mouth, whatever else he'd been planning to say about the weather forgotten.

"I invited Molly over to eat some leftover turkey. She helped cook everything, so only fair. Y'all can act normal for a little sweet potato casserole, can't you? Good." With that, Caroline swept off in the direction of the kitchen, Mia still attached like a starfish to her hip.

Which left Cooper and me to stare at each other. My legs stopped working one step from the bottom, putting me at eye-level with Cooper.

"You wrote Mia's story for her?"

"Yes," he said, cautiously.

"I should have known." How many uncles would have remembered to write up a story about a princess and a horseshoe?

"There's a lot of leftover food," he said, his face closed but polite. Even so, I thought I saw a little daylight under the door. This wasn't the kind of closed it had been on the dock. Hope began tiny vibrations in my belly.

I checked to make sure Caroline had gone around the corner. "You didn't tell her."

"No."

"Why?"

He ran a hand through his hair. "I thought . . . I thought it was for you to tell her, or not, if you don't want to."

I blinked. God, his eyes were so beautiful. His smell. I wanted to stand here and simply breathe him in. "Thank you. I didn't expect that."

"Y'all coming? This stuff isn't going to heat itself up!" called Caroline from the kitchen.

Cooper held out a silent hand, to let me go first. I glanced once more into his face and caught a glimpse of pain and frustration—

and longing. I saw the longing, too. He was still affected by me.

As if my body had no idea I was trying to protect my own feelings, heat and desire blazed over my skin until I wouldn't have been surprised to discover I was in literal flames. I paused, breathing deep, to let the overreaction die down.

In the kitchen, Caroline had gotten out plates and covered dishes from the fridge. We dove in and helped. Cooper heated the plates of food one at a time. I set up Mia with silverware and a paper towel for a napkin. In less than ten minutes, we were all seated around the island, eating a meal that was almost as good as the first one.

I couldn't keep my eyes away from Cooper, despite trying hard to follow Mia's story about the turkey her dad had burned, and how he didn't have any sweet potatoes or spoonbread at his dinner (poor fellow Yankee Danny—I remembered he was from Chicago). Cooper had tossed aside a half-zip fleece and wore only a worn T-shirt from a duck-hunting store. It hid none of his spectacular musculature. Every glance seemed to attract one in return.

I lost my appetite and unbuttoned my cardigan. Merely being in the room with him raised my temperature ten degrees.

"Mommy, what's a nullment?" asked Mia, watching the silent dance between Cooper and me.

Cooper's eyes widened and his fork froze in mid-air. I put mine down, suddenly freed from the need to look at Cooper. At all. Anywhere else would do.

Caroline's eyebrows drew together. "What's a what, sweetie?"

"A nullment," said Mia, stubbornly. "Uncle Coop says Aunt Molly has had enough and needs one."

Cooper met my eyes, panicked. "I didn't say anything since the time you were in the . . ."

"An annulment?" asked Caroline, ostensibly to Mia, but making clear her question had a wider audience.

"Yeah! That's a paper. A grown-up one. That's what Uncle Coop said."

"Pix, are you finished?" asked Cooper. "Why don't you go watch TV? Get out one of your Doc McStuffins videos."

"Can I, Mommy?"

"Sure. Go ahead." Mia scampered out of the room. Caroline waited until she'd disappeared from sight before turning on us. "What the frick? Are you crazy? You're going to get an annulment because you had a little spat? Cooper. How could you? I thought you were tougher than that."

Tiredly, Cooper dropped a bit of turkey to Mary Jane, who snuffled under his feet, hoping for a windfall. "We were married in Vegas, Caro. Of course we discussed an annulment. We got married drunk as skunks. We mentioned it in front of Mia on the way down to Charleston on Friday."

"Molly? Are you serious? After what we talked about?"

I said nothing. Everything in me screamed to say I didn't want one, that I loved him, that he had to forgive me, but as badly as I wanted Caroline to fix it for me, I could say nothing. Cooper had to handle it. It was for him to decide what his family knew.

"We talked about it, that's all," said Cooper. "As an option. We can't get one, now, anyway. That right there is way more than you're entitled to know. I love you, Caro, but butt out. Now. Molly and I are going to help you clean up and then we are going for a walk." He ruffled the dog's fur and gave her another piece of turkey.

I was very much afraid my entire heart wasn't just in my eyes but bursting out of every pore in my skin. He'd said we couldn't get an annulment. What did that mean?

And he'd asked me to go for a walk but he wouldn't meet my eyes.

"Go," said Caroline. "I'll clean up. I'm far more interested in you patching up whatever stupid fight you had than I am in having help putting this stuff in the dishwasher. Go. Get out of here."

I thought I'd been overcome with emotion before, until I heard the thickening of her voice. She turned away, raising a hand to her eyes.

"Go."

CHAPTER NINETEEN

Outside, the early darkness had fallen, and Cooper was right, the temperature had dropped. Wintry wind rustled branches in the canopy above us. I hugged my borrowed fleece jacket closer to myself, as protection against the weather. I wished I could protect myself from my own longing as easily.

We walked without speaking for quite a distance.

"Do you remember Hurricane Hugo?" asked Cooper, out of the blue.

"Um. The name sounds familiar. We didn't get many hurricanes in Michigan."

"We get them every now and then. Got one a couple months ago, actually; brought down a few trees and did some flooding. Nothing compared to Hugo."

"Tell me about Hugo." I'd have listened to any story he wanted to tell, as long as he kept talking.

He paused before speaking. A car door slammed down the block. In the darkness, the sound floated disembodied in the air.

"It was a huge storm, category four when it came ashore. One of the worst in Charleston's history—they still talk about it there, on the tours and what-all—but this is where the eye wall hit, the worst of the worst. I was seven. Caro was a baby. You can see there isn't any high ground around here. They told everyone to go to the high school for shelter, but the storm surge was so high it filled up the school. We were standing on tables, all the kids in our parents' arms. But the water kept coming, and the power was off. Everything was pitch black dark. It was so hot and humid. All those bodies so close together. Eventually, all the parents were pushing up the ceiling tiles—you know, the white ones you count the dots in during a boring class?—and lifting us into the space above the ceiling to get our heads to the air. It was so dark, and I remember how scared the grownups were. They tried to hide it, but I'd never been so scared in my life. Dad was holding Caro over his head. I stood on Mama's shoulders while she prayed. The water kept rising."

"Oh, my God. Cooper." His words, and the quiet horror in his tone, painted a vivid picture of a roomful of people expecting death. We walked on. The wind buffeted fallen leaves along the sidewalk under my feet. I tried to imagine it underwater.

"Everyone lived, somehow. The water crested and went down. Afterwards, though, things were bad. The shrimp fleet was destroyed. One boat landed in our front yard. The winds took out most of the woods around here. Nothing but broken trees for miles and miles up and down Highway 17. Live oaks that had stood two hundred years crashed all over the roads. Nearly every house in town had some damage."

I stayed quiet, waiting for the point.

We walked through the empty streets, under the branches of the huge oaks that had already been old when the storm came through and survived and thrived now. The chill in the air had silenced the insects. The only sound was the thudding of our feet on the sidewalk and the occasional creak of a faraway branch.

"After you left yesterday, after the . . . after the dock, I . . ." Cooper stopped walking. I stopped too and scuffed my toe in the cracked pavement.

"What?"

"This is hard for me to say. After the dock, after you left, I was afraid. Like I haven't been, since that day in the dark and the water."

I kept a careful distance from him, though inside me the flame of hope I'd been nursing leaped. "Of me?"

"No. Of myself, and the way I judged you without listening." He put his hands in his pockets. "And of you, leaving."

A gust of wind whistled through the branches and blew a strand of my hair onto my lips, where it got stuck. I was grateful to have something to take care of while I absorbed that. Somehow, though, pulling it loose didn't take nearly long enough.

"Wh-what?" I asked.

He avoided my eyes and rubbed the back of his neck. "It freaked me out. I thought you hadn't been planning to tell me. I know now you had. Miss Aurelia told me. And then I didn't even think to ask you questions. But I had a whole sleepless night to think about it. You said your mother wasn't maternal."

"No."

"I was right that the dream was about her, wasn't it?"

"Yes. It was."

"What did she do?"

I paused, the words choking me. I listened to the sounds of the night and fixed my eyes on a porch light down the block, flickering as a breeze blew a live oak branch in front of it. Cooper waited.

I'd never told anyone these things before. "I don't know when it started. When I was little she left me with my grandma a lot."

"Your grandma was different? Good to you?"

"Yeah. She was." I looked down, staring at my unpainted fingernails as if they were new. "My mother never hugged me or kissed me. She blew up at everything, and nothing. It was like living with . . . with a dragon, and I had to be ready to avoid the fire-breathing, all the time. I sound stupid. But nothing I did was enough. Everything I did was wrong."

Cooper let out a long breath. "It doesn't sound stupid. And it probably wasn't wrong."

"I know that rationally, but inside, it's different. She hated me. Other mothers didn't hate their kids. It actually took me a while to realize that, and then once I did I used to try to figure out what was different about me. What it was about me that . . . that couldn't be loved." I swallowed and answered his question. "She hurt me. A lot."

He was silent, absorbing what I'd said. "Last night, when I couldn't sleep, I thought maybe she had. I wondered. I can't believe I didn't even ask you, but I will now. Will you tell me what happened? So I can understand?"

I wanted to ask him if it would make a difference. If the explanation would wash the blood off my hands and strip off the orange jumpsuit, but I found I wanted to explain more than I cared about knowing the answer.

"I can't expect you to understand. You can't, growing up like you did. With a family to love you, with people not even in your family who love you. But I'll try."

"Will it be easier if we start walking again?"

"I think so." We set off down the sidewalk. It was easier, facing forward. "Grandma couldn't take care of me because she had macular degeneration and couldn't see. She needed help herself. She knew, kind of, what sort of daughter she had, but it upset her to know, so I didn't tell her the worst of it. She never saw the bruises and if I kept everything sounding fine, she didn't have to know."

"Oh, Molly."

I waved him off. "Let me get it all out, because if I stop it'll only be harder. Telling Grandma wouldn't have helped anyway, because when I was about eight, they fought and Ma stopped me spending time with her. I was the product of a one-night stand, so no dad was around. She'd gone to school to be a medical assistant, had good grades, even, but she got fired for stealing blank prescription pads. She got into drugs and alcohol early. Grandma tried to help out, but she used all of Grandma's money on more drugs."

I gave him a tiny smile, drawing strength from his nearby bulk for this next, much harder, part. "Somehow, Ma qualified for disability so she didn't have to work. We lived on what she got, and what Grandma could share from her own disability, and whatever I could earn from after-school jobs. It wasn't much. Not enough, she said, to pay for the fifth of vodka she wanted every day or the drugs. Whenever there wasn't money, she'd blame me, for eating, or needing clothes, or anything, really. For being alive. And then she'd blow up and come after me."

Cooper kept his face averted, though this time I thought it was out of respect and pity, and not out of contempt.

"When I was about sixteen, she decided what I earned from the after-school jobs wasn't enough. At first, she wanted me to drop out of school to get a full-time job. I refused, because I was in the running for valedictorian. I wanted the diploma."

"Did you get it?"

"No. I didn't. I got my GED in prison." I stepped over a broken branch in the sidewalk. "Right. Anyway, I made minimum wage at the grocery store, so she decided I could only keep that job if I supplemented it with one of her choosing."

Cooper stopped walking and turned a face full of dread toward me. "Wh . . ." He cleared his throat. "What job was that?"

Here it was. I swallowed, focusing my gaze on his chin, unable to meet his eyes.

"Not really a job, exactly. She said I was hot enough to bring top dollar. Said I had 'better tits than Jenna Jameson.'" I laughed, no mirth anywhere in it. "I didn't even know who that was."

Overcome, Cooper clasped my upper arms, making a literal protective shell with his body. "She didn't. Tell me she didn't make you . . ."

"No. I never did do it, but not because she quit trying. She made it clear it was that or the streets. My seventeenth birthday was on September twenty-first of my senior year. I had no intention of letting her turn me into a prostitute, so I'd started packing my stuff and making plans to talk to a teacher I liked about needing a place to stay. I went to the JV football game the night of my birthday with a friend to watch her little brother play, and I came home late. She was waiting."

Cooper stood still, his hands loose under my elbows, as if holding me up. Part of me thought he was.

"She was high as a kite and she wasn't alone. A skinny man was there I'd never seen before. She called him John, though that was probably more his title than his name. He had greasy gray hair in a ponytail, not much of it, and he was old. Yellow teeth and something wrong with his eyes so they didn't quite match. She told me I was going to be nice to him."

He made a broken sound and squeezed my elbows and tugged me closer. I let him hug me and then broke away to keep walking. I didn't think I could say this next part with his eyes, full of concern, on me.

"I said no. She said yes. I tried to dodge her and get back out the door, but she croaked out some command and the man grabbed me around the rib cage and held me. I remember his smell: dirty hair and gasoline. Then I jammed my foot down on his instep and he yelled and shoved me at her. He went and blocked the door. He said he'd give her two minutes to get me in line or he'd go. She yanked a kitchen knife out of a drawer and came after me. I tried to get behind the furniture, but he helped her corner me and she got me by the hair. The man kept laughing the whole time, like he thought it was a game. That's the last thing I remember."

It had been, until the flash earlier of the knife by my thigh. That memory sharpened. It was real.

Cooper shuddered, stopping behind me again. I halted in the shelter of a nearby tree, turning to see him pass a desperate hand over his eyes. "I hate that you're reliving this. I shouldn't have asked. Stop. Don't tell me any more." Anguish was written all over him. "God above, that anyone should have had to go through that."

Somehow the flood of words lifted something off me. Only once before had I told this story—to my lawyer who barely stayed awake long enough to hear it. Cooper was listening to me. I reached for a live oak branch hanging low and grasped it, thankful for the strength.

"The next thing I remember is the blood. A whole pool of it. The knife was on the floor nearby, half-submerged in it. I was on my knees with a red towel that used to be blue, pressing on the place in her upper thigh. If I loosened my hands at all, it spurted everywhere—I hit something big. I remember thinking that I should have known what—I'd only taken intro biology a year or so before. In the trial I found out it was the femoral artery."

"What happened to the man?"

"I don't know what he saw. He was gone. I must have pulled the knife out of her—I know now that was the worst thing I could have done, but I was a kid. I thought I could bandage it, but the blood kept pumping out, more and more of it. I called 911 and by the time they got there—took them forty-five minutes—she was gone. I was there, all alone, drenched in her blood. They arrested me two days later. I never saw the man again until the trial. Somehow the prosecution found him."

"Are you sure he didn't do it? Maybe . . ."

"He didn't. His fingerprints weren't on the knife. The only fingerprints on the knife were hers and mine. He was their star witness. He said he was her boyfriend and he'd watched me stab her in cold blood. I didn't have any wounds except a sore scalp from where she pulled my hair and that didn't show."

"God!" Cooper closed his eyes. "Why didn't your lawyer say you did it out of self-defense? How in the hell did they convict you?"

"I didn't know what had happened. I wasn't allowed to guess. The man testified and there was no one to say otherwise. My lawyer was court-appointed and overworked. His wife had cancer. He'd been staying up all night to take care of her and their new baby during chemo. I was hardly a priority and he kept dozing off. He missed parts of the witness testimony."

Cooper's fists clenched but he said nothing.

I kept talking. "And besides, nobody knew I'd been abused. I'd never said a word to anyone. We had a teacher to testify that my mother yelled at her once and generally wasn't a good mother, and my grandma to say she'd seen my mother high on drugs or drunk a bunch of times, but nothing else. And, Cooper, I did kill her. The fingerprints proved it."

"So you were convicted."

I pulled a leaf off the branch I'd been using for support, marveling at the smooth surface.

"They tried me as an adult. I was convicted. Off to the pen I went a week before my eighteenth birthday, right about a year after. You know all the rest."

Without a word, we resumed walking. He stayed quiet for a whole block. We walked in the chill breeze off the water to the public boat launch. It didn't escape me that Cooper headed to the water when he wanted comfort. Once we reached the end of the ramp where the water lapped against the wood pilings, he put his hand on my arm. For a moment we stared out over the creek toward the dusk to dawn lights at the waterfront houses.

"I couldn't be any more ashamed of my reaction when you told me on the dock than I am right now. Everything you said was true. I did judge you. You warned me and I judged you anyway. I am an absolute shit. You should never have gone to prison for that in a million fucking years. And, damn, you should never have had to go through what you did before prison. You were right. I can't understand, and it's not because I've had some special childhood. No one could understand that kind of life."

"There were plenty of women in prison who'd suffered that much or worse."

He squeezed his eyes shut. "I know you must be right and I can't stand it. I want to smash things, to burn down everything. If I could kill your mother again right now, I'd do it. With my bare hands. How could anyone blame you for that? Much less lock you up? You were a child! God!" He ran his hands through his hair, his face working, turning and pacing tight circles. "I'm so angry right now. I don't know . . . I can't handle how I feel right now."

I turned away, not sure whether to tell him what I was thinking.

"Molly," said Cooper, touching my arm, misinterpreting my movement. "I shouldn't have said that. How I feel doesn't matter at all compared to how you feel."

"It's not that. I don't remember what happened. What if I did wrestle the knife from her and jam it into her on purpose? Cold-blooded, like the man said? If I did that, Cooper, I deserved everything that happened to me. Prison. The punishment. And more."

"You didn't. It was self-defense, even if you did take the knife from her. Like you said, a spur-of-the-moment thing. You didn't plan it."

"What if I did?" I took a deep breath, determined he would know it all. "I did deserve it. Maybe I didn't make an advance plan to kill her that night, but I wanted her dead the day before that and the day before that. A hundred times I wished she would die. Be hit by a car. Overdose. Have a heart attack. I thought about it a lot. I wanted to be away from her so bad I could taste it. Then she *was* dead, and I did kill her. Isn't that just as bad as if I planned it?"

Cooper turned me to face him by pulling gently on my wrist. "No. It would be natural for you to have wished her gone from your life. But people don't subconsciously kill. You didn't do it on purpose. Your life was threatened. You were defending yourself. You did not deserve what happened to you."

I put a gentle hand on his arm. "It doesn't matter anymore. It's all a long time ago."

"It's not. They took your . . . your *years* from you."

"It's done. It's over."

"It's not. You still dream about it."

I stared out at the dark water, unable to deny it. In far too many ways, it would never be over. "I deal with it. I've been dealing with it for a long time. Like I said the other night, it's not new."

"You've been alone. All this time. What happened to your grandmother?"

"She died, six years ago. I was in prison. She wrote to me, but she couldn't come visit. She was pretty much house-bound, because of her eyes."

"I'm so sorry," he said, beginning to calm. "I treated you worse than anyone. I was supposed to . . . to care about you and I called you a killer. I'm so, so sorry."

"You needed time to think. I'm sorry that you found out on the Internet and not from me. I was a coward. I should have told you in Vegas. I'm sorry I let things go too far before I told you."

Remorse etched his features in the distant light. "That's my fault. I pushed you."

"You didn't push me anywhere I didn't want to go." I sat down on the end of the pilings, feet dangling above the black water. Cooper sat down next to me.

"What happens now?" he asked.

"With us?"

He nodded.

"I don't know. We consummated the marriage. I don't know if the fraud ground counts if you don't object," I said, carefully, afraid, so afraid he'd say he still objected.

"It's not fraud. We don't have any annulment grounds. That's what I meant before, when I told Caroline. You didn't commit any fraud as far as I'm concerned."

The flicker of hope burst into flames, and I began to fear they'd burn me up.

"So what now? Do we get a divorce?"

A silence hummed between us as he chose his words. Time stretched to an eternity. My whole being screamed *Please*. Please what, I didn't know.

"I don't know. I'd say we hold off for now. See what happens. I think we need time to get to know each other. To date, maybe. This was a big thing, but it means there are probably a hundred little things we don't know about each other. I . . ."

"I . . ." I started, at the same time.

"You first."

I took the leap. Damn the consequences. I had nothing—literally nothing—to lose. "I'd like to. Date, I mean." I took a breath, for courage. "The connection, like you said at the beach, is still there. With you."

He took my hand, lacing his fingers with mine. "It is. You're right. Let's take it slow, okay?"

"Okay."

"Come on. I think it's time to tell Caroline what you've been dealing with."

I paced back and forth in front of the windows in Cooper's bedroom. He'd been in the family room with Caroline for more than thirty minutes, telling her all about my history, our marriage, everything. No more secrets. Half an hour gave me plenty of time to bite all ten of my fingernails and wear a path in the plush of the rug.

In mid-hand-wring, the door burst open. Caroline, with red eyes and wet cheeks, charged at me with her arms open. She gave a loud sniffle as she squeezed me in a hug so tight I could barely breathe.

"I can't believe you didn't tell me. How could you think I would care about that? When I think about you all alone, trying to handle all that without family!" Caroline pulled back to look at me and then hugged me all over again. "Please, come back and stay here." Letting me loose, she turned to Cooper, who leaned against the doorframe with his hands in his pockets. "You are asking her back to stay, aren't you?"

He met my eyes. His gaze, so intense, sent a shiver down my spine. "Of course I am. Please come back."

The eye contact held and began to burn. I couldn't look away and my breath caught.

Caroline laughed, a happy sound tinged with relief. "Get a room. This one, I'd suggest."

Below, the front door banged shut. "Where's my family?" bellowed Ted, evidently done wining and dining the grocery store investors. From a greater distance away, he barked, "Where is your mother? Go find her." This last was followed by Mia's scurrying feet up the stairs.

Cooper raised an eyebrow. "While I think Caro's suggestion sounds great, looks like we might have to wait a few minutes. Come on. Let's go tell Dad you're staying."

I didn't think Ted would greet that news with undiluted enthusiasm. Still, I didn't mind doing anything that decreased Ted's happiness. I followed Cooper to the stairway. Caroline had already swept up Mia by the time I rounded the corner.

"What are y'all . . . ?" Ted's hands, loosening his tie, stopped moving as he spotted me at the end of the procession. "She's back."

Apparently Caroline didn't mind poking at Ted, either. Her

grin was wide. "Yep, Daddy. Coop and Molly made up. Aren't you glad?"

Cooper took my hand. A simple thing, really. He'd done it before. This time was different, though. This time it wasn't a performance for Ted's benefit. It was an announcement. A claim. Joy and import twined and turned into tears pricking at my eyes. I gave Cooper a watery smile.

Ted didn't miss any of it. His lips thinned as he stared at our joined hands.

"Welcome back, Mary. It's so nice to have you back under my roof."

CHAPTER TWENTY

"Hey," said Cooper, sitting on the edge of the bed, dressed in camouflage. He dropped a kiss on my forehead. "Good morning, sleepyhead. Dad invited you to go boar-hunting with us. You interested?"

I rolled over in the bed to face him. We'd slept together, but not *slept together.* Cooper had rubbed my back and then held me until I fell asleep, telling me that though he knew he'd have navy blue balls, he thought it might be better for us to start a little closer to the beginning.

It was the first time I'd ever shared a bed for a whole night, for the simple pleasure of sharing it. The intimacy and the trust seemed greater, somehow, than it had the night we'd had sex. The bed was as comfortable and luxurious as it had ever been, but this time I'd slept without dreaming of knives or hands that hurt. The warmth of Cooper's body where our feet touched or his hip brushed mine seeped all the way into my dreams.

I shoved my hair out of my face to meet smiling green eyes. "Hunting? For boars?"

"Yeah. It's kind of an honor that Dad asked me to ask you. He never invites women to go."

Knowing Ted, he had some ulterior motive, which could only be nefarious. He'd said my real name last night before retiring to his study. Ted didn't do things like that by chance. Danny's warning rang in my head. He would look for my weakness. And he'd find it: my weakness was Cooper.

"Ooh, I don't know. I'm not sure hunting is my thing."

"You don't have to carry a weapon. Just come along and be with me in the woods. You don't have to watch if you don't want to, but aren't you even a little curious?"

I was, actually. I'd never seen a wild boar. Or spent much time in the woods, hunting or otherwise, but . . . . "You're going? The whole time?"

"Of course. Please?"

I didn't want to go—I *really* didn't want to go. Ted combined with weaponry did not sound like any kind of a good idea. But Cooper had asked me. Cooper, who'd held me all night and rubbed my hair. Cooper, who'd brought me here, taken care of me, and carried me, literally and otherwise. Cooper, my weakness. We were only starting to feel our way back from the brink I'd taken us to with my silence about prison. I couldn't think of a single way to say no. I needed to talk to him about my worries about Ted, but if I did it now, if I used it as an excuse to skip out on spending time with him, I'd drive a stake into any chance we had together.

I'd have to go. I'd just avoid Ted and blood and dead things the best I could.

"Okay. I'll go if you're going," I said.

His smile lit up his face, lighting an answering glow in my chest. "And later, will you let me take you out to dinner in Charleston? On a date?"

That part would make up for the hunting. "I'd love that. Where will we go? Poogan's Porch?"

"I thought I'd see if I could get even fancier than that. Do you have a dress?"

"I can get one," I said, thinking of Miss Aurelia's black sheath.

"Okay. I'll go make some more coffee." He leaned down and gave me a shy, chaste kiss on the lips. I wanted to put my hands in his freshly-combed hair and pull him down to devour the little dent in his top lip and work my way around his stubble-free chin.

But we were "dating." I'd never done that before, unless you counted a movie or two I'd gone to with Logan Davidson in high school. Anthony and I had mainly hung out at body shops and our bedrooms. I'd never been taken out to a nice dinner before. I didn't know the rules for "dating." Confusing snippets of advice

I'd gotten from my grandmother came back to me: we weren't supposed to "go all the way" until some specific numbered date. And this was the first, officially.

I returned his chaste kiss. I may not have managed full-on chaste.

"Oh, no, you don't," said Cooper, pulling away with difficulty. "We've only got about twenty minutes to get dressed and get some coffee. But I might be able to work you in later tonight."

God, his smile.

When he was gone, I sped through the shower, tossing on the ratty old pink scoop neck and jeans I'd been wearing when I woke up married. Downstairs, Cooper and I gulped coffee and smiled shyly at each other. A note from Caroline said there were muffins in the pantry and that she'd see us later after some landscape appointments she had until lunchtime. I'd just gobbled down a pumpkin spice one when Ted came around the corner, wearing camouflage from head to toe and an orange trucker cap.

"Y'all ready?" Ted looked me up and down. "What you've got on is fine. Cooper'll get you some rubber boots and a camo coat. Come on, now. Coat and boots are out back in the shed, son. Hurry, now." He checked his watch. "Tide's right, and No-Neck'll be here with the boat and the dogs any minute. I'm going on down to the dock and start loading."

"We'll be back by afternoon, won't we?" I asked, thinking of dinner with Cooper.

"Yeah, Dad, I've got to be back early," said Cooper. "Got a call this morning. Floyd says his daughter talked to someone about that place I've got listed out on Isle of Palms and she found out the last owner died in it. She's apparently concerned about the 'aura.' I'll lose the sale if I don't deal with it. I've got to meet them out there at two."

Ted checked his watch again. "We should be back in time. If we can get going sometime this century."

Cooper took me out to Ted's workshop/man-cave and handed me white rubber boots and an over-large but warm camouflage jacket. We held hands down to the end of the Middleton dock, where a boat idled next to the one Cooper had taken me out on. Five metal dog cages covered most of the boat deck. Cooper hollered for Mary Jane and then put his hand on my back and helped me aboard. I peeked into the nearest cage and got an eyeful of the meanest-looking pit bull I'd ever seen. It made no sound, but the malevolent expression on its scarred face made the hair on my neck stand up. Ted and Cooper loaded gear while I gingerly took a seat some distance from the cage. The owner of the dogs gave me a mute wave from behind the wheel of the boat.

"Hi," I said to him. Nicknames are usually on the nose, and No-Neck's was no exception. He had a large bullet-shaped head and wore the green and brown layers of the woodsman. He must have garnered his nickname for the utter lack of any discernible indentation between acne-scarred chin and barrel chest. "I'm Molly."

No-Neck grunted in response and revved the boat engine. Cooper lifted Mary Jane aboard and dislodged a cage to clear room for her.

Ted hopped aboard and untied the rope connecting the front of the boat to the dock, casting a baleful glare at Mary Jane. "If you bring that idiot dog, son, you keep her on a leash and away from the hunting dogs this time." Cooper rolled his eyes and patted his dog, who'd curled at his feet.

No-Neck opened up the engine and the craft jerked forward. Ted chuckled and tossed me a life jacket. "If I remember right, you don't swim. Put that on and you'll be fine. It'll be an interesting experience for a city girl. No-Neck here don't say much, but he knows more about boar dogs than anyone in the county. These are the best-trained bunch I ever saw. Not like that mongrel of Cooper's over there. You'll see your first pig inside an hour after we cut the boat motor."

Cooper held my hand, giving me courage. Ted couldn't do anything to me with Cooper here. "How does this work, exactly?"

No-Neck's chest rumbled in a phlegm-riddled sound I identified as a laugh. Ted chortled along, the chill wind whipping his sleeves.

"We get off the boat," said Ted. "We check our weapons. We let the chase dogs go find the hogs, and then we follow the sound they make when they tear into one. If we need him after we get to the hog, we let Gator take a piece of him 'til we can kill him. Pretty simple."

"Gator?"

"Pit bull, there." Ted kicked at the metal cage containing the scarred dog. "Trained to fight the hogs. Pit bull's the secret weapon, but No-Neck's got 'em all trained so they don't make a sound until they come upon the hog. No warning until they've got him."

"What weapons do you use?" I asked. "Guns?"

"Naw," said Ted, enjoying himself as we sped over the gray waves. I tried to keep my seat and my dignity as the boat bounced. "Knives are more humane. Cleaner kill."

"Knives?" Bile began to rise in my throat. The wake from a nearby boat knocked me off my seat and forced me to uncross my legs.

In answer, he pulled back his coat to reveal a holster with three knife-handles sticking out of the top. The shortest blade was six inches long at least.

I didn't like knives.

After that, the surf got rougher and I leaned into Cooper's bulk for stability and protection from the cold wind. Conversation ceased until we landed at an island not too different from the one where Cooper had taken me to the beach, though this one was bigger, swampier, and covered in grasses and stunted-looking trees. It was sizable enough to justify a rough dock. No-Neck cut the motor and tied up the craft, working with Cooper to ready a pile of gear I assumed must be helpful in bringing back the kill. Cooper held Mary Jane's leash while No-Neck opened the cages to let the dogs out and harnessed the pit bull with an elaborate full-body leash. The other four dogs, though not as fearsome as the pit bull, were still hardly the kind of puppies anyone would want to cuddle up with at night.

"What kind are they?" I asked No-Neck, uninterested in any further conversation with Ted.

Not surprisingly, No-Neck ignored me. Cooper answered. "They're Catahoulas. They're the best for hunting boars." He bent to clip a leash onto Mary Jane's collar.

No-Neck lumbered off the boat and off the dock, dogs in close pursuit, the pit bull held tight and close by his plodding feet. He stood, wordless, waiting for Ted. Ted grinned at me. "Good golly, Miss Molly. You surely don't think I brought you all the way out here to sit on the boat all day, do you? Come on now. You'll get a sunburn on that pretty white skin of yours sitting here."

"Ignore him," said Cooper. "Stick by me."

I zipped my coat and followed Ted, No-Neck, Cooper, and the dogs into the woods.

Within a minute, it became obvious why I had on rubber boots. The fine black pluff mud, wet through from the tides, sucked at my feet, pulling the too-big boots half off with every step. I had to struggle to keep up with the men, moving much faster than my normal speed. Cooper stayed with me until Mary Jane yanked unexpectedly on her leash, startling Cooper, who dropped it.

"Gah!" he said.

"Go catch her!" I said. Cooper took off after the dog, who'd raced off toward the front of our entourage where No-Neck held Gator. The other dogs had streaked noiselessly into the distance, tracking the hog.

"Come on up here and walk with me," said Ted, glancing behind him as Cooper tore past. "You'll want to stick close—I know how to spot a gator slide."

"A gator slide?"

"Yup. Places where the alligators come ashore to sun themselves and then go back in the water. Island's covered with them."

Shit. Of course there were alligators. Between Ted and an alligator, I'd choose Ted. Though it was closer than you might think.

"There you go," he said, as I drew even with him, now watching the ground with far more attention than before. "I believe we may have gotten off on the wrong foot, you and me. I don't see any reason we can't be a little friendlier, now."

Ah. Here we go. He wanted something from me. I looked down at my chest. Not hard to guess what. "How's the Internet search going, Ted?"

"I'd say it's going real well, Mary Kathleen Todd. I found some right interesting things on the Internet. Real shame," he said, looking me over. "I don't think orange would have been your color."

He knew it all. And far from blowing the gasket I'd expected, he looked pleased as punch. A chill made me give a short shiver. I should have guessed. Leverage. He had leverage now. He thought Cooper didn't know. "What do you want, Ted?"

"You're my son's wife," he said, in a syrupy drawl that didn't suit him. "If he's happy, then I'm happy."

Uh-huh. I snorted. More likely he was horny as hell and I was the only woman in the house who wasn't blood-related.

"You and I are going to be close. Real close. I can feel it."

I gave him an incredulous look and veered away, alligators be damned.

He winked at me. "Cooper's a good boy. Ask yourself where he got his skills."

"Ew." I didn't even pretend not to curl my lip at that suggestion.

"Relax," he said, lapping up my discomfort. "I'm enjoying my new knowledge for now. Time enough later on to think of a good use for it. I'm hunting four-legged things today. Nothing comes before hunting. If it helps, No-Neck is happily married and the self-declared protector of four teenage daughters."

It did, but damned if I'd give Ted the satisfaction of saying so.

Off in front of us, the sudden yelping of a single dog in pain floated back to us.

"That's not the Catahoulas," said Ted, picking up the pace. "That's that damn dog of Cooper's. I've told him . . ."

Cooper appeared out of the woods in front of us, moving fast and carrying Mary Jane. "Pit bull bit her. Bad."

"Oh, my God," I said. Blood matted the fur on Mary Jane's front leg, which draped over Cooper's arm at an odd angle. "Why?"

"No idea. She got in Gator's way, I guess. Dammit. This is bad."

"There's a first aid kit in the cooler under the seat of the boat. Alcohol and bandages," said Ted, not making any moves to comfort the whimpering Mary Jane.

"I'll come with you," I said, automatically. Cooper over Ted and knives every day of the week.

"No, you came to see a boar hunt," said Ted. Cooper fought Mary Jane, trying to keep her from hurting herself further. "You haven't seen anything but mud yet."

"No, I'm going with Cooper. I can hold Mary Jane while he bandages."

"You'll get lost dragging along behind him," said Ted. "Cooper's wasting time here. He can run like the wind to that boat. You'd never keep up. Boots too big, am I right?" To Cooper, he said, "What are you waiting for, son? That dog's in pain."

Cooper glanced between me, the person he'd met the previous week, and his father, the person he'd taken orders from for thirty-four years. He shifted the weight of Mary Jane in his arms. "He's right, Molly. I'll wait for y'all at the boat. Stay with Dad and No-Neck."

That stung. Logistically, it made sense, but his choice of his father's demand over mine hurt. Even so, Ted was right. I'd hold up Cooper and Mary Jane. No way could I ask Cooper to walk slower for me when Mary Jane was wounded. Ted wouldn't do anything with No-Neck with us and with Cooper nearby.

Before I could say anything, the distant sound of dogs howling combined with the world's worst sound ever: the heart-stopping screech of something being attacked. The scream echoed in my ears: the full-throated volume of a large and powerful animal, signaling both terror and frightening aggression. I'd heard that pigs squealed or oinked. False. Little girls at birthday parties squealed. Pigs in kids' movies oinked. This sound—desperate, demonic, homicidal—was like something out of a horror movie. Ted disappeared at a full sprint in the direction of the noise. He'd meant what he said—for today, nothing came before the boar hunt.

"Catch up with them," said Cooper, unable to hide his concern for Mary Jane. "Get where you can see if you want, but stay the hell out of the way of the hog. They're ferocious and can take out a man a lot bigger than you." He leaned into me, touching my forehead briefly with his, asking a question.

I gave Mary Jane a pat. "Go. Go get her fixed up. See you soon." Cooper streaked off, toward the boat.

I really did not want to watch whatever was about to happen, but I also didn't want to be left here in the woods to pick my own way back through the alligators. Or past one of that shrieking thing's family members. The woods behind me had already swallowed up Cooper and Mary Jane without a sound. Ted had bigger fish to fry than me, right now. I'd be safe to follow him. The screaming pig left no doubt as to the direction he and No-Neck had headed and that nightmarish sound was all I had to go on to find humans in this jungle. Breathless, I struggled through wet spots and over fallen logs and underbrush and ducked under a low-hanging leafless branch. As I rounded a sucking mud hole, I came upon the scene and braced myself behind a tree trunk.

Judging from the way No-Neck held a straining Gator nearby but out of the immediate battle, the other dogs seemed to have the situation in hand. The pig, the size of a St. Bernard and covered with muddy bristles, fought with everything it was worth, surprising me with huge yellow-white tusks. Its muscles rippled as it thrashed in every direction. The dogs tore into whatever part of the hide they could grab, but the hog bucked, threatening them with the tusks, and occasionally managed to toss a dog off. If they were hurt, and they had to be hurt, the dogs kept at it anyway, shaking off the pain and jumping back into the fray with primal barbarity.

I'd seen animal fights on TV, and real fights in prison, but nothing had prepared me for the desperate need I had to turn away, to separate the combatants, to put someone, anyone, out of misery. I did nothing. I stood, rooted to the ground.

Ted pulled a long knife from his holster in a single motion, years of practiced grace in play. The sight of the blade churned my insides into a panicked nausea and I dug my fingernails into the bark of the tree. He strode up to the struggling animals, unafraid and unconcerned by their life-and-death battle. His face contorted into a kind of fierce joy, such an unmistakable bloodlust and resolve that my heart stuttered and a gasp escaped before I could stop it.

The word "Run!" had formed on my lips. I didn't even know who I thought should run.

"Stick it!" yelled No-Neck.

Ted moved with the controlled elegance of a big cat, arching to add strength and speed to his perfect strike. The blade flashed, driving into the struggling underbelly of the pig, straight into its heart. Ted pulled it out again; thrill making his every muscle more powerful. The blood spurted in waves from the animal's wound as its heart pumped itself into oblivion. My vision darkened and blurred.

"Dead pig, dogs!" commanded No-Neck.

The dogs subsided at the words, understanding that their job was done. I was surprised to find myself on the ground, the wet mud of the swamp seeping through the knees of my jeans. My fingertips were bloody, the skin and nails broken by the rough bark of the tree I'd been gripping.

Blood.

Kneeling in soaked pants.

Death spurts through sliced skin, following a departing blade.

The woods disappear and are replaced with peeling wallpaper. The smell of spilled alcohol shoves aside the pluff mud.

My scalp burns where she hauls my head back, exposing my throat. Desperate, I try peeling her fingers loose but she only grips harder. Hair begins to rip. I grab the soft underside of her arm and pinch with all the adrenaline I have. The knife clatters to the floor with her shriek and slides, like a miracle, toward my scrabbling feet. I'm faster. I get the handle and I back away, blade vibrating to the beat of my pounding pulse in front of me. She's thrown away reason or caution or humanity. She laughs, mouth a wide rictus. I can see the ravages the drugs have done to her teeth. Her cackle is terrifying.

The handle slides in my sweating fingers, but I don't drop it. She takes another step toward me and then another and another. I can't do it. I can't shove it in her heart. She's my mother. I lower the knife beside my leg, handle in a one-handed death grip, blade pointed at her. I back up until the wall stops me.

She's my mother. She won't . . .

She's my mother.

She turns away for a second. Just a second, as if to say something to the man. I think maybe it's over. Then she whips back. Goes for my neck, with the freak speed only addicts have, but she misjudges by millimeters. I avoid right and she attacks left and we move together like dancers in mirror-image tandem. Our bodies collide with a crunch and the outstretched knife slices into her leg, at the top. With an animal's grunt, she crumples to the floor. A door closes, as the man evaporates into the night, leaving me there alone with the blood and the ruin of her life.

And mine.

I'd killed by accident.

I'd never had the talent—the skill—Ted did. I turned again to look at the dead hog in its pool of blood. No-Neck bowed his head and said a mumbled prayer; some kind of thanks for the life of the animal that had died. The dogs paced, or rested, panting, on the ground near the dead pig.

None of that drew my gaze like Ted.

The sight of him made the contents of my stomach heave. His eyes glittered an unnatural blue. Covered in mud and blood, he vibrated with more joy than any hunter who wanted an exotic meal should. This was ecstasy. Ted was experiencing visceral, physical . . . I could think of no word for it but arousal.

I couldn't tear my eyes away. He held eye contact, his white grin undiminished, telegraphing something to me. He made no move to clean the bloody knife or to put it away. He stood there, electric eyes burning with almost sexual intensity.

Unable to move, I stared at him.

He raised the still-dripping knife to me, blade up and tipped toward me. The message was crystal clear: even at death-dealing, he was better than me, stronger, quicker, more vicious. The alpha killer. The blood made the knife shine, like a trophy.

Like a promise.

My hands went into the mud to keep me from collapsing. It wasn't just me he'd threatened. I wasn't the first to see Ted raise a knife as a means of control. *I knew it . . .*

My stomach gave a warning heave.

Because now I knew.

CHAPTER TWENTY-ONE

I knew in the oldest part of my brain, with the same certainty that I knew my name, that I knew ten times ten is a hundred, that I'd known I'd be convicted. *I knew.*

Lynette had never gone to the airport.

She'd said something Ted didn't want to hear. I'd never know whether she'd held him off and denied him one too many times, or told him she was done with him, or threatened to go to Cooper or Ted's business partners, or the police. It was possible she only told him Cooper had cut his hours and she couldn't come by as often anymore.

Nobody told Ted no.

He'd taken her hunting, under some threat from her diary or something, and come away with a bloody knife, a plane ticket to pay for, and a car to plant at the airport. Maybe he'd planned it and maybe it was the heat of passion. No way to know.

But I knew for sure Lynette had never left McClellanville, South Carolina.

I glanced around, panicked, thanking the lord that No-Neck was here. Watching. The island was deserted. It could only be reached by boat. It was swampy and alligator-ridden. Ted had said he knew how to recognize the alligator spots. An easy—and gruesome—way to dispose of a body forever.

Oh, my God, the alligators.

Wait a minute, screamed my evolved brain. Ted was Cooper's father. Caroline's father. He couldn't be a killer. He lived a normal life. He'd held Caroline over his head in a hurricane in the dark. He paid to have his house decorated for Christmas the way his wife used to do it. The town lined up to slap his back and depended on his businesses for its economy. I had to be overreacting. It wasn't possible.

Yet, it was.

I was a killer, after all. I wasn't the kind of person who cheats on my spouse, tries to rape my own daughter-in-law, or threatens to ruin my son's life, yet I still went to prison for fifteen years for killing. Almost every killer lived a normal life at some point. How much of a stretch was it to believe Ted—who'd practically had an orgasm in front of me while dripping in pig's blood—could be a killer, too?

Life was so fragile. Hadn't the pig been a fierce predator a moment ago? Death was so simple: a quick flash of a knife, blood frantic to escape. I hadn't even intended it. With a powerful body and a total absence of morals, Ted could kill as easily as flicking away a gnat.

And then no more thinking was possible. Absolute certainty and simple biology put an end to it. I lurched to my feet and raced to get as far away as I could. Bracing a hand on a tree, I threw up, retching up all the contents of my stomach but not the sick terror of my realization. That would stay.

"Aw," said Ted, far too close to me. "That's okay. Sometimes that happens to the girls. It's why I don't usually bring y'all. Little bit surprising on you, given what all you've seen, but I guess you never know."

I stood straight, wiping my mouth, and stared him down. A look I'd learned in prison, giving no quarter. "It was kind of a messy kill, wouldn't you say? That's never happened to me before. Let me know when you're ready to go."

Ted laughed softly. Appreciating my words. Believing my bravado.

For now.

I spent thirty more minutes crashing around in the swamp, careful to stay within three steps of No-Neck at all times. I asked him about his daughters and he paused to pull their pictures out of his wallet. I didn't quite catch their names given his mumble, but his affection was indisputable. On the way back to the boat, we saw one other pig, but it was small—an adolescent—and No-Neck deemed it unworthy of his dogs' attentions. They stood down with a single command.

Though I hated to claim any weakness, I pretended my over-large boots made it impossible to keep up with Ted. Whenever he spoke, I ignored him. I used my time bushwhacking in ankle-deep swamp mud to come up with multiple theories and ways to test them.

When we got to the boat, Cooper was asleep, Mary Jane by his side, neatly bandaged and calmed. No-Neck and Ted woke Cooper and they loaded the gear, the dogs, and the tarped pig carcass, and we were underway.

"How was it? Not too bad?" asked Cooper, holding my hand.

I had no idea how, or if, I should tell him what I'd seen, much less how I'd interpreted it. I couldn't do it now, though, with Ted feet away, still flushed with thrill and wearing an ugly knowing smile. "I don't know that I'd go again, but it was interesting."

"I prefer other kinds of hunting, myself. You never have to go again if you don't want to."

"Thanks. Is Mary Jane going to be okay?"

"I think so. I called the vet and they said I did everything right. She's got an appointment tomorrow."

"Poor baby." I rubbed the injured dog's back and held her in place as we flew over the water.

When the boat finally docked at the Middleton house, I jumped out. No-Neck and Ted planned to take the hog carcass up to No-Neck's place, further down the Intra-Coastal Waterway. Apparently No-Neck was a fan of butchering it and celebrating with buddies as they slow-cooked it right away. Cooper and I carried Mary Jane into her favorite spot in the back yard. I cleaned her up as best I could and fetched her water bowl, her blanket, and a treat, while Cooper hurried to change out of his hunting clothes for his client appointment. Once he left to calm the Isle of Palms woman concerned about auras, the house was empty. Caroline had left another note, saying she'd gone to run some errands and get Mia from school. She asked me to call her cell if I wanted her to bring me some dinner from Mt. Pleasant.

I was alone. Not wasting a minute, I ditched my hunting gear and borrowed Caroline's yellow dishwashing gloves. My first stop would be Ted's study, though I didn't really have any idea what I was looking for. When he'd retrieved his wallet before going with faux-helpless-female Miss Aurelia to check out her car, he'd unlocked his desk with a key that had either been on his person or hidden in the room somewhere. I prayed it was in the room.

Almost clinically, I noted that Leandra hadn't put any Christmas decorations in here. Interesting, given Ted's professed devotion to the holidays the way his wife used to do them. The room contained the sofa and two wing chairs, the coffee table with a glass top that displayed shells, the mini-bar and fridge, and the massive desk, desk chair, and credenza.

I'd learned all about fingerprints in my trial. I put on the gloves before I touched anything, the cheerful yellow rubber somehow making me feel even guiltier about what I was doing. As a preliminary, I ran my hands along all four walls to make sure there were no hidden panels or bookcases, then checked the desk and credenza. Locked. All the drawers and cabinets were locked. Ted was exactly the secretive sort who kept nothing on the surface of the desk except a green-shaded lamp, a closed laptop, a blotter, a landline, and a heavy crystal paperweight. The credenza had two more lamps and a printer. I checked around, under, behind and inside all of these and found no key. I lifted every bottle and can in the fridge, and examined all the liquor in the light. No key had been dropped into a bottle. I even ran my hands over the horrible elk head and its antlers. Nothing.

I pulled all the cushions off the chairs and the sofa and found nothing in the cracks except two dimes, a penny, and some crumpled foil from Hershey's Kisses. I even pulled up the rug's corners and checked under it as far beneath as I could without moving furniture.

Starting to feel desperate, I pulled out the drawer of the coffee table that held the shell collection and the baby alligator skeleton. When he went to get the wallet, it hadn't taken him long to find the key. I lifted the closest shell—nothing. Then another and another. This key had to be in this room. How had I missed it?

At the moment I decided I couldn't lift every one of the hundreds of shells in the glass display and praying I wouldn't have to touch the alligator skull, I knocked aside a large whelk like the ones Cooper and I had collected. It rattled.

Finally. The key dropped into my hand. I put the whelk back, careful to note the brown and white tortoiseshell markings on it.

Ted's desk, made of dark wood with brass drawer pulls, would have fit fine in Robert E. Lee's study. The key worked. I didn't find Ted's wallet—he must have that with him. The middle drawer held an assortment of normal office stuff: pens, Post-It notes, a stapler, some flash drives. The bigger drawers on either side held hanging files, all of it paper, mostly household things like insurance policies, deeds, bank records, contracts, manuals, and the like. One smaller top drawer held more of a mix of stuff—fishing lures, Christmas cards, loose ammunition, an empty needlepointed glasses case, a silver cup full of change. In the back, a pair of handcuffs, tiny key inserted, shocked me, though they probably shouldn't have. Ted would be into handcuffs.

Nothing except the paper, and I didn't have time to go through it all now. To be sure, I pushed it forward to see the back of the drawer. One volume of Lynette's diary had been stuffed down behind the hanging files. Nearly hyperventilating with excitement, I grabbed it, only to discover it was from her high school years. Clumps of pages at the midpoint and near the end had been torn out. I was tempted to read the teenage handwriting, but I'd be wasting time. She hadn't known Ted and Cooper then. There'd be no clues to the immediate problem in there.

Where were the other four volumes? Or was this not one of the ones that had been on the shelf? Disappointment settled over me. I'd found nothing useful, other than that Ted did indeed fetishize his son's wife by keeping her journal. What had I been expecting, anyway? A signed note on the top of a pile, confessing to murder with Ted's name signed in blood? I'd check the shed next. While I tried to regroup, I idly pulled out the handcuffs again, snorting in contempt. I tossed them back, where they bounced off the glasses case.

Wait. Ted didn't wear glasses. Everyone in the Middleton family had either perfect vision or enough vanity to wear contact lenses. The case was a soft one, empty, needlepointed in black, white, and dark blue swirls by a skillful craftsman.

Or craftswoman. The swirls gave way to initials in a clever way at the bottom edge. "L.A.N." Ted's initials were E.C.M, the same as Cooper's. Leandra, the only person I'd seen inside this house whose name began with L, was a Scott. I remembered, because of the sheer number of uncharitable thoughts I'd attached to it. Had Lynette's maiden name started with N? If so, what on earth was Ted doing with this in his desk? Lynette must have worn glasses, or sunglasses. Caroline had found a wipe for glasses and a frame repair kit in the Rubbermaid box that had belonged to Lynette.

I pocketed the glasses case and the journal, locked the desk, and replaced the key in the whelk.

Next, the workshop.

Which, of course, was locked. I spent fifteen futile minutes looking for one of those fake rocks that holds a key, even while knowing that this key would be on Ted's keyring, which he probably had with him. Nothing. I sat down, unsure what to do next, on an iron bench near a huge waxy-leaved shrub at the edge of the manicured garden.

With horror, I imagined the conversation I'd never be able to have with Cooper: "Your dad killed your wife after having sex with her for months. I know that because he hit on me and because he raised a knife after killing a boar and because he stole her diaries and because he kept one with torn pages."

I could never say those things. Even to me, it all sounded ridiculous. Even rearranged to sound less ludicrous, I'd be asking him to believe that his father was a rapist and a murderer. I pulled the glasses case out of my pocket and turned it over and over in my hands.

I'd known Cooper less than two weeks, and we'd had a major breach of trust in that time which was all my fault. This morning, he'd listened to his father's advice to take Mary Jane back to the boat unthinkingly. Trying to get him to believe something that preposterous would require a trust level that would take months to build.

In the meantime, I'd just have to stay far from Ted. I snorted to myself. Cooper couldn't have found a wife who was better at staying far away from someone in the same house. Ma had taught me that skill.

At loose ends, I wandered over to check on Mary Jane. She lay like a comatose frat boy with a bum basketball ankle in a patch of sunny grass, but she woke and sat up at my approach. I checked to make sure she had water and then crouched to rub her belly. I shifted the glasses case to the other hand to make it easier.

She took a good long sniff of it, then twisted away from my fingers behind her ears. She let out a low "woof" and struggled to stand.

"No, lay down, baby. You need to rest that leg," I said, as if she could understand me. She paid no attention. She took another sniff of the glasses case, and on three legs, limped away with more energy than she displayed most of the time.

With surprising success and with something resembling purpose, Mary Jane staggered in a straight line to a corner of the shed. Unable to take the weight off her good front foot, she nosed at a spot on the ground. She let out a series of short barks, the first noise other than happy welcome-home-Cooper whines I'd heard from her.

"What is going on with you, girl?"

On closer inspection, there was a faint difference in the grass color in a line about eight inches wide from the corner of the shed closest to the house running all the way to a utility area on the back wall of the main building. A utility trench, most likely to extend electricity or cable television or something from the house to the shed. It hadn't been recently dug. The grass grew thick across it and the ground was hard-packed under my toe when I kicked it.

Ted had told me he'd had water hooked up to this shed some years before for his sink. If I asked Caroline, I'd bet she'd tell me it was about five years ago. I had a strong idea I might find something pretty damn incriminating if I dug up the end of that trench.

I'd need a shovel.

I'd also need to work on arranging that imaginary conversation with Cooper into something less than ludicrous a lot earlier than I'd hoped.

Now I had no choice. I'd need to tell Cooper what I knew after all.

CHAPTER TWENTY-TWO

In my life, I hadn't spent anywhere near the hours primping that most girls do, but I gave it everything I had that night. I showered, shaved, plucked, perfumed, moisturized, used some kind of hair thickener and hair smoother and hair glosser Caroline had put in Cooper's bathroom and spent at least ten minutes—nine more than usual—on my makeup. Miss Aurelia donated a different sheath dress, this one a deep blue with a low neck that fit so perfectly over my chest and hips I wondered if she'd gone shopping with me in mind. I called Caroline and told her I'd skip the takeout and asked if she had tips for dressing up for a nice Charleston restaurant. She made me borrow her nude heels, which were half a size too big but much more comfortable than Miss Aurelia's.

By the time Cooper came pounding up the stairs at six, I looked as good as I ever had in my life. He came through the bedroom door, loosening an orange Clemson tie.

When he saw me, he closed the door and tossed aside the tie slowly, his eyes darkening. The room filled with unmet need.

"Aren't we . . ." I swallowed, finding my voice in the face of the concentrated desire radiating from him and the embarrassing reaction of my own body. "Aren't we going out?"

He gave me a rueful grin. "Oh, holy God. You're all dressed up. Yes, we have seven-thirty reservations at Husk, but I'd be happy, more than happy," he said, Adam's apple bobbing as he swallowed, "to change plans."

My turn to swallow. He'd begun unbuttoning his dress shirt. "Um. Are we changing plans?"

He closed his eyes and blew out a breath, a half-smile playing around the corner of his mouth. "No, we're going. I can be patient. I'm only changing my shirt." He tossed aside the shirt and yanked the undershirt off by the back of the collar.

I nearly gasped. Well-lit half-naked Cooper was even more glorious than night-time half-naked Cooper. "M-maybe we should stay here."

"Up to you," he said, advancing on me. He put a fingertip under my chin, tilting it up until our eyes met. Lowering his head, he kissed me, deep and sweet, being careful of my hair and eye makeup.

No. We needed to talk about bloody knives and needs for shovels. I pushed aside the delicious shudder at his bare-chested embrace. If we didn't get out of this room soon, I'd be hopelessly distracted. "We'd better go. This might be my only chance to eat in a fancy Charleston restaurant. If you take off any more clothes, we might have to stay here for a week."

"I don't think I'd mind. But okay. We'll go." He disappeared into the closet for a fresh shirt. From the depths of the closet, he said, "And this won't be your only chance."

I dug my injured fingernails into my palms, but this time, it didn't hurt.

Going out on a date in a dress and heels to a white tablecloth restaurant was new for me. It felt like being in a movie—one starring some Hollywood It-Girl with a perfect body and the face of an angel who you never doubted would get the happiest of endings.

I'd never yet seen a movie in which the female romantic lead is herself a killer and who has plans to suggest over dessert that perhaps she and her new father-in-law have that in common. I put it off, wanting the fantasy of sharing a table with a beautiful man who looked at me like he'd rather have me for dinner than any of the delicious farm-to-table food in front of us. We talked about teachers we'd loved and which superhero we'd be (Cooper: straight up Superman, me: Jean Grey), what food we could go without for the rest of our lives (Cooper: Brussels sprouts, me:

radishes). The dinner flew by.

"What three things would you take to a deserted island?" asked Cooper. His foot brushed my ankle, making it hard to think.

"Um. A really big book. A fishing net, maybe, and . . ." *You. I would take you.* "Um. I don't know. What else can I take? Oh, I know. I saw it on TV once. The world's biggest roll of duct tape. You can make anything out of duct tape. What would you take?"

"Duct tape is an excellent idea. That's one. A pot to boil water. What else?"

"Don't you need some kind of way to catch food?"

"Already got it. Third thing I'd take is you, and you've got a net." He raised his eyebrows to add a touch of lightness to it, but the hint of nervousness in his eyes told me he meant it.

Delight and hope and a jolt of joy lifted my insides, while despair at having to voice my suspicions about his father pulled me back down.

"Oh, Cooper. I wanted to say I'd take you too, but I didn't know if . . ." I reached for his hands. He took mine, heat spreading where our skin touched.

"Well, now you know."

Unable to speak, I stared at him, watching his pupils grow and blot out the green. My throat went dry and the blood rushed in my ears. *Oh, God*, I wanted him. Here. Now, in this former Charleston mansion with its heart pine floors and wide-spaced tables. My tongue came out to wet my parched lips and then the heat rose in my cheeks as I realized I'd actually licked my lips while staring at him like some cleavage-baring chick in an old hair band video.

Oh, shit, I had the cleavage going on, too.

He smiled at the blush. Or the lip-licking, I didn't know which. "Are you ready?" he asked, his voice husky and hot. "Or do you want dessert . . . here?"

I would have liked nothing better than to head straight home to McClellanville and have my dessert in the middle of Cooper's bed and then in the shower and then against the wall in the TV room and then on the pristine kitchen island and anywhere else we had the stamina to christen. But I had something that needed saying.

"Wait. Maybe we'd better order coffee. There are some things I need to talk to you about."

"Things?"

I would have laughed at the carefully-schooled terror on his face, if I didn't have to say the things I had to say. "Nothing about me. You know all my deepest secrets now. It's not that. It's your dad."

His face relaxed. "Dad?"

"Before I say anything more, you should know that Caroline and Miss Aurelia know part of this, but not all of it."

He didn't like it that they knew something he didn't. "What?"

"Okay. Please know how much I hate having to tell you the things I'm about to tell you."

"Say it."

I gulped. "The day before Thanksgiving, your dad invited me out to his workshop to watch him cut up the deer tenderloin we ate. When we were out there, he kind of hit on me."

Cooper's face closed over. "I think you must have misunderstood."

"No. I didn't. He put his hand on my face. He's said some other things since. But that's not all of it."

The waiter, another hipster who must have belonged to the same bearded waiter clique as the one at Poogan's Porch, approached and took my coffee order. Cooper sat impassive.

Oh, if only I didn't have to say these things.

"What is the rest of it?" he asked, stone-faced, when the waiter left.

"He told me . . ." I'd known he would not handle this well. So far this had gone about as badly as I'd imagined it the first time. I wiped my damp hands on my blue skirt under the table and then remembered it didn't belong to me. I clenched them again. "He said some things about Lynette."

Cooper folded his napkin tighter and tighter. "Go on . . ."

With the absolute worst timing, the waiter brought the coffee and made a huge fuss about scraping crumbs off the table, bringing me a clean spoon to stir in cream, naming the farm that was the source of the cream and the fact that the sugar was brown and organic. Every word out of his mouth made my blood pressure rise. "Thanks so much," I said, desperately praying he'd go away.

"No problem, ma'am. Will there be anything else?"

"Just the check," said Cooper, through gritted teeth.

"Will that be one check or two?"

"One," ground out Cooper. The waiter got the message and scurried away. "Dad said what about Lynette?"

Nothing to do but blurt it out. "Enough to make me absolutely sure that he and Lynette had something going on."

Time ticked by as I watched his face. I squeezed my hands under the table. What would I do if he didn't believe this much? With agonizing slowness, his emotions gave way, one after the other: first outrage, then disbelief, then consternation. Finally, the tiniest possibility that it was true—I assumed he'd recalled and considered all the evidence he'd ignored at the time—gained a foothold and his mouth dropped. "He said that?"

"Not exactly, but some of the ways he described her looks sent up red flags. I asked him outright and he didn't say no. He just smiled and said I had a vivid imagination or something. He also said that shortly before she . . . was gone, you changed your work hours to be home more with Lynette and she spent less time with him. Miss Aurelia and Caroline separately suspected something was going on."

Cooper's shoulders dropped. "My . . . my work hours?"

I'd gotten through. I couldn't have known he'd changed his hours around that time if his father hadn't told me. He propped an elbow on the table and rubbed his forehead hard enough to wrinkle it. "She . . ." His voice came out in a crackle of dismay. "She was so lethargic. Depressed. She slept all the time. Miss Aurelia spoke to me about it. She said I needed to be home more, to get her to go to the doctor, or to cheer her up." He looked up, eyes wide. "Oh, holy God. Did Miss Aurelia know and not tell me? Oh, I feel sick. Dad. With *Dad*. Under my nose."

"No. She didn't know at the time, only suspected something was wrong, but she didn't know. She said she saw Lynette feeding pages from her diary to a fire one day, after you found out some embarrassing thing. She thought Lynette might not have been a willing participant."

"Shit, Molly, I'm not under the impression that Dad has been celibate all these years since Mama died, but he's not the kind to force a woman."

Here it was.

"I think he is. Maybe not physically, but he is absolutely the kind to manipulate people to make them do things. He made clear he was interested in me, and when I told him no, he said if he chose, he could make me. He told me he could tell you that your mother slept around. I laughed at that; I knew you'd never believe that. So he tossed out another one: that he'd ruin your reputation at work. Lie and say you were a drunk or a drug addict. I never doubted for a second he'd do it if he felt like it. He knew that was something that would be guaranteed to hurt you, and he knew I . . ." I gulped water to fight off my dry mouth. "He knew I cared enough about you already not to let that happen."

"That client appointment today . . ." Cooper swallowed. "She's the daughter of one of Dad's friends. She said she got a call from a man who told her someone had died in the house she was about ready to buy. She walked away. I couldn't stop it." He gripped the table edge. "She said the man refused to give his name."

"We don't know that was your dad." But I bet it was. It happened right after Cooper moved me back into the house.

Cooper blinked. He was still absorbing. "And Mama didn't sleep around."

"No. Of course she didn't. I didn't know her, obviously, but Miss Aurelia told me about her. All good things. They were friends. Your mother was absolutely faithful to your dad. It was your dad who cheated. She knew about it and looked the other way. But she loved you. She stayed with your dad for you and Caroline, even knowing what Ted was up to. Miss Aurelia said she lived for you."

The waiter brought the check in the leather folder. Cooper slapped a credit card on it without even looking at it. The waiter rushed away, finally having sensed our desire not to linger. I stared unseeing at his back, the delay causing my brain to stick on the last thing I'd said. Something hovered beyond my reach, something uneasy and bothersome, like forgetting to turn off the oven or to write down that vital thing you remember right before you fall asleep. What?

"I don't even know how to handle this," said Cooper, fighting for control. That waiter had better bring back his credit card quick before Cooper lost it. And he would lose it—once he heard everything.

"That's not all, Cooper. There's more I need to tell you, but that's the part that Caroline and Miss Aurelia know. They agree that it's likely that Ted and Lynette had a relationship. Caroline saw her once, coming from his shed crying. Inside he was adjusting his clothes. They agree that whatever relationship they had made Lynette far from happy, and that it likely is at least part of the reason she's not here now."

"Oh, shit. Stop. I don't know if I want to hear any more. I need to be drunk to hear any more."

The waiter brought back Cooper's credit card. He signed the receipt in a daze, and I scooped up the card and handed it to him. "Let's go outside. Come on."

He followed, making it outside without stumbling or crying. Out on the street, the air was chilly and a fine rain fell, making the stone pavement shiny. I'd been too vain to wear a fleece jacket over my dress, but I figured the cold was the bed of nails I deserved for saying the things to Cooper that would hurt him. So far he hadn't asked me why I was telling him, but he needed to know.

We walked up King Street. Even at night, tourists still passed in groups and families, but most of our fellow pedestrians were either leaving work late or out on a date. Their smiles and laughter stung: I'd known this date had to end like this, but it didn't mean I didn't wish it had been different.

"Okay," Cooper growled, his anger only barely leashed. "Finish. What other life-wrecking things do you have to tell me?"

I laid a hand on his arm. He didn't shake it off, but he made no move to touch me. A sob rose in my throat, cutting off my air. This was it. Cooper loved his father. He would not take this well. He would not believe me. This was my last chance to turn back and hide—or do the right thing.

If I told him what I suspected about his father, it would break us. Only a fool would think he would believe me over his father. Cooper would cast me aside. It would be so much easier to keep it to myself. To let him continue to believe his father was one of the good people. To let him think that adultery was Ted's worst fault.

Yet if I kept silent, I put my own happiness above the safety of Cooper and Caroline and Mia and everyone they loved. If I said nothing, there might come a day when Ted decided he didn't want a half-Asian granddaughter going out in the world with his blood running through her veins. Or Caroline could marry someone Ted hated even more than Danny. Ted had experience now dealing with problematic people.

Cooper needed to know. During my trial and before, I'd done nothing to protect myself, but I could give Cooper the chance I hadn't taken. I could give him the information he needed to take action for his family.

Silence wasn't an option anymore. I took a deep breath.

"Something happened during the hunt today—after you took Mary Jane to the boat."

"Go on."

"Your dad stabbed the boar. When he did, I remembered everything about what happened with my mother. It was an accident; you were right."

"I told you," said Cooper, though waiting for the bad news. "And?"

"Your dad got kind of . . . excited about the kill. More than excited. And then he raised the bloody knife to me. In a certain way. He was telling me something with it. He knows about my crime, by the way. He knows it was a knife, I think. He was saying what he could do with a knife. Better than what I did. And suddenly I knew what he did do with it, five years ago. I think . . ."

Cooper stopped walking and swung me around to face him. He gripped both my arms hard enough to hurt. The oh-so-Charlestonian gas lanterns adorning the entrance of the shoe store in front of us lit the rain on his furious face in a flickering glow. It made me think of fire and flame and hell.

"Before you say another word," he hissed, his grip tightening to the point of pain, "you better make damn sure that what comes out of your mouth next is the absolute truth. Facts. Not guesses. Not opinions. Because if you're making this up, to try to gain some advantage, some . . ." He shook his head, the expression on his face as deadly as any I'd seen in prison. "I will walk away from you right now."

"Fine," I said, shaking off his hands on my frozen arms. I'd known he would react this way. Now all that was left was the words. "Facts it is. Here are the facts. Something was odd between your dad and your wife. Caroline saw her running out of your dad's shed crying. She was so depressed she slept all the time. He told me he'd ruin your life to get me to do what he wanted like it was nothing. He put his hand on my face. He hit on me. He told me if you had sex skills, you'd inherited them from him. He commented on the quality of my 'tits.' Lynette's diaries used to be in the spare bedroom, and then after I asked him if he had a thing with Lynette, someone moved them. It wasn't Caroline or Miss Aurelia. I'd bet you didn't even know they were there. He raised a bloody knife to me over the dead pig. Those things are all facts. All the truth."

I swallowed, knowing everything that had come to matter to me had gone—smashed on the rocks of my own choices. Every relationship I'd forged. Everything that kept me from being the lonely ghost drifting through life I'd been before Vegas.

"And here's one more. Caroline found an unused plane ticket in Lynette's box in the closet. A ticket to Roanoke through Dulles that was scheduled for two days after she left. She didn't change the ticket. Lynette—or someone—bought a completely new one to Charlotte. Today I found a needlepointed glasses case with her initials on it in your dad's office. Her maiden name started with an N, didn't it?"

"Nolan. It was Nolan." The words were an involuntary whisper.

"I was holding the glasses case when I went to check on Mary Jane and she sniffed it. She got up, even hurt, and limped over to the place where there's a covered-over utility trench going from the workshop to the house and barked to get my attention. She was showing me something. That trench is about five years old, isn't it? Your dad had water put into his workshop five years ago, didn't he?"

He had. I could see from Cooper's shell-shocked expression that he had. He nodded, confirming it.

"Mary Jane isn't a barker. You know she isn't."

In the lamplight, Cooper looked as old as the cobblestones. "No."

"I know it sounds crazy, but I think we need to dig there. There's something there."

Cooper drove all forty minutes back to McClellanville without a single word. He gripped the wheel tightly and drove way too fast. The rain dried up somewhere around Mt. Pleasant and the moon came out. I hadn't realized how much silence the windshield wipers had filled until they stopped. I kept from crying by reciting lists of states and U.S. presidents in my head. I'd survived alone before. I'd survive again.

Back at the house, Cooper stalked upstairs to make sure his father was still at the hog feasting. Apparently he was, because Cooper came downstairs in jeans and a hoodie and kept moving outside. He said nothing to me, but I scurried after him, kicking off the heels in favor of my flip flops. By the time the screen door banged shut behind me, Cooper had retrieved a shovel from somewhere.

"Where?" he demanded, rage written all over him.

"There. At that end." I pointed to the spot where Mary Jane

had barked.

Without another word, he handed me a heavy black flashlight, turned his back to me, and began digging in the dampened ground.

I wanted to ask him whether he needed to be careful, whether there were electric lines in there, but I figured he might take my head off if I said anything at all, and also that he probably knew what the trench had in it. Sure enough, after a couple of shovelfuls, he made more delicate stabs at the dirt, moving smaller heaps out of the way.

All I could do was stand there and try to keep my hand steady as I shone the flashlight, illuminating the movement of the shovel. If there was nothing in that spot, everything was over. Cooper and I would be done. I'd leave here and lose Caroline and Miss Aurelia, too. I'd gambled everything on this, but even so, part of me still hoped I was wrong. The pain Cooper would feel if I was right might kill him.

But I'd had no choice. Ted had killed Lynette. Every cell in my body knew it. He would know I knew it too. He would hardly welcome me into the family without expecting payment. I'd have to live with the knowledge that he was governed by no moral code and would ruin any of our lives whenever it suited him, if he chose to let us keep them at all.

I'd lived long enough fearing attacks that came with no warning. No more.

The shovel clanged as Cooper tossed it aside.

I stepped closer, in time to get a hand onto Cooper's back as he sagged to his knees.

At the bottom of the hole was the dirty white curve of a water pipe. Next to that, three inches of stained leather, shredded and curled by time and the shovel, poked out of the freshly-turned earth.

Pink leather, the shade a first-grade teacher might choose for a purse. The kind of thing that might hold a credit card, necessary to buy a plane ticket to Charlotte.

There was only one way that purse could be here, in this spot.

Cooper would know that.

Any tiny hope I might still have had that I'd been wrong evaporated with Cooper's anguished howl.

CHAPTER TWENTY-THREE

Cooper's spine seemed to melt as he pitched forward toward the hole in the ground, hands out.

"Stop! Don't touch it!" I leaped forward to grab his arm and yank it back, hard.

"I need to see it. I need to know for sure it's hers. I need to . . ." He muttered as if unhinged.

"No. Do not touch it with your fingers. You'll leave fingerprints. They'll have to eliminate you from the possible suspects anyway. You know they always think it's the husband. We'll have to call the police, but for the love of God, Cooper, please don't get your fingerprints on it."

With all my heart, I wished I didn't know these things; wished I'd learned them from TV crime dramas like everyone else. I'd had the dubious benefit, however, of listening to a fingerprint expert describe the unique swoops of my own fingerprints on a bloody kitchen knife in court and watching the judge nod along with his damning words. Fingerprints don't lie.

Cooper fell back on his heels, pain written all over him. He pushed the air in front of him away. "This doesn't make sense. This has to be something else. I didn't put this here. Dad's not dumb enough to put this here. If he killed Lynette, why would he bury her purse here? He'd get rid of it—burn it, dump it in Charleston Harbor. He'd never be stupid enough to bury it five feet from where he watches TV. Dad's too smart for that. Someone else must have put it here."

"Cooper . . ." I knew better than most that sometimes smart people do dumb things in connection with crime. And sometimes smart people do smart things they hope others will think are dumb.

I thought it likely that some kind of framing was going on here, but it might not be *of* Ted. It might be *by* Ted. Everyone knew they always suspect the husband. Why not add a little insurance to "discover" if the heat gets high?

"I don't know, Cooper. We'll have to figure it out." I reached a tentative arm to his bicep. He threw it off.

"I don't want to figure it out. Oh, holy . . ." A moan broke free of his throat, cutting off his words. "She's dead, Molly. This means Lynette is dead. All this time I thought . . . Do you realize she has to be dead?"

"Yes. I think that's what it means."

"But Dad couldn't have . . . He's not the kind who'd . . ." He glanced at me, the pain and helplessness not unlike that in the dying boar's eyes. "I need to . . ." He got to his feet like an old man. "I can't be around you right now. I don't want to . . . Go inside. I'm going for a walk."

"Cooper," I said, my heart breaking into deadening chunks. "We need to call the police."

"Oh. Yeah. You do what you want, then," he said, his voice hollow and robotic. "I'll just be . . . somewhere else." He stumbled a little as he turned. "I just need to . . . go."

I let him, knowing he might forever blame me for being the bearer of this worst news of his life. I'd learned he needed processing time, and I had to let him have it. He disappeared in the direction of the woods. Near the house, a car door slammed.

Ted had come home. I had to get away from here, but first, I had to get Caroline and Mia out as well. Ted would find that hole when dawn came.

I met Ted in the foyer. His gait was uneven—he'd been drinking, and driving, apparently, as well. Ted had the sort of skin that turned red as a beet when he was drunk.

"Well, well!" he boomed, too loud for a man in a house with a sleeping child in it. "If it isn't the big titty girl." He made an exaggerated movement with his head, looking me over. Instinctively, I stepped to the side, putting the round hall table between us.

"You, Miss Molly, are a vision. Look at that dress. You usually cover up too much, but damn, girl, look at the way those . . ." He waved his hand in the direction of my boobs, and I stepped back to avoid his unsteady stance before he swayed far enough toward me to actually make a grab for my chest.

He staggered badly. I backed up even more. "Oh, no, no. M'only complimenting your dress. You look lovely. You look like Barbara, that's m'wife, you know, below the neck, anyway. I've always been able to spot the hot ones." He retreated toward the newel post, which he clutched like a life preserver. "M'boy did tell you how hot you look, didn't he? 'Coop,' I tell him, 'you gotta tell the girl the clothes look good on if you want to get the clothes to come off.' Right? Right?"

"Ted. It's time for bed. Go. You're drunk."

"Yup. I sure am. See you 'morrow." He tottered up the staircase, but not before giving me one more lascivious look.

I stood still, watching his awkward ascent.

Cooper's face, so lost, so resigned, floated before me. I loved him. I'd give everything I never had to stop right here, find him and tie off his hurt with a tourniquet, not say another word—but I didn't have that choice anymore.

Life for Cooper would be so much easier if he could continue to believe that someone other than his father buried that purse. I wished he could keep believing, but that belief had hours, maybe minutes to live.

Over my head, the jagged edges of the cut-crystal chandelier shimmered in the dim light. I shuddered and climbed the stairs. Caroline and Mia could not spend another night under the same roof as Ted.

Twenty minutes later, I stood next to Caroline on Miss Aurelia's quiet front porch, still wearing the blue dress and the flip-flops. I'd called to tell her we were coming and given her the basic outline. It was after eleven, and Caroline carried a blanket-wrapped Mia, who drowsed in her arms, almost dropping a frayed pink rabbit.

Caroline had been silent when I showed her the contents of the hole. The silvery tear-tracks on her cheeks continually refreshed themselves, but still she said nothing. Ted was her father. I was a stranger, but Caroline knew that purse hadn't gotten into the ground by itself. She was still in a state of shock and I needed Miss Aurelia's help to know how much more she could take.

Cooper had not returned home and we had no idea where he was.

Miss Aurelia, improbably still wearing her jeans and turtleneck, opened the door and opened her arms. Caroline, Mia and all, fell into them. A single sob escaped her tight control.

"Mommy? Are you sad?" said Mia sleepily, strands of her straight dark hair falling around her face.

"No, sweetie. That was a cough. Let's get you up to bed."

"Why are we here?"

"We thought it would be fun to spend the night with Miss Aurelia. She'll let you play with her Legos tomorrow morning before school, won't you, Miss Aurelia?" Caroline's strength for Mia made the corners of my own eyes prick.

"Sure will, honey. Second door on the right. Washed the sheets today."

Caroline shot her a grateful red-eyed look and took Mia upstairs without another word.

Miss Aurelia turned a gimlet eye toward me, floundering immediately inside the door. She pointed at the couch. "Sit. I'll get the tea."

"Oh, that's all right," I said. "Please don't go to the trouble. It's late."

"You might not need it, but I do. Can't think without tea. Be right back. No point in talking until Caroline comes down anyway."

"Can I use your phone?" I asked, still standing. "I need to call the police."

"No, ma'am. Not yet. We're going to talk first."

Miss Aurelia returned with three large Mason jars full of ice and tea, managing it by sticking her fingers down into them and pinching the glasses together. It all looked deeply precarious, and I jumped up to take them from her.

"Sit," she barked. "I've got it." She deftly landed the glasses on the coffee table without a drop spilled.

Caroline came down the stairs, tears no longer trickling but dripping onto her T-shirt.

"Why do you want me to wait on calling the police?" I asked, wary. Maybe we'd made a mistake coming here. Maybe Miss Aurelia, despite every disparaging thing she'd said about Ted, believed in some kind of Omerta-ish protective code for Southerners of a Certain Age. Maybe her willingness to tolerate my murder made her totally fine with his.

"Because we don't have near enough evidence yet. We haven't figured out what happened. I know those damn cops. They're good guys, but they'll get their asses out to that hole in the ground, slow as molasses, they'll dig up Lynette's pocketbook with rubber gloves, probably find the cell phone and the credit card and the driver's license in there too, bag it up, find nothing else, and start looking at Cooper. And only at Cooper. He's the husband. I guarantee he touched some of that stuff before she went . . . missing. His fingerprints are bound to be on the pocketbook, the phone, maybe even the credit card if they used it at a restaurant and passed it around. You've seen all the same damn movies I have. We all know how this goes. We've got to have a reason they should start with Ted before we call them. We don't have it yet."

Caroline's silent sobs turned to small gasps for breath. Miss Aurelia moved off her perch on the yellow vinyl fishhook chair to sit next to her. She pulled Caroline into a hug and didn't let go.

"What if someone else buried that to frame Daddy?" asked Caroline.

"That makes no sense. If they wanted to frame Ted, they're awful patient. It's been five years and not a hint. No anonymous letters to the police. Nothing. You know that's not what happened."

"But Miss Aurelia, Daddy wouldn't bury evidence like that in his own yard! He loves crime shows. He'd know better than that," said Caroline.

"You're right he's not dumb," said Miss Aurelia. "If he put it there, he had a good reason. All right. Let's think this out. When did that trench get dug?" Miss Aurelia smoothed Caroline's hair as she wept.

"It was there before Lynette left," said Caroline, wiping her eyes. "I know that much. I remember being over there for some holiday and Mary Jane got muddy footprints all over the rug because of the open trench. Lynette had been scrubbing the carpet because Daddy said they shouldn't have brought the 'idiot dog.' I think there was some issue with the earth movers and the plumber coming at different times. It got closed over, but I don't know when. After, I'm sure. I didn't live there at the time."

"Just to be clear," asked Miss Aurelia. "There's no chance there's anything else in there besides the pocketbook, is there?"

The air in the room rippled in collective horror. My imagination went to a dark place, one with dirt-stained bones and decaying fabric, strands of hair caught in clumps of clay.

"I didn't see anything else. It wasn't that wide. I don't think . . ." I shivered.

"So Ted could have put the pocketbook in there and closed it up himself?"

"I suppose. But why so close to the house?"

Still businesslike, Miss Aurelia continued. "Molly, he said something to you to give you the idea to look?"

"Yes. Well, not exactly. He manipulated me, getting me to do what he wanted by threatening to ruin Cooper's career. He took me hunting and he showed me the knife in a certain way. A meaningful way. He said he knew where all the spots where alligators . . ." I broke off, the rest of that sentence too awful to contemplate.

"But he didn't say anything more."

"No. Nothing that would count as a confession."

As horrible as it was, it wasn't close to enough to hang him. Miss Aurelia was right. Ted had been careful to tell me things without saying anything that could incriminate him. They'd never find a body. We had almost nothing: only enough for his own family members to know that Lynette was dead and none of them had put that purse in the ground. I sagged backward.

"Yep," said Miss Aurelia. I spared a moment to thank God for Miss Aurelia's cool head and shimmering intelligence. "You know that's not enough for court. We need more, or they'll go for Cooper. There could be evidence: airline records could show someone other than Lynette bought the plane ticket, there might be a security video from the airport parking garage that shows Ted dropping off the car and hailing a taxi, but it's so long ago now. We can't be sure they still have it."

"I think Daddy must have buried it," said Caroline, her tears drying but still with a shaky voice. "Lynette would never have done it, so she must be dead. We know it, but you're right. The police won't."

"Problem is, we don't have much time," said Miss Aurelia, gulping her tea. Neither Caroline nor I had touched ours. "We have hours. Sun comes up at seven. When it gets light, Ted will be able to see that ground's been disturbed."

She leaned forward, resting her elbows on her graffiti-covered jeans. "I think we have to at least consider the idea that if they dig up that stuff, Ted will happily throw Cooper right under the bus." Miss Aurelia and I exchanged glances. Yep. She'd figured it out, too. "You're right that your Daddy is smart. I wonder if he put that pocketbook in the ground to be able to do exactly that if Lynette's death ever came to light."

Caroline's expression showed horror, but there was exhausted resignation there too.

"No two ways about it," said Miss Aurelia. "We've got to have more by sunup if they're going to haul the right person off to jail."

Caroline shuddered. "I don't even know how to . . . how to even make this fit in my head. I'm so glad Mama isn't around to see this. She loved him. She believed in him, even though she must have known he was cheating. It would kill her to . . ."

A silence fell, shouting words none of us had listened to before. My ears roared. The elusive thing I'd felt in the restaurant drifted just out of reach. I reached for it, chased after it, only to have it run further away.

It would kill her.

We stared at each other, eyes widening, blood draining. Caroline made a desperate sound in her throat. Miss Aurelia reached for her again, hugging her shoulders.

Kill her.

Miss Aurelia closed her eyes. "Did he kill her, too?" she whispered, getting there first. "Now that we know he's capable of it?"

That was it. The elusive thing. I'd told Cooper his mother "lived for you." Everyone had assumed that Barbara had been hiding a crippling depression, a depression bad enough to cause her to take her own life. Yet everything I'd heard about her indicated the opposite. She'd done everything for and with her kids. She'd known about Ted's infidelity long beforehand. She'd even decorated the house for Christmas. No one who was close to her remembered her as a depressed person.

The story of the lighthouse keeper who killed his wife replayed in grisly detail behind my eyelids. That husband got his wife's death labeled a suicide, too. Because of who he was, nobody questioned it. Dear God. Ted had told that story to Cooper and Caroline as kids. It had been right there, all along, and no one in town had seen it.

One glance at Caroline's face and I tensed, ready to call 911. Her face had bleached of color and her voice came out a choked keen. "Why? Why would he? He loved her."

"Did he? Or did he love her money?" asked Miss Aurelia, bitterness and revulsion souring her easy-going face. "She was rich. Her parents, your grandparents, had a lot of money and they died and left everything to her. Not long before she died herself."

"He told me he'd be willing to say your mother was a slut to get me to do what he wanted," I said, hating to speak the words.

Miss Aurelia's face had gone white. "He inherited the house when she died. The historic house in Charleston. He sold it for something like four million dollars."

"He used all the money to fix up our house," Caroline whispered. "The one here. The one that had been in *his* family for centuries."

"It was falling down at the time," said Miss Aurelia, her face setting in fearsome lines. "The part that's the TV room now had dry rot. It was unusable."

Caroline gave a sob.

"He made it into a showplace," said Miss Aurelia, looking sick. "Marble bathrooms. Parquet floors. Professional decoration. A monument to himself, with Barbara's Tradd family money. He built a workshop for himself. He quit his job as an engineer."

"He hired Etta, to do all the things Mama used to do for us. He had money to put in all the businesses and the shrimp boats and all over everywhere. He was nobody important before. He runs the town, now." Caroline's hands squeezed, knuckles turning white.

Miss Aurelia added, quietly, "Your grandparents left your mother a whole lot more money than simply the value of the house. Several million, I think. Barbara talked to me about it. She'd planned to put it in trust for the two of you. She never got the chance."

Caroline was openly sobbing now.

"Anti-freeze," fumed Miss Aurelia. "As if Barb would even have known where in the store to buy it. How easy, to get her to drink it in some sweet-tasting thing. Like tea," she said, glancing at the innocent glasses on the table. "All for that money." She paced. "For money. He let poor little Cooper find her body. An eleven-year-old child."

"The police will figure all that out after they arrest him for Lynette's murder," I said. "They'll get him."

"But how will they do that? We don't have any more evidence than we had when we sat down," said Caroline, a thin blade of steel shining through her dead-white expression.

"I'll go," I said, deciding. "I'll go up to his room and wake him up. He knows about my past. We're both . . ." I paused, unwilling to use that word in connection with Caroline's mother. "If I go there, pretend like we're in this together, like I've decided to give him what he wants, he might . . . I don't know. He might talk a little bit."

"But he can't hold your history over your head anymore. We all know about it and we don't care," said Caroline, somehow smaller in Miss Aurelia's embrace than she'd been before.

"Yes, but he doesn't know that. It's the only chance. We need the police to be pulling that purse out of the ground when daylight comes or Ted will know we're on to him. If we have nothing else, we might get enough to keep them from going after Cooper," I said. "But we have to try for more. All we need is one little comment to get them to focus on him. I'll have to focus on Lynette. For Barbara, we'd need to construct a long financial record of what he knew when. That will take detectives and technology and a lot more expertise than we have."

"We'll never know for sure what happened to Mama," Caroline said. "But it helps, maybe, to think that she didn't kill herself. I always used to wonder . . . if it was me. If I was too much. If she just didn't want to be a mom anymore."

"Oh, honey," said Miss Aurelia, smoothing back Caroline's hair. "Barb loved you and Cooper. You were her life. You have a child. Would you check out because of anything Mia did? Of course not."

"If I do this, I need witnesses," I said, to the room. "If he says anything, it needs to be heard by more than only me."

"Caroline can stay here with Mia. I'd like her out of that house until this is sorted. I'll come with you," said Miss Aurelia, clearing away the Mason jars in a single efficient motion. "I'll bring my cell phone. You can record him. I'll also bring my gun."

CHAPTER TWENTY-FOUR

One good thing about prison was I had endless time to think. Time in my cell with a book from the library. Time with pencil and paper to write ideas, memories, and conversations I wished I'd had. I never did a single thing without thinking about it first. Time is the one thing that prisoners have in abundance.

Now, for the first time, I wished for a few of those minutes to think. Soon, I'd be barging into Ted's bedroom to say . . . I had no idea what. I'd volunteered to talk him into saying something incriminating. Something loud enough for Miss Aurelia, stationed outside the door with her cell phone already recording, to hear. All I knew about investigatory technique was dim memories of being questioned about murder by a long-ago detective who brought me a hamburger and pretended to be my friend. If life ran on prison time, I'd have hours on my own to piece together a chain of topics to get him to admit the murder of his daughter-in-law.

But life ran at lightning-flash speed outside the four walls of prison. All split-second decisions and action out here.

We rode in silence in Miss Aurelia's Toyota to the Middleton house. On the front porch, I stopped, pressing my hands to my stomach.

"You don't have to do this," Miss Aurelia said.

"I do," I said, inserting Caroline's key in the door after several shaky failed attempts, "I have to do this for Cooper. I love him. I'm not going to let him go to prison. I'm not going to let him be suspected for even a minute. I will never let what happened to me happen to anyone else."

Miss Aurelia gave me a small smile. "You know, prison or no prison, you're one of the toughest people I know."

I didn't know what to say.

She seemed to understand. "Go on. I'll stay quiet in the hall listening to make sure you're okay. If he does anything at all that would hurt you, I'll break down that door before he takes another breath."

Soundlessly, we tossed aside our shoes and crept up the stairs. Ted's door stood ajar, a strip of moonlight stretching across the dark hall floor. Miss Aurelia took her place out of visual range against the wall. She saluted me with her phone.

I slipped inside and left the door open a crack. "Ted," I hissed. The room smelled like Ben-Gay and stale sheets. A bed so immense it had to have been built in the room dominated the space. "Ted!"

Despite the smell, a prickle of awareness told me the room was empty. He was not in bed. I dashed back into the hallway. "He's gone!"

Miss Aurelia met my eyes, aware we were now without a roadmap. "Shhh."

We listened for a few seconds to the house. Silence. Nothing but the humming of the heating system and the faraway ticking of a clock.

"He might have found the hole in the yard," Miss Aurelia said, glancing through the open doorway to the moonlight cutting through Ted's drape-less windows.

"Then we don't have any time to waste. He's got to be stopped before he hands Cooper over to the police gift-wrapped. We've got to find him. You look in the house. I'll go outside. Give me the phone."

Miss Aurelia handed it over automatically, then reached for it back. "No. We need to call the police now. It's not safe to mess around here any longer."

"We can't wait for them. Ted won't." I pocketed the phone. "I'm sorry. I have to do this." Evading her attempts to stop me, I slipped around her and ran down the stairs to where I'd left my flip-flops.

"Molly! Wait!" called Miss Aurelia from the top of the stairs, a note of fear in her voice I'd never heard from her before. The answering echo beat its wings inside my own chest.

"I can't." The door banged shut behind me.

Outside, I bolted straight to the shed. Ted was nowhere in sight, but the door to the empty shed was unlocked. If he'd gone in there, he'd turned the lights out after he got whatever he'd needed. I started around the side of the yard in the direction of the long dock. I rounded the dark wall of a dense magnolia tree, and there he was, wearing sweatpants and a Clemson sweatshirt. Cooper's Clemson sweatshirt. Some old guys look innocuous in tracksuits, even comical, but not Ted.

Even in the average-man getup, he radiated threat and cunning. His stagger was gone and his teeth shone white in the dim light. "Well, good golly, if it isn't Miss Molly, still with the tits showing, come looking for me. It's a dream come true."

My original plan had been to pretend to go along with his lurid attraction for me to get him to talk. Nothing better had yet occurred to me, so I ventured a little closer, even though my pulse felt like it would beat right out of my throat. "I want to talk to you and I wasn't sure how to get you alone any other time."

"Oh, you can get me alone any time. In fact, let's you and me go out and look at that beautiful moon on the water." He gestured toward the dock, a black arrow pointed at the moon and set off by tiny moon-shards reflected on the lapping water around it.

"On . . . on the water?"

"Sure thing. We'll take Cooper's boat for a little spin, see the reflection on the water. Nothing like a Lowcountry moon."

No. No boats. Not with Ted. Not alone. Hell, no. I began edging away. He followed me, all joviality and innocence. "Well, that would be great another time, but, um, I still feel a little queasy from dinner and I don't think . . ."

"Aw, now, darlin', where you going? You wanted to talk, didn't you?"

"Yes, but it's late. Maybe tomorrow?"

"We're going on the boat. I insist." He scratched his stomach so that the sweatshirt slipped up and I could see the glint of the metallic barrel of a small handgun in his waistband. Ted grinned, whatever effects of alcohol he'd been feeling an hour or two ago mostly gone. "I *insist*."

"Are you threatening me?" Even as the words came out, I realized how ridiculous they sounded given the gun, but somehow despite everything I'd learned I couldn't quite let go of the idea that Ted was reasonable.

He laughed. "Well, now, I gave you credit for being a lot smarter than that. Yes, darlin', I've been threatening you all along. Now you're going to get in the boat."

"No, Ted. You're drunk." I backed away toward the house. He reached for his hip and my muscles knew I'd failed; they bunched and coiled for flight. He wouldn't talk. I should have known. Miss Aurelia would know I was out here, she would . . .

She would not have time to save me.

Giving him no warning, I dashed blindly into the night, no destination in mind except away. I expected the lightning heat of a gunshot in my back at any moment; instead I heard only the pound of his footsteps and the low chuckle of his laughter, as if we were playing a game. The sound grew closer and closer. I made it maybe twenty feet before he grabbed my arm, spinning me like a top and throwing my momentum off kilter. A searing hot pain burst in my temple, transferring the starry night sky to my blackened vision. White fireworks exploded behind my closed eyelids as I dropped to my knees: he'd hit me with the gun. I should have known. I'd seen his reflexes on display with the boar. I opened my throbbing jaw to scream and he clapped his hand over it.

"Now, Miss Molly, you're going to need to shut the hell up. We're going on a boat ride." With one arm around my neck clamping my mouth shut and the other around my chest, he dragged me to my feet from behind. I tried to pry his hands off, but only succeeded in hurting my broken fingernails worse. My head throbbed and worked in slow motion. Plans for escape refused to take shape. The only thought I could form and hold was *Run*, but I couldn't get his hands off me.

Another thought formed out of the darkness: *Don't help*. I

straightened my legs and went limp, forcing him to drag me like a corpse toward the dock.

"Walk, you little bitch," he muttered. The hand over my mouth slipped as he struggled to make me move, and I wasted no time.

"Aurelia!" I screamed. Pain ricocheted in my head from the effort and then doubled and tripled as he smashed his open hand into the same injured spot on my head. Shock waves mushroomed outward from there and silenced me into a whimper. He yanked me up, replacing his hand over my mouth and dragged me unceremoniously down the long length of the dock, my legs scrabbling a grotesque and useless dance on the worn boards. The blow and the throbbing pain had slowed my thinking, but I forced myself to make plans.

I wouldn't be able to fight him off physically. After he threw me in the boat—and I'd be going in the boat—I'd have to figure another way to escape. He wouldn't be able to restrain me the whole time. There might be another boat to call to. Someone out in a nearby yard.

At the end of the dock, he squatted and used the hand over my mouth to jerk my head back so he could look in my eyes. "Get in the boat, or I will shoot you right here."

There was quiet as my brain took longer than usual to weigh those options. No one called my name. Miss Aurelia hadn't heard me. The only sound was the quiet slap of the water against the wooden pilings. As Ted turned to the boat, his hands loosened. I wiggled free, slipping down between his arms and away like a snake, but I didn't get far. He was too close to me; I couldn't scramble away fast enough. Ted sensed my movements and moved with astonishing quickness to stop me.

"You're beginning to be tiresome," Ted said. He grabbed me in a vise around my rib cage, tearing the side seam of my dress. He threw me to the floor of the boat. My bare arms and legs banged into metal railings, seat edges, and boat parts I had no name for and bruised. He stomped on the center of my back with one heavy boot, holding me in place as he connected himself to the kill switch with the lanyard clip, started the engine, and maneuvered the craft away from the dock.

"I don't guess I have to worry about you doing anything stupid and flinging yourself off, do I? Seems I recollect you can't swim." Cackling to himself, he flung the life vests over the side. They floated away, useless. The smell of dead fish permeated the boat floor.

I lay in silence, hurting, catching my breath, and trying to adjust to this insane reality. Something hard poked my hipbone and I felt for it. The phone Miss Aurelia had given me. Of course—something I could still do. A way to fight. I waited until Ted bent over some control at the wheel to slip it out of my pocket, hit "record," and hide it in the shadows of the rope coiled near my head.

Ted chuckled to himself as he ratcheted up the boat's speed until we were practically flying over the moon-brightened water. "Okay, darlin', you can sit up now. Right there, if you don't mind." He gestured at the seat at the front of the boat, on the other side of the console from him. I glanced at the phone, still well-positioned in the rope coil on the floor between us. I crawled up, refusing to give him the satisfaction of groaning, though I hurt in more places than I'd had time to catalog.

The size of the night sky made me feel even more powerless. The wind whipped by, bringing that organic smell of things growing and the Milky Way spread out above us without competition from the lights of town. Ted was going to kill me. He'd already hurt me and that meant he had no plans to let me show these injuries to a doctor. Exhaustion and pain deadened my limbs. I couldn't stop it. He was too strong. At least I'd die under these beautiful stars and not somewhere sordid and ugly like the woman in prison with the frozen eyes. Like my mother.

Even as the thought completed itself, I rejected it. No. I would not let him kill me that easily. My mother had not been able to do it. I had to get him to tell me enough to convict him, and then I had to—somehow!—get rid of him and save myself. The blows to the head had slowed my brain. It worked slower, but if I concentrated on making thoughts, almost like cookies, they still came.

"What did you want to talk to me about?" Ted asked, as if we were at a garden party instead of a midnight abduction at gunpoint. "I'm guessing it had to do with that hole in the backyard?"

Of course he'd found it. I clutched my knees, trying to keep my fear from flying loose. Panic would ruin everything. I had to force my brain into action. "How did you . . . ?"

"Went outside to take a leak. Sometimes it's nice to do that the way nature intended, out in the open. I noticed right away somebody'd got out the shovel. You find anything in that hole, darling?"

I had nothing to lose now. "Looked like Lynette's purse. Is that what it was?"

He grinned over the boat wheel, his graying hair flying in the rush of the wind. "She was a hot little thing, but dumb as a rock. She couldn't decide from one day to the next whether the sky was blue or green. One day she'd be in bed with me, the next acting like she'd never wanted to, making me have to persuade her all over again."

"Persuade her?" I asked, the words sour and thick on my tongue. I mourned again for Lynette, whose life had ended in terror and isolation.

"You know; remind her of what she stood to lose. She was stupid enough to write down all her sexual fantasies in her diary, years and years of them, and they made for real good reading. Let's just say, the Charleston County school system wouldn't have liked to find out about those. Not to mention Cooper. They didn't all relate to men."

He laughed and switched on a handheld flashlight he'd found in the console. He shone it on me, to see my face. "Oh, don't look shocked. If you've been to prison, you know what the real world's like. She wouldn't have let herself get in that situation if she didn't want to be there. She acted all shy, but I knew. You could tell with those short skirts she wore. Damn, she looked good in those skirts. Cheerleader skirts. Might as well have written 'do me' across her ass in black marker. She looked good in those skirts, but you look even better in that dress, with those huge tits all propped up like that." His tongue darted out to wet his lips.

Gorge rose in my throat. I could never have pretended to go along with his fantasies. Even if he'd been in his room where I'd expected him, Plan A had always been destined to fail.

He was going to kill me, but he was going to rape me first.

CHAPTER TWENTY-FIVE

I held on tight, the boat bouncing and flying over the black water. My skin crawled and my mind raced. The wheel. I needed to get control of the wheel. "That must have gotten old, Lynette changing her mind all the time." I had to scream out every word, to be heard above the wind. I'd have preferred to scratch Ted's eyes out with my ragged fingernails.

"Oh, yeah. Well, I won't lie," he said. "At first that hot/cold act turned me on. Kept me interested. Then as you say, it got old. One day she said she was finished. Said Cooper would be home more and she'd decided to tell him. Come clean. She said the guilt was eating at her and she didn't care what the consequences were."

"She never did, though. I feel like Cooper might have mentioned that."

"Naw, she never did. She left first."

How could I ever get control of this boat? Oh, my God. I couldn't do it. Before I could shove it down, terror roared up my spine, obliterating any thought. Biting my tongue hard to keep the nausea at bay and my brain functioning, I leaned forward to play his game. If I was going to die, I didn't want it to be in vain. "Oh, come on, Ted. I know you weren't going to sit by and take that chance. I sure as hell wouldn't have. That would be stupid, and you're a smart guy. You'd never forget to cover your ass. Some people need killing, is what I say. I think we understand each other. I know what happened to Lynette out at the island. I saw the knife earlier. I'll bet the alligators came in handy."

He cackled. "You like that trip?"

"You wanted to show me. That's my theory, Ted. You wanted

me to see. You wanted to tell me," I said. "Tell me now. You took her out hunting, and, well, things happen, don't they?"

He aimed the flashlight directly on my cleavage, spotlighting my only importance to him. We'd long since passed the point where he needed to pretend civility. Whatever he would do to me would hurt. Blood trickled from a broken fingernail where I'd clenched my hands too hard. "Hmmm. Sometimes they do happen. Cooper don't seem to be able to hang onto his women. Have I told you about Cooper's jealous rages around about the time Lynette disappeared? I told two or three of my partners about that way back. I may have found a piece of half-burnt khaki and a zipper in the bottom of the grill. I may just have kept that. Blood-stained, you know. Who knows? There might even be more of that kind of thing around here somewhere."

Horror dried my mouth. "You wear the same size clothes. You and Cooper."

His smile held grudging admiration. "You know, you're right. We do. On occasion he borrows my clothes. Or vice versa."

Mary, Mother of God. He'd planned it. He'd killed Lynette in Cooper's clothes and saved the burnt remnants of them. He'd planted stories others would remember that gave Cooper a motive. He'd definitely planted that purse as insurance for himself. He wasn't evil. He was satanic.

He was wearing Cooper's sweatshirt and driving Cooper's boat right now. He had planned to kill me too, as soon as he saw that hole in the ground. I was a problem to handle, and he must have thought of a way to frame Cooper for my disappearance as well. I could see nothing in the darkness beyond the ring of the flashlight but the dance of the moonbeams on the water, but we had to be heading toward that same island. This method of rape and murder had worked once; why fix what ain't broken?

I wanted to yell all that out, but I kept focused on the phone at my feet. Better. I needed better. I would take that wheel or die trying, or I would die anyway. I had nothing to lose. But first, I needed him to say the words. A rivulet of sweat trickled between my breasts.

"Clever," I said. "I wish I'd thought of that, but I was young. My mother was a bitch, but I didn't plan that well. I was a kid. I got caught. You're good. Much better than me. You planned it all out. No mistakes." I leaned back and put a foot up on the rail as if I didn't have a care in the world. The hem of my dress flapped in the rush of marsh air as we sped along. Ted shone the light on it, trying to see up it.

He smiled. "Smart girl. You're much smarter than Lynette."

God, I hoped so. It became harder to focus on anything but that wheel. Grasping, I tried for a Plan B. If I couldn't throw him off and take control, I could try flinging myself overboard to drown, but it wouldn't work. He would fish me out of the water and proceed with his original plan. Maybe I could do both. An involuntary whimper escaped me. I allowed myself a quick glance at the phone. Still there. While my mind raced, my mouth kept talking. "Let's be honest with each other, Ted. I know you killed her. You know you killed her. It was smart of you to set it up with Cooper to take the fall. I've got nothing but admiration for that. We both know we're on the way to the hunting island where we went this morning."

God, was it only this morning?

Unable to keep a slight wobble out of my voice, I continued. "And only one of us is coming back. Why don't you just tell me what it was Lynette did that pissed you off so much? You want to. I know you want to."

He stared at me. I watched him with my heart in my throat, waiting for his decision. My head throbbed. *Anything at all. Say anything at all.* I didn't think I could go much longer before the panic overwhelmed my injured and overtaxed brain.

He opened his mouth and closed it. My heart sank. What if he didn't say it?

"You figured out your mistake, I guess, all those years in prison, but you've got to plan. Lynette was hot when she was hot, but whiny as hell when she wasn't. She had an attack of conscience when Cooper changed his hours and told me she was done. She planned to come clean with him and let him decide whether he could forgive her. Said she was thinking about going home to her daddy if Cooper kicked her out. Well, I wasn't going to have that. I like my family to be close by. I can't have Cooper running around, connecting dots to other things. I decided a couple of days ahead, and spoke to a few people. Just little things, you know. How Cooper and Lynette had stormed out of my house after a dinner, how I heard him accusing her of cheating as they got out to the car. How I found the house a wreck one time and Lynette told me Cooper did it. That kind of thing. People remember that stuff if a body turns up, but it won't. They'll never find it. Put some things here and there, in case they need to arrest somebody—and it definitely won't be me."

Was it enough? Had he said enough? Did it matter? Maybe he'd still be arrested after he killed me if someone other than him found the phone. If he killed me, I needed to take him down with me. I needed these few more minutes to matter. *Keep talking.* "So you brought her out to the island and stabbed her?"

"Well, that sounds pretty heartless when you say it like that. I brought her out to the island—didn't need a gun for her—and we had a nice romantic interlude, then I did what I had to do as humanely as possible. Took her over to the alligator pit and weighted her down. Then I went on back, put stuff where it needed to go, and drove her car on out to the airport. Caught a taxi home."

"Cooper knows you did it. He knows he didn't kill her and bury that purse."

"Sure, fine. He's the only one who knows that for sure. Other than you, now, and soon you won't matter much. With the insurance I kept, his word against mine won't go real far. Too much points his way."

Enough. How could anyone be so sick? He talked about Cooper like he was a chess piece, not a person. Not a son. He'd said more than enough. I glanced at the phone. Time now to fight.

"And me? What are you going to tell Cooper about me?"

"You? Nothing. You're not his wife. You're a slut Vegas showgirl he's known a week. I'm going to tell everyone we went out to look at the moon and I told you I was cutting Cooper off if you stayed. You're a gold digger, of course, so when you heard that, you asked me to let you off the boat at Georgetown. I gave you all the cash in my wallet and I never saw you again. He'd be a damn idiot to think you'd stay around here if he had nothing. And besides, I saw him wander off into the woods. He's got no alibi for the time you're going to disappear if he decides to get vocal about things. Does too much thinking off by himself, that boy."

The insults rolled off me while I finalized my suicidal plan. I had no idea if I could drive this boat, but I'd seen Cooper and No-Neck do it. I'd have a better chance before we got off at the island than after, and a land mass was beginning to take shape on the horizon out of shadows where the moonlight went to die. I'd have to move fast. I retrieved the phone from the rope coil, unwilling to let it get flung off if I succeeded in throwing Ted off. I wanted to see him go down, and not posthumously.

The boat raced forward.

I stood up, the phone carefully hidden in my hand behind my thigh. "Well, Ted, this has been fun, but I think I'm getting off here. We're getting close to land. I can't swim, but I figure I die tonight anyway, right? I hear drowning isn't a bad way to go, and at least I'll save myself the rape. And I don't really like knives." I slung one leg over the side, watching his muscles tense, anticipating the direction of his movement. I had more practice at that than most people. And on a boat, I had an advantage. He had to unclip the kill switch lanyard first to get to me.

When he moved, I was ready. He unclipped the lanyard from his shirt and darted to his right. I shot to my right as well, with the skill born of years of evading drunken attackers. I put the console between us and yanked the wheel hard to the left and the kill switch key out of the dashboard at the same time. He never had a chance. The boat's engine died and what momentum was left over went into the turn. The force swept me sideways as well, scrabbling to keep my place at the console. Only the splash and the howl of outrage let me know I'd succeeded in knocking Ted over the side. He'd landed in the water between the bobbing buoys of three crab pots, two white and one orange.

I was alone in the drifting boat, though the splashing and cursing Ted wasn't the only thing in the water.

The phone had flown out of my hand as well. I abandoned the console to drop to my knees and peer over the rail into the black water that swallowed it without a bubble. A sob broke. It was gone.

I stood, cold and numb.

I'd lost Cooper for nothing. Ted's confession was gone. He'd get away with everything. I'd tried to have my cake and eat it too: live, and take Ted down. If I'd hidden the phone under the rope coil for Cooper to find someday, stayed politely on that front boat seat, and waited to be eviscerated mid-rape, Ted would eventually have been arrested—but I hadn't been willing to die. It turns out that a lifetime of minute-by-minute survival is a hard habit to break.

I was still alive.

I'd chosen my own life over protecting the confession. My life was all I had left now and I wasn't done saving it. I gripped the wheel.

CHAPTER TWENTY-SIX

I wouldn't have died if I'd jumped with the phone in my hand, though I hadn't been wrong about Ted fishing me out. The water wasn't deep. Ted was already on his feet, armpits out of the water, enraged, cursing, and wading through the sucking mud on the bottom toward the ladder at the back end of the boat. Wet, his hair was much thinner than it normally looked. It made him look less threatening. I reminded myself not to be fooled again and turned the key to start the motor like I'd seen Cooper do.

It didn't catch.

I tried again. Nothing. In a panic, I'd forgotten to insert the kill switch key. Ted continued moving toward me, assuming I'd have no idea how to start the boat. Fingers shaking, I dropped the lanyard twice before hooking it up.

"You fucking bitch! That was a very stupid thing to do!"

I tried a third time and it caught. The motor roared to life, and for one heady terrifying moment, I thought about pointing the boat straight at Ted and driving over him. I wanted him dead. He'd killed Lynette and probably his own wife, and he had every intention of killing me within the next half-hour. I might even get off with self-defense this time. I could get away with it. I could kill him and set us all free. He'd be coming for the others after me. It might be the only way to do justice now that I'd lost the phone.

No.

I would not kill. Not again. I would not live with the guilt. There had to be another way. I turned the wheel to get out of here.

Unfortunately, the channel was narrow and I had no idea what I was doing. I'd crash into the marsh grasses and run aground if I gave Ted too wide a berth. Mindful of the vicious propeller on the engine on the back of the boat, I didn't dare ratchet up the speed until I got past him. As the back end of the still-slow boat neared him, Ted launched himself into a strong swimming stroke and managed to catch the chrome ladder off the back corner on his side, allowing him to avoid the merciless grind of the blades. He brought the scent of the mud and the water with him.

His laughter rang cruel and triumphant as he maneuvered, hanging on but having trouble climbing up while the boat was moving. Frantic to shake him off, I revved the engine and swung the boat wildly. He fishtailed and let loose a string of profanity but didn't let go.

"Fine," he yelled, still splashing, unable to gain purchase as I picked up even more speed to throw him off. "You lose either way. Leave me here and take the boat on back. I'll tell the police you came out here with me, all hot and bothered, and then changed your mind. I'll tell them how you knocked me off the boat. It'll be you they arrest, not me. You go on and tell them what I said, see if anyone believes you. I own this town. I own the police. You're nothing!"

I kicked off my flip-flop and used my toes to bring the long pole from the floor of the boat, the one meant for saving people, and hit at him, trying to lash his hands hard enough to make him let go. He laughed harder. "Oh, that sounded good to you, did it? You try it, sweetheart. You have no idea who you're messing with here. This ain't gonna go well for you."

How could a man his age have a grip like that? The pole was long and unwieldy, and I had to repeatedly turn forward to keep from running aground on a marsh bank. He would climb up here and dismember me on the spot. I had no idea where I was. Finally, like a gift, the water opened up wider, enough that I could turn away long enough to whack Ted hard on the temple.

"You bitch!" Ted lost his grip. With a titanic splash, he fell back. The boat shot away from him. I risked one more glance back, to find him swimming with furious strokes to an isolated marsh bank, far from land. Pluff mud, to me, would now always smell like life.

It took me over an hour to find my way back to McClellanville. All along I could see the dimly-lit shoreline, but the marsh channels wound endlessly like a watery labyrinth, all wrong turns and dead ends and twisty canals to nowhere. The gas tank dropped steadily. At last the lights of the town drew close enough for me to recognize the town hall and the entrance to the creek where the shrimp boats docked. Unable to find the Middleton dock in the dark, I cut the engine almost to nothing and headed for the creek, where it took me four tries to get the boat close enough to tie it to one of the metal things bolted to the edge of the pilings of the public boat dock. I vaulted out and ran, panting and gasping, the half-mile to the Middleton house. Even the running didn't warm the coldness that had hardened all over me.

From a distance, I heard him.

"Molly! Where are you?" Cooper was calling my name, the desperation in his voice speeding my feet.

"Cooper!"

He appeared out of the landscaped darkness of the allée and swept me up without a sound. His smell, soap and sweat and warmth, helped calm the shaking.

Until I remembered that he knew nothing. He'd seen the purse and he'd dropped the shovel and gone. He had no idea what we'd figured out about his mother. He hadn't heard the chilling things Ted had said on the boat about Lynette. Slowly, I let go and stepped back to a careful distance.

"Are you all right?" he asked, his face gray and stark.

"I'm okay. I'm okay." I would tell him, no matter what happened to us. He had the right to know. Even if it meant I'd never see him again.

First things first, though. "Cooper. I need your cell phone. I have to call 911."

"The police are already here. Miss Aurelia called them when she couldn't find you. They've already bagged up the pocketbook—it was definitely Lynette's. They got the Coast Guard out looking for the boat. I assume Dad is on the boat?"

"No. The boat's at the dock. Your dad is out in the marsh. I can tell them where."

"Everyone is at the house. Come on." We started walking, not touching. "What happened, Molly? Where have you been?"

Here it was. "He kidnapped me, Cooper. He hit me and threw me onto the boat. Check the shed—he went in there and got a handgun. He was going to take me out to the island. He told me what he did to Lynette—took her there, raped her, then stabbed her with his knife. He weighted her body and threw it to the alligators. I recorded most of what he said, but the phone went overboard."

It took me more time than I wanted to find the courage to look him in the eyes. When I did, there was resignation there, but no anger. He didn't dismiss what I said, but he wasn't ready to embrace it, either. The disbelief had been washed away in the pain of the truth. He'd already pieced it together.

Even free of Ted, the fear kept up its roaring in my ears. I'd been afraid for my life many times before, but I'd never felt that kind of terror.

"Miss Aurelia told me some stuff. Everything you and Caroline talked about at her house. She said she lost you in the yard. We knew something was wrong." Cooper quickened his stride. The house came into view, lights blazing everywhere.

"We need to get the police out there to pick him up and see if they can find Miss Aurelia's phone," I said. "His plan is to frame you. He did it in your clothes. He's got your Clemson sweatshirt on right now." Cooper's jaw tightened and he nodded, without speaking. Inside, uniformed officers swarmed everywhere.

I swallowed hard. My experience with law enforcement had been bad without exception. I spent the night of my seventeenth birthday alone and terrified in a windowless room in a police station, swabbed and tested and accused. They didn't let me change out of the T-shirt and jeans that had stiffened to cardboard with dried blood for hours. Eventually they allowed my grandmother to take me home, and then had returned, the next day, to arrest me. My last view of my grandmother had been blocked by officers wearing uniforms like these. They didn't let me hug her goodbye and I never saw her in person again.

They hadn't cared about me then. And I had no choice but to hope they'd care more this time. This time, I had Cooper—maybe.

As calmly as I could, I told two detectives about the hunting island and the three crab pots where Ted, and the phone, had fallen out of the boat. I told them what the phone had recorded. They radioed that information—and the significance of the phone —out to whoever was offshore looking for us.

Miss Aurelia had gone home to take care of Caroline and Mia. Cooper and I took seats in the front hall side by side on an armless sofa Leandra had no doubt chosen but where no one ever sat. He stayed silent, his hands still, only his eyes indicating he wasn't asleep. They flicked back and forth, feverishly watching the movement of the police. Messages crackled in over their radios, garbled and shorthand, comprehensible only to them. Time passed and some kind of emotion stoked the furnace behind Cooper's eyes, building flames hotter and hotter.

Once, I touched his arm. "Do you want to talk?"

"No. Not yet."

A car door slammed. I startled awake from the light doze I'd fallen into on Cooper's shoulder. Ninety minutes had passed.

The door opened and Ted was there, wet through, shivering, and flanked on either side by officers, one local police, one Coast Guard. Cooper stood, unfolding his lanky frame slowly. He walked up to his father. The officers relaxed but did not release their grip. They seemed to know Cooper was due a reckoning.

Cooper paused a minute, to give an approaching detective an opportunity to do her job.

"Did you get it?" she asked the police officer.

"Yeah," said the officer, handing her the phone in a dripping plastic bag. "Found it with the tracker at the marsh edge, but it got wet. Don't know whether it can be saved."

"We'll see." The detective bustled off, holding the bag well clear of her dark pants.

Still insolent, Ted stared down Cooper as if the whole exchange hadn't even happened. "Did you want to say something, son?"

"You disgust me." The transformation from the controlled quiet to a fearsome anger was immediate and terrifying. Cooper's wrath grew and twisted, filling the room until he resembled a vengeful warrior from mythology.

"Son, I have no idea what you're talking about," Ted said.

"You killed Lynette."

"What? I did nothing of the kind. I'd love to see the lawyer who could prove otherwise. I expect you killed Lynette. You tried to frame me, burying that thing by my shed."

"You gutted her like a hog and threw her to the gators. My wife. You did that to *my wife*. You told Molly exactly how. After you kidnapped her."

Ted laughed. Despite myself, I had to marvel at his control. He'd clearly decided to bank on the hope that the phone would be unsalvageable. "Kidnapped? More the other way around. Your new wife there, she's got an itch apparently you can't scratch all by yourself. A tease, though. Got pissy and dumped me off."

"Don't you ever say another word about my wife. You're not good enough to lick her shoes."

Ted snorted, derision dripping off him with the marsh water.

"And you killed Lynette out at the hunt club island," said Cooper. "Because she wouldn't sleep with you anymore. You took her life, like she was nothing. You bury deer carcasses with more respect than what you did to her."

"You're nuts."

Like it was nothing, Cooper punched the doorframe, hard enough to leave a dent. Then with extraordinary self-mastery, he switched it off and turned all that heat to ice. "You know, I don't guess I honestly care whether they prove you did it or not. IPhones are pretty waterproof nowadays, and Miss Aurelia's was a good one. I think it'll tell an interesting story. And if it doesn't . . . well."

A chill went down my spine. Cooper was as grim and resolved as any reaper. He would kill Ted, and he didn't look at all concerned about the audience of officers. If they didn't convict his father, Cooper would be waiting. I read that knowledge in Ted's face, too.

"No, Cooper. It's not worth it. *And I would know.*" I spoke quietly, only for Cooper. He took my hand and squeezed it, a huge sigh gusting away a bit of the wrath. "Let the police handle him. Losing everything and going to jail will be worse than death for him."

Using astonishing restraint, Ted ignored me and modulated his voice to take off the skeptical edge, replacing it with the most reasonable of persuasive tones. "Cooper, let's talk this out. You're acting crazy. Lynette left you. She went to Charlotte. We know all of this. She was depressed and upset and she left. You've known all that for years. The only thing's changed is this one, here," he said, gesturing at me as if I were a piece of refuse on the floor.

"Don't, Dad."

"She's had a bad effect on you. She's a liar, son. A criminal."

Maybe he was right. I was a convicted criminal, but if things worked out well, it would be Ted's turn to learn about the real world in prison, and die there, given his age.

"Give it a rest, Ted," I said, a lifetime of stored-up bravado in my tone. "It takes one to know one, I guess."

Ted's shoulders sagged, the tiniest first hint that he might know it was over. "You've got nothing. Nothing at all."

The door slammed with a gust of cold air. Miss Aurelia entered, sweeping back her gray and white hair like a queen. Her eyes lit up when she saw Ted.

"Edward Middleton, as I live and breathe. You're a damn mangy flea-bitten cur. I knew you were a dog from the time we were kids. Look at you, burying your trophies in the yard, just like a damn stray mutt. It shouldn't surprise me that you were rabid all this time, but it did. It did surprise me. I have to admit it, Ted. You fooled me. You think you know a person because they dress nice and live in a nice house and marry a wonderful girl. I hope for your sake prison is comfortable."

She walked up to him where he stood, still restrained between the two officers, and without hesitating, drew back and punched him in the face. The impact snapped his head back. The police were too surprised to react.

"That's for Barbara. You better pray you're safe in prison when they prove you killed her, too."

As dawn broke, Cooper and I walked out of the police station where we'd given statements. The phone had been submerged, but not long enough to damage it much. Miss Aurelia apparently was one of those interesting people who kept a rotary dial phone in her house and bought the very latest model cell phone. The police were hopeful. We got into the cab of Cooper's truck.

"I wonder if I'm awake enough to drive home," he said, making no move to turn on the engine. "Think the police would mind if we crashed here in the parking lot for a couple of hours? I feel drained."

"No wonder," I said, rubbing his neck as he closed his eyes. He leaned back against the window as I stared at him, letting all the care and concern and feeling show, unmindful for now of any worry he didn't feel the same overpowering pull.

He opened his eyes, softer now with exhaustion and something else. "It's my turn to confess something."

"To confess something?"

"Yes. I remember our wedding. Parts, anyway. I told you I didn't, but I do remember it. We were drunk, no doubt about it, and acting stupid and loud, but I remember bits and pieces."

"You do?" Curiosity overwhelmed me. My memories were so sketchy. "All I remember is riding with the windows open, to the chapel, I guess."

He met my eyes, his expression direct and honest. "I don't remember deciding to do it, or who thought of it first. I don't remember if we brushed our teeth beforehand or combed our hair."

My lips tipped up as I remembered the stain on my shirt and

his mussed hair in the chapel parking lot the next morning.

"But I remember wanting it," said Cooper, his voice low and urgent. "Being glad about it. I remember staring at you in that tacky chapel and thinking I was lucky."

"Cooper." *Oh. My. God.*

"That's not all. The preacher, or the officiant, or whoever, was an old man with a stutter. Real bad stutter. He tripped over some words and got stuck on one for a long time. You put your hand on his and squeezed. Kind of like to let him know it was okay, that we could wait for him to get it. I remember thinking that I could do a whole lot worse than to marry someone as kind as that." At this, he took my hands in his larger ones, clutching them tight. Our fingers intertwined.

I couldn't speak. An new ease from within warmed me all over, erasing a tightness in my chest that had been there so long I didn't remember a time without it. I had no memory of the ceremony, but he was telling me that he'd wanted to marry me. That he hadn't regretted it. It hadn't been my hair or my bra size.

He'd seen me. The real me. I hadn't been invisible after all.

I leaned forward and gave him a long kiss. He pulled me against him and slung one arm around me.

We drifted off together, once again, in a parking lot.

CHAPTER TWENTY-SEVEN

Six Months Later

We met for lunch in Charleston. Cooper's office was still in Mt. Pleasant, but he crossed the bridge to join me near my office. I'd gotten a job working as a legal assistant for the Charleston Legal Aid office, which provides free legal services for low-income Charlestonians. I'd been forthcoming about my status as a felon, but CLA was dedicated to social justice and improving legal access for the underprivileged and they had no problem with it.

We'd gotten sandwiches on King Street and went to sit on some nearby marble steps to eat outside in the heat that already teetered on the edge of oppressive.

The Lowcountry is spectacular in the spring, if you don't mind thinking of spring as March and April. May, on the other hand, is as sweaty and hot as July in Michigan. I didn't mind. I'd spent so much of my life indoors that I still enjoyed every ray of sunshine and the splash of every lap of water on the marsh grasses and every whiff of pluff mud.

"So, you probably already know all about it, but I think Caroline and Danny are up to something." Cooper side-eyed me, watching to see if I'd give anything away.

I pressed my lips together to maintain my poker face. "What makes you say that?"

"Well, Caro asked if we could watch Mia tonight. I don't know that she's ever asked me to do that other than for the transport, because usually Danny wants to have her if Caro has something at night." He tipped my chin up and narrowed his eyes at me playfully. "Come on, now. You know something. I can see it in your eyes."

I closed them and stuck my tongue out at him. "Um, she might have said something about needing a babysitter tonight. Possibly."

"Tell me." He brought his mouth close enough to mine for me to feel the feather of his breath on my lips.

I opened my eyes. "Maybe we could just kiss a little bit instead."

"Come on. Spill. I won't rule out the kissing," he said, his lips widening into a smile.

"Okay, but she doesn't want you to know. She's nervous. After all the stuff with your dad went down and he was out of the house, I called Danny and said Caroline had seen a few things clearer and he might want to give her a call. He hung up on me, but a month later, he called me and asked for specifics. I told him all the things Ted had done to manipulate people to do what he wanted and that he might consider the idea that he and Caroline had also been manipulated."

Cooper let out a breath. "No doubt."

"He said he'd think about it. I didn't hear any more until last week, when Caro said she and Danny had actually talked when she went to pick up Mia. Tonight they're going out to dinner."

"Is it a date or a negotiation?"

"Oh, I think it's a negotiation, but Caroline hopes it will turn into a date. I think she's gone to get a manicure and a blowout while Mia is in school."

"Aw. I would say Danny's an idiot for treating her that way, but maybe I might revise that opinion if he's willing to listen."

"He gets major points for being willing to consider admitting he was wrong. About Caro, at least. He was right about Ted." I checked my phone. "I've only got five more minutes if I'm going to get to the prosecutor's office by one-thirty."

"Are you nervous?" asked Cooper, scooting closer to play with a lock of my long hair.

I relaxed my knee to touch his. "About talking to them? No. I don't have anything to say that isn't the truth."

Ted sat in jail, awaiting trial, charged with the murder of Lynette. The recording had survived the water, but some of the words had been drowned out by the wind. Enough remained that the prosecutors were hopeful I could piece together what was missing: I'd be the star witness in this trial. Ted's fingerprints had also shown up on the credit card that they found in the pink purse in the ground. He'd been denied bond because the prosecutor argued successfully he was a flight risk. The trial had been scheduled and continued once already, and the prosecutor's office was re-interviewing their witnesses. Only the previous week, we'd heard that detectives had begun a look at the death of Barbara Tradd Middleton, previously ruled a suicide. They'd asked Cooper for permission to cart away all the financial records in Ted's desk, and he'd given it, gladly. They came in with boxes and emptied the desk and the workshop and took the computer and all the flash drives he'd locked up. After I'd showed them how Ted had hidden the desk key in a whelk in the coffee table, they emptied all the shells, one at a time, taking over an hour to find another flash drive hidden inside a whelk. We hadn't heard yet what they found on that.

"The prosecutor was tough on me," Cooper said. "She made me go through the timeline of the whole year before Lynette disappeared. She kept asking why I didn't figure out that something was up with Lynette before she . . ." Cooper's phone rang. When he saw who it was, his serious expression turned to a grin. He showed me the screen before answering it and hitting speaker so I could hear it too.

"Gibbes DuPre. Hey, man."

"Coop. My assistant's been harassing me—that's right, Ada, I said harassing—to clean off my desk, and I found a folder here under an ungodly tall pile of shit with your name on it and an unsigned annulment complaint in it. From last November. You know anything about that?"

Cooper smiled at me and ran a fingertip up my bare arm, making me arch my throat and shiver. "Yeah, Gibbes, I think you can toss that. I don't think we qualify for an annulment anymore. Go on and send me the bill for your time, though."

I let my fingertips brush my midsection. No, we didn't qualify for an annulment, not if the next few months passed the way I hoped they would.

Cooper still had trouble adjusting to the knowledge that he was the son of a sociopath. He lapsed into odd silences on occasion and woke sometimes out of bad dreams. He'd started seeing a counselor in an office down the hall from mine, who, he said, helped tamp down the worry that his dad's sickness had been genetic.

It hadn't been. Few men on earth cared more about other people than Cooper Middleton. And I knew how to help him after the bad dreams. He did the same for me. Our child would have the best of fathers.

"Well, damn," said Gibbes, cackling. "I could have told you that back at Thanksgiving. Anyone could see you were whipped within an inch of your life. Like being in the room with two nekkid . . ."

"Uh, Gibbes, you're on speaker. Say hello to Molly."

There was a pause, then more formally, "Hello, Molly, it's nice to speak to you. Everything going all right?"

I laughed. "Yes. Thank you."

"So, Mrs. Middleton, it's my legal duty to inform you that if you don't qualify for an annulment ground, you've got no choice but to divorce that bastard when he gets out of line."

"So I hear, Gibbes. I appreciate the advice. I'll be sure to call you if I need it."

Gibbes let loose with his rusty cackle. I could picture him cleaning his glasses on his dress shirt. "You do that. Listen. I'm going to toss this file in the closed files—yes, Ada, here it is, I'm letting you have it—and hey. Y'all be good, okay?"

"Okay, man," said Cooper. "We'll be good." He slipped his hand into mine.

"More than good, Gibbes. Thank you." I caught his eyes and held them, reveling in the intensity of the mossy green depths. Heat began to build in my skin. Tourists passed, eating pralines and carrying shopping bags from expensive stores. They took no notice of me as I scooted close enough on the marble step to press the length of my thigh against his.

"And hey, Coop," continued Gibbes. "Don't worry about the bill. Not gonna charge you for the annulment complaint. I should pay you, to be honest. I drafted it at my wife's mother's house in Greenville over Thanksgiving. Bought myself a whole hour in a room all by myself. It was a gift. In-laws. Sweet Baby Jesus. In-laws'll drive you crazy. Y'all have a good day, now."

Cooper pushed his fingers into my hair, his thumb brushing my lips.

"We will," I breathed, hitting END on the phone and tossing it aside.

Around us, sweltering strangers passed, gawking at Charleston. The stranger I'd married only pulled me closer as I lost myself in his kiss.

THE END

Acknowledgements

I started writing late in life and I didn't know how much blood, sweat, and tears—and love—went into every book on the shelf. This one is no different, and it wouldn't exist without all the help I received along the way.

Thank you first and foremost to my parents, Bob and Nancy Button, who put their skills as former English teachers to amazing use reading—and marking up with a red pen—an early draft of this book. More importantly—maybe most importantly—thank you for raising me in a house where books were sacred and proof of immortality.

Thank you to my husband, Frank, who urged me to write a book years before I dared try and who never stopped believing and encouraging on all the dark days when things got hard. Thanks also to my sons, Austin and Matthew, for whom I kept going to prove that perseverance and hard work matter. If I can do this, boys, *you* can do anything. I love you all as high as the sky, as deep as the ocean, and higher than the moon.

Thank you also to my aunt, Judy Oswood, who gave me my first Pat Conroy book and introduced this Midwestern girl to the South Carolina Lowcountry.

To Mary Ann Marlowe, Elly Blake, Jennifer Hawkins, Ron Walters, Summer Spence, and Kelly Siskind, you are my second family. "Critique partners" doesn't adequately describe what you mean to me. You didn't let me quit. You didn't let me walk away. You read my words and demanded more from me. Molly and Cooper would be a badly-written Word document without you.

Writing is a big community, and I have to thank Brenda Drake and everyone involved with the online contest Pitch Wars.

Without you, I might never have taken myself seriously as a writer. To my gang of fellow mentees in Pitch Wars 2014, hang in there with me. We are in this together. Kelli Newby, Susan Bickford, Margarita Montimore, Kellye Garrett, Kelly Calabrese, Kara Leigh Miller, Laura Heffernan, Roselle Lim, Mairi Kilaine, Jennifer Camiccia, Rachel Lynn Solomon, Ruthanne Frost, Meghan Crowther, Sherry Harding, and Cathy Moore—support means everything. You might not have known it, but you each said or did something (or more than one thing) that kept me writing. Thank you so much for everything you've done.

Thank you to the community of McClellanville, SC, for being an amazing setting. Nowhere on earth is less likely to harbor a real-life Ted (at least not now—the Cape Romain lighthouse story is still told to children there and is by all accounts true). Please visit: the people are wonderful and the scenery is stunning.

Thank you to Rod Hunter and the brilliant editors at Bella Rosa Books who saw something here worth reading. Your edits were indispensable. I weep to think of what this ending would have been without you.

A special thank you to my incredible agent, Sarah E. Younger, who told me once she'd never give up on me and therefore made it impossible to give up on myself. I'm so lucky to have you.

To my readers, wherever I may find you—you're the reason. Thank you, most of all.

About the Author

Kristin lives in rural Virginia with her husband, two sons, and two beagles. She is a graduate of the University of Michigan Law School and works as a local government attorney. This is her first novel.

CPSIA information can be obtained
at www.ICGtesting.com
Printed in the USA
FSHW010627150119
55035FS